CHRISTMAS AT
Glitter Peak Lodge

Christmas at Glitter Peak Lodge

A NOVEL

KJERSTI HERLAND JOHNSEN

Translated from
the Norwegian by
Olivia Lasky

HARPERVIA

An Imprint of HarperCollins*Publishers*

CHRISTMAS AT GLITTER PEAK LODGE. Copyright © 2022 by CAPPELEN DAMM AS, Oslo. Translation copyright © 2024 by Olivia Lasky. All rights reserved. Printed in the United States of America. No part of this book may be used or reproduced in any manner whatsoever without written permission except in the case of brief quotations embodied in critical articles and reviews. For information, address HarperCollins Publishers, 195 Broadway, New York, NY 10007.

HarperCollins books may be purchased for educational, business, or sales promotional use. For information, please email the Special Markets Department at SPsales@harpercollins.com.

Originally published as *Jul på Himmelfjell hotell* in Norway in 2022 by Cappelen Damm.

FIRST HARPERVIA EDITION PUBLISHED 2024

Designed by Yvonne Chan
Illustrations © Olha/Adobe Stock

Library of Congress Cataloging-in-Publication Data

Names: Johnsen, Kjersti Herland, author. | Lasky, Olivia, translator.
Title: Christmas at Glitter Peak Lodge: a novel / Kjersti Herland Johnsen; translated from the Norwegian by Olivia Lasky.
Other titles: Jul på Himmelfjell Hotell. English
Description: New York: HarperVia, an imprint of HarperCollinsPublishers, 2024. |
Identifiers: LCCN 2024016673 (print) | LCCN 2024016674 (ebook) | ISBN 9780063339293 (trade paperback) | ISBN 9780063339231 (ebook)
Subjects: LCGFT: Christmas fiction. | Romance fiction. | Novels.
Classification: LCC PT8952.2.O63 J8513 2024 (print) | LCC PT8952.2.O63 (ebook) | DDC 839.823/8—dc23/eng/20240624
LC record available at https://lccn.loc.gov/2024016673
LC ebook record available at https://lccn.loc.gov/2024016674

24 25 26 27 28 LBC 5 4 3 2 1

To Mom

One day as I sat musing, sad and lonely without a friend,
a voice came to me from out of the gloom saying,
"Cheer up. Things could be worse."
So I cheered up and sure enough—things got worse.

CURLY HOWARD, AS QUOTED BY
JOAN HOWARD MAURER

The solution of every problem is another problem.

JOHANN WOLFGANG VON GOETHE

Contents

CHRISTMAS AT
Glitter Peak Lodge

PROLOGUE:
AVALANCHE

As soon as she hears the faint rumbling, she knows they've made the biggest—and maybe the last—mistake of their lives.

At first, she can only hear it. Then she sees it. The avalanche is a white sheet racing toward them, breaking up into small ivory flakes, a spiderweb getting bigger and bigger as it hurtles down the mountainside.

She's completely paralyzed for what feels like an eternity. Then she hears shouting—from Giovanni, from Sherpa Pertema, from the others in the group. Preben is first in the procession, and she can't make out what he's saying. He said it was safe before they left base camp. He said he knew what he was doing. That was only a few minutes ago—and now the avalanche is coming. It's all happening so fast. She thinks someone's going to die. She just doesn't know who it is. But she isn't afraid. Not yet.

The white snow is the most beautiful thing she's ever seen. It's also the most terrifying thing she's ever seen. It's a train barreling toward her at a hundred miles per hour. It's a wild animal that's been hibernating in the mountains, furious that it's been awakened from its slumber. It's a monster, a yeti . . . no—it's a glittering, white dragon. That's what it is.

Suddenly, she's no longer paralyzed. Her body wakes up, and

she wants to run, but the ground is disappearing beneath her; it's crumbling to pieces. The dragon gets hold of her and lifts her, and she floats on its breath at first. Then it dances with her—a frenzied dance, around and around, moving faster and faster.

There's snow and ice on all sides. She's lost control; she can't breathe; she's in a maelstrom; she's pushed down into the mass of snow, locked in, shoved under. And then—silence.

Is she dead? She can see a few streaks of light. She's not in any pain. She's not cold. But she can't move her legs; it's as if they're cast in stone. She tries her hands, which are up by her face, and is able to move them an inch or two in each direction. So she's not dead after all.

She's able to create only a small space by moving her hands. But the cracks start filling up with snow and the light disappears. Now it's getting hard to breathe. She can't get enough air. Her lungs start to burn. *Which way is up? Which way is down?* she thinks. *How deep am I? How many minutes do I have left? Was this how it was supposed to end?*

Then everything goes dark.

DECEMBER 1

Ingrid Berg sits up abruptly. It's the same dream as always, the one that comes to her again and again. The rumbling. The white dragon. The snow on all sides. The shouting. The others disappearing. The darkness, the lack of oxygen, the panic. The pain. In reality, that had come later—after they'd dug her out and she woke up in the hospital.

She doesn't remember much from those first hours and days, but the bright lights, the people in white bustling around her, the pain, and the blood—so much blood—she'll never forget that.

She gets control of her breathing. She isn't there now. Not under the snow, not at the hospital. She's in her bed at the Glitter Peak Lodge. She's surrounded by darkness, and she's alone.

Ingrid was a climber from an early age—first on the rocks near the hotel where she grew up, then in the mountains. There was something inside her that drove her forward, ever steeper and ever higher. People were surprised that her grandmother, Nana Borghild, allowed it—*especially after what happened to her parents!* But her grandmother had always been perfectly at ease. "Ingrid was born to climb," she would say calmly. "Not letting her climb would be like not letting a mountain hawk fly."

The people of Glitter Peak had always been climbers; both Nana Borghild and Ingrid's mother, Angelina, had been up in the mountains since they were old enough to walk, even though it was somewhat unusual for women in those days. So the last thing Nana Borghild wanted was to keep Ingrid from pursuing her passion. Of course, she made sure that Ingrid went to climbing courses, learned how to belay and rappel, wore a helmet, found responsible climbing partners, and did whatever else it took to make climbing as safe as possible. Nana Borghild trusted Ingrid. Ingrid had always trusted herself, too. She felt confident in her abilities. She understood the mountain: her fingers instinctively knew where to hold, and she always knew where to place her feet.

Over time, climbing became her whole life. She explored the world, sought out new challenges, and always felt safe—invincible, even.

But then last year, her life had changed in a matter of minutes up there in the Himalayas. The images surged through her like the avalanche they'd barely survived. Preben's failure, the fatal consequences . . . she'd never get over it, and every time she thought about what happened, it felt as if she was once again trapped beneath feet of snow, gasping for air.

SHE LET THE HOT WATER flow over her head and body as she sang along to the song streaming from the radio: "All I Want for Christmas Is You." It was almost as though she'd forgotten that she couldn't carry a tune. It was the first Sunday in December, and Christmas songs had already been playing for weeks. Shampoo, rinse. What a luxury it was to be able to take a hot shower every day! To let last night's nightmares run down the drain. Ingrid had been on enough expeditions to be able to *really* appreciate the comforts of indoor life. Clean, dry towels. Hot water. Scented soap. She squeezed a generous amount of conditioner into her hands and ran them through her long, curly hair to try to get some control over the tangles.

Turning off the water, she reached for a towel. For a fleeting moment, the hot water and the cheerful, jangly music had taken her back to a time when life was completely different—when *Ingrid* was completely different. A time when she'd loved this song and the person who'd sung it to her, even though he couldn't sing, either.

She stopped and wrapped herself in the towel, suddenly feeling as though she was getting cold. Her body tensed up. It normally did that when it remembered.

She threw on some clothes before applying a thick moisturizer to her hands and face. After a few intense minutes with the hair dryer on full blast, her hair was dry enough to tuck under a hat. Ingrid looked at herself in the mirror, the one that had been hanging next to the door for as long as she could remember. As a child, she had lived with Nana Borghild here in the manager's apartment at Glitter Peak Lodge—"The Residence," as the hotel staff called it. Now, Ingrid was living here alone. Her grandmother had insisted on it when Ingrid came home to take over running the hotel. Nana Borghild had moved into a smaller apartment on the same floor, "The Pensioner's." The rest of the staff lived in the annex, with the exception of the hotel facilities manager and the chef, who had their own apartments in the main building, and the caretaker, who had a kind of bachelor pad in the basement.

Ingrid put on her lace-up boots and a thick wool sweater, ran down the stairs to the reception area, and strode out to greet the morning light. She had time for a quick walk before she had to get started on the day's work.

THE SUN WAS RISING OVER Glitter Peak. Pink rays broke through a thin layer of clouds and silhouetted mountain peaks and trees. Just under two hundred miles from Oslo and an hour's drive from Lillehammer, through valleys and up steep mountain roads, Glitter Peak Lodge was close to the tree line. Only birches and pines grew up here—no big spruces as on the slopes down toward Dalen. That made the view all the better. The colors of the sky were constantly in flux, and the very shape of the massif in front of her seemed to be changing with the light.

There was a crunching beneath her boots as Ingrid crossed the heather on her way toward the scree. The moss and lichen on the ground were covered in frost that glittered in the early morning light. The berries that still hung on the blueberry and lingonberry bushes were encased in a thin layer of ice and looked like works of art, more elaborately and delicately designed by nature than anything a human could have created.

It was unusual for the ground to be so bare in December, but despite a cold autumn, there'd been little snow so far this year. Only the peak high, high above was covered in an icy white. The enormous mountaintop stretched up toward the sky. Sometimes you couldn't even see the top because it was shrouded in clouds—like a dwelling of the gods high above the human world. It was no wonder it was named Heaven's Horn and had so many associated myths and stories.

Below Heaven's Horn, the waterfall, Styggfossen, was a blue-white, monumental cascade frozen in time.

The sun melted through the cloud layer, and the light changed color, getting warmer. Ingrid shut her eyes and let the sun's rays warm her face. More birds and animals were starting to wake up now. A small flock of Siberian jays fluttered from the top of a birch and darted past her. She knew they were headed for the door to the kitchen, where there might be breadcrumbs from the hotel staff, although the chef was wary of the little jays, which she called "bad luck birds"—an unfair name, really. Bad luck wasn't caused by birds.

Ingrid looked around. If you were lucky, you could spot herds of wild reindeer on the mountainsides. This morning, however, there weren't any to be seen.

The sun rose, and the light grew whiter, the glittering sharper. The winter sun wouldn't stay above the horizon for more than a few hours before it warmed up in color once again, said a sleepy "good night," and went down in a sea of red and orange. Dusk would then send colorful streaks over the horizon before the darkness returned—a long, cold, and dark winter night in the mountains of Norway.

BUT—INGRID TOOK A DEEP BREATH—there was much to be done at Glitter Peak Lodge before then. The jays weren't the only ones who had business to take care of. The hours between sunrise and sunset also meant a lot of activity for Ingrid and the staff at Glitter Peak Lodge; Christmas was rapidly approaching and they had to prepare for the arrival of the holiday guests and test the dishes that would be served in the restaurant. In just a few weeks, they would find out whether everything they'd worked for over the past months could really succeed.

Ingrid turned abruptly and walked back across the heather toward the hotel, which dominated the landscape. No matter how familiar the colossal building was, Glitter Peak Lodge never ceased to impress her. It was tall and wide, solid and walnut-stained, with white window frames and dragon-style carvings. The Berg family had been living at the foot of the high mountains for hundreds of years and running the hotel for 130 of them. Glitter Peak Lodge had been there ever since the very first tourists had set foot in the mountains in the 1800s; it stood at an altitude of four thousand feet, where the paved road ended and the ascent to Heaven's Horn began.

The hotel had grown over the decades, and several extensions and annexes had been built in the same style as the main building. As a result, the hotel now had several apartments and family-friendly accommodations in addition to twenty rooms and two suites in the main building. Ingrid thought the extensions had been nicely done. A place like this should have a traditional building style. Here, there were none of the ugly additions you could see in some chain hotels. No, this was the family-run Glitter Peak Lodge, and Nana Borghild had made sure to maintain the original style.

The large lot in front of the hotel was covered with gravel, and a wide staircase with ramps on both sides led to the entrance, which was protected by an awning and flanked by large, wrought-iron lanterns.

Upstairs, many of the rooms were still dark and had their curtains drawn. Not all of the guests had gotten up yet, but the hotel was far from full occupancy anyway. The windows on the ground floor were fully lit, though; the staff was already hard at work there. Chef Maja Seter had probably been in the kitchen since around five. *The early bird gets the worm* was one of her favorite sayings. When the other employees came into the kitchen around six thirty, Maja was usually ready with freshly baked rolls. She would also have had time to empty and reload the dishwasher, knock over a saltshaker and throw a pinch of salt over her shoulder to prevent bad luck, set the table for her coworkers, light the first candle in the Advent candleholder, and make coffee. And now that the sun was fully up at nine o'clock, she would already be well underway with preparations for tonight's dinner as well.

IT WAS THE RIGHT CHOICE, Ingrid thought. *It was the right choice to come back here.* It wasn't that she was exactly *happy* about the choice she'd made—to the extent that she'd actually had a choice. Running the hotel involved too many worries, too much work, and too much uncertainty to make her truly "happy." Still, something swelled inside her every time she looked at the hotel—a seed of something that she might even call contentment. There was something about venturing out, having a look around, then coming back. On her morning walks, she sometimes even found an inner calm that complemented the cold, glittering silence around her.

But the peace rarely lasted long. And today it was particularly short-lived. Before Ingrid had even reached the front door, a loud scream cut through the silence.

❄

"MOUSE! *Mouuuse!*" The old kitchen table creaked beneath Maja Seter's considerable weight. The chef's sturdy legs were shaking in her clogs in the middle of the checkered tablecloth. "Get it out! Get it *out*! We can't have any mice in this kitchen!"

"Mouse? Where is it?" Ingrid had sped straight to the kitchen when she heard the shouts, and she was now standing in the doorway, looking up at the terrified chef.

"It ran right in front of me when I went to turn on the oven!" Maja shouted. "I'm telling you, it stared at me with these big, red eyes . . . then it disappeared under the stove! It was *huge*! A real beast! Actually, maybe it was even a rat . . ."

The chef was breathing heavily and clutching her chest. "We should have taken a couple of Meowgret's kittens up here," she continued before Ingrid could even answer. "We never had any mice or vermin back when we had a cat."

Ingrid wasn't totally sure whether having cats in the kitchen would be fully in line with food hygiene regulations but didn't have the energy to get into that discussion right now.

"I think the mouse is cute. He likes it here."

It was only now that Ingrid realized Hussein was also in the kitchen. The six-year-old was sitting on the bench at the window and smiling at her with two missing front teeth. She looked at him, one eyebrow raised.

"Have you seen the mouse before, Hussein?" she asked.

"Yes, his name is Speedy because he's so fast. He likes bread. And cheese."

Ingrid looked at him for a long time.

"You haven't been feeding Speedy, have you?"

"No, Auntie Ingrid!" Hussein quickly averted his eyes.

"You can't feed mice, you know. Maja doesn't want them in the kitchen."

"You can be sure about that," Maja said from atop the kitchen table. "They're deadly! Don't you know they carry the plague? We need traps! Or cats! Or poison! Or all of it! *Now!*"

"What's going on?"

Aisha Mansour was standing in the doorway, a confused expression on her beautiful face. Aisha was otherwise the epitome of order and control. Her long, straight hair was gathered in a clip at the base of her neck, and she was wearing black pants and a navy blue blazer. Aisha was new to the role of facilities manager at Glitter Peak Lodge—the first person Ingrid had hired when she took over as manager.

Aisha and her son, Hussein, had arrived in Norway in the spring and moved into the hotel in time for the first day of school in the fall. Ingrid was happy she'd been able to give them this opportunity, but it wasn't charity: Syrian-Jordanian Aisha had excellent references from previous jobs; she was educated, spoke good English, and had extensive experience in the hotel industry. After only a few months in the country, both Aisha and Hussein could speak fluent Norwegian as well. Hussein's father, Mohammed, was from Syria, but was currently living in Jordan.

"Hussein, what have you gotten up to now? And why is Miss Maja on the table?" Aisha asked.

Before Maja could shout "*Mouse!*" again, Hussein had hurried over to his mother and buried his face in her blazer. "Miss Maja wants to kill Speedy!" he sniffled. "Just because he's fast and likes cheese!"

❄

When the situation in the kitchen was under control again—after Aisha had taken Hussein to her office, Maja had climbed down from the table, and the mouse hadn't shown any signs of returning—Ingrid served herself a big mug of coffee. Now she needed to find Nana Borghild.

Around now, Ingrid's grandmother would be done with the inspection round she made each morning. Ingrid could picture her stroking her finger over moldings and railings. They would be dust-free today, just as they'd been every day for the fifty years Borghild had been manager—with the possible exception of a few chaotic weeks in the early 1990s. She usually greeted the staff in the kitchen while Ingrid was out for a walk. Then Borghild would bring a cup of coffee into the library, and Ingrid always looked forward to sitting down with her.

Ingrid had grown up with Nana Borghild; she was Ingrid's rock, her steadfast pillar. Borghild had been widowed quite early, when Ingrid's grandfather Christian died of a heart attack at only fifty. By then, Borghild and Christian had already been married for almost thirty years and had run the hotel together for more than twenty. Borghild continued to run the hotel with her daughter, Angelina, and her son-in-law, Marius, Ingrid's parents.

But misfortune struck again when Ingrid was three years old. Just a few years after Christian's sudden death, Angelina and Marius were killed in a car accident when they drove off the road coming home from a summer party. There was no explanation, and no other cars had been involved. Was it a moment of inattentiveness, or perhaps an animal had run into the road? No one knew. In the midst of her grief, Borghild was left in charge of both the hotel and a toddler at the age of fifty-three.

Borghild had then run the hotel on her own for the past thirty years.

Ingrid admired her grandmother more and more as she realized the many challenges of running a hotel. Nana Borghild had preserved Glitter Peak's traditions as a family business while simultaneously facilitating skiing, hiking, ice climbing, mountain climbing, and all of the other activities the terrain could offer.

There'd been ups and downs. Competition from larger hotels, fluctuations in bookings, the need for expansions and improvements, bureaucratic challenges and changing economic conditions—Nana Borghild had been responsible for absolutely everything. Until now, when Ingrid had come home to take up the baton.

Every morning since Ingrid's return, she and her grandmother had met in the library after breakfast. They used these meetings to go over practical issues and discuss how to deal with crises, big and small. And in the category of big crises was the issue of the mouse; pests in the hotel actually *were* a real problem, no matter how calm Ingrid had tried to appear in the kitchen. The health inspectors would definitely *not* be impressed by mouse droppings in the corners.

The door shut with a creak behind her, and even though the entryway was beautifully decorated with spruce branches and candles for Christmas, Ingrid let out an exasperated sigh as she passed the reception area and headed toward the library. She smiled at the new girl standing behind the desk, but Ingrid's mind was occupied with practical matters. She had to remember to ask Alfred to oil the door hinges. Or maybe it was just as easy to do it herself. There was also the matter of checking those planks in the basement wall that might be rotting. The list of tasks was never-ending. There was so much to take care of, so many things that could go wrong in a hotel. As if the physical maintenance weren't demanding enough, you also had to make sure that the website was up-to-date and that the booking system worked, and preferably keep up an appealing social media presence as well. You were responsible for ensuring that the right number of staff showed up at the right time, that the food orders made sense, that hygiene rules were observed. Then there were all the things you couldn't do anything about. Closed roads. Power outages. Illness. Conditions that kept people away.

In her darkest moments, she feared that something would happen that was beyond her control, something that made their guests abandon Glitter Peak Lodge so that she'd have to throw in the towel and sell the hotel to cover its not-so-insignificant debts. There were quite a few people who wanted to buy Glitter Peak Lodge—she knew that. She'd been contacted by almost all of the hotel chains that had established themselves in the mountain valleys in recent years and that increasingly dominated the Norwegian hotel market, but the prices they'd offered had been absurdly low.

Ingrid had made up her mind that she wasn't going to give up so easily, though. Once she'd decided to take over running the hotel, she did it wholeheartedly. The stakes were high, and the risk of failure just as lofty.

She opened the door to the library and found her grandmother sitting in one of the large armchairs by the fireplace.

"AH YES, IT'S A MOUSE YEAR. I've spoken to Barry about it," Nana Borghild said, setting a large book on the table next to her—a tome about the history of the area, which she was so interested in.

"Nana. Barry is a stuffed bear," Ingrid said. She sat down in the chair beside her grandmother and looked up at the big bear next to the fireplace, its mouth open and its paws stiff. Tall and dark, Barry stared at them wordlessly, his gaze steady.

"Yes, I know that," her grandmother continued, straightening her cardigan. "Do you think I've gone completely senile?" She gave Ingrid a stern look. "Barry's been at the hotel almost as long as I have, you know that. But he's holding up a lot better. He also says he's seen worse. In the great mouse year of 1961, for example, there were so many mice in the hotel that the cats couldn't keep them away. There were even some here in the library, gnawing at his foot. Just look. You can see the marks there in his fur."

Ingrid looked at her grandmother again and saw a twinkle in her eye. Ah, she was joking! Thank goodness! Ingrid had to laugh. She'd been away for so long that she'd almost forgotten her grandmother's subtle sense of humor. No, Nana Borghild was still "all there," to be sure—but Ingrid did think that her grandmother might actually exchange a few words with the stuffed bear every now and again.

"AND HOW ARE PREPARATIONS GOING otherwise?" her grandmother asked, stroking a hand over her snow-white hair. "Your friends will be arriving in a few days, too, won't they?"

Well, perhaps Nana Borghild really did still have just as much control over everything that needed to be done. But her grandmother made a point of the fact that she was now stepping down and that Ingrid was the new manager of Glitter Peak Lodge, with all of the responsibility that entailed. And it was a *lot* of responsibility. There was a reason Ingrid had run away from it once upon a time—down from the mountain and into the city, and eventually up to other mountains all around the world.

But the time felt right now. Her grandmother was over eighty, and Ingrid needed a fresh start.

There had been quite a lot of stress after what happened in the Himalayas, and Ingrid had just wanted to get away—away from Preben, away from the attention, away from all the memories, and, perhaps most important, as far away from the international mountaineering community as possible. It was a bit paradoxical, then, that she had come back here to Glitter Peak Lodge with its view of Heaven's Horn, which she'd climbed so many times in her youth and which she now, at the age of thirty-three, was sure she'd never set foot on again.

Nana Borghild had once told her that the most important thing for a climber is to be good at forgetting. Anyone who climbs mountains needs to be able to forget the fear, forget all the falls and frozen fingers and battles and impassable obstacles— and try again.

And that's exactly how it was. You had to learn to forget the pain in order to keep going. You had to find the joy in the sense of achievement, to push away the difficult memories, over and over again. And Ingrid had done that, until something happened that was impossible to forget.

She lifted her gaze. Her grandmother had asked something. Ingrid had to pull herself together, focus on what was happening here and now.

"The preparations . . . yes, they're moving forward. Tonight, we're tasting the *pinnekjøtt*. If the mice haven't eaten it up, that is. We want to make sure it's just right before we serve it to the guests," Ingrid said. "Do you think it'll be a hit, by the way?"

"I should think so! People want hearty, traditional food when they come up here."

"I remember we used to serve meatballs when I was little," Ingrid said. "And then there were lots of ribs and *medisterkaker* at Christmas. And sausages."

Nana Borghild smiled. "You loved sausages! And the ribs were popular, of course. In the old days, it was traditional to have a *møljefest* one of the days before Christmas Eve."

"Møljefest? What's that?"

"Well, in those days, we boiled the ribs before baking them and served the stock—the *mølje*—with *møljebrød*. It was wonderful! And then we had *rakfisk* one day during the holidays. Maybe that's something you could try on your tourists? You have to be pretty tough to eat rakfisk!"

Ingrid raised an eyebrow. "I don't know if I'll risk it. Can't you get poisoned if you prepare it the wrong way?"

Borghild laughed. "Maja doesn't make mistakes. You know that. And it certainly sounds like you two have control over the menu." Borghild stroked her stomach. She'd always been careful about maintaining her figure, and even now, at her advanced age, she had only a slight hint of a roll over the waistband of her tweed skirt. "There'll be a lot of samples for us in the next few weeks, then," she added, smiling. "With all of Maja's cakes and cookies as well. Not that it will matter for you, Ingrid. Fat never sticks to you. You don't have any extra lumps or bumps. But the rest of us have to be careful, you know."

Ingrid instinctively touched her belly. Her grandmother was

just trying to give her a compliment, but she had no idea how hard the well-intentioned words hit home—because this was the one thing Ingrid had never spoken to her grandmother about. Ingrid had to look away. No, she didn't have any lumps or bumps. And she probably never would, either.

She'd set aside the time between breakfast and lunch to do some work in the office, but she found it difficult to concentrate on her long to-do list, which included budgets, menus, invoicing systems, and letters from the tax authorities. She felt the restlessness creeping up on her, and her eyes kept wandering out the window and across the beautiful terrain outside. Was this really how she was going to live her life from now on? What she appreciated so much about being here—in addition to the hotel and her grandmother, of course—was first and foremost the nature: the challenging terrain, the light in the mountains, the changing seasons, the fresh air . . . But now Ingrid spent most of her time indoors, staring at a computer screen.

While nobody had said so outright, she was expected to contribute her experience as a mountaineer as well. She was so well known as a climber and expedition leader that a lot of people would find it exciting to meet her and benefit from her experience, and perhaps even to have her as a guide on trips in the area or hear her give lectures. Her friend and business adviser Vegard Vang had suggested this. Theme weekends. Inspirational seminars for businesspeople. There was real money in that kind of thing!

Sure, but if only they knew how she *really* felt, she thought.

Who would be inspired by a mountain climber who was now afraid of heights?

SHE'D JUST COLLECTED HERSELF AND logged into the accounting software when her phone rang. It was Aisha.

"I saw something strange up in the attic," she said. "I think it might be dry rot."

"Oh no!" Ingrid exclaimed. "Mice, dry rot . . . What's next?"

She put her head in her hands. Would this even be possible—this attempt at revitalizing the hotel and bringing it into a new era? Or was she in over her head?

She wanted to just walk away from the whole thing—to tell her grandmother that it was all too much, that they had to sell the hotel.

But she couldn't. She couldn't give up now.

"I'll look at it with Alfred," she said.

Keep going, said a voice in her head. *One foot in front of the other.*

DECEMBER 2

The sun takes its time coming to Glitter Peak in the winter, Borghild Berg thought, *but when it does, it's with a flourish.* She stood at the window, gazing out over the mountains—a sight she'd never grown tired of and couldn't live without. Ingrid had heard her grandmother say it a thousand times: she'd lived up here, and she'd die up here. Some nursing home down in the valley was completely out of the question.

The panorama stretching out before her this December morning was frozen, yet still full of life. Was that an arctic fox slinking around by that ridge? Yes, it looked like one. If it were to look toward the southeast, it would see that the night sky was developing a reddish stripe close to the horizon. The ribbon of budding light was ever so slowly broadening into a wide band that spanned all the colors of the rainbow—red, orange, yellow, green, blue, and purple that faded into grayish pink and blue shades if you turned your head to the north or south. A lone star still shone brightly in the dark azure high above, but the mountain fox probably didn't notice that. If it *had* thought about that kind of thing, it would see that the constellations were starting to fade, and that Ursa Major and Minor were heading back into their sky dens for the day.

For a while, it seemed as if the sun was going to change its mind; the sky was growing brighter and brighter but there was no glowing orb to be seen. A bleary-eyed person might have thought that the sun hadn't been able to resist the temptation to go back to bed—to sleep just a *little* bit longer—in that plush duvet of stratus clouds that had collected in the valley below. But the mountain fox didn't have any concept of what a duvet is and probably wasn't the least bit bleary-eyed. Borghild watched as it trotted purposefully toward its den in the scree beneath the rock face. Perhaps the fox had been lucky today and managed to take its morning walk without running into either a big red fox or a human. With an extra dose of luck, the fox might have even managed to catch a lemming for breakfast as well. It wasn't hard to imagine that the fox was perfectly content on a morning like this.

But it wasn't the only early riser. The people at Glitter Peak Lodge had already been up and at it for several hours when the orange sphere finally made its way over the horizon and its rays started to creep up the side of Glitter Peak.

Borghild Berg was one of them. Most days, she did her rounds of the hotel as soon as she'd gotten dressed, but today, she'd sat down at her desk in the little apartment and spent some time writing in her journal.

Borghild turned away from the window and caught sight of her reflection in the mirror next to the wardrobe. She plucked a bit of lint off the blue-and-white cardigan she'd knitted a few years ago and tucked a loose strand of hair into the bun at the nape of her neck. Her clothes fit her well and her hair was still thick, even though it was completely white. *Not bad for eighty-three*, she thought, before scoffing at her own vanity.

On her way to the door, she paused by the two pictures hanging on the wall—just as she always did. The black-and-white wedding portrait of her and Christian. The small oil painting of two young girls clad in *bunads*, the Norwegian national dress, in front of a freshly sprouted birch tree. She'd taken them with her when she left "The Residence" for "The Pensioner's." She and Christian had moved into "The Residence" as newlyweds what felt like—and practically was—a lifetime ago, and it had been her home until last fall. She'd looked at these pictures every day for sixty years but still couldn't pass by them without a pang in her chest that was a combination of love and melancholy. An aching grief over what had been and what had never come to pass.

The photograph and painting were memories from a completely different time, a time when she herself had been standing on the precipice of adult life, just as Ingrid was now. Well, strictly speaking, Ingrid was already well into her adult life. She was over thirty, after all! Borghild had been much younger than that when the photo was taken. Young people were taking longer to become adults these days. So much had to be done before they could settle down; they had to study for ages, travel farther away, and try out different ways of living. Back in her day, there were fewer options and more obligations. There was so much you simply had to deal with, whether you wanted to or not.

And yet—life had still felt so open back then, as though the world were her oyster. It had given her a lot, but she'd also had to give up a great deal.

She returned to her desk and wrote a few more lines. She sat there for a few seconds with the pen raised—as if in reflection—before she clapped the journal shut, placed it inside the rolltop desk, and locked it with the key that hung on a gold chain inside her blouse. Some things were best kept to oneself.

Borghild stood up and took a breath. She cast one last glance at the pictures before stepping into the hallway and locking the door behind her. Only she and Ingrid had the key. Borghild cleaned the apartment herself, just as she had when living in the manager's residence. She didn't think it was appropriate for the maids to go in there and clean up after her, and she stuck to that belief after she'd taken over the smaller apartment.

AT THE BOTTOM OF THE STAIRS, she met little Hussein, his backpack packed and ready. His mother had gone out to warm up the car before driving him to school. The six-year-old was so bundled up that he was round as a ball, but that didn't stop him from trying to climb the banister from the wrong side.

"Good morning, Hussein. What are you doing?"

"Good morning, Miss Borghild! I'm just bouldering a little!" the boy shouted, hopping down and exposing his missing front teeth in a big smile. His face glistened with cold cream and was barely visible between his fuzzy hat, which was pulled down over his ears, and the many scarves his mother had tied around his neck.

"I see," Borghild said. "Are you ready for school?"

"Yeah! We're going skiing today!" Hussein beamed.

"Is that so?" Borghild said. "I suppose they've been running the snow machines down by the ski stadium for a while now. But do you have skis?"

"No, but we can borrow some."

"I'm sure you'll have lots of fun! But you might be a little too warmly dressed for skiing," Borghild said. "You'll see when you get started."

"Mommy says you can never be too warmly dressed in Norway," Hussein replied.

Borghild smiled. Aisha had heard lots of stories about careless people who got injured and froze to death in the inhospitable Norwegian outdoors, especially from Maja Seter. The chef always had a good disaster story up her sleeve, and Aisha was terrified that something would happen to her son here in this new, cold, and wild country.

Borghild understood Aisha's concern; she recognized something of Ingrid in Hussein. She'd also been this kind of child, the kind who could never sit still and was always climbing—on furniture, rocks, railings, and trees. A few weeks ago, Aisha had gotten a call from Hussein's teacher; her son had climbed up the big statue in the village when the class was on a field trip. The teacher had been worried—not that Hussein would get hurt, because he always got down safely, but that the other children might try the same thing.

Borghild followed Hussein to the exit and waved at mother and son as they started the twenty-minute drive down to Dalen. Then she went into the kitchen to get her coffee.

Ingrid walked resolutely up the stairs, with caretaker Alfred Haug's heavy footsteps behind her. *Those with a lot to do get a*

lot done, a voice said inside her—Nana Borghild's words. Alfred Haug said nothing. On the top floor, they turned down the corridor, reached the stairs leading to the attic, and started up the dark steps. A bit of light came through an opening in the wall at the top.

Ingrid hadn't had time to check the attic the day before and really didn't feel like dealing with it now, to be honest. Alfred clearly didn't either. But it had to be done. Since Aisha had discovered the possible fungus when she was up in the attic looking through the old linen chests, Ingrid knew she didn't have the luxury of simply shutting her eyes and pretending this wasn't happening. It was just that she couldn't really afford to do anything about it if she actually found fungus, either. She'd googled *dry rot* and shuddered at what she'd read: "Once it gets a good grip on your house, the consequences can be dire. It spreads rapidly, and often in concealed areas. You don't have much of a chance of discovering it before it's done a lot of irreversible damage."

She took the last few steps, pushed open the heavy attic door, and fumbled for the light switch. Bare bulbs hung from heavy timber beams, creating small, dim circles of light. The corners of the room were still dark, so she could only just make out the outlines of boxes, cupboards, and miscellaneous furniture that had been retired but not yet discarded. The air was freezing cold. Ingrid held the door open until Alfred had also made it up the stairs. He was panting after tramping up four floors with his heavy toolbox. He'd snorted when Ingrid had told him that Aisha had seen some strange growths along the skirting boards and protested against the whole expedition. But you could be darn sure he was going to take a look at this. He was the caretaker, and it was his job.

"Alfred, look! Could this be real dry rot?" Ingrid asked.

"What kind of dry rot would it be otherwise?" Alfred replied. "A replica? Made in China?"

Ingrid sighed. She didn't know whether Alfred was being stupid or was trying to tease her, but right now, she wasn't really in a joking mood.

"Dry rot is a nightmare!" she exclaimed. She looked around. "But I wouldn't have thought the hotel was particularly prone to it. The building is so solid . . ."

"Yes, exactly," Alfred said.

"And it's odd that it would grow up in the attic."

"Yes."

"You'd think it was pretty dry up here."

"Yes."

She turned to the caretaker and studied his bushy gray sideburns and eyes buried deep under folds of skin. How old was Alfred really? Impossible to say. Anywhere between fifty and a hundred, she thought. Could he have started neglecting his maintenance duties in recent years? Nana Borghild was a resourceful woman, but with limited income from hotel operations and a small staff, there were limits to how much she could realistically manage to keep track of. She was also over eighty. Perhaps the decay had been able to go too far.

Ingrid pointed her flashlight at the wall again.

"Have you been up here lately? Checked the moisture levels?"

Alfred stared at her without responding and walked over to the area she was shining the light on. He squatted down painstakingly and tentatively felt the rot or whatever it was with one finger. He loosened a small piece and lifted it to take a closer look. He sniffed it. Then he put it in his mouth.

Ingrid could hardly believe her eyes. Admittedly, she'd always thought Alfred Haug was a bit odd, but was he really *this* foolish? Why had Nana Borghild kept him as caretaker and handyman for so many years—a guy who sat on the floor eating dry rot?

Alfred's weather-beaten face broke into a big smile. He reached out, picked up another piece of the orange substance, and stood up heavily, supporting himself on his left knee. He walked toward Ingrid, grinning like a fool. When he got to her, he lifted what he had between his fingers up to her face. She squinted. It was orange and looked dry and porous.

"Take a bite!" Alfred said. "This is a very special kind of dry rot, I'd say!"

She took a step back, but he continued, "Don't you like Cheetos?"

Alfred's booming laughter resounded until the attic door shut behind them and they headed back down the stairs to the kitchen.

Ingrid took a five-minute break in the kitchen with Hussein. The chef had cleaned up after "nons"—as she called the after-school meal—and retired to her room for a while. Aisha had gone back to her office. The facilities manager had flexible hours so that she could take care of Hussein, but plenty of tasks needed her attention, and she had orders to go through. There was a lot to buy for both the hotel operations and the outdoor restaurant for ski tourists, which would open as soon as the snow came and the trails were prepped.

Hussein's cheeks were still rosy-red after the activity day at school. He was enthusiastic when Ingrid asked him how it had gone.

"I think I was pretty good at skiing," he said. "And the teacher thought so too. Even though Mikkel said I was just *trudging*. And then he started singing the Arabian Nights song from Aladdin."

Mikkel. That had to be Mikkel Dalen, son of Freddy Dalen, whom she remembered from school. So Mikkel was—*what would he be?*—the great-grandson (*yes, that must be it*) of the famous, and infamous, Hallgrim "Muskox" Dalen.

Hallgrim was a kind of village king, clan chief, and owner of the most prominent business in town, Muskox Machinery. His family dominated the village and had done so for as long as Ingrid could remember—and certainly long before that, too. She'd always thought the Dalen family was unpleasant, especially the boys. At school, they always had a snide comment at the ready. If you had gotten a new piece of clothing or a trendy backpack, you could be sure that it would be sneered at and possibly even damaged by the end of the day. She remembered the time Freddy Dalen and some of his friends tried to hoist a boy up the flagpole in the schoolyard. He was wearing expensive new jeans and had to be punished for thinking he was better than them. The boy fought back, but the older boys overpowered him and threaded the flag cord through the loops of his pants. The other kids just stood there and watched, their faces shining with terrified delight. But suddenly, a fair-haired boy came running through the schoolyard. It was Thor Seter, Ingrid's classmate. He was much younger than Freddy, but big and strong for his age, and he jumped on Freddy from behind. "Let him go!" Thor roared. "That's dangerous!"

Freddy let go of the boy and threw himself at Thor instead. "Why the hell do you care?" he shouted, shoving Thor to the ground. "Stupid sheep farmer!" He sat on top of Thor and made faces. "You smell like shit! Sheep shit!" Even though Thor was big, Freddy Dalen was bigger—and he had a whole gang with him. The bullies let go of the first victim, who darted off with his new pants intact, and turned to backing up Freddy, who was beating up Thor. No teachers were to be seen, but suddenly, a thin voice cut through the commotion: "Freddy! Stop!" It was Freddy's little brother, Karl, who was in Thor and Ingrid's class. Karl—the "Muskox Calf," as he was called—was small and thin, quite unlike his enormous brothers and cousins. "There's something off with that one," people in the village said. He mostly kept to himself, but Thor looked after him. Karl was usually quiet, but now, his voice echoed through the schoolyard: "Thor is my friend! I'll tell Mom if you hurt him!" Freddy laughed loudly but stopped hitting Thor, stood up, and wiped his hands on his pants before calling Karl a whiny brat and leaving the schoolyard, his minions at his heels.

It was as if the Dalen boys simply *had* to be nasty back then, and apparently, they were still the same way. Or maybe Ingrid was seeing ghosts in broad daylight? It didn't sound as though Hussein was taking the teasing to heart, but she'd definitely be keeping an eye on this. She was well aware of the way bullies could have a firm hold on small villages, and because Hussein was from elsewhere, there was extra reason to pay attention.

Ingrid knew that Nana Borghild also had a strained relationship with the Dalen family. She didn't even say hello to Hallgrim if they ran into each other down in the village, even though they were the same age and must have known each other since childhood. It was strange, really. It wasn't like Borghild to be impolite, so there had to be some reason for it. Had they also disliked each other during their school days, or was there something else? Ingrid had asked her grandmother about it once a long time ago but didn't get a clear answer. Nana Borghild had just shaken her head and said that some people were best to stay away from. Ingrid knew that Hallgrim Dalen and his sons had a reputation for being crafty in business situations—perhaps a bit *too* crafty sometimes. Apparently, they also didn't shy away from forcing people into deals that always worked out in the Dalen family's favor.

"HE SAID I WAS GOOD at shooting bears, though," Hussein said.

Ingrid looked at him, confused, before she realized what he meant.

"But that's a weird thing to say," Hussein said. "The only bear I've ever met is Barry, and he was shot long before I got to know him."

Ingrid could have told Hussein that *shooting bears* was local dialect for falling on skis, but he'd surely figure that out with time.

"Hey, Hussein," she said. "Does Speedy have any relatives up in the attic?"

Hussein looked at her quickly with his big, dark eyes before his gaze darted over to the stove and then back to her. He didn't answer immediately, just concentrated on the carvings on the back of the bench.

"The thing is, Alfred and I found some Cheetos in a mouse hole up there," Ingrid said. "And cookie crumbs on the floor. I was wondering if you had any idea how they could have gotten there?"

"His little cousins were hungry, too," Hussein explained, not meeting her eyes. "You have to feed the hungry!"

Ingrid had examined both the woolen blankets in the corner

and the food on the floor once she'd gotten over the initial shock of the "dry rot." The Cheetos had been stuffed into a small hole, which was why it looked as though something was growing out of the wall. On closer inspection, the brown powder had turned out to be crumbs—not fungal spores, as Ingrid had feared. When she kept looking, she'd also found a comic book and half a package of chocolate chip cookies between the blankets.

"Did we find your secret hideout up there, Hussein?" she asked, taking his hand. He looked at her with a shy smile.

"You know, it's okay," Ingrid said. "You can hang out in the attic when you need some time to yourself. Even though it's terribly cold up there right now. But you have to promise you won't feed the mice anymore."

Hussein nodded weakly and not entirely convincingly.

Ingrid continued, "And the next thing I have to say is even more important. I found a candle and matchbox up there, too. You *cannot* use matches! We'll get you a flashlight instead. Candles are a real fire hazard, okay? Imagine if the whole hotel burned down!"

Hussein looked at her in horror. "I'm sorry, Auntie Ingrid!" he exclaimed. "I won't burn down the hotel!"

Ingrid saw that he had tears in his eyes and regretted how stern she'd been. Besides, she always softened a bit when he called her Auntie Ingrid. She wasn't really his aunt, of course, but she considered it a declaration of love. She put her arm around him, and he rested his head on her shoulder.

They sat that way until Maja came back into the kitchen and started unloading groceries energetically. She occasionally cast a glance at the floor by the stove as if preparing to attack any rodents that might venture out from there.

"We really should have kept Meowgret's kittens," Maja said. "It's like my grandmother always said—when the cat's away, the mice will play."

Ingrid grabbed a caramel from the bowl on her desk and popped it in her mouth while her computer started up with a bit of fanfare. Even though Ingrid now heard this sound almost every day, it still caused her some discomfort. For months, she had associated both her computer and phone with social media, unwanted attention, and bad memories. Last year's experience had taught her that there was no limit to the amount of speculation and gossip people could spew about people they didn't even know.

Celebrity climber in deadly accident. Climbers criticized after fatal avalanche. Defied warnings. Uncertain if deceased climber can be retrieved from avalanche area. Lost close friend—and love. Speculations about the breakup. The media had been intrusive, and the comments sections even worse. Ingrid felt physically ill just thinking about it, her pulse speeding up and nausea setting in. She'd learned which sites to avoid and had reduced her use of social media to a minimum. She had to if she didn't want to fall into the black hole again and again.

But an internet-free life wasn't an option, and she had to use Messenger and Snapchat, which were her friend Vegard's preferred methods of communication. Vegard Vang had been there for her all along, and he still was.

Vegard and Ingrid had instantly become best friends when they met at a hotel in the Alps years ago. Vegard was working for an event agency that had organized a big conference for business leaders at the hotel, and Ingrid had been hired to give an inspirational speech. She wasn't particularly fond of such jobs, since these kinds of conferences were often filled with pretentious jerks, but it was incredibly well paid, so she'd said yes anyway.

Vegard had stood out among the conference participants. He was dressed informally (but still expensively and fashionably, she'd later realized; she was clueless about that kind of thing). He had tousled medium-blond hair, blue eyes, and a contagious smile. There was something eager and boyish about him that made him particularly charming, and after the conference was over, they spent a fun evening together at the hotel bar. At first, she'd thought Vegard was trying to pick her up, but she'd known him for only a few minutes when she realized he was never going to be interested in her *that* way.

"You're the sister I always wanted!" Vegard laughed as they hugged each other goodbye after the conference. "To be fair, I already have a sister. But you're better!" She had to laugh, too. She'd love it if Vegard were her brother.

Since then, they saw each other as much as possible when they were both in Norway. Vegard said she could always crash at his place when she was in Oslo. When they couldn't meet in person, they texted and talked on the phone. They'd supported each other in both professional and private situations. When Ingrid started dating Preben Wexelsen, she'd noticed he was skeptical of Vegard, and vice versa. Even though Preben quickly realized Ingrid's friend was by no means a competitor in the romance department, their relationship had never gotten past cordiality. Preben and Vegard tolerated each other, but no more than that. Ingrid had found this difficult because they both meant so much to her—but it was her friendship with Vegard that had stood the test of time.

They were quite different, she and Vegard. She was interested in the outdoors, he in city life. Where she preferred practical outdoor gear, he read up on trends and fashion. But they had something deeper in common, something that inspired confidence, goodwill, and trust. With time, Vegard came to know everything about her. She'd even shared the most difficult things with him—things no one else knew.

She was always happy when her friend was close by. With a friend like Vegard by her side, she felt she could handle anything.

And when Vegard got a boyfriend, it was completely different from when Ingrid got together with Preben. Ingrid had liked David Wong from the moment she met him. This actually came as a bit of a surprise, because when Vegard had told her that he'd started talking to the wealthy Chinese-Norwegian investor at a nightclub in Oslo and that they were now a couple, she'd been far from convinced that it was a good idea. But as soon as she met David, she immediately knew it was a good match. There was something about his attitude, his voice, the warmth in his beautiful eyes when he looked at Vegard.

She hadn't seen David as much recently because he was so occupied with his businesses, but he'd helped from the sidelines and given her lots of good advice, both practical and financial. Wisdom and economy seemed to merge in David. Vegard sometimes affectionately called him "the Owl," and David called Vegard "my squirrel." A bit ridiculous, but an appropriate nickname nonetheless—Vegard was social and sharp-witted, while at the same time hardworking and good at planning.

Had it not been for Vegard and David, Ingrid never would

have dared to take over the hotel. "Go for it!" Vegard had said with his characteristic enthusiasm. "I'll help you!" And help he had. Inspirer, strategist, and media adviser—Vegard Vang was worth his weight in gold. Perhaps even more than that, considering his modest weight. He and David had gone through both Ingrid's personal finances and the hotel's accounts for the past few years and helped Ingrid and Nana Borghild come up with a plan for refinancing and continued operations. The couple had also offered to invest some of their own money in the hotel, but Ingrid hadn't been keen on accepting charity and had gratefully declined. Besides, the best help from Vegard and David—or Vang & Wong as they were known in business settings—wouldn't be a direct investment, but rather support to make the hotel viable in the years to come.

Social media, which Vegard was so keen on, would also be crucial. She needed it for marketing the hotel and the Glitter Peak brand—or the Ingrid Berg brand, really, if you chose to look at it that way. Vegard helped her handle that part.

The program for Christmas and different events at the hotel had been posted on various websites and on Facebook. Instagram and Snapchat would help them reach the younger target audience. Although the current number of bookings wasn't exactly unmanageable, to say the least, interest in Glitter Peak Lodge had increased considerably after Vegard had started helping her promote the business through the right channels.

At that very moment, the Messenger symbol lit up on the screen. Speak of the devil—it was Vegard himself. *Great news!* the message read. *Call me!*

DECEMBER 3

"But what do *you* think about incentives?" the new maid, receptionist, and all-around assistant, Sunniva Pedersen, was asking Alfred Haug as Ingrid entered the kitchen.

Alfred didn't reply. He raised a hand in greeting to Ingrid and nodded good morning before he continued chewing on his slice of bread with sheep sausage, looking at Sunniva from beneath heavy eyelids.

"You know, what's most important when it comes to internal and external incentives, for example? A lot of research has been done on it but not that much in the hotel industry," Sunniva said eagerly, pushing her blond curls behind one ear with her left hand while gesticulating with the butter knife in her right as though it were a state-of-the-art presentation tool. "I'm writing about all of the different types of incentives for my bachelor's thesis on employee-involved innovation. External incentives can be financial rewards, for example."

Yet another blank look from Alfred.

She went on, "Like salary. Or bonuses. Internal incentives can be the experience of satisfaction or pleasure from the activity you're doing."

Alfred didn't have a response to this, either. Perhaps he didn't get any particular satisfaction or pleasure from his work, Ingrid thought as she leaned against the kitchen counter after pouring herself a cup of coffee. Or maybe he did. He enjoyed chopping wood, she knew that. And drinking a beer afterward. Maybe Sunniva could include those activities in her thesis as examples of internal and external incentives.

SUNNIVA PEDERSEN—OR SUNNY, AS HER friends called her—was a rising star in the field of work-life research and management philosophy. She already had a considerable following on social media and was determined to grow it further. While she was writing her thesis and waiting for her career to take off, she was also employed at Glitter Peak Lodge in a fairly flexible role. Sunny cleaned rooms, made bookings, and did pretty much whatever was needed. She thought of it as research. The hotel had been going through a bit of a slump but had recently been looking for more staff, with plans to make a new push after several years of reduced operations. At her interview, Sunny had said that working at Glitter Peak would be an ideal way for her to combine fieldwork and income, but as she sat here at the breakfast table with the taciturn caretaker, Ingrid realized that Sunny might not be too sure about that anymore.

"Hey, Maja." Sunny now tried to address the chef, who was relaxing with a large mug of coffee and cream. "How do you think we can expand our innovative toolbox?"

"Our innovative toolbox?" Maja asked, setting her coffee cup down on the table. "Isn't the toolbox we have enough? Has it gotten too small, Alfred?"

The caretaker snorted. "No, no, that's nonsense. The toolbox is just the right size, like it's always been. It's enough for me, just like it was for my father before me. I can't see any point in expanding it."

Sunny tried to formulate a few sentences about thinking outside the box—or toolbox—but her attempts fell on deaf ears, and she instead concentrated on spreading butter on a slice of bread.

Ingrid almost felt sorry for Sunny. She was so enthusiastic about her studies and genuinely interested in understanding the mechanisms behind the development of the tourism industry, but if she thought she could discuss innovation processes with old-timers such as Alfred and Maja, she was barking up the wrong tree. Figuring out your audience was something you needed to learn if you wanted to achieve your goals. Perhaps Ingrid should talk to Sunny about that some other time, but right now, she had good news.

"Sunny," she said. "Guess who's coming here this weekend!"

"Vegard?" Sunny suggested with a hopeful smile.

"Yes! But not alone. He's bringing Pia Pihlstrøm!"

"*What!?* Are you kidding me?"

Sunny looked so ecstatic that Ingrid had to laugh. It was fun to share the news with someone who really knew how to appreciate it. The visit from the famous influencer had been on Ingrid's mind ever since her conversation with Vegard last night.

"Yeah, she saw his last posts and thought the hotel seemed really nice. They agreed she'd come up with him this weekend.

Vegard was so excited. You know he's pretty proud of being friends with her."

"Of *course* he is!" Sunny shouted. "Pia Pihlstrøm! She has, like, almost a million followers on Instagram, you know that, right?"

Ingrid grinned. "I *knew* you'd be excited!"

Maja and Alfred looked as though they had no idea what was going on. "Pia Pihlstrøm—who's that?" Maja asked.

Sunny was quick to answer. "Well, first she got famous as a model, but then she started a blog where she shares stuff with her followers. Everything from skincare routines to animal welfare. She's *super* popular."

"Okay," Maja said. "But what does she *do*? Does she *make* anything? What does she do for a living?"

"She lives off her blog and social media," Sunny said. "And different jobs and ads and that kind of thing. But she doesn't share absolutely everything. She kind of has a mysterious private life."

"Oh?"

"Yeah, she never says anything about boyfriends or stuff like that," Sunny said. "Has Vegard told you anything, Ingrid?"

"No, but apparently there are a lot of rumors," Ingrid replied. "She doesn't tell him much either."

"I think it just makes people even *more* curious, if you ask me," Sunny said. "Everyone loves speculating about what she's hiding. I mean, why doesn't she ever just come out and say she's fallen in love?"

"Maybe she's one of those . . . lesbians?" Alfred interjected.

"No," Sunny said. "That's not something people think they need to hide anymore. But maybe she's asexual? Or polyamorous?"

"Or secretly married?" Ingrid laughed.

In any case, she knew what Sunny was saying was true. Every one of Pia P's photos and updates was scrutinized, and "everyone" was watching to see whether she ever hinted at something private. Well, not Ingrid, but she was totally behind the times anyway, as Vegard liked to point out.

"But apart from her love life, she shares a ton," Sunny continued. "She posts tons of things from her travels and restaurants and stuff. So if she comes here, it's *super* cool! There are thousands of people out there who want to do whatever Pia P does."

"Yeah, it's no wonder Vegard is so happy!" Ingrid said. "But of course, that means it's even more important that everything goes well when she's here."

The thought was overwhelming. Pia Pihlstrøm was used to traveling the world in first class on sponsored trips. She probably wouldn't be all that impressed by a rundown hotel with Cheetos in the corners and mice in the kitchen—and probably not by a rustic pinnekjøtt dinner, either.

Ingrid finished her coffee, grabbed a banana from the fruit platter on the counter, and left the kitchen after saying goodbye to the others. She knew what to do when she started getting stressed like this: get outside.

THE GROUND CRUNCHED BENEATH HER BOOTS, and the air was freezing cold. Ingrid pulled her buff up over her chin and her hat down over her ears. It was still dark outside, but the light was growing over the horizon, ready to unleash a new day. Today, she wanted to see the sunrise from Angelina Hill, and she walked the familiar path along the edge of the big ravine. It was dangerous for untrained hikers with its steep rock face down one side, but it was Ingrid's old stomping ground. She could have walked the path blindfolded. She'd walked here in all kinds of weather and all kinds of moods. The others had always thought it was a bit odd that she plodded around like this all by herself, but walking gave her peace and comfort.

A lot of things had changed in her life, but the landscape at Glitter Peak always remained the same. It was wild and over-whelming with the gray rock masses and steep, sharp summits, with Heaven's Horn towering above the rest. At the same time, the mountains were also full of detail, and they had all kinds of secrets you had to be a local to know about—where the reindeer usually grazed, where you could take shelter if you were caught in a storm, where it was safe to walk, where you needed to be extra careful. She passed Troll Rock, which Maja Seter claimed an old troll had thrown when humans settled near Glitter Peak and started build-ing there. As a child, Ingrid had always shuddered at the thought. It was terrifying that the troll had been so angry—and it was lucky that the rock hadn't hit the hotel! She'd also wondered where the troll went after that. Had it retreated to another mountain area, or had it forgotten to hide when the sun came up and turned into a stone itself? Perhaps it was lurking somewhere between the moun-tains, waiting for the right time to take its revenge?

The sky was starting to lighten as Ingrid set off up toward An-gelina Hill, which had been named after her mother. Ingrid had called it "Angel Hill" when she was little, imagining her parents rising like angels into the big, blue vault over Glitter Peak. Even now, it still felt as though she could sense their presence here more than anywhere else. She'd been so young when they died that she couldn't really remember them properly—except as a safe and warm presence. Occasionally, a scent or thought might flash through her like a bolt of lightning, a reminder of what they had once been.

Her heart rate rose in the demanding terrain, and she started to warm up. She was still wearing her advanced sports watch, a Garmin Tactix that Preben had given her. She stopped at the top of the hill, took it off, and put it in her jacket pocket. She stretched her arms up in the air and took a deep breath, taking in the view and enjoying the cold air flowing into her lungs. Her worries, her everyday problems, the practical challenges of the hotel—everything seemed so small when she was standing up here. On one side, she stared straight down into the dark gorge. On the other, the scree continued all the way to the base of Heaven's Horn, now silhouetted against the brightening sky.

She looked up at the summit, which would soon be bathed in golden light. Ingrid used to love climbing on Heaven's Horn. She'd summited for the first time at the age of twelve, guided by an experienced mountaineer from the village. Nana Borghild had said that as far as she knew, Ingrid was the youngest person to have made it to the top. It was a challenging route, and Borghild herself had been fourteen the first time she made it up. Ingrid had been surprised when her grandmother told her about her own ascent. She'd been in her sixties at the time—an age that seemed ancient to a twelve-year-old. It had been impossible to imagine that Borghild had also once been an enthusiastic young climber. But she had been, just like Ingrid. At some point, however, Borghild had also stopped climbing. There was a lot Ingrid didn't know about her grandmother's life and past. Ingrid made a resolution: she was going to ask her more now, while she still had the chance.

The fact that her grandmother knew the wild and dangerous

joys of climbing had certainly contributed to her giving Ingrid the freedom to pursue the hobby. Nana Borghild understood the rewards it could bring and the draw of the mountains. Over time, climbing had become Ingrid's life, and she had summited many other peaks—the wildest and most challenging in the world. But after what happened last summer, she hadn't climbed a single mountain.

A piercing noise broke her train of thought—her phone. How silly of her to forget to put it on silent; she usually did that when she was out walking. Her walks were her way of meditating, and she didn't like to be disturbed. But when she pulled her phone out of her jacket pocket, she saw that it was Vegard. She might as well answer.

"Hi, Vegard!"

"Good morning, hon! What are you up to?"

"I'm out on a walk."

"Oh, sorry! I didn't mean to disturb you. Should we chat later?"

"No, it's fine. I'm taking a break now. Standing and looking at the view of Heaven's Horn and Styggfossen."

"Oh. Do you think . . . would you ever want to try climbing them again?"

Not only had she climbed Heaven's Horn in her past life, but she'd also loved ice climbing Styggfossen in the winter—a challenge that often attracted groups of climbers to the hotel. She suddenly recalled the one time she'd brought Preben up here and how much fun they'd had. Styggfossen was a challenge even for an experienced climber like him, but they'd made it to the top and warmed up their frozen bodies together afterward . . .

She brought herself back to the conversation with Vegard.

"Do I want to climb them again? Nope. I'm done." She could tell that her friend wanted to say something but was holding back. He probably knew that there was no point and changed the subject.

"There were a few things I wanted to discuss with you before Pia and I come up on Friday. I was wondering who else will be at the dinner. Are any locals coming? What about that sheep farmer?"

"You mean Thor Seter?"

Vegard liked to tease her about her childhood friend Thor: "How are things with that cute farmer, hmm?" Thor was one of the few friends from her school days with whom she still had contact, and Vegard had met him once or twice and gotten it into his head that Ingrid had gone "home to her childhood sweetheart." Or he pretended to think so, at least. Vegard knew that wasn't really the case, even though she and Thor had sort of been "boyfriend-girlfriend" for about three weeks in the fifth grade.

"Why on earth would I ask him to come to dinner?"

"Well, I mean, he *is* handsome. And maybe he could be an exotic escapade for Pia?"

Ingrid snorted.

ONCE THEY'D FINISHED TALKING, she stayed there for a while longer, watching the sun coming up, before she turned and started heading back home. She really did want to imagine that she might climb Heaven's Horn again one day. She'd lived with and for climbing for almost her whole life and came back home to find what she'd lost along the way. She'd thought it would be waiting for her here—the peace, the anchorage she needed, the roots. But panic rose just at the thought of the steep wall, the gorge below her with its frozen waterfall, the masses of snow that could break loose and bury her . . .

Deep down, she didn't think she'd ever be able to climb the mountain again.

DECEMBER 4

Some things are so beautiful that they can't be photographed without losing their essence. Thor Seter had had this thought time and time again. The pale sun shining through the fog like a silver button. The spruce forest, dense and bewitching, branches heavy with snow. The bare deciduous trees, brown at the base of the trunks and gradually lighter toward the tops where the frost had covered them, their upper branches fully encased in a heavenly glaze.

The fact that he couldn't quite capture the beauty with his camera lens was a source of eternal frustration for Thor, but also inspiration to try again.

As a sheep farmer, he didn't have much free time, but photography was a hobby that meant more and more to him over the years. It was as if he saw the nature around him differently after he started taking pictures. He noticed the changes in the light and where the shadows fell; he saw motifs everywhere—in the mountains and rivers and sky, in the interaction between animals and humans and the surrounding nature. Now he even saw his sheep as models as well—and he'd actually sold some pictures of them to tourists at an exhibition at the community center last summer. Sandra should have seen that. She'd always just scoffed at "those silly photos" of his. But when the exhibit opened, it was too late for Sandra to scoff, because she'd gone back to Oslo long ago.

Now, Thor was sitting perfectly still at the edge of Dalen River, aiming his camera at something he'd never seen in real life: a kingfisher. These birds tended to favor warmer climes and were therefore rarely spotted in Norway. It was hard to grasp that it was really here on the Dalen River in the middle of winter, but the river hadn't frozen over yet, and the bird must have found something to eat up here. It had flown across the water like a bolt of royal-blue lightning and was now perched on a low-hanging branch above the river. Thor stayed as still as he could as he pointed the camera. He snapped a few times, but the result wasn't good enough. He pulled off a glove and turned one of the knobs on the camera. He wanted to try his luck at burst mode to try to capture the bird's movements. Now it had settled down over by the old bridge. This could be good. But then—*bang!*

A sound echoed across the valley, and the bird was gone in a flash of blue. *Dammit! Seriously? Right now?* Another bang sounded.

It had to be Hallgrim "Muskox" Dalen or one of his sons out hunting.

Everyone in Dalen had grown up with hunting, and you'd have to look hard to find someone who was against it on principle. Thor wasn't either. As a rural sheep farmer, he was used to animals having to be killed, recognizing that life and death were closely intertwined. Nothing to pout about. That was simply the way it was. But the Dalen family's love of hunting was unusually strong. They hunted game birds until Christmas and grouse all winter. They shot hares, beavers, marten, badgers, deer, elk, and reindeer. No creature on four legs—and hardly anything on two, for that matter—was safe when the Muskox and his herd were out hunting. Whether the hunt was legal or not wasn't of particular concern to them.

Hallgrim had to be around eighty now, but he was big and strong and still worked several days a week at the family business, Muskox Machinery, which sold and repaired tractors and other machines. Thor was unsure whether it was Hallgrim's nickname that had inspired the company's name or vice versa. Either way, it wasn't difficult to understand the name when you saw the man, enormous and bull-necked as he was. His sons Arthur, Bernt, and Cato had all joined the company, as well as his grandson Karl, who was a mechanic and assistant of sorts.

Hallgrim was the great-grandson of the fabled Old Hallgrim, who, according to legend, had lived to be 112 and killed a bear with his bare hands when he was 110. Thor had his own opinions about the tale, but there was no getting around the fact that the younger Hallgrim was a prolific hunter.

The Dalen family's enormous log house could be seen on the hill on the other side of the river. It was on one of the nicest plots of land in the village, and practically every square foot from basement to attic was filled with skins and antlers from animals that Hallgrim and his family had killed. Thor had been there often—and never without getting a bit scared—when he went to school with Karl Dalen. Back then, he'd seen the occasional glimpse of another side of Hallgrim Dalen. The Muskox, who otherwise had the social skills of a bulldozer, had a gruff affection for his grand-children, the spindly little Karl in particular.

Thor listened attentively. It had been quiet for a while now; the two shots must have been enough. Perhaps luck wasn't on the hunter's side today, or perhaps it had been a direct hit off the bat?

The kingfisher was nowhere to be seen, even though Thor stayed squatting on the riverbank until his feet fell asleep. Well, he couldn't spend any more time here anyway. He had to head back to the barn. It had been a snowless fall, and the sheep had been able to graze until November, but now there was frost on the ground, and that meant indoor feeding for a few months to come.

He strolled the few hundred feet along the gravel road back to the farm. Yesterday, he and Aunt Maja had spoken about making deliveries to Glitter Peak. He'd already sent up a selection of the finest meats he had, and Maja thought there would be opportu-nities to sell more. She wanted him to stop by with samples of other meats as well. Lamb steaks, for example, and maybe some of the sausages he had made. Yes, he was more than willing to do that. If Glitter Peak was happy with what he had to offer, it could be the start of bigger, more regular deliveries to the hotel. God knows he could use the money. Running a farm wasn't easy these days. As a farmer, he was his own little business, holding all the responsibility for everything from maintenance and animal care to finances and paperwork. He could easily wind up working 70 to 80 hours a week. Practically no free time to speak of. But in the few hours he allowed himself to take photos, he got a bit of a reprieve from his worries.

It wasn't until Thor was approaching the yard at home that

he saw a car parked there, a car that sent a pang of—was it nostalgia?—through him. The unmistakable shape, the bright blue color, so well maintained it almost hurt to look at it. There was only one person in the village who still drove a Volvo Amazon. Even the older men who once swore by the reliable classic had replaced it with newer models by now, but you could still find the occasional Amazon in the barns around the village. They were polished and waxed and given an airing for holidays and parades.

Thor didn't even need to get close enough to read the license plate to know that the figure sitting on the steps of the farmhouse was the Muskox Calf.

Karl was a simple man, but he had been a faithful friend to Thor throughout elementary school. A person didn't have that many friends to choose from in a small place like Dalen. Nowadays, the two of them mostly met only when Thor stopped by the workshop to have some machines serviced or buy some parts. They always exchanged a few friendly words, but they didn't have that much in common anymore besides the machines and their childhood days.

Once Thor had brewed some coffee, they sat down at the old kitchen table, both with steaming hot mugs in front of them.

Karl squirmed in his chair and looked out the window at the bird feeder. "Blue tit," he said.

"Huh?" Thor said, following his gaze.

There was indeed a tiny Eurasian blue tit sitting on the feeder.

"Aha. There's quite a lot of great tits and blue tits around here right now," Thor said.

Karl nodded. "They like lard."

"Yes," Thor replied. Then they sat in silence for a while.

"I saw a rare bird down by the river earlier," Thor said. "A kingfisher. But it got scared off by gunshots before I could get a good picture of it. Were you the one out hunting?"

Karl shook his head.

"Do you know who it was?" Thor asked.

Karl shook his head for a while longer before it gradually turned into a slow nod. "It was probably Uncle Bernt," he said. "He wanted to shoot a buck he saw over on the south side."

Silence again.

"Was there anything you wanted to talk about?" Thor asked. "Since you stopped by?"

Karl shook his head again. "No . . ." Then he nodded. "Are you up at Glitter Peak much these days?"

Thor was a bit surprised by the question. "No . . . well, it depends on what you mean by *much*. I stop by every once in a while. Why?"

Karl fell silent and looked out the window again. The blue tit was gone. "I have to get back to the workshop," he said suddenly, standing up. "Gotta fix Mikalsen's headlight and straighten out a dent in the fender."

"But what did you mean about Glitter Peak, Karl?"

The Muskox Calf just shook his head again. "Nothing. Gotta head out now."

THOR WATCHED THE BLUE VOLVO as it turned onto the main road, following the oval taillights with his eyes until they were swallowed up by the darkness. It wasn't easy to make sense of Karl, but if he had something on his mind, he'd get it out eventually.

❄

It had been a long day. Ingrid kicked off her shoes and hung her jacket in the closet. She opened the kitchen cabinet and reached behind the bags of almonds and cartons of raisins. The plastic crackled as she pulled out the bag of caramels. She didn't know why she hid it; it was probably a remnant from her time with Preben, when caramels were a "guilty pleasure." He would have had something to say about carbs and saturated fats—but *God*, the way they melted in your mouth was pure heaven! She unwrapped a golden candy and popped it in her mouth. *Mmmm.* It was a taste she experienced only on Saturdays as a child, but now she could indulge herself whenever she wanted. Being an adult involved a lot of hassle, but there were some advantages, too.

Her phone buzzed. *Remember to rest!* Vegard's message read. It seemed he'd taken it upon himself to be her life coach now, too, in addition to acting as her financial adviser and social media manager. But Vegard knew her, and he was right; she wasn't good at taking breaks. Breaks were important, she'd learned that much. Okay, then, maybe she *should* listen to him. Rest. How were you supposed to do that, though?

She hesitated a bit before taking a bottle of white wine out of the fridge. *Yes, dammit.* Now she was going to sink down on the sofa with a glass of wine and watch TV—before dinner! She'd never been much of a TV watcher; she'd always been too busy and found it strange how people could spend so much time on it. She thought TV was a poor substitute for real life. Soaking in hot springs on the way up Kilimanjaro or camping in a tent in the Arctic with a storm raging outside and the northern lights glittering above, she hadn't needed that kind of entertainment. Life itself was more than enough.

Now, however, she saw things differently. She was neither in Africa nor the Arctic. She was in her apartment at Glitter Peak Lodge in the middle of the Norwegian mountains, in the middle of the Norwegian winter. It had been a long day of work, and she deserved a break.

Ingrid sat down on the sofa and lifted the glass of white burgundy. She still had a bit of caramel taste in her mouth, but when she inhaled deeply, she could make out the fresh scent of apple mixed with something reminiscent of toast. She could picture her old climbing partner, the Benedictine monk Giovanni Orlando, with his nose buried deep in the glass. *Toast with a hint of wood,* he would have said before taking a generous sip and letting it linger in his mouth. *Creamy, minerally, fruity—and what a balanced freshness, Ingrid!* She would have smiled at him and pretended to have recognized the same scents in the wine, but over the years, she actually *had* learned quite a lot from the delightful, kindhearted food and wine lover.

She and Giovanni had met years ago in the climbing village of Arco on Lake Garda. She was surprised that a monk could also be a mountain climber, but he'd said that he learned as much about God in nature as inside the monastery.

He'd also told her that he worked with Catholic charities in the places he went to climb. He tried to be a force for good everywhere he went. He was one of the few people she knew who could say something like that without sounding pompous. He'd been involved with so many things, things that might otherwise seem to be contradictory but that, with him, were natural parts of a complex personality. God and nature. Wine and asceticism.

Living life to the fullest and caring for his fellow man. He'd encompassed all of these things.

And now he was gone. God, how she missed him.

Ingrid took a sip of wine, grabbed the remote, and turned on the TV. She stretched out her legs and pulled a blanket over her. Ahhh, this *was* pretty nice. The way people watched TV had also changed during the years she'd been abroad. Before, you had to take what you could get from a handful of channels and watch at the right times if there was something you were interested in, but now, you had all kinds of streaming services, and "bingeing" a show had become a phenomenon. Vegard was constantly enlightening her about things she simply *had* to watch. A couple of years ago it was *The Kardashians*; now it was a series about amateur chefs. There was probably something even newer than that, but she at least hadn't had to watch *The Bachelor*— even though there'd been a sly twinkle in Vegard's eye when he'd suggested that Glitter Peak could be the perfect location for the next season. She usually just laughed at him. When were people supposed to have the time to watch all of these programs? She certainly didn't have that luxury. But right now, at this moment, after hours of menu planning and staining the stairs and setting mouse traps, a little relaxation was exactly what she needed. Some mindless entertainment might be just the trick to silence the voice in the back of her head that kept nagging her about how much she had to do.

She took another sip of wine and flipped through the channels at random, landing on the celebrity edition of a popular outdoor reality competition show. The irony of sitting and relaxing with this show in particular struck her, but she decided to watch anyway. At first, she thought it was pretty boring—a group of people in colorful hiking clothes struggling up a steep hill. The camera zoomed in on a dark-haired woman sobbing about her fear of heights. Then it cut to a monologue with a young redhead complaining about how tired she was of hearing about the dark-haired woman's fear of heights. The team spirit had clearly worn a bit thin here. Ingrid knew all about how that could happen, and how dangerous it could be—if the climb was for real, that is. *These* particular participants weren't in any real danger. They were surrounded by invisible helpers and assistants, the climbing gear would have been checked and double-checked, and the rescue helicopter wasn't far away if anyone panicked or had an accident.

There was one team at the top. They were waving a red flag and producing tears of joy that the cameras skillfully captured. But—

Ingrid flinched when she saw a familiar face, sloshing wine all over her lap. She set her glass down on the table and dabbed at the spreading stain on the blanket as the narrator announced: "And at this stage, the participants get a surprise! The judge of the summit competition isn't just anyone . . . because when the participants reach the top of Frost Peak, they are welcomed by Preben Wexelsen, international globe-trotter, expedition leader and adventurer, and regular on lists of Norway's sexiest men."

Preben's face came into focus.

Ingrid felt her heart beat faster. Preben looked into the camera with a crooked smile on his rugged face, a hint of wolf in that smile. It somehow felt as if those green eyes under those dark brows were staring right out of the TV and straight at her. Suddenly, he was there. The man she'd once loved.

This was unbelievable. She couldn't even get five minutes of relaxation before her past appeared on the TV screen. What were the odds of that happening? Well, there he stood, so confident, arms crossed, welcoming the expedition members as they trudged to the top.

It's not just the juries of the women's magazines who think he's one of Norway's sexiest men, Ingrid thought. *He thinks so himself, too.* And Preben *was* nice to look at, no doubt about that. He also had charm. Charisma. Preben always knew what to say and do, how to get people on board, to help them perform their best. He was tough and inspiring. But she also knew he wasn't as invincible as he liked to make himself out to be. Even Preben Wexelsen could make mistakes. He was a human being, with strengths and weaknesses. But he was reluctant to admit that.

His competitive instinct, for example. He had needed it in order to achieve as much as he had, but sometimes it could overshadow his judgment and cause him to make the wrong decisions. His stubbornness verged on childishness, and he had a hard time listening to others and taking advice.

This stubbornness was what had brought misfortune upon them in the Himalayas. That was the bitter truth. That and the fact that she had been so incomprehensibly dazzled by him that she hadn't put her foot down when he wanted to start the ascent, despite warnings from the Sherpas that the weather and snow conditions weren't optimal. "There's *not* going to be an avalanche," he'd said firmly. She and the others had believed him, and they'd set out from base camp. A day or two of waiting would have saved them. A day or two of Preben listening to the others and not being so unbearably self-righteous—then everything could have been avoided. But they went out. Disaster struck. There was indeed an avalanche.

And now, here he was on TV, smiling that wolfish smile as

if nothing had happened. She couldn't believe he was able to do that—make entertainment out of climbing after what they'd been through, after the accident where they'd lost so much. They'd lost Brother Giovanni and barely escaped with their own lives. The local development projects they were involved in had come to a standstill. The tragedy and all of the media coverage in the aftermath had put an end to, or at least a strong brake on, her career as an expedition leader and had taken away her passion and joy for climbing—while Preben apparently just continued on as usual.

She turned down the volume on the TV. It had gotten harder to breathe. She could hear her breaths as though they were gusts of wind. Was she crying? She didn't know. Her hands were shaking when she picked up her phone and called Vegard.

"Hey, sweetie!" He picked up on the second ring. "What's up?"

She couldn't answer in the same upbeat way.

"Vegard!" she sobbed. "Preben. He's on TV right now. I . . ."

"Oh no. Wait a sec, let me just go to the other room."

She heard the sound of a door closing before he continued.

"Okay. You saw Preben on TV?"

"Yes!"

"Is it that reality show?"

"Yes, have you seen it, too?"

"No, but I've seen some commercials. Maybe I should've warned you. Are you okay?"

"No. Or—I don't really know."

She paused for a moment and tried to control her voice.

"I . . . Vegard, it makes me sick to look at him. He's just like . . . moved on. 'Norway's sexiest man and globe-trotter and expedition leader,' the presenter called him. Has everyone totally forgotten about the accident? I just don't get it." A terrible suspicion dawned on her. "Could it be that Preben has gotten even *more* interesting for TV producers after the accident? Like, the scandal made him exciting and sexy somehow?"

Vegard hesitated for a moment before answering. "I don't think so. And I don't think they've forgotten about the accident, either. But they probably think that accidents happen and that you can't blame people forever."

"A year and a half. That's not forever. We lost a friend in that accident. A good friend! And I lost my career, my network, the life I built."

She heard Vegard take a deep breath. They'd been through this before. Vegard also knew she'd lost more than just this. Shortly after the accident, as soon as she'd gotten home and seen Vegard again, she'd told him about the loss that neither Preben nor Nana Borghild had been informed of. But he also knew that it was too difficult for her to talk about.

"You haven't lost your career, Ingrid. Or your life. You're thirty-three years old! Life has only just begun! You have your skills, your experience, tons of job offers. You have me and Nana Borghild. And of course, you have Glitter Peak Lodge."

"Yes. But there are so many obstacles all the time. In the hotel business, too. Something is always coming up. I'm tired. I don't know how much more I can handle."

"But isn't that just like climbing, Ingrid?"

"Climbing?"

Vegard continued, "When you've been up on a difficult wall and encountered obstacles, you want nothing more than to try again the next day, right?"

"Yes. Or . . . it *was* like that. It isn't anymore."

There was silence on the other end.

"Listen, Ingrid," Vegard said after a moment. "I have to run, but we'll talk again soon, okay?"

"Okay," she said. "I didn't mean to bother you."

"You're never a bother, honey!"

She knew it wasn't true; Vegard was simply too nice to say that it wasn't a good time to talk. And she was grateful for that.

She blew her nose, suddenly embarrassed to be feeling so sorry for herself. This wasn't her. She was alive, after all. And fully aware that she had a lot to be grateful for.

She put down her phone and had just taken another sip of wine when there was a knock at the door.

Nana Borghild was standing with Thor Seter in the doorway. Now, the tall, fair-haired farmer towered more than a head over Borghild.

"Hi! What are you doing here?" Ingrid exclaimed. Then she caught herself, hearing how rude it sounded. "Sorry, I mean, please come in."

They both stepped inside, and Thor shut the door behind him. He was holding a brown paper bag in one hand.

Of course someone comes by at this very moment, Ingrid thought. She scanned the scene as it must have appeared to the other two: the bottle on the kitchen counter, the wineglass on the coffee table next to the sofa. The muted TV, still playing that damn show. And she probably looked like a mess to boot. She felt her face grow warm and guessed her hair was probably sticking up in all directions. She instinctively pushed her curls behind her ears as if that might help her make a somewhat more presentable general impression and quickly picked the used tissues off the sofa.

Nana Borghild looked at Ingrid in surprise and put a hand on her shoulder.

"Are you all right?" she asked quietly.

Ingrid nodded, and her grandmother turned to the guest: "Thor here came with some more pinnekjøtt and a couple other things from the farm. He wanted to hear what we might need in the future as well."

Thor smiled. "Only if it's a good time, of course. I don't want to intrude."

His voice was deep and solid. So different from Vegard's.

"Of course," Ingrid said quickly. "It's no bother at all. I was just . . . relaxing. But come in," she said again.

She located the remote between two sofa cushions and turned off the TV. "Have a seat. I just opened a bottle of wine. Would you like a glass?"

"Thanks, but I'm driving," Thor said.

It almost looked as if he was embarrassed to decline. He wasn't at the hotel that often, and he'd never been here in "The Residence," at least not since Ingrid had moved in. She and Thor had been good friends throughout their childhood and adolescence, even though their fifth-grade romance had been short-lived. She broke it off after a few weeks for reasons she no longer recalled, and she didn't remember how Thor had reacted, either. He wasn't exactly the type to talk about feelings. Thor mostly stuck to the practical, really—just as she did. But their friendship had lasted until she moved to Oslo for college. Or it had lasted to some extent, even though they hadn't had much contact after she left the village. Perhaps it had just been in some kind of hibernation.

"Of course, sorry," Ingrid said. "You can't drink when you're driving. I should've thought of that. Would you like a cup of coffee instead?"

"Yes, please," Thor replied. "You can never go wrong with coffee."

He did as she'd suggested and sat down on the sofa, placing the brown paper bag on the floor beside him before taking off his blue jacket and hanging it over the armrest. His big, weathered hands opened and closed, and he put them on his knees.

"Well, *I* would like a glass of wine," Nana Borghild said with a smile, settling down in one of the armchairs. She placed one leg neatly over the other and wiggled her foot.

INGRID SLIPPED INTO THE BATHROOM and splashed cold water over her face while the coffee brewed. She looked at herself in the mirror. She didn't look as bad as she felt, actually. A little tired, maybe. Bushy hair. No makeup. A hint of dark circles under her eyes. Maybe she should start using something to cover them up—one of those products Vegard was always hinting at. But she wasn't too fond of that kind of thing. She'd always thought that natural was best.

She got a cup of coffee for Thor and a glass of wine for her grandmother and sat down on the sofa. Nana Borghild spoke eagerly about the deliveries from Thor's farm. She was really talking him up. Thor and Borghild could have discussed the deliveries with Aisha or Maja. But Thor was of course welcome to come to her, by all means. It was nice that he was here, actually. It gave her something to think about besides that damned Preben Wexelsen.

The meat from Seter Farm was always high quality, and if they could help Thor keep the farm up and running, nothing could be better. She knew that he—like so many farmers—worked a lot and still struggled to make ends meet.

"I have more pinnekjøtt in storage, and more sheep and lamb meat as well," Thor explained. "And Aunt Maja has helped me make cured sausage using the traditional methods. I brought some samples."

He reached inside the bag he'd placed on the floor and took out a couple of plastic boxes.

"This one is pure sheep meat," he said, taking the lid off one box. "The other is a mix of deer, pork, and sheep. Have a taste."

He held the boxes out to her. Ingrid took a bite of the sheep sausage first. It was salty with a strong gamey flavor and was slightly acidic. The mixed sausage was milder.

"Mmm! This is really good," she said once she'd finished chewing. "But what do you mean by 'traditional methods'?"

"It means that the minced meat is left to mature for several weeks before the sausages are stuffed," Thor replied. "That helps the pH values drop slowly so the lactic acid bacteria can develop. That's what gives it that nice, cured taste."

"Do you add any spices?"

"No, you can use pepper and garlic and wine if you want, but I don't really think these sausages need it. The flavor is so good on its own. We don't use any other additives either."

"And you can be sure that the meat will keep when you don't add any preservatives?"

"Yeah, this is traditional knowledge. Salt and lactic acid bacteria keep bad bacteria away, and maturing takes place in airtight packaging. After the sausages are stuffed, they're dried and cold smoked. The method is even approved by the food safety department."

"I'm glad that sheep meat is back in fashion," Nana Borghild said. "So much has gone to waste because people only wanted to eat lamb."

"Yeah, there's no point in making pinnekjøtt or sausage from lamb, in any case," Thor said. "The meat is dryer and has less flavor. Old ladies taste best." He paused. "I mean ewes, of course."

Ingrid had to laugh, and Thor turned bright red. Nana Borghild took a sip from her wineglass, her eyes sparkling with laughter.

"How's the photography going, Thor?" Ingrid asked after a moment.

"It's going well," Thor said. "I'm hoping to set up an exhibition soon. Maybe in the summer."

Thor told them a bit about his hobby and the kingfisher at Dalen River. Nana Borghild scoffed loudly when she heard about the shots that had scared off the rare visitor.

"Yep, that's typical of Hallgrim Dalen and his gang. They just bulldoze right through. No consideration for people or animals."

The last traces of light disappeared as they chatted about food and sheep and life in the village. Ingrid stood to turn on another lamp, but Thor got up as well.

"Well, I should get back home," he said. "It'll be pitch-black out soon." He put on the blue jacket he'd hung over the armrest of the sofa. "By the way, Aunt Maja says it's *Barbromesse* today. Saint Barbara's feast day. Legend says the sun disappears and won't come back before Saint Lucia's Day. Aunt Maja knows all about these old holidays."

"Yes, Maja knows a lot about many things," Nana Borghild said. "Shall we stop by the kitchen before you head home?" She waited until Thor was at the door, then whispered to Ingrid, "Was that Preben Wexelsen on the television when we arrived?"

Ingrid just nodded silently and glanced at Thor; she didn't want to talk about Preben while he was there. That conversation could wait for later.

Then, remembering what Vegard had mentioned earlier, Ingrid held Thor back on his way out the door. "Hey, do you want to join us for dinner on Friday? So you can make sure the pinnekjøtt has been prepared properly."

She thought that he looked pleasantly surprised when he accepted the invitation; there was a twinkle in his blue eyes. She'd almost forgotten how cute he was when he smiled.

DECEMBER 5

Ingrid looked at herself in the mirror. The green silk draped softly over her body. Vegard had helped her pick out the dress the last time she was in Oslo, at an exclusive shop she never would have set foot in on her own. Vegard and the shop assistant had practically clapped when she put the dress on, and she could see that it looked good on her; it accentuated her slim figure and toned arms, while the simple draped neckline and luxurious fabric created an elegant effect. But she could never get used to seeing herself in this kind of outfit. Pants and T-shirts, solid shoes, wool sweaters, anoraks—that type of clothing was more her style. Clothes you could work and walk in, not the kind of thing you had to send to the dry cleaner and worry about the sequins falling off.

The woman staring back at her was tall and angular, with curly, sandy blond hair that flowed down her shoulders. She had strong arms and long fingers with short nails. Her calves, which showed beneath the hem of her dress, were slender but toned.

She raised herself up on tiptoe and her calves bulged even more. In high heels, both her muscles and her height became even more pronounced, so she tended to avoid heels. Besides, they were painful to walk in. Preben had always preferred that she wear flats; he wanted to be the tallest in the relationship. Vegard, on the other hand, claimed that stilettos gave you power and a real beauty boost. "Keep your heels, head, and standards high," he said, quoting Coco Chanel. Ingrid had told *him* to try wearing five-inch heels if he thought they were so sexy.

Ingrid had never been much of a dress girl. Painful memories flashed through her head: senior prom her last year in high school, when she'd been convinced to wear a strapless dress in shimmering red fabric. Freddy Dalen, who was hanging outside the school with his gang, laughed when she arrived, saying she looked like an overgrown candy cane. The dress kept threatening to slip down over her almost completely flat chest, and she'd ended up sneaking into the arts and crafts room to tape it with double-sided tape, which caused a rash that lasted for days.

Then there was the cocktail party at the Norwegian embassy in New Delhi, where she arrived in an expensive, newly purchased skirt. She'd forgotten how tight it was as she took the stairs to the roof terrace two at a time. She ended up with a rip up the back that she had to hide by borrowing a shawl from the ambassador—a stylish woman in her sixties—that Ingrid tied around her waist. *Ouch.* What good were clothes designed to inhibit your ability to move? Nice pants and simple, stylish tops were pretty much her go-to when she was forced to go to parties.

But these were new times with new expectations. If Glitter Peak Lodge was going to stand out on social media, the hotel manager had to "put herself out there," Vegard said. Gorgeous photos of food and interiors were a given, but pictures of Ingrid in simple but elegant dresses were apparently also a must. ("But they've only seen pictures of me in outdoor gear. No one is coming to Glitter Peak to see me in a dress," she said. "People should come to Glitter Peak to live out their fantasy," Vegard replied. "And that dream might involve anything from climbing to nature to food to peace and quiet to beauty and elegance. You have to show them that you don't need to choose—you can have it all." He pointed at the slogan he'd come up with for the hotel: *Glitter Peak—Where All That Glitters Is Gold.*)

Well . . . she'd decided to do what needed to be done. She really *was* going to put more effort into being well-dressed, hence the shopping trips with Vegard that had resulted in a handful of dresses in her closet. Now she just needed to figure out what she was going to wear to dinner this weekend, when Vegard and Pia P were coming to visit. And Thor.

It would of course be hopeless to ask her grandmother for advice. Nana Borghild's standard answer was that bunad was best—for Constitution Day, confirmations, big birthdays, and Christmas, the Norwegian national costume was her go-to garment for any kind of celebration. She'd also told Ingrid that a bunad would be a stylish choice for festive occasions when she made her debut as manager of the hotel. Ingrid had to try her best not to scoff. She didn't want to hurt her grandmother's feelings. But the idea of waltzing around the hotel in a pile of brocade and silver was downright ridiculous. And it wouldn't exactly help anyone "live out their fantasy" either.

She opened the smaller closet, where her bunad was hanging inside two heavy garment bags: one for the embroidered wool skirt with an attached bodice and one for the shawl and cape.

There was a separate jewelry box for the silver brooches—*sølje*—and cuff links, and the belt and bunad purse with its large silver clasp.

Ingrid always felt like she was playing dress-up when she wore a bunad—as though she was in a national romantic fantasy she had no desire to be a part of. Worse than that: it felt like she was dressing up like her own mother.

Ingrid had inherited Angelina's bunad, which Borghild had embroidered for Angelina's confirmation. Nana Borghild wanted nothing more than for Ingrid to wear it, and Ingrid could understand why: the loss of her daughter, all the love that Nana Borghild had put into the garment that Angelina had gotten to wear for far too few years. So Ingrid had agreed to wear the bunad for her own confirmation, as well as a few other occasions since then. Angelina had also been tall, so the garment had fit Ingrid without needing many adjustments. But it mostly stayed in the closet. It smelled like mothballs and sadness. She shut the closet door.

She squirmed out of the green dress and laid it on the chair behind her. Then she looked in the mirror again, placing a hand on her stomach. Other women had often told her that it was enviably flat, gesturing to their own rounder bodies. But a few years ago—when did it happen, really?—she'd apparently reached an age when a flat stomach had become a source of pity, while other women's round bellies and bulging breasts had become something they carried around with pride. Ingrid had never cared about this much—until suddenly she did.

She walked over to the large wardrobe and tentatively pulled out a formfitting blue dress that Vegard had also chosen. She held it up in front of her and met her own gaze in the mirror.

Stop feeling sorry for yourself, she thought. *You've had an incredible life. And it will be incredible again. Maybe. It could be pretty good, at least.*

And the start of her new life was this first winter season as manager of Glitter Peak Lodge. The encouragement from Vegard and David helped Ingrid believe—at least in some optimistic moments—that a miracle actually *could* happen and that the family hotel would be able to survive in the years to come and not be swallowed up by the competitors who were constantly making offers to buy them out, especially during periods when the market was particularly difficult. And it had been difficult for as long as Ingrid could remember. Maybe even always? When she'd left home, she hadn't been mature enough to get involved in the hotel business; she traveled out into the world, confident that her grandmother could handle both the practical operations and hotel finances. Surely Nana Borghild had always done so? It was only now, when she stood with her own feet planted firmly in all of the work, that she realized how difficult it must have been. How much her grandmother had kept from her, even though they were so close.

Ingrid pulled the blue dress over her head and zipped it up the side. It fit nicely, but was it right for the occasion? Was it too short for a dinner party? Too tight? It was more of a cocktail dress, perhaps. Vegard had tried to give her advice and tips on what was appropriate when, but she still felt unsure. Ingrid was terrified at the thought of Pia Pihlstrøm being here to judge both her and the hotel, but Vegard was right; it would be good advertising for Glitter Peak if Pia liked it here.

Pia would get the nicest room. It was on the top floor, but walking up all those stairs was good exercise—maybe that was how they could sell it to her? Ingrid had stopped by today to check that everything was dust-free and that the bedding didn't have a single wrinkle. The bathroom had a selection of products that Vegard had convinced Ingrid the hotel had to offer for sale—Glitter Peak birch soap and hand cream with heather extract. Wine, snacks, and flowers had been put in the room that morning as well.

The evening's menu would be the same as on Christmas Eve: pinnekjøtt with Christmas sausages and mashed root vegetables. Opinions on what to serve to drink were divided, so there would be plenty to choose from. The traditional alternatives— beer and aquavit—would of course be available. Nana Borghild scoffed at the suggestion of wine with pinnekjøtt, but Ingrid wanted to balance the heavy fare with a nice amarone. Maja favored the nonalcoholic malt beer they brewed at the hotel or alternatively a glass of fresh black currant juice. Ingrid wondered what Pia P would prefer. Champagne, perhaps? Fortunately, there was plenty of that in stock.

Ingrid hoped, hoped, *hoped* that everything would go smoothly now—that she would manage to represent the hotel in a positive way and attract new guests. Deep down, she knew the dresses had little to do with it. That's not what people came to see. Traditionally, it was mostly hikers and climbers who came to Glitter Peak, and if they associated anything with Ingrid, it was her climbing career. They'd probably want to talk to her about expeditions and climbing tips, perhaps with the hope of joining a trip she led herself.

So many hopes. So many things that could go wrong.

She looked at herself in the mirror and pulled the zipper down. She took off the dress and hung it back up on the hanger, leaving it and the pale green silk dress to hang outside the closet door. She would go for the green one tomorrow—since hope was green, after all.

It was early evening, dinner had been eaten, and Sunny and Ingrid were carrying boxes of Christmas decorations down from the attic (where neither dry rot nor Cheetos were to be seen). They put them in the foyer. Ingrid opened one and pulled out a soft white blanket. She draped it over the table Alfred had carried up from the basement.

"This'll be the snow!"

She pushed the table against the wall and set up the vases of spruce twigs that had been collected for the occasion.

"And here's the forest!"

BORGHILD, WHO WAS ON HER way down to get something in the library, stopped on the landing and clutched her chest. It was all so familiar, the tableau taking shape in the foyer. She stood there, watching Ingrid and Sunny. They were rummaging through boxes while Ingrid instructed Sunny on how she should set up the fairy-tale forest. They placed small elves and skiers on the white blanket. Borghild knew every single figure. Hares and reindeer would also find their places. A whole forest of characters in miniature would teem between the trees.

Setting up the winter forest was a cherished tradition, and Borghild remembered its humble beginnings well. It was the last Christmas that Angelina and Marius were still alive. Back then, they didn't usually keep the hotel open for Christmas, so the staff had been given the day off and it was just Borghild, Angelina, Marius, and little Ingrid. To think that it was thirty years ago . . .

Ingrid had been so excited, like most three-year-olds around Christmas. She sprinted up and down the stairs and in and out of the rooms all day, looking forward to opening presents. To slow her down, her father had brought out a box of elf figurines he'd bought in a gift shop in Oslo. Ingrid gave every elf a name (Mrs. Claus, Mommy, Daddy, Theodore, Bjarne, and Poopy) and placed them between some spruce twigs that had been brought in as decoration. This was the forest where they lived, she explained, describing their life there with great enthusiasm. Then she asked where the elves' reindeer were. Marius had said they might come next Christmas.

But the next Christmas, Angelina and Marius were gone, and a heartbroken Borghild had bought reindeer for little Ingrid and the elves. Over the years, they'd been joined by many more figurines—animals and people, sleighs and houses. Borghild had made it a Christmas tradition to add one or more items to the collection each year. It had become her and Ingrid's little ritual, and as the collection grew, they'd found that the foyer was the best place to display them.

A couple of guests also stopped to admire the small display. Borghild watched as Ingrid chatted with them as she set up elves and adjusted the sleds. It was nice to see the glow in her grand-daughter's cheeks when she occasionally managed to forget her worries. Borghild even saw some of the same eagerness in Ingrid as she herself had felt in her childhood. It had already been a long, dark winter, and there were many difficult days, but these glimmers of light gave her hope.

For the first time in many years, Borghild felt that she was actually looking forward to Christmas.

DECEMBER 6

Things could have been so different, Ingrid said to herself. She pulled off her paint-stained work clothes and tossed them in the laundry basket. She could have accepted the job in Thailand that she was offered last year. (*Who said your career is over?* she heard Vegard's voice say at the back of her head.) The company, Thai Climbing, organized trips to summit mountains such as Doi Inthanon and rock-climbing courses in Krabi. She could have lived in a beachfront bungalow, guiding adventurous tourists during the day and relaxing in the evenings when the buses had gone and the dive boats had docked for the night. She could have felt the warm sand between her toes as she walked down to the sea at sunset, floated on her back, and looked up at the sky. Eighty degrees in the water, eighty degrees in the air. Perfect. She could have had a coconut drink when she came ashore, looking forward to a long evening on the terrace with only the crashing of the waves to accompany her.

She put on clean pants and a T-shirt and looked out the window at the parking lot.

Or she could have accepted the offer from New York, the one from the center for nature conservation run by one of her sponsors. It wasn't hard to imagine—finishing off a run around the Reservoir in Central Park before work, looking around in amazement at this vast green space in the middle of the city, luxury high-rises on all sides. What amazing foresight the city planners had had when they'd set aside this enormous green area in the middle of a place where apartments were now going for some of the highest prices per square foot in the world. She imagined a gray squirrel darting up a tree trunk, a man on roller skates gliding past, a saxophonist playing on one of the walkways. The images flickered away, and she once again saw only the gray parking lot at Glitter Peak, frost-covered bushes and heather surrounding the area. The trees in her imaginary scene had been green. It was easiest to imagine New York in the summer.

But it isn't summer, she thought as she shut the door behind her and headed for the stairs. *And I'm not in New York. Not in London, Paris, or Sydney either, for that matter.* But she *could* have been in any of those places if she'd wanted to. Because even though she felt as though it was all over after the accident and was sure that her career was ruined, that wasn't actually the case. All kinds of possibilities had been open to her after she came home from the Himalayas. That was exactly what Vegard kept trying to remind her about. She had friends and contacts in all kinds of places after her years in the climbing and expedition worlds. Her commitment to climate and environmental work had helped her get to know people in environmental organizations, and you couldn't deny that her years in the limelight with Preben had also contributed to her receiving even more inquiries. *Ingrid Berg* was a name that a lot of people wanted to be associated with.

But what had she chosen to do? She hadn't accepted any of the offers that could have given her a more comfortable life in a better climate. No, she'd fled from the mountains that had ruined her life—for another mountain. Home to Glitter Peak, where her grandmother and the hotel were waiting and had been waiting for years. Somehow, it felt as if fate had finally caught up with her.

She walked onto the porch and looked out over the square. They should be arriving soon.

The black Audi SUV crunched over the gravel and swerved elegantly before coming to a stop. The driver's-side door opened, and out hopped Vegard Vang, his dashing figure clad in a down jacket and suede shoes. His medium-blond hair was fashionably tousled, and he was suspiciously tan for mid-December. Vegard grinned and waved at Ingrid before he walked around the car and opened the door on the passenger side.

Ingrid's first glimpse of Pia Pihlstrøm was of a pair of elegant cognac-brown high-heeled leather boots. (*I hope she brought better hiking boots*, Ingrid thought. *She won't get far in this terrain with that kind of footwear.*) The boots continued up a pair of long legs to a wide, white coat. The feet were placed tentatively on the frozen ground, and Vegard stretched out a hand. A tall figure stepped out of the car, and Pia Pihlstrøm revealed herself in all her glory.

She was truly beautiful. Her face was sculpted, her eyebrows two pronounced arches over large eyes, a surprisingly prominent nose, and full lips. Her honey-blond locks flowed down to the waist of her white coat.

Vegard shut the car door behind her, then dashed over the courtyard and up the stairs to Ingrid.

"Hi!" he said, hugging her tightly. Ingrid hugged him back, feeling the warmth of his smooth cheek and breathing in the fresh scent of his cologne. She wasn't usually a hugger; it somehow felt too intimate, like an invasion of privacy, when you pressed yourself up against other people like that. She usually preferred a polite handshake, but it was different with Vegard.

"So good to see you!" she exclaimed. "Welcome!"

"Thanks!" He beamed. Then he jogged back to the car and opened the trunk while Pia waited next to him. *Wait a minute . . . what is this?* Ingrid thought as she fixed her eyes on the influencer again. The elegant white coat showed an obvious bump—like a mountaintop—around Pia P's midsection. Surely it couldn't be . . . ? Yes, it was. Someone had forgotten to tell Ingrid something. Admittedly, the female body wasn't Vegard Vang's primary area of interest—but surely he hadn't failed to notice that Pia Pihlstrøm was pregnant?

"Of course I knew! I'm not blind," Vegard exclaimed with a roll of the eyes when Ingrid got him alone for a moment. They were sitting on the couch in her apartment, and she fixed him with an accusatory stare.

"You don't think you could have mentioned it, then? She must be . . . six or seven months along!"

"I promised I wouldn't say anything." Vegard shrugged.

He took a sip of water from the glass Ingrid had placed in front of him and ran a hand through his hair, tousling it even more.

"I'm sorry," he said. "I've known for a while but I promised I wouldn't tell anyone. And I didn't consider the fact that . . . that . . . you might think it was an uncomfortable surprise. That was thoughtless of me."

Alfred had carried the luggage up to the rooms, and Ingrid, Pia, and Vegard had agreed to meet down in the bar later that afternoon so Pia could rest for a bit. Vegard had joined Ingrid in her apartment after a warm greeting from Nana Borghild and the rest of the staff.

Ingrid had to quickly find Pia a room on the second floor instead of the one they'd originally prepared on the fourth. She couldn't make her walk up all those stairs with that belly. Sunny had made the change at record speed while Ingrid kept Pia and the others busy in the foyer. Sunny was excited about the urgent assignment, and when she saw their celebrity guest, she'd practically lost her ability to speak. Ingrid had to take her aside and remind her that as a hotel employee, she should never, never, *ever* post anything about their guests on social media. When she saw the disappointed look on the young girl's face, she realized that it had been a much-needed reminder. Anything about Pia P's stay at Glitter Peak Lodge had to be posted by Pia herself.

"It wasn't exactly *uncomfortable*," Ingrid said to Vegard. She wasn't sure whether that was totally true, but what she felt was irrelevant. "I was thinking more about the practical side of things. How far along is she?"

"Relax, she isn't due for ages," Vegard said.

Ingrid scoffed. "Since when have *you* been an expert in this kind of thing?"

"Well, I'm actually pretty familiar with it now because of Pia. She doesn't have many people she can count on. She hasn't told anyone she's expecting. It's a little . . . complicated."

"Seriously? She hasn't told anyone?" Ingrid widened her eyes. "But how on earth has she managed to hide it?"

"Well, when you live most of your life on social media and aren't out much otherwise, it's not that hard. She's good at cropping photos, and neither her face nor her home look particularly pregnant."

"But she *does* have some friends, right? Besides you, I mean? A social circle? And . . . there must be a father of the child somewhere?"

Vegard set his bright eyes on her. "Well, maybe there is. But whoever it is . . . that's a well-kept secret."

"So she hasn't even told you?"

He let his gaze drift across the living room and over the green dress, which was still hanging outside the closet door.

"Nope, not even me."

"Oh, this looks amazing!" Pia Pihlstrøm exclaimed when they entered the dining room.

She was right—it really *did* look amazing. Tall candles flickered in the candelabras on both sides of the room, and the long tables were decked with white linen tablecloths and the hotel's finest glassware and tableware. The napkins were also linen, and the silver napkin rings, freshly polished by Maja, glittered in the glow from the dancing candles. The sun had long since gone down, and the view through the large windows revealed a dark blue sky above rugged peaks.

The furniture was solid and handmade, and the high-backed chairs had carvings in the national romantic style and had been in use since the late nineteenth century. Ingrid felt a sudden sense of pride that the furniture had been so well cared for.

Alfred had been down in the forest to collect spruce branches for decoration early in the day, and their fresh scent mingled with the enticing aromas wafting in from the kitchen. Birch logs crackled in the fireplace.

A few hotel guests were already in the dining room, and the sound of chattering and clinking glasses and cutlery could be heard over the soft background music. Their own small group headed for a reserved table at the back of the room and took their seats as directed by Nana Borghild. There were seven people in addition to Ingrid: Vegard, Pia, Nana Borghild, Aisha, Hussein, Alfred, and Thor Seter. Thor had arrived half an hour before dinner and had a drink at the bar with the others before they went to the table. Even though she'd invited him at the last minute and because of Vegard's nagging, Ingrid thought it was nice to have him here, actually.

Maja and Sunny were busy cooking and serving. Maja had brusquely rejected Ingrid's suggestion that they should join the meal afterward. Maja believed a certain professional distance should be kept and hinted that she didn't think it was entirely appropriate for the caretaker to participate in the dinner either, but Ingrid wanted to fill up the table. It made it more credible as a kind of rehearsal. There would be more guests closer to Christmas, additional staff would be hired, and they would have several full tables like this one every single evening! A lot of things had to go right.

Ingrid stood at the end of the table with her back to the wall and tapped her glass once the others had taken their seats. Seven pairs of eyes were fixed on her. Vegard's alert Muppet-like peepers; Pia P's gray-blue eyes framed by long lashes beneath well-shaped brows; Nana Borghild's sharp and familiar gaze between smile lines; Aisha's and Hussein's warm, brown eyes; Alfred's indeterminate look beneath bushy brows; and Thor Seter's bright blue optimism. Thor's look hadn't changed since he and Ingrid started in the same class at Dalen Elementary School twenty-seven years ago.

Ingrid cleared her throat.

"Welcome everyone. This is a big occasion, even though we're a small gathering," she said. "We've eaten a lot of dinners in this hall before, but this is my first dinner party as manager. As you know, I grew up here, under Nana Borghild's wing, after my parents passed away."

She felt her voice trembling and fixed her gaze on her grandmother, who gave her a reassuring smile.

Ingrid went on, "Nana Borghild has run the hotel since the 1960s. First with her parents, then with my grandfather until his passing. She's been the manager of Glitter Peak Lodge for fifty years, in other words. I would therefore like to start by toasting to Nana Borghild."

Ingrid raised her glass of sparkling wine. "Cheers!" Hussein shouted, raising his glass of juice. Everyone laughed and lifted their own glasses—filled with wine, apple cider, black currant juice, or a nonalcoholic mojito.

"And cheers to the new manager," Borghild said, raising her glass again.

Ingrid put her glass down on the table while the others toasted a second time. She cleared her throat and paused before continuing her welcome speech.

"Now, I have—*finally*, some might say—come home to Glitter Peak to take over the running of the hotel. We will both continue the traditions of the past and introduce some new ones. This year, we'll be staying open through Christmas and New Year's, with a program that includes everything from beer tasting and skiing courses to dancing and the classic Norwegian tradition of walking around the Christmas tree. I'm excited, and I know that this never could have happened without all of your help. I'm so happy every one of you could come—and a special welcome to you, Pia, here for the first time."

The influencer smiled and nodded.

Ingrid continued: "So, a little bit about the food we'll be eating tonight. For the starter, we're having smoked trout with apple salad. And Thor here delivered today's main course, pinnekjøtt, which was prepared by his aunt Maja and her skilled kitchen assistants. I hope and believe you'll enjoy it. Bon appétit, dear friends."

"Thank you!" and "Cheers!" resonated from the others once again, and they drank and looked into one another's eyes, excited that the meal was officially underway.

NANA BORGHILD STOOD UP WHEN they were finished with the starter and leaned toward Ingrid.

"This is going spectacularly," she whispered.

Ingrid nodded happily. She'd placed Pia P between herself and Vegard, with Alfred the furthest away since he wasn't exactly the most skilled in the noble art of conversation. She had poor Sunny's attempts at conversation about incentives fresh in her mind. Pia was easy to talk to; she was friendly and interested in everything having to do with the hotel—so Ingrid didn't mind that she kept pulling out her phone to take pictures of drinks and decor. That was her job, after all, not to mention the reason that Vegard had invited her here in the first place. Pia was wearing a lovely green velvet pantsuit, her cheeks were aglow, and her blond locks were gathered in a loose braid down her back. She really was extraordinarily beautiful, Ingrid thought, and not just that; she also seemed sharp and intelligent. Ingrid was almost ashamed to find that surprising.

Thor was sitting opposite Pia. He was handsome and friendly, a little taciturn when he met new people, perhaps, but now he was talking enthusiastically about animals and photography with both Pia and Hussein, who was sitting next to him.

Maja and Sunny came in with pinnekjøtt, sausages, almond potatoes, and mashed turnips, and a collective murmur of excitement spread through the group. Ingrid saw Thor studying the meat extra carefully. She took a bite, met his gaze, and nodded happily as she savored the delicious, salty flavor. This was top-notch pinnekjøtt, and it boded well for the future Christmas dinners.

Aisha was sitting between Hussein and Alfred, across from Nana Borghild. She seemed a bit quiet today. Could it have something to do with the food? When they'd spoken before she was hired, Ingrid had gently touched on food customs, and also how Aisha, as a Muslim, felt about Christmas and other traditions. "We don't celebrate Christmas ourselves, of course, but both my family and Mohammed's family have been in the tourism industry for decades," Aisha had said. "So we're used to making arrangements for all kinds of holidays! At the hotel in Aqaba we even have gingerbread houses—the biggest in town!"

Maybe there was something else that was bothering her. Aisha's husband was still in Jordan. Who knew how things were going with him and the rest of the family, some of whom were in Syria as well? Aisha didn't talk about it much, and Ingrid wondered whether her reticence might be some kind of self-preservation. It had been a long time since she and her husband and child had been a nuclear family; when Ingrid got to know Aisha and Hussein, Aisha was working as the manager of a catering company in Kathmandu. She and her husband hoped to live together again at some point, but everything was still unresolved. It must be hard, Ingrid thought, living with such uncertainty—especially when you have a child.

Aisha took the napkin from her lap and wiped a bit of dried turnip mash off Hussein's chin. She was wearing a beautiful black long-sleeved dress with red and white embroidery. Nana Borghild had stopped and admired it when they'd met in the bar. The traditional Arabic patterns weren't so unlike the bunad embroidery she did herself, and Borghild recognized good craftsmanship when she saw it.

Ingrid turned her attention to Pia when Sunny and Maja reappeared with another round of pinnekjøtt. "Would you like some more?"

"Yes, please, it's delicious," Pia said. "I probably shouldn't take that much, but I suppose I'm eating for two now."

It was actually the first time Pia had alluded to her pregnancy, and Ingrid hadn't wanted to ask. She wondered whether this was her chance to find out more, but Pia was concentrating on her food, savoring every bite. "You know, I've never actually had pinnekjøtt before!" she said.

"Really? Well, I guess you probably grew up with ribs for Christmas dinner, then?" In Norway, families usually ate one or the other.

"Yeah, we'd have all kinds of things. But to be honest, my family wasn't all that into Christmas traditions."

Ingrid could tell that Pia didn't really want to talk about her family, so she steered the conversation toward Glitter Peak instead. Perhaps it could be inspiring for Pia to hear about the history of the place and all the famous people who'd skied and climbed here over the years.

"And I'm hoping to show you some good photo ops tomorrow," Ingrid said. "We really do have to try to create a *little* Christmas mood even if the snow is taking its sweet time."

"There *has* to be snow for Christmas," Vegard broke in. "Otherwise it'll be pretty hard to organize skiing courses and sleigh rides, and we've been posting everywhere that you'll be running those."

BY NOW, PEOPLE HAD WORKED their way through two or three portions, and a blissful mood settled over the table.

"Well . . . does anyone have room for rice pudding with red sauce?" a smiling Maja asked as she and Sunny cleared the dinner plates. "I know that *you* definitely have an extra stomach for dessert, Thor," she said, ruffling her nephew's hair. Thor blushed and looked at Ingrid and the out-of-town guests, clearly embarrassed.

"Do you have an extra stomach?" Hussein asked enthusiastically. "Cool! Did you know that camels have *three* stomachs? So they can eat a *lot* of dessert!"

Thor smiled slyly. "My sheep actually have four stomachs. So they win! But I don't want to share Aunt Maja's rice pudding with them. It's so good that we need to keep it for ourselves, Hussein."

He nudged the boy with a wink.

Everyone laughed. Alfred pulled out a handkerchief and dabbed at his forehead before bending over the dessert. Ingrid wondered whether he was too hot in his seldom-worn suit—which had a cut that was probably fashionable in the 1970s—and having had a couple of glasses of aquavit to boot. Alfred lifted his spoon, ready to tackle the dessert with the same gusto as he had the pinnekjøtt—but then suddenly raised a hand to his forehead again. He stared at it in surprise before lifting his gaze.

"It's dripping!" he exclaimed. "The ceiling is *dripping!*"

Such an abrupt departure from the dinner table had never been witnessed before. Cutlery clattered and chairs scraped.

Ingrid was on her feet at the same time as Alfred and stared up at the ceiling. Yes, it was true: there was a wet spot on the wood up there, and a drop that grew until it dripped right into Alfred's beer glass with a *splash!* And *splash!* Another drop.

The other guests in the restaurant had begun to look toward their table with growing curiosity, and Borghild went over to re-assure them while Ingrid and Alfred headed for the floor above, where the leak must have been coming from. Alfred huffed and puffed up the stairs. They stopped for a moment before he led the way into the corridor and stopped abruptly outside Pia P's room.

"This must be where it's coming from," he said.

"Do you think it's Pia's bathroom?" Ingrid asked. "Could she have forgotten to turn off the water in the bath?"

Alfred tried the door, but it was locked. For a moment, Ingrid considered asking him to break it down, but Alfred beat her to it and pulled the universal key from his suit pocket. He unlocked the door, and they both entered the room and stood on the threshold of Pia's bathroom. It wasn't clear what had happened in there. Ingrid had been expecting to see water gushing down from an overflowing tub, but it was empty and the taps were turned off. However, the floor was covered in at least an inch of water, some of which was flowing out into the hallway as well.

Ingrid heard someone come in and turned around. Pia was standing behind her with a horrified expression, looking at the mess.

"I . . . I took a bath before I came downstairs," she said. "But I didn't notice anything wrong then."

Alfred took off his shoes and socks and waded resolutely into the bathroom.

"Something's going on down here," he said, flipping the drain grate in the floor open with a small screwdriver he pulled out of his jacket pocket. Apparently wearing his best suit didn't stop the caretaker from carrying the right equipment at all times. "It almost looks like the water is coming back up. The drainpipe from the bathtub must be leaking, or maybe one of the branch pipes has come loose."

Ingrid went in and squatted down next to Alfred. He tentatively reached his right hand down the drain and grabbed a clump that he pulled up with a grimace. It looked like hair and wet paper. No wonder the water hadn't been draining properly. It was now flowing down slowly, but it would be a long time before it was all gone. The water had also obviously collected under the bathroom floor and dripped through the joists to the dining room below. Ingrid shuddered as she thought about the potential damage and expenses. How much could actually go wrong in such a short time? It almost felt like a cruel joke considering that not five minutes ago, she'd been sitting there, reveling in how well everything was going.

She suddenly noticed that her feet were wet. The suede ballerina shoes were dark with moisture and would never look right again after this. Her green silk dress was also soaked through at the edges. It was probably ruined as well. That green hope of hers wasn't looking all that good anymore.

DECEMBER 7

You can always tell who works with what, Ingrid thought as she and Alfred welcomed the workers the next day. The carpenters were almost definitely the two blond guys, one bigger and more muscular than the other, like two brothers in a cartoon. The plumber had to be the older fellow in the blue overalls, which meant the young, skinny one in the beanie was probably the electrician.

It really was lucky that they'd been able to come on such short notice, on a Saturday and everything—but Alfred had said it was incredibly important to start the drying process right away. Mold could start growing after just a day or two of moisture, and mold was a real problem that could be bad for your health and destructive ("as opposed to Cheetos," Alfred pointed out). They had to break open the floor in Pia's bathroom to see whether there was water collecting under there and possibly put in dehumidifiers.

The evening had rapidly shifted from dream to nightmare.

The rice pudding had been left half-eaten when the water started dripping and the party broke up. They'd pushed the table aside and placed some buckets and towels on the floor—all as discreetly as possible, of course, so as not to spoil the mood for the other guests in the dining room. Not much water had come through the ceiling during the night, and that was a relief. Everything seemed to indicate that a drainpipe was broken. Ingrid just hoped they wouldn't have to tear down the old ceiling over the dining room.

Once the worst of the chaos had subsided last night, Ingrid found herself consoling a weeping Pia, who had been given a new room after poor Sunny had to go upstairs for the third time that day to set up a room farther down the hall. Pia repeated that she'd taken a bath but that she was absolutely certain she'd turned off the water and pulled the stopper before getting ready and coming down to the bar. There was no reason to believe that Pia had done anything wrong. The incident was clearly just a stroke of bad luck—or rather, it was probably due to the general maintenance backlog at the hotel. Ingrid had the nagging feeling that such problems would happen again and again.

Vegard came down the stairs, and she left Alfred to deal with the workers.

"I was just in Pia's room," Vegard said when he'd given Ingrid a hug. "She's a total wreck and wants to go back home."

"Oh no!" Ingrid cried. "Her stay can't end like this. Is there anything we can do?"

"Maybe you can stop by her room later," Vegard suggested.

Ingrid sighed. They'd been dreaming of good publicity and viral posts on social media, but they might just have to settle for being happy if her visit to the hotel wasn't mentioned at all. It seemed as though there wouldn't be a line of Pia Pihlstrøm fans out the door anytime soon.

Her phone rang. *Thor Seter*, the screen read. Thor had actually been offered a room so he wouldn't have to drive back to the village after dinner, but his friend Roger picked him up when the party came to an abrupt halt.

Ingrid glanced at Vegard apologetically and walked to the front door before answering.

"Hi, Thor," she said, walking outside with her phone against her ear.

"Hey, you!" the deep voice on the other end replied. "I just wanted to check in on how things are going up there. See if there's anything I can do to help."

"That's really nice of you, but the workers are already here. Sorry about yesterday."

"Don't worry about it," Thor said. "The food was great and the company even better."

She smiled. "Yeah, it just ended a bit too abruptly."

AFTER HANGING UP, INGRID WENT upstairs and cautiously knocked on Pia's door.

"Come in," a weak voice sounded, and Ingrid tried the door, which wasn't locked. It was dark inside.

"Sorry, it's probably pretty stuffy in here. Just open the window if you want," Pia said. She was still in bed. Ingrid opened the window, and drew the curtains to let the light flood in.

Pia looked considerably less glamorous than she had the day before. Her hair was disheveled, her eyes swollen, and her skin pale.

"How are you doing? Are you sick?" Ingrid asked.

"No, I'm fine now, but I got so tired all of a sudden," Pia replied.

"I was going to come downstairs, but I was too tired, and my stomach is like . . . tight. I don't really know how to explain it. Anyway, it's hard to move. So I lay down for a bit after Vegard stopped by and fell asleep again. Now I'm totally out of it. And then I started thinking about what happened with the bathtub yesterday . . ."

"It wasn't your fault," Ingrid assured her, trying to hide her concern that Pia wasn't feeling well. She certainly didn't want the star blogger to get sick here on top of all the other problems. That would almost make it seem as though there was a curse on the whole hotel.

"I'll come back with something for you to eat," Ingrid said. "And a cup of tea, maybe? Or is there anything else you want?"

Pia smiled weakly. "A cup of tea and some toast would be lovely. Thank you so much. I'll come down eventually so I can talk to Vegard about our plans."

WHEN INGRID FOUND VEGARD AGAIN, he was sitting in the library with Nana Borghild, a stack of old books and a plate of dried dates and figs—her grandmother's favorite snacks—on the table between them. Nana Borghild was probably educating him about the history of the hotel and village.

"Sorry I can't help more, Ingrid," Vegard said as she came over to them. "But you know how hopeless I am when it comes to practical things like this."

"Yeah, I think it's best that you stay away from the repairs," she laughed. "Otherwise we'll just make things worse. But there are other things you can help with. Maybe you want to come on a walk and have a chat?"

"I'd love to," Vegard replied. "Let me just run up and get my coat."

"See you at lunch in a little while, Nana," Ingrid said, kissing her grandmother on the cheek.

Her grandmother nodded, smiled, and put one of the books in her lap. She pretended to be engrossed in her reading again before they were out of the room, but Ingrid could feel her grandmother's eyes on her back on the way out.

THE SUN WAS AT ITS highest point, which, to be fair, wasn't particularly high at this time of year. The air was crisp and clear.

"It's so beautiful here," Vegard said, looking up toward the mountains. He wasn't wearing a hat, but Ingrid had given up nagging him about it. "I wish David had come with us."

His boyfriend hadn't visited Glitter Peak yet, even though Vegard had been to the hotel several times. David worked long hours and rarely took time off.

"It would be great if he could make the trip sometime," Ingrid said. "But I understand that he's busy. On the other hand, it means I get you all to myself!"

She patted Vegard on the shoulder, and they set off across the heather while she explained the many practical challenges at the hotel—the leak, of course, but also other issues. For example, a large group of travelers had recently canceled their stay without any explanation. That kind of thing happened at hotels all the time, but she'd calculated for more guests than they had now.

"We need to increase revenue," she told Vegard, and he nodded in agreement.

He knew just as well as Ingrid that times had been tough for a while, with few guests and reduced operations. The picture was dominated by expenses, expenses, expenses—for salaries and purchases and renovations and food and transportation and taxes and God knows what else . . .

"Vegard," she said. "I'm kind of at the point that I'm doubting that this is going to work out at all."

"No, no, no! You can't think like that," Vegard protested. "The advertising has already started working, and the number of guests will increase soon. I'm sure of it. Then your numbers will start changing from red to black."

Ingrid nodded. That wouldn't happen this year, though, and probably not next year, either. It would take a long time before all the bills were paid off and salaries covered. If, on top of everything else, unforeseen expenses kept coming in all the time, it might *never* happen.

"I'm not expecting you to solve this," she said. "But it's nice to be able to talk about these things. I don't want to burden Nana Borghild with everything I'm worried about."

"No, I get that," Vegard replied. "And the reason you took over here is probably *specifically* to relieve her worries! But remember that she's the one who knows the hotel best, too. Don't count her out completely. I bet she still has a lot to contribute."

There was a ding, and Vegard pulled his phone out of his pocket. He grinned.

"Reply from Hanna," he said. "She and PX will try to make a trip up here later. But they're not sure if they'll manage before Christmas."

"Hanna? As in Hanna and the Hearts?"

"The one and only."

"That would really be something!"

The artist Hanna and her photographer boyfriend, Per Xandersen, known as PX, were currently among the brightest stars on the Norwegian celebrity scene. Ingrid knew that Vegard got a lot of requests from people who wanted to visit the hotel, but that it usually didn't work out. She still appreciated that he tried, though.

THEY HEADED FOR THE KITCHEN when they got back to the hotel, and Ingrid prepared a simple meal of whole-grain bread, cheese, and salad. Alfred briefed her on his conversations with the workers. It didn't seem as though the damage was as extensive as they'd feared, he explained between mouthfuls. They'd opened up the floor and put in dehumidifiers, and they would come back later to fix the rest.

"It's going to be costly," he said grimly.

Ingrid nodded but didn't say anything. She was painfully aware that even such "minor" damage could cost tens of thousands of kroner—kroner she didn't have.

They had two new kitchen assistants who took care of the food for the guests on the weekend. Ingrid, Vegard, Sunny, Borghild, and Alfred were the only ones sitting around the kitchen table today; Pia was still in her room. Maja and Aisha had the day off, and Aisha had taken Hussein to Lillehammer. She'd made a friend when she was learning Norwegian in the small city, a Syrian woman who now worked at one of the larger hotels there. Now, mother and son were going to spend the night at the hotel and return on Sunday evening. Aisha wanted to buy clothes and winter gear for Hussein while they were in town. "You can never be dressed warmly enough in Norway," Hussein had said, grinning at Ingrid with his two missing front teeth. He'd also confided in her that they knew of a shop where they could get *much* better dates for Nana Borghild than the variety available at the shop in Dalen.

The door opened slowly, and Pia P came in. She'd combed her hair and put on a simple gray wool dress.

"Honey!" Vegard was on his feet as soon as he saw her. "How are you feeling?"

Pia smiled a bit weakly. "A little better. At least now I can bear the thought of eating a little bit."

Vegard offered his chair to Pia. He pushed it in gently as she sank down, then sat on the bench next to Ingrid. Nana Borghild smiled approvingly, while Alfred looked at Vegard in surprise. Alfred probably thought this was a strange gesture, Ingrid thought. Both in Dalen and at Glitter Peak, women had mostly managed to sit down on chairs without any help.

"HELLO!" THEY SUDDENLY HEARD A voice in the hallway. "Hello?"

The bell on the reception desk rang, and Ingrid was about to stand up when the kitchen door flew open with a bang. A slim, tan woman in a green wool cape, lace-up boots, and what appeared to be a real bearskin hat over her blond hair sailed into the room.

"Hello!" she said in broad American English, then clapped her hands together excitedly when she saw Pia's stomach.

"Are you married?"

Pia looked at her in amazement and shook her head slightly.

The woman smiled. "Isn't that great? You don't have to be married these days!" She waved in a silver-haired man in a dark blue double-breasted wool coat. "Look at her, John. Isn't she lovely?"

"She is indeed," the man said, raising his eyebrows slightly.

Turning to Pia once again, the woman said: "Well, if you

decide to get married, I can highly recommend it. John and I have been married for thirty years, so I know what I'm talking about!" She flashed her blindingly white teeth. "It's so wonderful to be here! Who can check us in? We're Mr. and Mrs. Wilkins," the woman declared in a tone of voice that sounded as if she were announcing that they were royalty. "Dr. and Mrs. John Wilkins."

"Wilkins?" Ingrid said, standing behind the counter and looking through the reservation system. "Welcome. But we weren't expecting you for another two weeks . . . on the twenty-first?"

"I know!" the woman exclaimed excitedly. "But we heard there were rooms available here, and these chain hotels are so terribly *boring*, so we thought we could come sooner. Isn't that great? We bought a car in Lillehammer."

"You bought a car? To use while you're on vacation? That must have been . . ."

Ingrid swallowed the rest of the sentence. There wasn't any point in commenting on how expensive it must have been. There was nothing to indicate that these people cared much about costs.

"Yes, wasn't that a brilliant idea? Then we can sell it again when we leave. Or keep it here for when we come back. John got all the paperwork done in record time. You know, then we don't have to take taxis or drive any of these terrible rental cars."

The woman took off her bearskin hat and ran a hand through her hair.

"It was a lovely drive! So many trees! And don't get me started on those beautiful old houses. Wasn't thrilled with the roads, though. I actually would have expected them to be quite a bit better. But I guess that's just how it is here in Europe. That's why we wanted a decent car. We parked just outside, by the way. Maybe you can send the porter out for the luggage?"

"Porter?" Ingrid looked up. "Yes, of course."

Frantic plans were forming in Ingrid's head as she went back to the kitchen to ask Alfred to fetch the luggage. They had to prepare the best room on the top floor. These guests seemed more than energetic enough to manage the stairs, even if they were on the older side. Maybe Sunny could help with the food, too, so they wouldn't have to ruin Maja's weekend off.

In the meantime, they placed the new arrivals in the library and gave them something to drink. Ingrid wondered what kinds of expectations they had when it came to the standard of the hotel and level of service, but she'd do her best.

"A brand-new Range Rover," Alfred muttered to Ingrid when he came in from the parking lot with two enormous suitcases that looked as though they weighed at least sixty pounds each. "Costs an arm and a leg."

"Let's hope they can afford to tip well, then!" Ingrid said quietly, nodding at the stairs Alfred would have to drag the suitcases up.

"Fourth floor!" she said with a wink.

Alfred just grunted.

"DO YOU HAVE A CREDIT CARD for the registration?" Ingrid asked once she'd returned to the guests.

"Yes, of course. *Jo-ohn*, come and pay!" Mrs. Wilkins shouted, still at full volume. Ingrid wondered whether the new guest was even capable of anything else.

John Wilkins, who'd barely said a word, took a black Amex card from his inside pocket and handed it to Ingrid with an almost inaudible sigh.

❄

"Hey, Ingrid, shouldn't we put up the Christmas tree soon?" Sunny asked later that afternoon. "It would look really nice in the pictures if everything was already decorated in the dining room."

"I thought we'd wait with the tree until the last weekend before Christmas," Ingrid replied. "One of the activities that Saturday is to go out and cut down a Christmas tree. Won't that be fun? And according to tradition—and Maja—you're not actually supposed to decorate the tree before Christmas Eve, you know."

"That's what my mom and dad say, too," Sunny said. "But I've managed to get them to agree to do it earlier in December. Having a decorated tree is *so* nice. That, and lights on the bushes outside. Then I can really get into the Christmas spirit! Can we put up some more lights out by the entrance?"

"For sure," Ingrid replied. She poured two cups of coffee and offered Sunny a cookie from one of Maja's many cookie jars. *Saturday night in the mountains*, Ingrid thought. She would have thought that Sunny would rather have the night off to be with people her own age, but she'd said she was fine with working.

Sunny took a bite of the cookie and looked at Ingrid as she chewed. Then she said: "Hey, I was wondering if I could use the old guest books and scrapbooks for an assignment I'm working on. It's going to be about guest reviews of hotels and how they're combined with advertising and used as part of marketing. I've seen some clippings from old newspapers and stuff in the library, and there are tons of nice greetings from guests in those books.

I thought it would be cool to compare it with today's ads and Tripadvisor and that kind of thing."

"That's a great idea!" Ingrid said. "Of course you can use the old materials. Nana Borghild or I can help you find them."

"Cool!" Sunny said. "Maybe we could even use some of it on social media too if we find something fun."

DECEMBER 8

Nana Borghild took a sip from her cup of coffee and set it down on the tray with a faint clink. She stared into space. Barry watched them from his nook by the fireplace.

Ingrid looked at Nana Borghild's neatly arranged hair and the exhaustion in her body that she couldn't quite conceal despite her upright posture. Her grandmother suddenly seemed so old, Ingrid thought. She *was* eighty-three, but amazingly, Ingrid had never thought of her as old before.

What had changed? Was her grandmother getting worn down from all of the work and practical problems at the hotel? Ingrid felt a tenderness for her and a pang of guilt for not having come back sooner. Her grandmother had always taken care of her. Maybe she should have realized long ago that *she* was the one who should be taking care of her grandmother.

They'd sat down in the library that morning to discuss the

plans for the coming days, but Nana Borghild seemed a bit distracted. Ingrid reached out and took her grandmother's hand. Her hands had always been so small and delicate, but now the joints were more prominent than before. Her wedding ring, which she'd kept wearing for decades after Grandpa Christian's death, had recently been coaxed off and moved onto a long gold chain that Nana Borghild wore around her neck along with a small key.

Ingrid closed her eyes and squeezed her grandmother's warm fingers. She missed the intimate moments they used to have when she was younger. They still talked a lot, but now it was mostly about practical things. Ingrid wasn't sure why this had happened, but she somehow didn't find it as easy to open up to her grandmother anymore. Her life had changed while living abroad. *She* had changed. She wasn't the same girl who'd sat with her grandmother, drunk hot chocolate, and chatted about school and climbing and the stupid boys at school. She'd been through such dramatic things since then—and what could her grandmother understand of such things? After all, she'd only experienced a sheltered life here at Glitter Peak.

Ingrid was about to ask whether Nana Borghild had anything particular on her mind today when they heard a loud, peppy voice from the doorway behind them.

"Good morning!"

Ingrid pulled her hand away.

Mrs. Wilkins came striding in. She had a cup of coffee from the buffet in the dining room and was walking toward them with quick, purposeful steps.

She was dressed in jeans and a green wool sweater. Her wavy

blond hair was gathered in a braid at the nape of her neck, and she looked younger than when she'd arrived yesterday in her bearskin hat and full getup. *I wonder how old she really is,* Ingrid thought. *Somewhere between fifty and sixty, maybe.* She had a fresh complexion and few wrinkles, but there were remedies for that. And there was no way of knowing whether her hair color was real.

"How lovely to be able to chat with you a bit," Mrs. Wilkins said as she settled into one of the big leather chairs without any kind of invitation.

"Good morning, Mrs. Wilkins," Ingrid said.

"Please call me Freya. It's wonderful to be here! I feel so at home."

"That's nice to hear," Ingrid replied.

Freya Wilkins set her coffee cup on the table. "I've been looking around the hotel. This lovely building, the smell of wood. These mountains around us. It's all so *real*, all of it. I feel like my roots are here, even though I've never been here before. It's in my blood."

Borghild nodded thoughtfully but didn't say anything.

"So you have Norwegian roots?" Ingrid asked.

"Yes, my parents were Norwegian." It looked as if Freya was about to say more before she changed her mind and took a sip of coffee instead. "But what were you two talking about?"

Nothing, Ingrid thought, *because we were interrupted before we could get started.* She and her grandmother hadn't had more than a few minutes in peace. Ingrid noted that they'd have to move their private talks to one of the apartments in the future. They couldn't chase the guests away from the common areas, after all, and now they had no choice but to include Freya Wilkins in the conversation.

As briefly as possible, Ingrid told her about the flooding on Friday night and all of the extra work it entailed. Not her favorite topic, but with workers coming and going, there was no point in pretending nothing was happening. Mrs. Wilkins also seemed to be the sort of person who generally found out whatever she wanted to if she set her mind to it.

"How unfortunate!" Freya Wilkins exclaimed, leaning forward.

Her eyes sparkled in the morning light. Ingrid hadn't noticed them before, but she now saw that they had a unique play of colors: deep gray with golden flecks, like polished granite.

Nana Borghild also seemed to have noticed them. She sat there, staring at Freya without a word. *What kind of strange behavior is this?* Ingrid thought. Her grandmother wasn't normally impolite.

Freya Wilkins was still looking at Ingrid, wanting more information. "How could it have happened? The leak, I mean?"

"It was strange, really," Ingrid replied. "We think a water pipe may have burst when one of the guests drained the bathtub. It's not the kind of thing that normally happens here. Just bad luck, really."

"Yes, that's for sure," Freya Wilkins replied.

Nana Borghild stood up.

"I have to go speak with Maja," she said. "She wanted to discuss something about the menus for the coming weeks. You'll have to excuse me."

"Oh, I didn't mean to be a bother!" Freya exclaimed.

Ingrid was perplexed. It was obvious that her grandmother had just made up an excuse to leave the room. She and Freya sat there for a while without saying anything while Barry watched them from his nook.

Borghild stopped on the landing and leaned on the banister. The stairs seemed particularly steep today, even though she normally scaled them with ease. She felt that her breathing was heavier and her heart was beating faster than usual.

She realized that it must have seemed odd that she left the library so abruptly, but she had to get away—to think in peace.

Could things really be connected the way she suspected?

She felt dizzy just thinking about it.

She had a strong feeling that she was now going to have to deal with what had weighed upon her so heavily all her life. What she'd told herself was over, a closed chapter.

But it wasn't over. Of course it wasn't.

She'd been so naive to believe that the mistakes of the past would stay there—in the past.

Dalen, Spring 1962

The bells echoed across Dalen. From the tower of the old brown church, the deep sound resonated over fields and meadows, over farms and forest. Come-come, come-come, come-come, they rang.

And people came. They flocked there from the big farm up the hill and from the gas station by the main road, from neighboring villages, and even from Glitter Peak. People came dressed in their finest, driving and walking, some on bicycles, between the birch trees in all their spring glory down the avenue, through the big gate and up the gravel road across the churchyard, and through the church doors, which were wide open — because there was going to be a wedding in Dalen today.

The bells went silent for a while. The priest stood ready in his cassock in the sacristy, going through the day's sermon in his head. In the doorway, the usher was handing out programs with ornate lettering. There was muffled chatter and creaking as the narrow old wooden pews were filled with people in bunads, people in dresses, people in suits. At the very front of the church, by the altar, the groom and his best man stood sweating in their finery. Their new suits were itchy, and it was unusually warm for so early in the spring.

The bells rang for the second time. Ribbons of multicolored sunlight stretched across the wooden floor from the tall old windows. A newly awakened fly buzzed woozily through the gallery, and the organist absentmindedly waved it away as he flipped through his notes.

The bride's maid of honor came through the door and walked up on the left side of the pews. The young, dark-haired woman seemed to be deeply affected by the occasion, greeting friends and family sitting in the pews with a serious face. The sunlight made the silver on her bunad sparkle, spreading small flashes of light throughout the church as she sat down on one of the chairs by the altar rail.

The usher closed the doors from the outside and stood on the church steps, ready to open them again shortly. After a few minutes, the chiming of the bells stopped. An expectant silence settled over the congregation. Soon, the doors would open, and the bride would enter, surrounded by sunlight and the majestic chimes of the organ.

But nothing happened. The silence was deafening at first, but gradually, people started to turn toward the door and one another, exchanging glances and hushed murmurs. The benches creaked uneasily. A minute passed. Two minutes. Then the door was opened, but only a crack. The usher slipped inside and motioned to the best man, who gave the groom a pat on the shoulder before walking down the aisle. By now, the murmuring in the pews had developed into nervous chatter.

"What's going on?" the best man asked as he entered the porch. "Why aren't you sending the bride in?"

"There's no bride to send in," the usher replied. "She isn't here."

DECEMBER 9

"I think it's kind of hard to tell with the kids in my class. If they're my friends or not, I mean. I've never gone to school before. And I haven't lived in this country before either."

Ingrid looked at Hussein in surprise. She'd run into him in the parking lot as she was coming back from her morning walk and he was waiting by the car for his mother, who was on her way out of the hotel. Ingrid had asked some casual questions—"How's it going at school? Have you made any friends?"—and received answers that were weightier than she'd been prepared for.

Ingrid put a hand on his shoulder, or at least roughly where she thought his shoulder was beneath all the layers of jackets and scarves, and looked at the boy seriously.

"Are they not being nice to you?"

Hussein looked at her a bit shyly.

"I don't know, really," he said. "Maybe that's just how friends are here."

———

INGRID WATCHED AS THE CAR drove off toward Dalen, lost in thought. How was Hussein *really* doing? She had to find out. She wrested herself from her thoughts and went through the back door to the kitchen, where Maja was busy baking. It smelled wonderful, and Ingrid helped herself to a fresh roll cooling on a rack.

The radio was on in the background, playing the usual morning chatter between music and news reports. "Yes, that was Hanna and the Hearts with 'Let it Snow,'" a woman's voice said. "But what do the meteorologists have to say about the weather ahead, Halvor? Any snow coming?"

"Well, Kristine," a man's voice replied, "it's true that winter hasn't really taken hold around here. Some people are probably missing the snow, while others think it's nice to have clear roads. But with the precipitation coming now, the risk increases for freezing rain. So we should probably tell listeners who are planning on driving over the next few days to keep an extra eye on the weather reports and drive carefully."

The chef looked sternly at Ingrid and the roll she had in her hand.

"Ingrid! That'll give you a stomachache! It's not done. I freeze half-baked rolls so we have something on hand. We don't know how many guests we'll have all of a sudden!"

Ingrid laughed and put the roll back down. "No, you're right about that. But there won't be many new guests for a few days. As far as I know, at least. But don't you have any fully baked rolls somewhere?"

Maja nodded at a rack on the other side of the counter, where there was an inviting pile of golden rolls. Ingrid grabbed one, broke off a piece, and spread on a generous dollop of butter, which quickly melted into the bread. *Mmmm!* Delicious.

"Mrs. Wilkins asked if she could come and help me bake *goro* and *lefse* one day," Maja said.

"Really?" Ingrid asked. "She wants to bake? That's kind of an odd thing for a guest to ask."

"Well, she seems to be into that kind of thing. Everything traditional and everything Norwegian. Bunads and handicrafts, *lutefisk* and lefse. Old Norwegian customs. She has Norwegian roots, you know—that's why they're here. After Dr. Wilkins retired, they started on a big tour—under her direction—to 'find their European roots.'"

"Yes, I can picture her at one of those Daughters of Norway meetings in California," Ingrid said with a smile.

"Yeah, she told me she's actually the head of the Hulda Garborg Lodge," Maja said, rolling her eyes. "But I'm happy to bake with her. It needs to get done before Christmas anyway. As long as she doesn't insist on following some Norwegian American recipe that's been handed down for generations. I've dealt with that kind of thing before."

"I have a feeling that your recipes will be the ones being followed, Maja," Ingrid said.

"Yeah, you can bet on that," Maja said.

From Borghild Berg's diary:

I can't be completely sure that things are as I think they are. For now, it's just a gut feeling. But what if I'm right? What should I do then? I can't dig into it any deeper until I've made up my mind. In the meantime, though, I need to keep my distance.

These are tough times. I'm worried about Ingrid. About the hotel. What if it doesn't work out? It's gotten close to failing several times over the past few years. If Ingrid hadn't come home now, I would have had to sell. Ingrid knows a lot about the hotel and our challenges, but I don't think she <u>quite</u> realizes how demanding it's actually been to stay open all these years. Or—maybe she's starting to understand now.

Oh, my dear little Ingrid! I fear that it was duty and not desire that made her come home to Glitter Peak. She was so rattled after the accident. The lively girl who just wanted to go out and climb was almost unrecognizable. Not surprising, though. It took weeks before she was able to even talk about what happened. She came here pretty soon after she got out of the hospital over there. I wanted to go there and see her, but of course I couldn't. It was too far of a journey, and someone had to keep things going at Glitter Peak as well.

Then she came home—thin, drained, quiet. When she finally started talking again, she said she was going to take over the hotel. And I agreed. But I said yes with a heavy heart, even though I've been longing for her to come home. Now, I almost wish she'd stayed out there instead. It might have been better than coming back only from a sense of duty.

And then there's the breakup with this Preben Wexelsen. She tries to pretend that she's doing better now, but I can see the grief is still eating away at her. She'd been crying the day we came in and he was on TV. I'd always felt that he wasn't the right man for her and that this celebrity life wasn't what Ingrid was meant to live, either. But what could I do? In any case, there's no doubt that she feels burdened by the loss.

Worst of all, she's not climbing anymore. It truly goes against nature. Ingrid, who was born to climb! But she's scared. Scared of heights, avalanches, losing control.

I wish I knew what I could do.

I'm old and I'll be out of the game soon, but my greatest wish is that the hotel business can live on after me. And for that, Glitter Peak Lodge has to have a manager with vitality and energy. But right now, Ingrid walks around with this dark cloud over her.

Is there something else, I wonder? Something she hasn't told me?

Well, I suppose I have my secrets, too. Some of them I've been keeping for all my adult life. Maybe it's been wrong of me to stay silent for so long. But I haven't felt that I've had a choice. I had to keep my word. I had to protect Charlie.

Charlie . . . Even after all these years, it still hurts.

I had to protect myself, and Christian too. Create a future for us, protect the others from the painful truth. But maybe I only made matters worse.

It should have been buried and forgotten. All of this. I had no intention of bringing it back into the light. But now it's happening all on its own—the past always comes back.

The road was slippery, and Thor Seter was furious. That wasn't typical of him; he was mostly a pretty even-keeled guy. He was raised on the motto *roll with the punches*, and he mostly tried to avoid both the high peaks and deep valleys—emotionally speaking, that is, if not literally. He could get excited about spring days and good photo opportunities, he experienced joy when the lambs were born and when he heard good music, and he could feel his pulse quicken when he was watching an exciting soccer match. But violent emotional outbursts? That wasn't his thing. And he was brought up to never swear.

Still, when he lost control and slid several feet forward, a *God dammit!* slipped out of him.

He hadn't even made a scene when Sandra left for Oslo for the very last time. If she wanted to go, she had to go. The worst part was that he had no problem understanding her choice when she had decided to leave both him and the village. For a few years—when they'd first gotten together—Thor had thought that their love would make up for everything else, for everything she'd given up when she moved from the big city. He'd imagined that they would create their own happiness, maybe with a couple of kids someday, too. He thought that this life, in nature and on the farm, would compensate for everything she'd missed out on. But it couldn't, she'd said the last time. She was sick and tired of Dalen, tired of his grumpy parents in the neighboring house, and tired of all the sheep shit. She was also tired of him. There weren't any children, either. And he never bought her flowers.

Flowers? Was he supposed to buy flowers? He knew he'd disappointed her in many ways, but this was the only complaint that came as a surprise. Thor had never bought flowers in his life—not for anyone. Keep the farm and house in order, take care of the animals, be a good husband, love her. Watch movies that she liked, sometimes go into town and eat at a fancy restaurant even though they couldn't really afford it. He'd done all that. But buy *flowers*? When you lived in the middle of a field full of them? That was the kind of thing people only did in the movies. Or was it? Maybe he'd misunderstood. He could try flowers the next time he had a girlfriend—if that ever happened.

It hurt when Sandra left, but he hadn't shown it. Anyway, it wouldn't have helped if he had made a scene. If anything, it would have made things worse. So he swallowed his tears and questions, loaded her suitcases into the back of the pickup truck, and drove her to the train station. He stayed in the car for a long time afterward.

That was how Thor was, just like all of the men he'd known— his father, his uncles, his grandfather. Stoic. When challenges came their way, they dealt with them in stride. They grabbed the shovel or the saw or the pitchfork, or the sandbags when the Dalen River flooded. They didn't buy flowers, but they did do what needed to be done—without big gestures or big words. At least that was how Thor had perceived it. For a long time.

But then it turned out that these men also had sides that weren't quite as Thor had thought. His father, for example, had caused problems for both himself and the family. Behind his controlled facade, he'd gotten involved in gambling and bad investments. He'd been too proud to tell anyone about it until the debt was almost drowning them. Hallgrim Dalen and Co. had also been involved—with predatory loans camouflaged as friendly help and advice. They never hesitated to profit from others' misfortune.

Thor preferred not to think too much about the matter—but they'd been deceitful, treacherous. A lot like this damned shitty weather.

Little infuriated him as much as freezing rain, this unpredictable phenomenon that made cold roads function like flash-freezers for precipitation. The roads went from dry to skating rinks in a matter of seconds, and even cars like his own—solid, with the best studded tires on the market—were sliding around like Bambi on ice. Storms had been in the forecast, and no sensible person would think of driving right now unless it was absolutely necessary. But when Borghild Berg called from Glitter Peak, he knew he had to show up.

"Aisha doesn't have enough experience with driving in these conditions," Borghild had said on the phone. "And Alfred has the day off today. Could you pick Hussein up from school and drive him up here? We would be forever grateful."

It was an unusual request, but Thor would never even consider saying no to Nana Borghild. He had more experience with the weather and roads around here than most others—but he still *hated* it.

He'd taken his father's Škoda; it smelled less like sheep than his own pickup. He already noticed how slippery the roads had gotten on his way to the village center, and it only got worse over the few hundred feet to the school. He drove carefully all the way to the schoolyard, where he found Hussein standing alone beneath the awning at the main entrance. Most of the other kids lived down in Dalen and walked to and from school on their own. Hussein grinned at Thor as he ran over to the car and got into the passenger seat.

"My teacher said you were going to pick me up today! Cool!"

Thor had to smile, too. It wasn't often that anyone used the word *cool* to describe anything he did.

"What did you learn at school today?" he asked as they turned out of the schoolyard.

"We've been learning about old Christmas traditions," Hussein replied. "And folklore and the Runic calendar and stuff. There's a lot that's kind of spooky. Have you heard about the underworld?"

"Yes, tons," Thor said. "Maja's my aunt, you know!"

"Oh, yeah," Hussein said. "She knows a lot about scary stuff from the old days. But I don't think I should tell my mom about the underworld. That would only make her even more scared."

"Creatures from the underworld don't have to be scary. They can be nice, too," Thor said. "But maybe you can tell her about Anna pissihose instead, if you want."

"What?"

"That's what Aunt Maja calls today," Thor said. "Anna's Day. It often rains a lot on the ninth of December, and that's true today, for sure. That's why it's a good day for washing clothes and brewing beer—because of all the water."

"Rain, frost, sleet, hail, snow," Hussein rattled off. "All of that is water."

"That's right," Thor said.

"And rain like this, that covers everything in ice," Hussein said.

"Yep," Thor confirmed.

"Is it hard to drive?" Hussein asked.

"It would be easier if it didn't freeze and get so damn . . ." Thor cleared his throat. "If it didn't freeze and get so slippery."

Hussein laughed.

"I heard that you said *damn*," he giggled. "But I won't tell anyone."

"No, that's probably for the best," Thor muttered.

Up at the hotel, Vegard and Ingrid had been working separately all day. Ingrid was still trying to get an overview of the financial consequences of Friday's flooding. She'd just finished a long phone call with the insurance company and was studying the estimates from the workers when there was a knock on the office door. Vegard stuck his head in.

"Hi, Ingrid!" he said. "Want to grab some lunch?"

Ingrid looked at her watch. It was already two o'clock. Time also flew when you *weren't* having fun. "Sure, let's go downstairs and find something in the kitchen. Do you know if Pia's eaten?"

"Yeah, she's eaten . . ."—he pulled out his phone and opened Instagram—". . . venison carbonnade and home-baked wholegrain bread with pickled onions."

He grinned and showed Ingrid the picture, which already had hundreds of likes.

"Awesome! Let's see if Maja has any leftovers for us."

Maja did indeed. And it was delicious—even without any likes besides the ones they got from their own stomachs.

Afterward, they met Thor Seter in the foyer as he came through the door with Hussein. The boy waved and ran up the stairs while Thor stood there, looking a bit lost.

"Hi, Thor!" Ingrid said as she walked toward him.

He smiled. "Hi!"

Vegard punched Thor lightly on the shoulder and said he had to get back to work.

Ingrid got the feeling that he wanted to make sure that she and Thor got some alone time. *You little matchmaker,* she said to herself, but to Thor she said, "Thank you for driving Hussein back home. Aisha gets so scared when the weather's like this, understandably."

"No problem," Thor said. "Happy to be able to help."

He ran a hand through his light bangs, tousling his hair even more. He *was* pretty cute.

"Are you hungry? Thirsty? Want some coffee?" Ingrid asked. "Why don't you come to the library for a cup?"

"Yes, sure, that . . . that would be nice. Thanks," Thor said.

She came into the library, placed two steaming mugs on the table, and sat down next to Thor on the sofa. She pulled a small bag out of the pocket of her cardigan. "Do you like caramels?"

"They're my *absolute* favorite candy," he said.

Thor was such a likable guy. She'd always thought so.

It was so nice to talk with him that she almost forgot how busy she was. They chatted about the weather, the new guests, Hussein, the hotel. It was almost as though she hadn't ever been away from the village when they sat here like this. It was different when it was just the two of them.

Thor talked enthusiastically about the farm and sheep but didn't have much to say when it came to topics such as relationships and family. Thor had been young—in his midtwenties—when he got married, and Ingrid had felt a little sorry for him when she heard about his divorce. She'd never really known Sandra but had heard a little about what happened from her grandmother and a bit from Maja. Well, quite a bit from Maja, really. She'd been upset that her nephew had been abandoned that way.

Thor didn't seem to have any need to talk about the divorce himself, and Ingrid wasn't going to nag. She of all people knew that breakups and heartbreak weren't something you wanted to talk about with just anyone. But Thor was handsome and had his own farm, so surely there must be a woman for him somewhere out there? She knew that many girls in the village had been interested in the past.

Ingrid had never come close to getting married or settling down. Her relationship with Preben was the closest she'd gotten, but it had been—or so she thought in retrospect—based on physical attraction and a shared sense of adventure. Preben had been married before and had never hinted that he wanted to try it again. His divorce from Sylvia had probably been too public and painful. And when things ended between him and Ingrid, it seemed as though everyone in the world was a part of the breakup somehow. Even though Ingrid felt that the biggest blow in *that* context had been to her and not him, she didn't really know how Preben had felt afterward. She hadn't wanted to speak with him.

WHEN THEIR COFFEE CUPS WERE EMPTY, Thor started looking around the library. She followed his gaze. Large, custom-built bookshelves covered one wall. Row after row of fiction and history.

"I'd almost forgotten how many books you have here," he said. "Has anyone ever written about the hotel? Books to commemorate one of its anniversaries, or anything like that? I've been getting more and more interested in that kind of thing lately. Pretty soon I'll be one of those old men who trawls through archives and writes about local history."

"I'm not aware of anything written about the hotel apart from some old newspaper articles," Ingrid replied. "No anniversary books." She thought for a moment. "The hundredth anniversary of the hotel was around the time when Mom and Dad died. Nana Borghild probably had other things to deal with then."

Thor's face fell. "I didn't mean to . . ."

"No, of course not!" Ingrid said. "It's totally fine for you to ask. I think it's interesting, too. We have a lot of historical materials, like the guest books, for example."

She stood up and walked over to the bookcase. "That reminds me, Sunny asked if she could look at them for a paper she's writing. I guess she wants newspaper clippings and such too. It's a bit of a mess here, but I'll see what I can find for her."

She opened the bottom cabinet—solid wood, creak-free hinges.

On top of the large stack of old guest books, there were also a couple of yellowed paper folders. Ingrid knew there were more in the archive, but apparently some had ended up here as well.

"Maybe Sunny could combine her homework with a tidying project," she said over her shoulder. "That could be the seed of a history book, too!"

She took a couple of the books and the two folders back to the table and opened the top folder out of curiosity. It contained old newspaper clippings. She picked up the one on top.

Thor stretched his neck to look. "That's the old logo for the *Daily.*"

"Yeah, kind of weird seeing it again. I remember it from when we were kids."

The Dalen Daily was written in Gothic letters beneath a logo of a sun over mountain peaks.

64th Volume. Monday, March 5, 1962. 75 øre.

The top of the right-hand side had an advertisement with a picture of the "Volkswagen Family Deluxe": father, mother, three children, and a dog with a pile of luggage in front of a Volkswagen Beetle. "Put Volkswagen wheels on life," it read.

But the headline just below stood in stark contrast to the family idyll of the ad:

YOUNG GIRL MISSING

"What's this?" Thor asked.

Ingrid read on. Beneath a photo of the main road through Dalen with houses on both sides, the story read:

> The sheriff of Dalen and Innviken is searching for a young woman who went missing from her home two days ago without a trace. See page 5.

But she couldn't find page 5 because the rest of the newspaper wasn't there. Ingrid flipped through the rest of the stack, but it looked as though the other clippings were from other years and about completely different things.

"I vaguely remember hearing about this, actually," Ingrid said. "There was a disappearance in Dalen sometime in the '60s. But I don't know much about it. Do you?"

"No," Thor said. "I'd think that Aunt Maja would've told me about it in detail if something exciting happened . . . but I guess she had barely even been born at that time. And it could be that the girl turned up the next day, and it wasn't a big deal."

"Yeah, maybe," Ingrid said. "But I'd like to know what happened."

"Do you think it has something to do with the hotel?" Thor asked.

"I don't know. But otherwise, it's weird that someone would have saved this front page, isn't it? I'll have to ask Nana Borghild!"

"Yeah, do that. And I can ask the *Dalen Daily* if they have the old newspapers downstairs at the editorial office," Thor suggested. "Or maybe there are some libraries or archives that keep that kind of thing? Like I said . . . I'm going to become one of those old local history guys. Or maybe a detective? I'm already excited about it!"

His blue eyes shone eagerly. Ingrid caught a glimpse of the boy she'd known in her childhood—adventurous and optimistic. He was still there.

Ingrid sat down at her computer again once Thor had left. Her task truly felt Sisyphean. For every estimate from the workers that she read through and every form she filled out, another estimate and another form awaited—like an eternal uphill battle.

When she'd gotten as far as she could for the day, she slammed down the lid of her computer and rubbed her hands together. Now, a more joyful task was on the horizon: she'd been summoned to sample Maja's *krumkake*.

She jogged down the stairs and into the kitchen, where Maja and Hussein were already waiting. Maja had made coffee and set out cups and plates. This had to be one of the very best parts of being the manager of a hotel, Ingrid thought as she squeezed in next to them on the bench. They hadn't seen Nana Borghild since breakfast. Ingrid didn't want to bother her; they could catch up early tomorrow morning.

The cookies were exactly as they should be: golden, light, and crispy, with a taste of butter, cream, and vanilla. *It's nice that something can be so simple*, Ingrid thought. Just sitting here in the warm kitchen with completely uncomplicated people, eating something good and looking forward to being able to go to bed soon.

She heard a car outside—probably the Wilkinses returning from one of their excursions.

Hussein grabbed another krumkake.

"Auntie Ingrid," he said. "I've been thinking about something. Could Mrs. Wilkins be one of those people from the underworld? Or maybe a *hulder*?"

Ingrid laughed out loud, but Hussein just looked at her gravely.

"We've been learning about them at school," he exclaimed. "Wood nymphs. They live in the forest and they try to be like ordinary people, but they aren't. They have tails, and hair that looks like gold. So does Mrs. Wilkins, even though she's old."

"She is *not* old!" Maja exclaimed. "Around my age, I suppose. Even if she does dye her hair."

Ingrid laughed again, but Hussein looked a little embarrassed.

"I'm sorry, Miss Maja. I didn't mean it like that. But Mrs. Wilkins has green clothes, too. And she's kind of nice, but weird."

"I think she wears a lot of green because she likes nature colors. But why do you think she's weird?" Ingrid asked.

"She smiles sooo much and asks lots of questions."

"What does she ask about?"

The six-year-old took a bite of krumkake while he thought. "All kinds of things. Where I'm from, who works at the hotel, and about people down in Dalen. But she doesn't have a tail. I think."

"I agree," Maja said. "I get a strange feeling about that woman. It's like she has something to hide. She's not totally normal, that's for sure."

DECEMBER 10

The day was gray and Ingrid's mood even grayer. She'd been in such good spirits yesterday after the cake tasting and the nice afternoon with Thor. She was sick of the dark clouds that always drifted over her after periods of energy and sunshine. What had happened to good old vivacious Ingrid Berg?

She'd been planning on going to bed early the night before but ended up sitting up late, obsessing over renovations and bills and missing orders, eating caramels until her stomach protested and her mouth felt glazed in fat and sugar.

She was lethargic when she woke up. Her battery level was close to zero. Three cups of strong morning coffee had helped a little, but not as much as they should have. Apparently Nana Borghild wasn't feeling great either; she had asked whether they could postpone their daily chat until later in the day. So after breakfast, Ingrid had taken a trip down to the basement to look at some walls that needed painting. She'd noticed not only that the paint was peeling, but that the wood was bulging in some places. Was the drainage system not functioning properly? Had water gotten in from outside? When she stuck her thumbnail into the wood, it had given way. Was it rotten? Oh no . . . she couldn't take any more of this.

Her phone buzzed. It was a text from Vegard: *Can you come up to Pia's room?*

Coming!

What was it now? Pia and Vegard couldn't possibly already be ready to leave. He was notoriously slow-moving and always took forever to pack. Ingrid always wondered how he could take so long; it was just a matter of throwing everything you'd brought into your suitcase! To be fair, though, Vegard packed more clothes for a weekend than she would have packed for a week, and he had so many skin and hair products that the shelves in the bathroom usually didn't even have enough room for everything.

Ingrid knocked on Pia's door, bracing herself for another disaster, but found Vegard and Pia sitting by the small table in front of the window. Vegard had clearly brought breakfast upstairs, but Pia didn't seem to have eaten much. The juice glass was half empty, and only a few bites had been taken from a roll lying on the plate. Pia looked pale, even though she seemed to be freshly showered and made up, and her hair was just as beautiful as when she'd arrived.

"Are you all right?" Ingrid asked. "Or is something wrong?"

"No, not really, but I feel a bit off," Pia replied. "Nauseous and dizzy. I don't think I can drive all the way back to Oslo when I'm feeling like this."

She almost looked like she was going to cry, and she shut her eyes for a moment before looking at Ingrid again. "I guess I just need to rest. Is it okay if I stay until tomorrow? Or maybe the day after? I'll pay for my stay, of course."

Ingrid looked at Vegard. He gave her a *pretty please?* look, which was really quite unnecessary. Ingrid would never say no to paying guests or Vegard's friends, and *definitely* not to famous influencers. And Pia P—she was the whole package.

"Of course you can stay until tomorrow," Ingrid replied. "You can stay as long as you want! You're more than welcome here. But let us know if there's anything we can help with."

Pia nodded. "Yes, I will."

"You . . . don't need a doctor or anything?"

Pia shook her head energetically but stopped quickly. "No, no, it's not *that* bad! Don't worry. I just don't feel quite ready to travel. It's probably better to stay here and gather my strength. I think I'll try to go outside and get some fresh air later."

"You should definitely rest," Ingrid said. "And I hope you feel better soon. And it's a good idea to take a little walk outside later, if you feel up to it. Silver linings and all that. We've been really looking forward to showing you Glitter Peak at its finest, and now maybe we'll have the chance!"

Pia smiled weakly.

"What about you, Vegard?" Ingrid asked. "Will you stay a little longer, too? And keep Pia company?"

Vegard's work mostly took place online, so she knew he didn't have to return to the capital to get back to the office or anything like that.

He smiled and nodded. "I might as well work from here for a few more days," he said. "If you have room, that is."

"Of course I have room," Ingrid assured him. "You know I'm just happy to have you here."

"Then I'll tell David right away."

Her gray mood was brightened by a glimmer of sunshine. Vegard would stay here a little longer! That warmed her enough to be able to bear the thought of finding Alfred and getting him to take a look at the wall in the basement.

"That is *insaaaaanely* cool!" Vegard practically shouted when she showed him the front page of the newspaper about the young woman who disappeared in 1962. They were drinking coffee together in the library.

She shushed him, but he didn't seem to notice.

"I mean, we should do a podcast or something," he continued. "That's the big thing now, you know. True crime."

"Okay, you have to stop," Ingrid laughed. "We're not going to be making any podcasts here. At least not until we know what this is all about. We don't even know if there even was a crime to begin with!"

"That doesn't make it any less exciting, though."

"No, I guess not. But I'll ask Nana Borghild about it. And Thor is going to try to help find more newspapers."

"Trustworthy ol' Thor," Vegard said. "He has a crush on you. You know that, right?"

Ingrid snorted. "Oh my God, now you really have to knock it off, Vegard. Thor and I were boyfriend-girlfriend when we were about . . . eleven. I think he's gotten over it."

"Do you think so? And what about you? Have *you* gotten over it? He *is* pretty cute. If it weren't for David, I might've considered going after him myself. Sheep and all."

Vegard had put on his most coquettish voice.

"You goofball," Ingrid laughed.

❄

Ingrid was sitting on the sofa in Borghild's apartment with a pile of insurance papers that she intended to go through with her grandmother. But of course, she had to ask about the mysterious disappearance first. Borghild stood with her back turned, looking out the window.

"Yes, a young woman disappeared," she said. "She was only nineteen. It was her wedding day. The groom was waiting at the altar, but she never showed up."

"And no one knows what happened to her?"

"At least no one who wants to talk about it."

"So the mystery was never solved?" Ingrid asked.

Her grandmother turned around.

"No, it wasn't solved."

"But who was it? Did you know her?"

"Yes, I knew her. She was from the village."

"Oh, wow. It must have been pretty . . . I mean, what do you think happened?"

Nana Borghild sat down next to Ingrid and put her hand on hers.

"Some people think she ran off, others think she jumped into the falls. Or that something happened to her. Why are you asking about this now, sweetie? It was a long, long time ago."

"I found some newspaper clippings in the cupboard with the guest books. Someone kept the front page of the paper that said she was missing. Was it you?"

"It could be. I . . . don't really remember. Like I said, it was a long time ago."

"So you don't know if we have the rest of the paper some-where?"

"No, I don't know . . . I can't remember what was saved de-cades ago."

"Of course," Ingrid said. "Thor's going to help me investigate some more. Did you know he's interested in local history?"

"No, I didn't," her grandmother said. "Your grandfather was, too, in his last years. He was always talking about wanting to write Glitter Peak's history, but he didn't get around to it before he died."

"Do you think about him a lot?" Ingrid asked.

Nana Borghild looked at her, clearly surprised. They didn't usually talk about Grandpa Christian.

"Of course I do," Borghild said. "But I've lived longer without him than I did with him."

"Why didn't you ever remarry after he died?" Ingrid asked.

Borghild had never even had a boyfriend or "friend" after she was widowed—at least not that Ingrid knew about.

"It might have made things easier up here if you had a hus-band? For support? A kind of partner?"

Nana Borghild shook her head.

"No, that would only have complicated things. For me, life is easier without a husband getting involved in everything."

Ingrid wasn't sure whether she was joking or serious. For all she knew, her grandmother could have had romances without Ingrid being aware of them. She felt that she'd already gone a bit too far with the questions now. Maybe a person didn't always want to tell her grandchild absolutely everything.

Ingrid knew that love and romance were elements that had to

be pushed aside when life demanded something else of you—and life had indeed demanded a lot of Borghild.

"But what about you, then?" her grandmother's lively voice said. "You're the one who needs a husband—not me!"

"Me?!" Ingrid couldn't imagine sharing her life or job with a man right now. "Oh no, no, no . . . taking care of myself and the hotel is more than enough. I can't imagine having to nurture a relationship as well."

She paused for a moment before continuing. "I guess I've never really pictured it either. I've never really longed for a partner the way other people seem to. The thing with Preben was kind of . . . something else."

HER JOBS AS A MOUNTAIN GUIDE and expedition leader had always been lonely. True, she'd been surrounded by teams, but she was the leader, she was the one making the decisions: where they were going, who could join, when they should attempt a summit, when they should wait. She listened to other people's opinions, but she had to be strong. Not just strong—she knew a lot of people thought she was cold, too. But she had to be that way. As a leader and as a climber, you had to be focused and disciplined. You had to be in control of yourself in order to lead others.

At least that's how it was until she met Preben Wexelsen. At some point in their relationship, she'd lost her focus, and she'd definitely lost her leadership abilities. She'd let her feelings for him get in the way of her judgment.

She noticed that he was someone who took charge as soon as she met him—maybe even the first time they were in the same room. It was at a convention—"Nordic Summit: The Elevating Experience"—where they'd both been hired to speak about their expeditions. She was standing in a crowded room full of climbers and tour organizers, and the volume of the chatter and laughter around them almost seemed to lower a bit the moment Preben entered the room. She recognized him from TV and newspapers, but he was even more good-looking in person: tall, handsome, strong. He had dark, slicked-back hair and clearly chiseled features with prominent cheekbones and a defined jawline. He looked around, and when his eyes met Ingrid's, she felt it like an electric shock. A bolt of lightning. She'd never experienced anything like it before.

Later, she thought that her fate had been sealed at this moment. If she'd known how it was going to turn out, she would have walked out of the conference room right then and there and never looked back.

But she didn't know. And she didn't leave the conference room. On the contrary, she kept looking at Preben even after they broke eye contact and he turned to greet someone from the company organizing the conference. She felt an immediate urge to go over to him but controlled herself for as long as she could. Everything about him appealed to her. The tall figure, the confident posture. The piercing gaze. She later found out that his eyes were green—and that his mouth was the only thing that was soft about him.

"It's you and me now," he said as he kissed her and left her room the next morning. And so it was.

Preben had a natural authority that made it easy to trust him, to let him have the final say in things. If she wanted to climb

Kilimanjaro from the south and he from the north, she would argue against it, but they'd most likely end up climbing from the north anyway. As their partnership and relationship developed, it became more and more natural for her to give in, to let him take the lead. She started to suppress her gut feeling if they disagreed, thinking that he must know better. An expedition couldn't have two leaders anyway, and he had more experience than her. For a while, it felt right to do things that way. But in the end, it turned out to be catastrophic.

If she'd learned anything from all this, it was that she had to be able to make it on her own. The decision to give up climbing and focus on running a hotel was related to this insight—except for the fact that she didn't really have much of a choice, either.

Vegard, who was the world's biggest Disney fan, said that Ingrid was like Elsa from *Frozen*, sitting up here in her hotel: an ice queen on Glitter Peak. But she wasn't a queen. She didn't have any magical powers. She'd simply learned from hard-earned experience that you couldn't trust anyone but yourself. With Preben, she'd let go of control, allowed someone else to take charge, and it had ended in disaster.

Spring 1962

"She's not here? What do you mean she's not here?" the groom's best man growled. He was also the bride's older brother, and his broad shoulders were hunched, as if he were preparing to attack.

The usher took a step backward, tugged at his lapels, and widened his eyes, clearly frightened by the young man in front of him. This wasn't a guy you wanted to mess with, but the usher could do nothing but tell the truth.

"She isn't here," he said. He was clutching a bundle of songbooks in a sweaty hand and set them on a shelf in the armory. He fixed his gaze on the big, burly man who towered in front of him. "The driver came with an empty car," the usher stammered. "He waited outside your house for a long time, but she never came out. He went and knocked, too, but nothing happened, and the house seemed empty. So he drove over here to see if he'd misunderstood and she'd come to the church some other way. But she's not here."

"She's not here. She's. Not. Here." The bride's brother had turned red in the face and was breathing heavily. "What the hell has she gotten herself into now?"

The usher couldn't answer and therefore settled for shaking in his boots.

The bride's brother ignored him and glanced into the crowded church, where the groom was still standing at the altar rail, sweating in his slightly too-tight suit, and where more and more people in the pews had turned around to see what was happening.

The only person not looking toward the back was the bride's maid of honor. She was sitting on a chair in the chancel, staring straight ahead.

Rage flared up in the bride's brother. That bitch. He

would deal with her later. He'd never felt so humiliated in his entire life, and he had a strong feeling that the girl sitting right there was partly responsible for this scandal.

But first, he had to find out where his sister was.

Because she was going to regret this.

DECEMBER 11

"Almost everything else has changed," Nana Borghild said. "But the mountains are the same as always."

She and Ingrid were standing at the panoramic window in the dining room, watching the first rays of sun over Glitter Peak. Sunny smiled at them as she carried in trays and plates, setting up breakfast for the day.

"What a lovely girl!" they suddenly heard behind them.

They exchanged glances. It was Freya Wilkins, and it was too late to get away.

"Always so enthusiastic!" the American practically shouted, gesturing toward Sunny, who smiled and waved back.

"Yes, she's fantastic," Ingrid replied.

"I hope you take good care of her so Glitter Peak Lodge will be a place she'll look back on fondly," Freya said. "As the first part of a brilliant hotel career. Good morning, by the way. How are you?" She smiled, her teeth gleaming white against her tanned face. "I slept terribly myself, but it's because John keeps nudging me all the time. He says I snore! Have you ever heard such a thing?"

Ingrid had no trouble imagining that Freya Wilkins was loud even when she was asleep but wasn't planning on communicating that.

She settled for a simple "Good morning!" while Borghild contented herself with nodding at the new arrival. Her grandmother was usually good at chatting with the tourists, even though they hadn't learned much English at school back in her day. Right now, though, it seemed that she didn't feel the need to say anything.

Freya still looked sharp and alert for someone who'd slept poorly. Her golden hair was gathered in a ponytail, and she was dressed in surprisingly modern hiking pants and a beautiful green-and-white knitted cardigan in a traditional pattern from Fana. She saw Ingrid's approving look and beat her to the punch.

"Isn't it lovely? I knitted it myself from a pattern from a friend in Daughters of Norway. I didn't care about such things when I was young. I just thought it was embarrassing with all the fuss about the motherland and traditions and lefse and lutefisk. But when I started searching for my Norwegian roots, I found the joy of knitting, too." She pointed at the T-shirt under the open sweater: *Knitting keeps me from unraveling.*

Ingrid smiled. "You know all about that, don't you, Nana?"

She turned to her grandmother, who didn't have to answer because Freya kept on talking.

"John and I are going on an expedition today," she declared. "We're going to the old farmhouse up at Storebru. We heard it's a spectacular example of the traditional log cabin style in this area."

"That's a nice trip," Ingrid replied. "But the road is a little tricky between Dalen and the parking lot at Storebruveien."

Freya laughed loudly.

"I'd say that *all* of the roads are tricky here in the old country! But what a godsend that we got hold of that Range Rover—and that John is such a good driver."

"Yes, that's lucky . . . So Dr. Wilkins is on his way down to breakfast soon?"

"Yes, he'll be down any minute," Freya replied. "*Uten mat og drikke, duger helten ikke!*" she proclaimed in Norwegian with thick American *r*'s. "An army marches on its stomach. That's what my mother always used to say. And John has taken a liking to this milk of yours, *skummel kulturmelk*. Eats a big bowl every morning with his oats. You'd think he was the one with Norwegian roots."

"Skummel kulturmelk?" Ingrid repeated. "Scary cultured milk? You must mean *skummet* kulturmelk—skimmed cultured milk!"

"Yes, *skummet* kulturmelk!" Freya said enthusiastically. "I've heard you can use it to make pancakes, too?"

"Yes, absolutely," Ingrid confirmed. "We can get Maja to make some one day if you'd like."

"Great! We love pancakes, especially if they have a taste of Norway," Freya said. "I'll tell Miss Seter that we can do it together one day. I can teach her some American cooking tricks, too."

"I'm sure she'd like that," Ingrid said.

Ingrid thought she saw her grandmother's face twitch but pretended not to notice. Freya Wilkins certainly didn't seem to see it, at least.

"I thought I'd ask you something," Freya said. "That painting hanging in the stairwell, is it the same view we see here from the dining room?"

"Yes, it is," Ingrid confirmed, pointing out the window. "That's Heaven's Horn that you see towering over there, and Styggfossen is the waterfall."

"We thought we'd go check out the waterfall one of these days," Freya continued. "It's so big and wild! I've heard it's taken quite a few lives."

"Probably mostly legends," Ingrid said. "Though of course you need to be careful when you go close to such a waterfall. But it's frozen right now, so you can climb it."

"I don't think that'll be something for me and John," Freya laughed.

As they were heading up the stairs afterward, her grandmother stopped on the landing where the oil painting of Heaven's Horn and Styggfossen hung. Neither of them said anything at first; Ingrid stood and waited while Borghild stared at the painting. Ingrid had walked past it every day of her life but never really thought much about it. Like many of the other paintings in the house, it had simply always been there.

Now, she looked at it more closely. It was an early summer scene in an elaborate gilded frame. The pointed, snowcapped top of Heaven's Horn towered against a clear blue sky, the moss and grass in the foreground were light green, and the water in the waterfall was light, almost white. So different from the ice castle it became in the winter.

"Yes, this painting's been hanging here for more than sixty years," Borghild said.

"Really? I thought it was even older," Ingrid said. "It's kind of old-fashioned."

"No, it's from 1961, but it was painted in a traditional style," her grandmother said. "I'll never forget the time it was painted. The painter was a popular fellow, you see, during the months he stayed in the village. Antonsen was his name. Everyone who could afford it bought one of his landscape paintings. He was quite the sensation, and my mother and father really got caught up in the frenzy." She smiled again. "They commissioned another painting, too. The one I have in my room."

"The one of the girls in bunads?"

Her grandmother nodded, her face suddenly serious.

"It doesn't seem so long ago," she said. "But at the same time, it was a whole different lifetime."

Ingrid went through the reservations for the coming weeks. People were coming and going, but she would have liked to have even more bookings. It wasn't exactly jam-packed here. On the plus side, she noted that the Wilkinses had come a whole two weeks early. *Lucky for them we weren't full—unlucky for me that we have so few guests*, Ingrid thought. The Americans were planning on staying here for Christmas and over New Year's, and that was good for the hotel; guests who stayed for weeks meant much less work than the short weekend visits, which made up most of the bookings.

On Friday the thirteenth—*good thing I'm not superstitious,*

Ingrid thought—the hotel was expecting a group of young men who'd be staying from Friday to Sunday. Ingrid looked through the list of names and wondered who they were and what they were expecting in terms of amenities. This wasn't exactly Hemsedal or Geilo with hot tubs and wild après-ski parties. Would they like staying at a traditional old hotel like this? At the same time, she had to assume there was a reason they'd chosen Glitter Peak in the first place. The climbing, perhaps. Two couples from the Hamar region would also be arriving for the weekend, as well as a British family, who were apparently pretty outdoorsy.

There were a number of guests who came here just to climb, even now during the winter season. Ice climbing was becoming increasingly popular, and Styggfossen was an exciting challenge. Some came to hike and enjoy the peace and quiet and the views. On the weekends, the premises were also open to guests who just wanted to have lunch or dinner in the restaurant. There weren't many such visitors because the hotel was pretty off the beaten track, but the pre-Christmas festivities—and perhaps curiosity—enticed some locals to give it a try. On Friday evening, six people would be dining here in addition to the overnight guests, and ten people were booked for lunch on Sunday. Ingrid recognized several of the names from her school days in Dalen. They probably wanted to check out how things were going up here.

She felt uneasy at the thought of seeing her old schoolmates again. Thor was the only one of them she had any contact with. She'd become a little wary after the avalanche and the public breakup with Preben. She got anxious when she had to meet people, especially old acquaintances who often asked how she was *really* doing—people who'd read about her online and took the information they found there as an invitation to stomp into her personal and emotional life. They'd probably seen the headlines in the gossip magazines. *Dramatic breakup after accident. Left the country in a hurry. Friends losing hope: she won't speak to him.*

She shook it off. Curiosity and feigned concern were things she'd just have to deal with. She was trying to secure the future of the hotel, she needed guests, and she was going to be happy about every single one who came—no matter what their motivations for visiting might be.

Friday, December 20, was the last big arrival day. One of the groups from Hamar and one from around Drammen were expected that weekend, along with two families from Oslo who would be staying in the apartments in the annex. Vegard and David would be coming up that day as well—if Vegard even managed to go *back* to Oslo before then. That depended on Pia P. Ingrid got the strange feeling that Pia was dragging out her visit. Perhaps she was planning on moving in? Anyway, she'd said she would pay—although Ingrid didn't know how to bring that up again.

Ingrid was the one who'd decided that the hotel should stay open for Christmas, but now she regretted the decision. It was strange to think that she and Nana Borghild would be celebrating Christmas with the Wilkinses. *That* would be a pretty special experience! She wished Vegard could be here then, too, but of course he had other plans with David and his family.

Glitter Peak used to have guests during Christmas, but not since Ingrid's parents died. Nana Borghild had had enough to deal with taking care of little Ingrid in the years after the accident, and celebrating Christmas with strangers hadn't felt natural after Angelina and Marius had passed.

More than ever, it struck Ingrid how dramatic and demanding

life had been for her grandmother—what with the sole responsibility not only for the hotel but also for Ingrid. Her paternal grandparents in Oslo had also been there for her, and Ingrid had had a good relationship with them until they died a few years ago. But it was Nana Borghild who in practice had been both mother and father to Ingrid when she was growing up, and it was Nana Borghild who stood on the hotel steps and waved goodbye when Ingrid headed out into the world. Her grandmother had carried everything on her shoulders, and Ingrid had never once heard her complain.

Thank you, Nana, Ingrid thought. *Now, at well over eighty years old, you'll finally be able to bow out while I take over. It's really not a moment too soon. I'm sorry I didn't come back before.*

Borghild went into the library. It was empty. Perfect. She wanted to look through the guest books in peace and quiet before handing them over. Sunny wanted to write term papers about the hotel's history, and Ingrid had started asking questions about what had happened in the 1960s. Borghild needed to think carefully about which story she wanted to tell.

Here they were, on the bottom shelf of the bookcase: several stacks of books in worn brown leather bindings. She picked up the oldest and carried them over to the sofa by the fireplace. Initially, she'd planned on reading through the books between 1960 and 1962, but as she ran her fingers over the leather covers, she couldn't resist the urge to start at the beginning.

Glitter Peak Lodge was written in gold Gothic letters on the oldest volumes. She flipped through the pages in Volume 1. The first entry was dated August 1, 1893, in elegant calligraphy:

"Grand Opening of Glitter Peak Lodge." The thick book was filled up by New Year's in 1899, then a new one was started. There'd been about twenty books so far. For 130 years, hikers and tourists had written their names and observations within the heavy leather bindings. Hiking trails were described, good and bad weather noted. Holiday menus were pasted in, and sketches of plant and animal life were drawn in the corners: heather and lichen, mountain birch and cloudberries, animals ranging from lemmings to bears.

She lifted her gaze and looked at the stuffed bear in the corner by the fireplace. Barry was an *Ursus arctos arctos*—a Eurasian brown bear. Not as large as the American grizzly or Kodiak, but big and scary enough. Borghild clearly remembered when Barry was killed. It was Dalen's self-proclaimed legendary huntsman who'd shot it. Bear hunting was legal at that time, and the hunter was young. He'd been Borghild's friend. He no longer was.

She shuddered and continued flipping the pages of the guest book, put it down, and picked up the next one, then the next. These books really were a treasure trove! Here was a greeting from the British mountaineer Sir Peter Downsize, who in 1919 had found Glitter Peak to be "magnificent" and the hotel "splendid."

And here, in 1921, an envoy from the Royal Norwegian Automobile Club had visited the hotel, which he found "very satisfactory," even though he had a lot to criticize about the "macadamization" of the roads in Dalen and the surrounding area. It was like listening to Freya Wilkins complaining about the Norwegian roads. Some things never changed. A clipping from the local newspaper with a picture of the proud motorist in a hat and driving gloves was pasted on the next page.

Her gaze stopped on a picture of a woman in a white blouse and long skirt hiked up above her ankles, heavy boots underneath. Ingbrita Berg, Borghild's own grandmother, had been one of the very first female climbers in the country. People in the village told tales of her escapades: she wore a skirt when she posed in the pictures, but she'd been so wild that she climbed in pants. She was the first woman to climb Heaven's Horn and one of the first people in general to climb it. She'd also been up Store Skagastølstind—Norway's third-highest and most difficult peak—at a time when mountaineering itself was completely new.

Borghild hadn't climbed since Angelina and Marius died; the responsibility for Ingrid had made her put climbing aside. It simply felt too risky. Giving up climbing had been a great loss, but Borghild had been careful not to let it overshadow Ingrid's own love of the sport. Someone else had taken that away from her.

They were a part of a long tradition, she and Ingrid. All these women who ended up in the shadow of men. She looked at the photo of Ingbrita again. This was a story more people should know about. It occurred to Borghild that someone should write the history of the mountain women and the hotel based on these entries. Perhaps she could do it herself? Yes. That's just what she wanted to do. Even in her eighty-third year on this earth, she still had the energy and willpower to keep working. Now that she'd been relieved from her duties as hotel manager, writing the history of Glitter Peak would be her next project.

But first—first, she had to deal with what was happening around her now. She shut the book and looked for the one that had records from the first half of the 1960s.

The sketch on the page she opened to was funny; it was supposed to depict "Sofie, Borghild, Christian, and Charlie on a mouse hunt in the hotel." That was what was written in ornate handwriting beneath the picture. She remembered that winter well. Winter tourism was booming at the time. Starting around 1960, new and better roads had been built from Dalen and upward, and more and more people from the cities wanted and could afford to go on mountain vacations. Borghild and her friend, Christian Stugu—who had not yet become her husband—had therefore convinced Borghild's parents that the hotel should stay open during Christmas and New Year's to make the most out of the new business. This had turned out to be a good idea. His cousin Sofie had come from Bergen and worked there for several seasons. And Charlie . . . she imagined Charlie's blond hair and contagious laughter. Charlie had been a natural part of the team. They'd been a group of young people working together while the townspeople had flocked to the mountains. The hotel had been full of guests and the atmosphere was fantastic.

Unfortunately, it wasn't just the tourists who'd flocked to the hotel that year; the mice did as well. They'd found their way into the buildings when the frosty nights set in, and as the weeks went by, the problem only got worse and worse. Borghild would never forget the night Sofie had found a mouse in the bedroom she shared with one of the maids and ran out into the snow in sheer panic, dressed in nothing but her nightgown. The others had laughed their heads off at the scene, though Sofie hadn't found it the least bit amusing. But it was. Even all these years later, Borghild still found herself smiling at the memory.

Otherwise—apart from the mice—they'd had a wonderful time! There was no distinction between work and play back in those days; everything was work, and everything was fun. They washed the floors and carried luggage, guided tourists up to the

tops of the mountains and skied back down. They peeled potatoes, changed sheets, and manned the reception area. And in the
evenings, there was dancing. So much dancing.

Her gaze stopped on an entry, and Borghild stood up abruptly
and shut the book. She didn't want to sit here in the library any
longer. She wanted to take the book up to her room and prepare
herself for what she would have to talk about soon—for the first
time since it all happened.

DECEMBER 12

It was getting dark, and Maja Seter made the sign of the cross over the doors. She said the Lord's Prayer as she polished the glass in the lanterns she'd be setting outside. Ingrid knew the chef would also be putting a knife in the wall above her bed. She'd explained that when dark forces were near, you needed to protect yourself in every way possible.

"And the dark forces are coming, whether you believe in them or not," Maja claimed.

To be honest, it wasn't all that hard to believe that evil forces were approaching at this time of year, when the sun hardly showed itself and the shadows were long and deep. They were coming from all sides, said Maja, since the distinctions between the world of the spirits and the world of humans became less defined during the dark winter months. And especially tonight. It was *Lussi langnatt*, Saint Lucia's Day—the scariest, most dangerous night of the year. That was why Maja was so busy; there was a lot that needed to be done before nightfall.

"How do you know all this?" Sunny asked. She and Ingrid were sitting on the bench, watching Maja's preparations.

"I've always known about these kinds of things," Maja replied. "I learned them from my mother, who learned them from her mother."

It was knowledge passed down from a time when everyone knew such things. Knowledge or superstition—whatever you chose to call it—that had long since been forgotten by most people. But not by Maja Seter.

"I remember, and I take care of what needs doing," Maja continued. "I'm sure I've prevented all kinds of evil by using what I know."

"But not everything can be prevented," Ingrid objected.

"No! For example, this morning I had to make *lussekatter* with Freya Wilkins," Maja replied with a grimace.

Ingrid laughed. She knew that Maja hadn't wanted to bake today; the Christmas baking had really been finished long before Saint Lucia's Day, as it should be. She'd always taken pride in that, and this year, the Christmas treats were once again neatly stacked in their own boxes in the pantry according to tradition: goro and *bordstabler*, *sandkaker* and *krumkaker*, *sirupsnipper*, *hjortetakk* and *fattigmann*.

"But now there will also be lussekatter," Maja said. "Even though that particular Saint Lucia's convention is best suited for children and Swedes."

"But Freya wants to take part in that *beautiful Nordic tradition*," Ingrid said with a smile.

"Yes, and Sunny and Vegard, too," Maja replied.

"Yeah, it'll look great on socials," Sunny said.

"Socials! It took me a while before I understood that's supposed to mean *social media*," Maja scoffed. "My goodness. It's not a real job, this posting pictures on Instagram and Snapchat."

"Sure it is. Just look at Pia," Sunny objected. "She makes her living being an influencer."

"An *influencer*!" Maja repeated with the exact same contempt as she'd said the word *socials*. "I guess she does look like she's doing pretty well with it, that Pia. Great clothes, always looking like she came straight from the hairdresser. But she's sickly, the poor thing."

"Sickly?" Sunny asked.

"Yes, I heard she isn't feeling well," Maja replied. "But it wasn't so bad that she couldn't come down to breakfast this morning and eat three rolls while taking pictures of her food and tapping around on her phone."

Sunny beamed.

"But that's awesome! She has like a million followers!" she chirped. "I mean, it's just *soooooo* cool that she's here, you know? And tomorrow she's gonna post stories from the Saint Lucia's celebration. Imagine that, Maja. Your lussekatter will be famous."

"Famous! Yeah, yeah. I won't stand in the way of that," Maja said. "If you want lussekatter, you'll get them, buckets of them. They're ready in the pantry."

She set down the last lantern, its glass now perfectly shiny. "But now I need to run an errand down in the valley. There's something I have to pick up."

"What?" Sunny asked curiously.

The chef gave her an inscrutable look. "You'll find out soon enough."

❄

"There's a lot that needs to be done with the equipment here," the electrician said. It turned out that he *wasn't* actually the young and thin one who wore a beanie indoors, but rather the older fellow in blue overalls. "I'm writing a preliminary report since there are some things you need to get fixed." He'd been at it all day, first with the wiring in the floor they had to break open after the flooding, then with checking out other things "since he was already here," as he said.

He beckoned her into the back room. "Look," he said, shining a light into the fuse box by the stairs. "Nobody has this kind of thing anymore, with fuses that need changing. When you replace the box, you can also change the circuits. They're not rated for the current usage. It's not so urgent that it needs to be changed immediately, but you should definitely do it within the next year. And there are some connections here and there that weren't done by a registered electrician. I've fixed the ones I've come across."

Ugh. Yet another expensive project. Shouldn't Alfred have dealt with this a long time ago? Had he tried to repair the defects by doing the electrical work himself? While she was abroad, Ingrid had believed—or chosen to believe—that Alfred and Nana Borghild had been taking care of hotel maintenance. But . . . with the mice and flooding and poor electrical work, she wasn't so sure of anything anymore. Admittedly, people had always been handy up here at Glitter Peak, herself included. She could replace rotten trim and change a water trap. But electrical work wasn't something you could do yourself. Everyone knew that. You got professionals to check the system at regular intervals and fix what needed to be fixed. Right? She needed to have a chat with Alfred.

She just had to hope that things kept going well for a little while longer so they could manage to make a bit of money in between all the expenses.

It was already getting dark when Hussein came home from school, and now it was evening. He sat in his nook in the attic and thought he could hear them outside. The dark forces. *Åsgårdsreien*—the Wild Hunt. At least he thought it was them. The wind howled around the corners, and something slammed against the wall. Was it just the storm, or was it the jinn Lussi and her entourage? Hussein had heard Miss Maja talking about them. The night between the twelfth and thirteenth of December was the darkest and most dangerous of the year, she'd said. That was when Lussi came to check whether the work that needed to be done before Christmas was on schedule. If you hadn't cleaned, baked, and brewed, you might see her scary white face pressed against the windowpane. In the worst-case scenario, she might take the Wild Hunt down the chimney with her. They could even destroy the whole house in their fury!

But that wasn't the only thing that was special about this night, Lussi langnatt. No, Miss Maja had also said it was the only night of the year when animals could talk. Could that *really* be true? That was why Hussein was in the attic now. He hoped that Speedy would show up tonight so he could find out whether Miss Maja had been telling the truth. He'd put a piece of a lussekatt in his pocket and scattered crumbs in the corner of the attic. He didn't want to let his little friend starve, even though he knew it was wrong to defy what both Miss Maja and Auntie Ingrid had told him. In any case, Speedy had stayed away for now. He wondered what the little mouse would say if it came. Hussein was pretty sure it would thank him for the food.

What was worse was the thought that the people of the underworld could also come out tonight—and they might already have one in the hotel! That weird American lady with green clothes and yellow hair and a smile that was way too big. Hussein shuddered.

What Miss Maja had told him had been exciting earlier today, when Hussein was sitting on the bench in the nice, warm kitchen, surrounded by grown-ups and the smell of baking, a delicious saffron lussekatt in his hand. Up here in the attic, though, he really wished he hadn't heard it at all. It was a little too easy to believe in dark forces now that he was all alone. He stood up and shone the light around. You had to light candles against the dark forces and let them burn all night, Miss Maja had said. But he wasn't allowed to bring candles up to the attic. Then the whole hotel could burn down! Auntie Ingrid had told him that. But he wasn't sure whether flashlights worked against the dark forces . . .

There was no Speedy to be seen. After a while, Hussein folded the wool blanket he'd been sitting on and put it and his Donald Duck comic neatly in the corner. It was probably best to go down to his mother now. He hoped she was finished working for the day.

As he made his way downstairs, he heard something—a deep rumbling coming from outside. Music. Voices. It sounded more like people and cars than dark forces, but these weren't regular cars. These cars kind of roared sometimes. They had a completely different energy from his mother's and Nana Borghild's electric cars, which were small and cheerful, or Auntie Ingrid's SUV, which was big and safe. He'd heard these kinds of car sounds before, down in Dalen. He thought about the big boys who drove around with girls riding along. Both the boys and the cars were scary. They revved their engines and made lots of noise on purpose. Sometimes they said things that weren't that nice, too. The big boys, that is.

He didn't know any big boys who had their own car, but his cousin Ahmed in Aqaba had been allowed to drive Uncle Abdel's Hyundai when he turned eighteen. Hussein remembered that well, even though he'd been only four at the time. Ahmed had been so proud when he skidded into the courtyard and got out of the car, proudly dangling the car keys in one hand and pushing his sunglasses into place. Hussein had never seen anything so cool. From that moment on, he'd looked forward to turning eighteen and driving his father's red Land Cruiser. But then he and his mom had moved abroad, first to Nepal and then to Norway, while his dad stayed at home. He had things to take care of. He would come to Norway when he could—at least that's what Mama said.

Now, Hussein was absolutely sure that it was the roar of car engines he was hearing outside, and music that seemed to be pumping out into the air. *Thump thump thump. Thump thump thump.* Hussein didn't know whether the big boys in Dalen were mean to all of the younger kids or just him. Did adults think they were scary, too? In any case, he avoided them as best he could, and he'd never heard them up here before.

Hussein walked toward the window at the end of the hallway but quickly retreated. He couldn't bear the thought of seeing a white face pressed against the windowpane. He hurried into the apartment, slammed the door behind him, and felt his heart hammering in his chest. *Thump thump thump. Thump thump thump.*

What was all this racket? When Ingrid ran down the stairs and flung open the front door, she saw Alfred was already outside. The caretaker was leaning toward the rolled-down window of an old, orange Volvo 240 with the word *Jägermeister* written in Gothic letters on one side and what looked like deer antlers attached to the hood. Alfred looked gruff, and before Ingrid had even managed to cross the square, the car was already moving toward the road. Three other cars that had been parked next to the hotel with music playing at full blast revved their engines before following.

"What in the world is going on? Were those boys from the village? What did they want?" Ingrid was full of questions, but Alfred just grunted.

"Kids. Messing around. Just trying to show off."

"But why? Why now? They've never come up here before."

"I guess they'll have to find something else to do now, then," Alfred said, heading back inside.

Ingrid didn't move, though. What was the reason behind this noisy visit? Was it meant to frighten the guests?

Speaking of guests, here came Freya Wilkins, striding out of the dining room in a long teal dress and gold Skechers. She was heading straight for Ingrid. Her blond hair hung down her back, and her eyes shone with delight—perhaps combined with a bit of fear, but mostly just excitement.

"Oh, dear me!" Freya exclaimed. "What was all that about? Was it a gang from the neighborhood? Is there some kind of feud brewing?"

Feud. What a strange choice of words. As if they were in the middle of a gangster film! The *West Side Story* of rural Norway! Gang loyalty, love, passion, knives, and death. No, Ingrid didn't think the boys from Dalen were out to kill anyone, but she didn't doubt for a moment that they were capable of stirring up some trouble.

She put on what she hoped was a reassuring tone. "No, no. Just some local boys who wanted to come up and say hi."

It wasn't exactly a lie. She forced out a smile as she took Freya by the elbow and led her back toward the dining hall.

"Have you finished eating? I hope you've gotten to taste Maja's delicious caramel pudding. No? Then you *must* treat yourself. On the house, of course! And you'll have a second helping, too. Nope, no protests, no one can stop at just one when they've tasted Maja's desserts."

It took Ingrid a while to make her way out of the dining room again. When the manager first makes an appearance, she has to take the time to chat with everyone, something Nana Borghild had been careful to instill in her granddaughter. First, Ingrid sat with Freya and John Wilkins to make sure they hadn't been too upset by the visit from the village boys. They hadn't been, and they also agreed that Maja's caramel pudding was "marvelous." Vegard and Pia at the neighboring table were also enthusiastic, and it was nice to exchange a few words with them after she hadn't seen them all day.

She was so lost in her thoughts on her way up to the apartment that she didn't see the dark shape in the shadowy corridor until she stepped on it. Something soft scurried away, a shadow that disappeared down the hallway. She heard a sharp hiss and her own startled gasp. *Shit!* What the heck was that? She thought she spotted a pair of yellow eyes glowing in the darkness before the shape merged with the shadows once again. Ingrid felt her heart pounding, and she stopped by the wall for a moment to regain her composure.

It was too dark here; no one had turned on the lamps in the corridor. Ingrid found the switch and pressed it, and the shadows in the hallway vanished—as did the dark shape.

Thor turned off the main road, swung in toward the workshop, and looked at his watch. Yes, they should still be open. They often worked pretty late, and there was a light on inside. He could pop in and see whether he could chat with the Muskox Calf in private.

He didn't know what Karl would be able to tell him, but he'd obviously had something on his mind the day he'd come to visit. The Muskox gang was up to something—Thor was sure of that. Did it have something to do with the farm? Had Thor's father gotten them tangled up in even more sticky financial situations Thor didn't know about? His gut feeling told him it had something to do with the new initiatives at Glitter Peak. Karl *had* asked whether Thor was spending more time up there these days, and Hallgrim Dalen was usually quick to get involved if there was talk of money and property. But what were they up to? And how much did Karl know about it?

Thor parked his pickup by the old building. A couple of old lowriders drove past and idled on the other side of the lot. They were the kind of cars that only had two speeds: 10 or 100 miles per hour. Then two Volvo 240s came along with music blasting: one blue and the other bright orange with antlers on the hood. *Talk about needing to show off!*

Thor knew what this was all about. Racing, doing donuts, sitting in the car, blasting music, driving to the closest fast-food restaurant. The way young people in Dalen spent their free time hadn't changed much since he was their age. He couldn't make out who was in the cars, but it was probably the gang of Muskox grandchildren. They drove around a lot, and it wasn't uncommon for them to get into mischief from time to time. There were a lot of people in the village who were afraid of them—and some with good reason.

When he entered the workshop, he saw Gunnhild Dalen, Karl's mother, behind the counter. She was small and thin and had short brown hair with a bit of gray. She was knitting something purple and barely even looked up when the bell rang and Thor came through the door. *Even more wizened and grumpy than before*, Thor thought, then felt a bit ashamed of himself. He'd probably also be wizened and grumpy if he was married to Arthur Dalen and had the Muskox as a father-in-law. There wasn't much space for other people around that kind of person. It seemed as though that space had gotten tighter and tighter over the years, and Gunnhild Dalen had gotten smaller and smaller and drier and drier. Now, she'd probably catch fire like a bundle of twigs if she got close to an open flame. Maybe that was why they kept her in here.

Thor greeted her as cheerfully as he could—which was pretty cheerfully, to be honest. Gunnhild barely dignified him with a glance and a nod before she turned her attention back to her knitting.

He cleared his throat. "Is Karl here?"

Gunnhild shook her head. "No, Karl . . . he . . . has the day off."

She was concentrating intently on a stitch that was apparently quite obstinate.

The day off? Thor couldn't quite believe that Karl had time off. Maybe they didn't want him to speak with Thor? He was on his way out when Gunnhild spoke again.

"Someone from Glitter Peak was here and asking lots of questions. An American woman. And her husband. They had something they wanted checked on a Range Rover. But she practically wanted the whole history of the village, too."

She laughed a small, dry laugh that sounded like sticks breaking. "She was asking about old things from the '60s and who was related to whom here. Arthur's English isn't that good so he came and got me. But I didn't have much to tell them."

"No . . ." Thor shook his head, not really knowing what to say.

"She should probably talk to Hallgrim, I guess, but he's not interested in being a tour guide."

Gunnhild clearly had nothing more to say after that because she focused her attention back on her knitting once again. Thor was deep in thought as he walked out the door toward his pickup.

"THERE, THERE. COME HERE, GRETE."

Thor gave his favorite ewe a handful of oats and scratched her neck. He'd already removed the old straw, brought in new hay, and changed the water in the troughs.

Thor had spent a lot of money rebuilding the barn so the sheep had access to a yard. His father had thought that was nonsense, but everything indicated that the sheep's health was better if they were allowed outside a bit even during the winter, when they were fed indoors. This kept them in better shape, and the lambing in the spring also went more smoothly. He could see they enjoyed their time outside. "How would *you* like to be locked up for months?" Thor had asked the last time they'd discussed the matter, but his father had just grumbled and turned up the sound on the TV. He wasn't fond of change, so Thor had to do this on his own. He'd been to a couple of farming conferences before, and it had been nice to talk with other sheep farmers about how to run things as effectively as possible. But he had neither the time nor the money to do this too often. His father considered himself done with farm work. He stepped in only if there was an emergency, and it was expensive to use temporary workers. So for the most part, Thor just stayed at home and went about his business.

But he also enjoyed trying out new production methods and working on new meat products with the butcher. They were able to sell to some local customers and a bit to Glitter Peak. Everything that was happening up there was a nice change. A joy to see, actually! Ingrid's return had brought new life to the place. He was happy she wanted to continue running the hotel, even though it seemed as though it might take a miracle for it to be financially viable given the way things were now. They needed a *lot* more guests. That went without saying. And some of the guests they had now were quite strange, to be honest—especially this American couple. Why were they so interested in the history of the village?

He also had his own history projects going on. The newspaper page he and Ingrid had found in the library had renewed his interest in local history, and in a few days, he had an appointment with the old editor in chief of the *Dalen Daily*. Thor was looking forward to telling Ingrid about what he'd found out, both about the disappearance and about the history of Dalen and Glitter Peak in general.

"Maybe I should have been a historian, Grete," he said to the ewe. "But I can't deny that I'm mostly doing this for Ingrid now."

The ewe had nothing to say about that—at least not out loud. She just stared at him enigmatically and kept chewing on her oats.

DECEMBER 13

As usual, the workday at the hotel had started long before sunrise. Maja had been up at the crack of dawn and made coffee, prepared breakfast, and brought out lussekatter. She'd been in a surprisingly good mood when Ingrid came down to the kitchen around seven. Ingrid had quickly understood why. There, on the bench next to Hussein—who was already dressed in his star boy costume for Saint Lucia's Day—was a cat. An enormous, black, purring cat, who was enjoying scratches from Hussein and who barely bothered to lift its head when Ingrid came in. It stopped purring when it regarded her with its narrow yellow eyes.

Ingrid took a deep breath. So *that* was what Maja's errand had been last night. She'd quite simply gone to pick up a cat! A few things started to make sense. Ingrid hadn't just imagined that shape in the corridor last night. What had frightened her in the darkness was this enormous feline beast that Maja had let loose in the hotel. The cat's skepticism toward her was probably due to the fact that it recognized Ingrid from the night before, when she had accidentally stepped on it. "This here is Mewsephina," Maja said, looking pleased. "Now she can take care of those pesky mice."

Hussein stopped petting the cat for a moment when he heard Maja say this, and he looked up at the chef, horrified, but Maja continued.

"Mewsephina is Meowgret's daughter," she explained, glancing at the black animal, who was now curled up in a ball on the bench. "And Meowgret was the daughter of Tabbytha, who lived at Glitter Peak when you were growing up, Ingrid. You remember Tabbytha, right?"

And just like that, Ingrid was suddenly thrown thirty years back to her earliest memories. Ingrid had only been three years old when her parents died, but she still remembered that time well. She'd cried herself to sleep night after night because her mother and father were gone. Had she understood that it was forever at such a young age? She didn't know, but she remembered their absence being like a great darkness that had opened up in the middle of summer and consumed them. Nana Borghild had come to Ingrid every night, sat at the edge of her bed, and stroked her hair, singing to her. Tabbytha would also hop into Ingrid's bed and curl up close to her like a purring bundle. So nice and warm and soft! Borghild had let Ingrid keep the cat there all night long.

She'd loved Tabbytha—a beautiful, cuddly kitty who was a mouse hunter at one moment and Ingrid's best friend the next. The cat had lived a long time, until Ingrid started high school. She cried when Tabbytha died, but she was old and full of days, and they buried her by a downy birch near Troll Rock.

And it was precisely because of her memories of Tabbytha, and because Hussein was there, and because Maja was so determined to have Mewsephina (*what a name!*) there that Ingrid didn't have the heart to say that they weren't allowed to have cats in a hotel kitchen, mice or not.

VEGARD WAS THE ONE WHO persuaded Pia P to be their Saint Lucia, even though it was practically the middle of the night the way she saw it. But they needed to be finished before Hussein went to school, and at half past seven, Pia was ready at the kitchen door, clad in a white Saint Lucia costume. Hussein put the crown of lit candles on her head, his eyes sparkling.

"You look like a princess," he said admiringly before turning away shyly and standing close to Ingrid.

Now, the candles flickered in the dark corridors. They illuminated the white robes of the two star boys. Vegard and Hussein wore white hats with gold stars that they'd spent the previous afternoon making. They walked solemnly through the hotel corridors, each carrying a basket of lussekatter.

"They're so cute!" Sunny whispered, and Ingrid smiled and nodded.

Behind the star boys, Saint Lucia came in her long, flowy white clothes, the wreath of candles on her head. She was radiantly beautiful. Ingrid hadn't seen much of Pia in recent days, but she seemed to be feeling better again. Her skin glowed, her eyes were fresh and clear, and her honey-blond hair was flowing beautifully down her shoulders, perfectly curled.

Sunny, Ingrid, and Borghild wore ordinary clothes but had candles in hand. (*At least Nana Borghild didn't suggest we wear bunads today,* Ingrid thought.) Maja had said she didn't have time to walk in the procession; she needed to prepare breakfast for the guests. She had sent Ingrid with a cup of coffee for Alfred, though, which she was now balancing in her right hand while holding a candle in her left.

Sunny danced around excitedly, taking pictures with her phone. Portraits of Pia and the star boys, close-ups of the lussekatter, short video clips of candlelight in dark hotel corridors. This would be going out on Instagram. And Snapchat. And TikTok. *#stluciasday #lussekatt #morningmood #starstruck #glitterpeaklodge @piap.*

If you counted everyone on social media, thousands of people were present today, especially when you included all of Pia P's followers—and that was the whole point, Vegard and Sunny had explained. If it wasn't on social media, it didn't happen.

Sunny had gotten access to the hotel's social media accounts shortly after she started working for them. Ingrid thought it was nice to be able to outsource this kind of thing to someone who was so enthusiastic about it. Sunny had proven herself worthy of the trust and created a lot of nice posts, often with Vegard's advice. Pia had made it a condition that they should under *no circumstances* share any pictures showing her belly. She'd emphasized how important this was several times. She would be responsible for publicly announcing the pregnancy herself.

When, though? Ingrid had wondered. *You'll have given birth before you've even told anyone!* Then it hit her: Maybe that was the plan? Was Pia planning on having a completely secret pregnancy that no outsider would find out about—all while still seemingly sharing everything with her followers just as before?

Pia must have lived a pretty secluded life in the city if she'd managed to hide her pregnancy for this long, and here at the hotel, there weren't that many people who knew who she was. Pia's target audience wasn't exactly hikers and climbers. So maybe this could actually work: sharing carefully composed photos of details of interiors and clothes, views, selfies with and without sunglasses, glasses of wine no one knew she wasn't actually drinking—all while the secret grew and grew beyond the reach of the lens.

Alfred almost looked gruff when he opened the door, but Ingrid still thought she saw a glimmer of laughter in his gray-blue eyes beneath his bushy brows as he took a lussekatt from Hussein's basket.

Some doors opened as the procession moved through the corridors. Smiling guests helped themselves to pastries. Hussein had been looking forward to serving a lussekatt to his mother, and Aisha clapped her hands in excitement when she opened the door and saw her little star boy. When they got to the Wilkinses' room, he insisted that Vegard knock, because Hussein was still a bit afraid of Freya Wilkins.

But Freya—whom this whole procession was essentially in honor of, along with Pia's Instagram followers—was thrilled when she saw the little group outside her door, candles flickering in the darkness. She was clearly moved when they sang the Saint Lucia song, and she kissed both Vegard and Hussein on the cheek. Dr. Wilkins, still wearing striped pajamas, wasn't quite as enthusiastic, but he smiled warmly and thanked Hussein when he was handed a lussekatt.

Ingrid walked with long, energetic strides, and when she reached the top of Angelina Hill, she stretched her arms over her head and greeted the day. She was warm from the brisk walk up, even though the air was crisp and cold. The sky was almost cloudless again, and the mountainside was colored pink by the first rays of sunlight.

She saw some movement to the left out of the corner of her eye and turned toward Kvitfonna on the other side of the scree. Some dark dots were moving against the white surface of the glacier. A herd of reindeer!

The wild reindeer ran across the mountains, constantly on the move, looking for food and shelter. Moss and lichen in the winter, grass and leaves in the summer. If there was snow on the ground, they dug through it to find something to eat. The reindeer had been here for thousands of years, probably before any humans lived here. There were traces of reindeer hunting around Glitter Peak from as early as the Stone Age. Arrowheads and spearheads kept turning up in the barren terrain, as well as occasional bows and scaring sticks. The hunters of the Migration Period—in the very olden days, before the Vikings even, her grandmother had told Ingrid when she was little—used to set up rows of these tall poles, which had birch bark pennants on the top, to guide the herds of reindeer to where the hunters wanted them to go. The reindeer were easily frightened, then as now, and would try to avoid these moving things. The reindeer then ran straight to where the humans wanted them. It was paradoxical, really; the reindeer avoided one danger and went straight toward a much bigger one.

It was strange to think that people had been roaming around here for such a long time, in this inhospitable landscape. They'd walked with leather shoes, woolen clothes, and weapons they made themselves. It must have been a difficult life—difficult and cold. Archaeologists knew—unfortunately, one might say—

more and more about the past as the snow and ice caps melted and the remains of bygone days came to light for the first time in hundreds of years. That included the microbial life of the past: in Siberia, there had been cases of anthrax infecting both humans and animals when centuries-old reindeer carcasses turned out to be carrying the deadly bacteria—a rather disturbing manifestation of ever-increasing global warming.

But Ingrid's biggest concerns in this area were related to the changes she'd experienced on her expeditions in the Himalayas. In these vulnerable areas, she and her companions had seen how quickly the glaciers were melting. Combined with state-led development and a lack of dam maintenance, the melting created a huge risk of landslides and flooding. There had already been several terrible accidents. The avalanche Ingrid and her companions had endured was minor compared to the catastrophes that affected the local population. Continued development in the wrong direction threatened the lives and livelihoods of millions of people in India and Pakistan, not to mention the mountainous countries of Tibet, Nepal, and Bhutan.

One of the things Ingrid had wanted to do as an expedition leader in this area was to shed light on the critical situation. She, Preben, and Brother Giovanni had been in contact with several organizations working to spread awareness and help villages and families affected by climate change. She had indeed leveraged Giovanni's considerable network to convince Preben to let him join the expedition. Giovanni was a less experienced climber than them, but he had access to people and resources in Christian communities, which was invaluable when it came to offering help to those in need.

As a privileged tourist—which is essentially what you are as a climber and participant in expeditions—you should use your energy, both mental and physical, to give back to the areas you visited. Ingrid was firmly convinced of this. And she and her team had several promising collaborations underway—but then events unfolded as they did. The avalanche hit, and everything came crashing down.

She thought about the mountaineer-priest Abbot Henry, who'd been one of Giovanni's biggest role models. "It's better to fail a hundred times climbing a mountain than to succeed at losing your life once," he'd written somewhere. How bitterly ironic.

Ingrid practically collided with the Wilkinses as she entered the foyer. Freya Wilkins was wearing a green coat with a matching hat and had a large bag under one arm. She was making her way toward the front door at an astonishing speed, with John Wilkins at her heels, but stopped abruptly in front of Ingrid.

"Good morning!" she crowed. "I hope driving conditions are good out there. We're going on a trip to Hamar!"

"Hamar? What are you doing all the way down there?"

"We have some research to do at the National Archives. And then we're going to buy some presents."

She tucked her bag extra firmly beneath her armpit and continued toward the door, which her husband was now holding open for her. He lifted his hat and nodded at Ingrid before they disappeared into the cold.

Ingrid stared at the door that closed behind them. The National Archives? Well, maybe that wasn't so odd; after all, Freya had said she had Norwegian parents. Maybe they were getting some help going through old church books to learn more about her family.

The door opened again almost immediately, and in came the young men from Oslo, who'd booked a room and lunch. They turned out to be geology students and enthusiastic ice climbers who wanted to try their hand at Styggfossen, and they had no expectations of hot tubs or après-ski whatsoever. *As far away from table-dancing partiers as you can get,* Ingrid thought with relief.

They carried in bags and equipment and chatted away about the weather and practical preparations.

"You're Ingrid Berg, aren't you?" one of the young men asked. He seemed to be the leader of the group.

"Yes, that's right."

"Cool! Then we can ask you for climbing advice."

"Sure, go right ahead! Was there anything in particular that you were interested in?"

"We're especially interested in metamorphic rocks and steep ice walls."

"Right. You'll find both in abundance here," Ingrid said with a laugh. "Just let us know if you need help finding either. Styggfossen is the place for you."

She hoped no one saw how she shuddered at the thought of the frozen waterfall. The deep gorge. The heights. The snow on Heaven's Horn that could come tumbling down. She knew some of the recent guests might have chosen to come here to the hotel not only because of the spectacular climbing opportunities but also because of her reputation as a climber. She couldn't let them know how things were *really* going for her.

She saw how Sunny's eyes widened as she came out of the dining room, where she'd been setting the table for lunch. Had

Sunny finally realized Vegard wasn't batting for her team and started looking for other romantic opportunities? Or was she looking for Insta-material here, too? These boys were living illustrations of *#getoutside*.

Several more arrivals showed up early that afternoon, including a minivan from the car rental agency in Lillehammer that turned out to contain a British couple with four children—two boys and two girls—and an enormous amount of luggage, which Alfred carried in with the husband. Maybe Hussein could get to know the youngest of the children over the weekend, Ingrid thought. She often wondered whether it was too lonely for him at Glitter Peak, but when she thought back on her own upbringing here as the only child, it wasn't loneliness she remembered. It had felt natural for her to be here, and she had friends down in Dalen. It wasn't *that* far.

She went into the kitchen, where Maja and one of the young extra helpers were busy preparing dinner. She breathed in the delicious scent of meat sizzling in iron pans and potatoes with garlic and butter baking in the oven. Sunny was pulling glasses out of the cupboards for the sparkling wine that would be served before the meal.

"Looks like you have everything under control here!" Ingrid said to Maja.

"Things can still go wrong," Maja said. "After all, it's Friday the thirteenth."

Mewsephina opened her yellow eyes and stared at them from the bench. Ingrid shrugged and went back out to the reception area. The bell above the front door rang, and in came a couple from Dalen who'd booked a table for dinner, Aslaug and Svein Slettebakken. Ingrid remembered them from her school days, even though they were a few years older than her. Aslaug had had a different surname at the time, of course.

"We thought it would be exciting to see how things are here," Aslaug said with a saccharine smile as she pulled off her leather gloves. "Despite what they say. We came early so we could have a look around."

"Welcome!" Ingrid said enthusiastically, but she was thinking about what Aslaug had said. *Despite what they say?* She chose to ignore it, and instead put on what she hoped was a friendly smile. "Perhaps you'd like to have a drink in the bar while you're waiting? You can bring drinks into the library as well."

She was eager to send guests to the bar, especially since they'd actually hired a bartender, Tom Hansdalen, who started today. He was hired to work starting at three every afternoon, but so far, he'd had an alarming amount of time to polish glasses and study drink recipes. Today, only the Wilkinses had been in for a drink thus far. Fortunately, the Slettebakkens did want to take a trip to the bar, as did the group of four dinner guests who arrived just after them. When Mr. Taylor from England also came strolling in and asked whether it was possible to get a "pint of lager" anywhere there, Ingrid finally started to feel a little more optimistic. She showed him the way and glanced happily at Tom, who was suddenly quite busy behind the bar.

When she was back at the reception area, Nana Borghild came down the stairs in her coat and boots, her back straight and a determined look on her face. She stopped at the reception desk.

"Hi Ingrid," she said with a smile. "Everything okay here?"

"Yes, everything's fine. All of the guests have arrived and the food is ready. But where are you heading off to?"

"I'm just headed down to Dalen," Nana Borghild replied.

Was her grandmother's voice trembling?

"Down to Dalen? Now?" Ingrid asked. "It's almost six o'clock."

Now Ingrid could see that Nana Borghild had her car keys in her hand.

"Is there anything we need for dinner?" Ingrid asked. "Alfred can probably drive down and get it. Or I can do it. You don't need—"

"No, no, nothing like that," Borghild said. "Just something I have to take care of. Be back soon, sweetie." She patted Ingrid gently on the shoulder and turned toward the door.

When Borghild came back from Dalen, she went straight up to her apartment. She sat down at her desk and took out her diary, but realized she didn't actually have the energy to write anything. She couldn't bear to talk to anyone either—especially not Ingrid. Not quite yet.

Things hadn't gone the way she'd hoped they would.

But what had she been hoping for, really? What had she thought would come from this visit? Now, she wondered why she'd even gone in the first place.

It had seemed obvious that she needed to go down and speak with Hallgrim. She'd felt that it was absolutely necessary now—that the time had come. She'd gone over it in her head again and again: how she would present it, how she would make him understand that everything was connected.

But she'd regretted going as soon as she pulled up in the yard. The house loomed tall and massive as ever, with lights on only above the front door and in an upstairs window. There were several pairs of reindeer horns mounted on the black-stained garage, a monument to hunting and death.

No one answered when she rang the doorbell, so she opened the door and stepped into the hallway. The door creaked. *Isn't it a bit odd that such an important man with a house full of sons and grandsons can't even manage to oil the hinges?* she thought.

God, it had been so awful to walk inside! The house completely overwhelmed her. It had been such a long time since she'd been there, and it filled her with grief and painful memories.

It had already been a dark house when they were young, when she was there all the time. A massive old log house with small windows that towered over the village, full of taxidermied animals. But at the time, she'd never thought of the house as bleak. Back then, she associated her visits with other things—completely different things! The bleak feeling had come later.

She shuddered. All of these dead animals everywhere. Hares and weasels staring at her with blank button eyes. A stuffed badger. Deer and elk heads on the walls of the hallway. Reindeer skins on the benches. But a bear—Hallgrim didn't have one of those. Because *that* was at Glitter Peak Lodge.

She'd shouted, "Hello?" several times but there was no answer, so she went up the stairs with her coat and shoes on—ready for a hasty retreat. Halfway up, she was startled by an ugly, dark-brown animal snarling at her. It was a stuffed wolverine, but for a moment, it had looked as though it was alive.

Up on the second floor, there he was: Hallgrim Dalen, sitting at a kind of worktable that would have had a nice view of a valley had it not been pitch-black out. He sat with his back to the stairs but didn't turn around or say anything when she came up.

Perhaps his broad shoulders tightened a little, but she could have imagined that.

Hallgrim "Muskox" Dalen still lived up to his nickname. His body was so compact, his neck so hunched. His hair was more brown than gray, shaggy on the sides, balding on top. But there was nothing decrepit about this man. Old, yes—almost primordial. But not decrepit.

"Hallgrim," she'd said.

No reaction. She knew he was aware she was there, but he wouldn't acknowledge her presence.

She walked toward the desk, and he slowly spun his chair around and looked at her with his small, black eyes. He exhaled loudly through his nose but said nothing.

"Hallgrim," she said again. "What's happened has happened. Both you and I have been grieving for many years. You have your reasons to be bitter, and I have mine. But it has to end. This can't ruin things for the hotel and Ingrid."

Silence. Only the sound of breathing. She stayed completely motionless, her eyes fixed on Hallgrim.

"There's something I need to tell you," she said.

She'd hoped that her statement would make him say or do something, give her an opening somehow. But nothing happened besides the airflow through his nose that seemed to increase and eventually approach snorting. If Hallgrim had had horns, he would have been rubbing them against his front legs and stomping his hoofs by now. But he did nothing except to sit with his huge arms on the armrests and stare at her—stare and snort.

NOW SHE WAS GOING TO SAY IT. At long last she was going to—she simply *had* to—tell him the truth.

She stood there for a few moments to collect herself. Then she felt the determination drain out of her. No. She couldn't do it. She couldn't say what she'd come to say. She just stood there.

The tension was broken when the door opened downstairs, then slammed shut with a bang. Men's voices could be heard from the hallway, and Arthur and Cato came stomping up the stairs.

Borghild had noticed the puzzled looks on the faces of Hallgrim's sons when they came up and saw her standing there, but she didn't feel that she owed them any explanation. They said nothing as she walked past them and went down the stairs.

It hadn't been the right way to do it.

She had to find another way.

And then she had to talk to *her*.

DECEMBER 14

Ingrid's email pinged. A cancellation from two people who were supposed to have arrived this week, once again without any explanation.

Ingrid looked up from the screen and shifted her gaze out the window. She stared at the mountaintop to her left. The one to her right. The heather stretched out before her. The scree. The mountaintop to the left again, right, left, right, left. She'd read that it was important to look up and stretch the eye muscles. It was supposed to help prevent visual damage and fatigue.

Despite Maja's ominous predictions, Friday the thirteenth had passed smoothly, at least as far as Ingrid could tell. The ice climbers had gone out after a quick lunch and came back in the evening, flushed and excited. Today, they'd headed out again at dawn to get the most of the daylight. The British family had expressed their satisfaction with both the apartment and the hotel itself. The first service of Glitter Peak Lodge's pre-Christmas menu had surpassed all expectations. The dinner guests had heaped praises on the food, and even Maja, who was always good at finding problems, had to admit that it had been successful. Happy visitors and an efficient staff—you had to be pleased with that. Ingrid had therefore allowed herself a bit of an internal celebration and a glass of wine at the bar with Vegard in the evening. Nana Borghild had gone straight up to her room when she came back from Dalen. Ingrid hadn't been able to extract any more information about what her grandmother had been doing. Perhaps it had something to do with a secret Christmas present?

Anyway, it was now Saturday morning, and Ingrid had been sitting at her computer for several hours, going through insurance plans. Her hand had gone back and forth to the bowl of caramels almost automatically as she worked. A small mountain of wrappers had piled up on the desk beside her—a typical sign of stress, she knew that. She should drink water and get some fresh air, but now she just *had* to get this work done. She'd just stood up from her desk to stretch her stiff back when there was a gentle knock on the office door. She strode over and opened it.

Sunny was standing outside with some papers in her hand. She had the day off but had chosen to stay at the hotel to go through old hotel advertisements for her paper.

"I thought you might want to see this," she said eagerly when she came in. She handed Ingrid a thick yellow sheet of paper.

Ingrid took it and looked down at what seemed to be an old promotional brochure. The sheet was folded in half, with a border in the shape of a stylized mountain range at the top and bottom of the pages. On the front, it said:

I love to go a-wandering
Along the mountain track
And as I go, I love to sing
My knapsack on my back

And where can you find better mountain
tracks than on GLITTER PEAK?
Do you want to get away from the hustle and bustle
of the city?

Welcome to Christmas celebrations
at GLITTER PEAK LODGE
Come to the mountains and enjoy the peace
and quiet of nature. Skiing lessons. Christmas
service. Delicious food from local farms.
Learn to waltz, swing, and folk dance every
afternoon in the hotel's dining room.
Instructors: Borghild Berg and Hallgrim Dalen

"Hallgrim Dalen," Sunny said. "That's the old guy down in the village, right? I thought it was kind of weird, and a little funny, to think that he and Borghild held dance classes up here."

"Come and sit," Ingrid said, gesturing toward the sofa in the corner, still staring at the paper in her hand.

Dance lessons with Borghild Berg and Hallgrim Dalen? What on earth was this about? It was difficult enough to imagine the Muskox waltzing and swinging and jumping—she could feel the floor shaking just at the thought—but had he really danced *here*, together with Nana Borghild? It would have been like dancing polka with the devil.

"I CAN'T MAKE SENSE OF IT," Ingrid said, slumping down on the sofa next to Sunny. "If there's one man Nana Borghild can't stand, it's Hallgrim Dalen."

Hallgrim was the only person her grandmother—who was usually perfectly polite and friendly toward everyone—didn't greet when they happened to bump into each other down in the village. This coldness was so striking that even newcomers such as Sunny and Aisha had taken note of it. The village was small enough that you were bound to run into most people from time to time, even if you did your best to avoid them. At National Day celebrations you were guaranteed to see people you knew, but you could just look straight ahead and pretend you didn't notice. At funerals and on Christmas Eve, everyone gathered in Dalen Church—young and old, from Glitter Peak and from the village—but you could stay on opposite sides of the aisle and not exit at the same time.

"But why?" Sunny asked.

Ingrid looked at her. "I really don't know," she said.

She didn't have any good explanation for the animosity between Nana Borghild and Hallgrim Dalen. Perhaps she'd just attributed it to the quirkiness of the elderly? But now, she realized there must be something more behind it. It was clear that at some point, the relationship between the two of them had been completely different—and that something or other had made things change.

When was the brochure from? Ingrid turned it over. "Christmas at Glitter Peak Lodge 1961" was written on the back. Such a long time ago! Her grandmother had been around twenty at the time. She married Christian Stugu in 1962, and they had their daughter, Angelina, in 1964. Even before that time, though, Borghild—the only child of the owners—had been a central part of the hotel. Not just her, but Hallgrim Dalen as well, it seemed. Ingrid scratched her head. Nana Borghild had told Ingrid quite a bit about the running of the hotel in the past, but she'd never heard anything about these dance evenings.

"Where did you find this?" she asked Sunny.

"It was in the archive folders you brought me," Sunny replied. "I thought I'd look through them before I got started on the guest books. It's all so exciting!"

"Yeah, it really is," Ingrid said thoughtfully. "Thank you so much for bringing this to me."

One more thing to ask Nana Borghild about, Ingrid thought. *And tell Thor about!* She looked at the brochure again. She wanted to call him. Maybe he had found out more about the newspaper as well.

"Mmm! The soup and the bread are just as delicious as you said," Pia said at the lunch table. Her cheeks were rosy after a morning walk with Vegard, and she was eagerly eating Maja's forest mushroom soup and homemade bread.

"Here you go, dear." Dr. Wilkins held out the plate of bread for his wife—after making sure that the other women helped themselves first. He was an old-fashioned gentleman that way. It seemed to come so naturally to them, Ingrid thought as she watched the Wilkinses. At first, she'd thought of Dr. Wilkins as a rather sulky type, but the way he and Freya spoke to each other was full of warmth and respect.

That was how a relationship could be, even after many, many years together. Could she have grown old with Preben? The tone between the Wilkinses was so different from what Ingrid and Preben had had. They had desired each other—perhaps even loved each other—but at the same time, they'd been rivals. Both wanted to lead, and both wanted to win. They hadn't been able to find a proper power balance. She didn't know how to avoid arguments with Preben without compromising herself. No wonder their relationship ended in tragedy.

As they were finishing the meal, Ingrid turned to Pia and asked whether she would help with something. "I'd love to discuss our range of skincare products with you," Ingrid said. "We've gotten some samples from suppliers, and I think you're just the right person to give me an opinion on them."

She was pleased at having come up with an excuse to talk to Pia privately. What she *really* wanted to find out was how the influencer envisioned the days and weeks ahead, and how long she was actually planning to stay at the hotel. It wasn't easy to bring it up without seeming rude, but she thought it might be easier if it was just the two of them.

They went up to Ingrid's apartment, where she'd fortunately remembered to clean up the candy wrappers and used cups and plates. She'd started seeing everything through Instagram eyes when she was with Pia, which made it easy to be self-critical. Ingrid brought out the samples and set them up on the table while Pia found a comfortable position on the sofa.

"It's an income opportunity I wasn't aware of before," Ingrid said. "But several cosmetics manufacturers have actually contacted us to sell us their products."

"How fun!" Pia exclaimed, picking up a skin cream with honey extract. "Glitter Peak's honey cream. What kind of suppliers have gotten in touch?"

"There are some local companies and individuals, and some bigger and more commercial firms as well," Ingrid said. "But it has to be local if there's any point in doing it."

"Agreed," Pia said. "Then the guests can go home with unique products, while farmers and small businesses get a nice additional income. Can I open this?"

They applied honey cream to their hands and put beeswax pomade on their lips. Pia seemed to be quite enthusiastic about the products.

"This one's great!" she said, holding up a jar of cream. "It smells so good and makes my skin feel really soft."

"Only local ingredients," Ingrid said with a smile. "Easy to produce, too."

"You know," Pia said, "you could hold classes here! Weekend courses where guests get to make products adapted to their own needs. Combined with a yoga and wellness retreat or something."

Ingrid nodded slowly. She was still getting used to how different the hotel business was from when she was growing up, not to mention how much more prosperous Norway had become. She'd learned that the profit margin of luxury products could be enormous, and guests found things that they perceived as healthy and natural to be particularly attractive.

In addition to the skincare products, including Glitter Peak Balm (a muscle oil for relieving soreness after long hikes), they also planned out how they could sell food and drinks with a sort of souvenir feel to them. So far, they had thought of Glitter Peak honey and Borghild's raspberry soda.

"You could sell clothes, too!" Pia suggested. "Hats, scarves, and mittens would make total sense up here in the mountains."

"Yeah, that's a great idea," Ingrid said. "Hand-knitted by locals, maybe?"

And art. What about Thor's photos? She could ask to see some of them.

"This oil is supposed to be good for pregnant women," she said, handing Pia a dainty vial. "It has a special combination of plant extracts and vitamins that are supposed to help with stretch marks. Well, not that you have them, of course," she said, cursing her own clumsiness. But Pia eagerly accepted the bottle.

"I'd love to try it," she said. "I've gotten a lot bigger lately, and my skin is so hot and tight in some places. It almost feels like it's going to burst. It's actually kind of scary."

"Then you have to take this!" Ingrid exclaimed. Maybe now was her chance to ask some more questions. "But are you feeling okay otherwise? Please don't be afraid to ask for help or a ride if you need anything. Vegard and I are both here to help you."

"Thank you. That's very kind. But I feel fine," Pia said. "I've just been a little . . . tired . . . for a while. I haven't been sleeping or eating well. But thank you for your concern. You and everyone else here at the hotel have been so nice to me."

Pia fell silent and fiddled with the little vial. She set it down on the table and picked it up again.

"I get that it seems weird that I just keep staying," she said. "I was really just supposed to be here for a weekend. But I've been keeping out of the public eye for personal reasons, and I feel as if I can handle it better up here. Like I've risen above it all—literally. And since I'm dreading going home and dealing with reality again, I've been putting off my departure . . . and maybe making myself out to be a little weaker than I really am. So I can have an excuse to stay."

She smiled quickly and apologetically. It was strange to see her fumbling like this, Ingrid thought. She'd always perceived Pia P—with all her charm and followers—as fiercely self-confident.

"So . . . I guess I'll just come right out with it," Pia said. "So you have to say no if it's not okay. But I'd really like to stay here until after Christmas."

Ingrid was almost speechless. She would have thought that someone like Pia would have her calendar filled to the brim and have all kinds of plans with family and friends for Christmas.

Ingrid glanced at Pia's belly, and Pia noticed.

"I'm not due for a while!" she assured Ingrid with what was an almost apologetic smile.

Ingrid felt embarrassed. "No, no, that's not what I was thinking," she lied. "But yes, so you want to be here for Christmas? Of course you can! We'll be open."

Pia looked pale and tense now, almost on the verge of tears. What was going on with her?

"You're more than welcome to stay," Ingrid said. "Of course! But . . . well . . . you don't have anything else planned? Someone coming to visit, or . . . ?"

And that was all it took to make Pia P's whole perfect facade fall apart. She squeezed her eyes shut, and her face flushed red beneath her meticulously applied makeup. She made some sounds that Ingrid needed a few moments to realize were sobs. Then the tears started to flow.

"No!" Pia exclaimed. "I have no plans, no visitors, no one to see. I don't have anyone I want to be with at all. And definitely not someone who can help me with everything that's on my mind. That's the problem. Everything's a mess!"

Pia sniffed, and Ingrid scurried to the bathroom to get some tissues, which Pia gratefully accepted. Ingrid got her a glass of water and sat back down on the sofa.

"But what about your parents? Or . . . the father of the child?" Ingrid dared to ask.

She knew it was a sensitive topic, because Pia still hadn't said a word about the man with whom she was having a child. Ingrid had tried asking Vegard again, but he only said that Pia didn't want to talk about it and that he respected that.

"The father of the child!" Pia sobbed. "There is none. At least not one who knows he's going to be one. It was totally random. I like being on my own and have always thought I would continue to do so. I like running my own life. I never really had any desire for children either. I got an IUD a long time ago, so I've always felt I was safe. But obviously it didn't work."

She picked up another tissue, wiped her eyes, and blew her nose.

"It was a guy I met at a fashion party," she said. "It was great for one weekend, but it was never meant to be anything more than that. He's with another woman now. So I can't really just tell him he's going to be a father out of the blue. When I went to the doctor and got confirmation that I was pregnant, she assumed I wanted an abortion. And I thought so, too. But right then and there, when I saw the little creature on the ultrasound, I knew . . . I knew I didn't want that. Suddenly, I was sure that I was meant to have this baby. So I went from being scared of being pregnant to suddenly being scared of losing the baby. I was so relieved when the doctors were able to remove the IUD without me miscarrying! Isn't that crazy?"

Pia smiled at Ingrid, her eyes shining. A tear rolled down her cheek. "So now here I am. Single and pregnant. I thought it would be fine. I've been so confident. I was going to make it without the father, and it didn't matter what my parents thought about it. It didn't matter what the whole world thought. And I still kind of feel that way. But I also feel so very, very alone."

AS SHE WATCHED PIA SITTING there with the tears streaming down her face and her hands wrapped around her round belly, Ingrid could almost feel the physical void within herself. She could feel the uterus where once—for a few short months—a small being had clung on, a tiny life that could have become a child but that she lost in the avalanche. It had bled out of her in the white hospital sheets while knives of pain cut through her body and mind.

The avalanche. The great turning point in her life. The white dragon.

The dragon had wanted to destroy her. It had destroyed Giovanni. And it had killed the child she was expecting and her love for Preben. The dragon still came to her at night and made her wake up gasping, suffocated beneath tons of snow. It had taken away the joy of climbing and replaced it with paralyzing fear.

The pregnancy had come as a surprise and lasted for such a short time that she never even got used to the idea of being a mother. Ingrid had never wanted children, but she hadn't actively rejected the idea, either. She'd just lived her life and, over time, considered parenthood to be less and less relevant. So when she found out she was pregnant, it came as a shock. She and Preben were preparing for the trip, having just arrived in Kathmandu, and were heading to Lukla to start the trek to base camp.

In hindsight, it was obvious that she should have figured it out long before. She'd missed her period a couple of times, but that wasn't unusual for female athletes who worked out a lot and had low body fat. The nausea and an upset stomach weren't unusual for her, either. As much as they'd traveled in recent months and as many feet of altitude as they'd climbed, it would have been strange if she *hadn't* had any kind of reaction to that kind of physical stress.

She was at a reception at the Norwegian embassy when she finally realized she was pregnant—or rather, someone told her. After a standing buffet, fragrant Nepalese coffee and large platters of cakes made from boiled milk and syrup were brought in. The specialty was deep-fried sweets that looked like fried orange spaghetti, dripping with fat and sugar. The effect on Ingrid's sense of smell was powerful and immediate. She sped out of the elegant room and threw up behind a plant in the atrium.

"Please, madam, you must take care," said a voice behind her. She turned and found herself staring straight at a beautiful Middle Eastern woman, who handed her a napkin and a glass of water. "Please come and sit down."

The woman led Ingrid toward a bench and sat down next to her. "Excuse me . . . May I loosen this a bit?" The woman carefully took hold of the belt that was tied at the back of Ingrid's silk trousers, and which had been a bit too tight across her stomach. It felt good to have a bit more room to breathe. The woman went on, "I don't mean to overstep, but you shouldn't wear such tight clothes when you're pregnant. It's not good for you or the baby."

Pregnant? The word echoed against the stone walls and in her head. Ingrid had wanted to laugh, but the laughter stopped in her throat. She realized that the woman might be right. How had Ingrid not realized this earlier?

She took another sip from the glass of water and looked at this beautiful stranger.

"Thank you," she said. "I . . . What would I have done without you? My name is Ingrid, by the way."

"And my name is Aisha. I'm in charge of the catering here tonight. I'm very pleased to meet you."

Their conversation was interrupted when a boy who couldn't be more than four or five came running from the kitchen and started climbing up a trellis. "Hussein!" the woman exclaimed, launching into a long tirade in Arabic.

The boy climbed down and came toward them, seemingly crestfallen, but with a mischievous twinkle in his eyes.

"Hello, Hussein," Ingrid greeted him. "My name is Ingrid."

He put his right hand on his chest. "Hi, Auntie Ingrid," he said.

Later that evening, Ingrid came up with an excuse and took a taxi to a twenty-four-hour health center, where she breathlessly asked for a pregnancy test. She'd taken the test right then and there, in the health center's bathroom, and sat staring at the two lines for such a long time that the staff had finally knocked on the door to ask whether she was all right.

She hadn't said anything to Preben when she returned. Nor did she the next day. The preparations were well underway, and she never seemed to be able to find the right time to say anything. It was so big, this project of theirs. It had originally been Preben's dream to set a world record for climbing the Seven Summits, the highest peaks on every continent. Together, they'd further developed their vision: they would be the first couple—man and woman—to do so in less than one hundred days. Their preparations had been going on for a long time, and they'd heard rumors of at least one other couple with the same plans. It had been so important to be the first. Their sponsors had promised them an extra bonus if they made it, and the prestige would be unparalleled.

Of course she was always thinking about telling Preben about the pregnancy; she just had to find the right moment—the right opportunity.

And maybe Preben wouldn't have allowed her to continue if he'd known she was pregnant. She couldn't deny that the possibility had contributed to her keeping it a secret. She felt strong, though, and was sure that it wouldn't be an issue. It was still quite early, and women had worked and struggled through pregnancies since time immemorial and still had healthy babies. So she would wait to tell him, maybe when they were up on Mount Everest. On top of the seventh mountain. What a wonderful surprise that would be!

But they never made it that far. She never got her chance. The avalanche took that away. The avalanche, the loss, the blood, the hospitalization, the chaos, and the news that Giovanni hadn't survived. And then it was too late. She couldn't tell him then.

For a long time, Aisha had been the only one who knew anything. Ingrid had never forgotten the care she got from the stranger that night in Kathmandu—her eyes that saw what no one else did. When they happened to meet again at the embassy before Ingrid was due to leave the country after the accident, Aisha was also the first, apart from the doctors, to find out about the miscarriage. The doctors had told Ingrid she was four months pregnant.

Tears had welled up in Aisha's eyes as Ingrid told her about everything that had happened. "You poor thing," she'd said. "But Allah will give you new chances."

They made a connection that day, and it almost seemed like fate when it turned out that Aisha was looking for a job in Europe. It had taken a lot of work and even more dealing with bureaucracy, but as a Syrian with refugee status, she had been granted a work permit in Norway and was able to bring Hussein to Glitter Peak. She and Ingrid didn't talk much about what had happened but carried the secret like something fragile that still bound them together.

INGRID HAD LATER CONFIDED IN VEGARD, and he'd told her several times that she had to tell Preben about what had happened. He had the right to know about it, and it might ease the burden for her, too. But no—she didn't want to talk to Preben about it. She didn't want to talk to Preben about anything at all.

So, Preben was never going to find out that he might have been a father. And Ingrid would never know what it would have been like to be a mother. In retrospect, she somehow thought it was a punishment she'd brought upon herself. Punishment for setting out on the expedition without taking this new life into account. For not involving Preben and making him take responsibility. For not letting the child's well-being take precedence over what she wanted to do. It was this selfishness, this overconfidence, that had caused her to lose all three: the child, Preben, and climbing.

Not even Nana Borghild knew about the child. Ingrid didn't know why she hadn't told her grandmother; they'd always been so close. But this was too painful. It was Ingrid's own sorrow to bear. Perhaps she and her grandmother were *too* close for Ingrid to put this on her. For her grandmother, the loss of her great-grandchild would also be a reminder that the family at Glitter Peak was dying out. After Ingrid, there wouldn't be anyone left.

PIA AND INGRID SAT IN silence for a while. Ingrid felt the tears welling up. Why was she still so affected by this? It had been a long time—more than a year and a half now. It also wasn't the first time someone had been through an accident or a breakup. It wasn't the first time someone had miscarried, either. Miscarriage was actually pretty common, even though the fourth month was relatively late. People went through this kind of thing all the time. Most people moved on and tried again. For some, such an event might even have been the impetus for a change in their lives.

Ingrid had thought that moving back to Glitter Peak could be a completely fresh start. She wanted to build a new life on the roots of her old one, on her family's traditions. This was where she belonged, high up in the Norwegian mountains. She would put the drama behind her now. She was done with what had happened out there in the big world. Now she was here. And that was a good thing.

But apparently that wasn't the case after all. Every time she got her period, the thought of all the blood from that time came back. The pain. The nausea. The fear. The grief.

And now this. Pia, sitting here in front of her, lost in her own despair and confusion. For a moment, Ingrid was tempted to confide in her, to tell her she knew what it felt like to carry such a secret. Pia had probably heard about the dramatic accident in which the Norwegian-led expedition was involved and a member of the group had lost his life. She'd probably also read about the breakup and all the speculation about why Ingrid had withdrawn from the public eye. This was Ingrid's chance to shed some light on that.

She reached out to Pia and took her hand in hers. She *could* tell Pia what had really happened . . .

But she didn't. No good would come from it, and it was too late to do anything about it anyway.

In an attempt to hide her own tears, Ingrid wrapped her arms around Pia, who leaned her face against Ingrid's shoulder.

"What do your parents say?" Ingrid asked, stroking Pia's hair. She regretted the question as soon as it crossed her lips.

"My parents . . ."

Ingrid could have slapped herself. Vegard had once told her that Pia's parents were a bit odd and that she had very little contact with them.

Pia straightened up and dabbed at her face with another tissue. A small pile of used ones was growing on the coffee table.

"My parents don't know either," she said. "I haven't seen them in years, actually. They're really conservative and made it quite clear early on that they don't approve of the way I live my life. I should've married young, like them, and gotten a 'real job.' Blogging and social media and the *extravagant jet-setter life* they think I live aren't things they can acknowledge."

She cleared her throat and took a sip of water. "My mom and dad and I haven't had anything to say to one another for a long time. The gaps between each time I had the energy to talk to them got longer and longer, and they never called me. So one day, it was just over. I'd given up, and there was total silence from their end. It didn't exactly feel natural to drop by to tell them about the pregnancy. They're not going to be pleased that their daughter is about to be a single mother."

"I lost my parents when I was three," Ingrid said, and Pia looked a bit taken aback. Ingrid herself was surprised at having blurted this out. Why was she saying this? The answer came when she said it out loud: "As long as your parents are alive, you still have the chance to reestablish contact. After all, they are your child's grandparents."

There was silence.

Ingrid knew she'd gone too far. "I'm sorry," she said. "It's none of my business."

"It's okay," Pia said. "You're just being honest. And you're absolutely right. They're alive, so it's not too late. But there's more, you see. I really don't know whether I can handle establishing a relationship with them again."

Pia took yet another tissue and rubbed it between her fingers as she searched for the words. "They've . . . kind of gone down a rabbit hole. When I was younger, I just thought they were old-fashioned and conservative. But recently, they've been getting more and more influenced by friends and started believing all sorts of conspiracy theories. You know, the kind of thing that you read about in the newspapers but can't imagine anyone would *actually* believe. Chemtrails. Pandemics made up by the government. My father claims that the US government was behind 9/11 and that the Labour Party is collaborating with Arab countries to turn Europe into an Islamic colony. And my mom supports him. All of it. The whole package. And they can't stand being contradicted about any of it because whoever argues against them has been brainwashed, they say. I honestly don't know whether that kind of grandparent would be good for a child."

But maybe better than no grandparents at all, Ingrid thought. But instead, she said, a bit hesitantly, "Maybe it's for the best that you aren't in contact with them . . . but do you have anyone else who can help you? Siblings? Friends?"

"My brother is almost as bad as our parents," Pia sighed. "I mean, I guess he doesn't really believe their nonsense, but he manages not to argue with them. I think he's a coward, and he's never supported me when we've disagreed. He just sort of . . . slips away. But he doesn't spend much time with them anymore, either. I think his wife put her foot down. She can't stand all their BS. And who wants in-laws who teach their grandkids to believe such deadly lies?"

Ingrid looked at her watch. *Shoot!* It was already half past three, and she still had a lot to do.

Pia took the hint and got up from the sofa.

"Should I walk you down to your room?" Ingrid asked.

"No, thanks, it's okay. I'm doing fine now," Pia said. "Thank you for listening to me. I don't really know how to deal with all of this. But what I really want right now is to be here."

"And you're welcome to stay for as long as you want," Ingrid said with a smile. "On the condition that you promise to let me know if you need help."

"Deal!" Pia P said.

DECEMBER 15

Some days you wake up and just know it's going to be a shitty day. You can hope you're wrong, you can try to change it, or you can be like Preben Wexelsen: accept that the day is what it is and try to make the most of it. After all, shit works well as fertilizer, and that means that the shittiest days can also be the most fruitful.

Preben Wexelsen was pleased with this metaphor as he sat up in bed. He noted that it was something he should use in a lecture sometime.

He'd been giving a lot of lectures lately. And he'd had a lot of shitty days, weeks, months. Actually, it had been a pretty shitty year in general. He didn't let those around him see that, though. To most people, he was the same as always: a successful, strong, and enterprising mountaineer, leader, motivator, and businessman. Whatever was bothering him, mentally or physically, was something he kept to himself. He always chose to try to make the best of everything. And more often than not, he succeeded.

He swung his legs out of his plaid Hästens bed—more than a hundred and fifty thousand well-invested kroner—and put his feet on the floor. He looked at his own naked, sinewy body in the mirrored door of the closet as he stood up. He hadn't changed much; he was still a tall, slim man with piercing eyes and a sun-tanned face that contrasted with the pale skin on the rest of his body. A few scars here and there.

A jolt went through his body as he put his weight on his right foot, but he quickly straightened himself up. That ankle would never be quite right again after it broke in the avalanche last year. He rolled out his shoulders. They ached, too, as did his right wrist and most of his fingers. Decades of climbing in subzero temperatures had taken their toll. The tendency to osteoarthritis that he'd inherited didn't make things any better. He had good days and bad. Today was clearly going to be a bad one.

He heard the rain pattering against the window and opened the blinds, listening to the town hall bells playing a tune he remembered from his childhood: "Ingrid's Song." Maybe it was a sign.

He made himself a double espresso and drank it as he gazed out over the lead-gray Oslofjord. Was this supposed to be winter? Everything was foggy, gray, and wet. But he'd never been one to let the weather stop him. Preben always had places to go and people to see—even on a Sunday, like today.

He whistled along to the melody from the clock tower—terribly off-key, he could hear that himself—as he got dressed. Nothing flashy: a suit, but no tie. He thought about going in a sportier direction for a moment, but today's meeting required just the right amount of formality. He checked his teeth in the mirror after brushing. They gleamed white, just as they always did.

He never would have admitted it, but he actually felt some nerves ahead of the meeting. Nothing he couldn't handle, but it was an important conversation. He'd sat up late the night before, preparing for what he had to do today.

Getting here had taken some time. At first, he'd been too sad, then he'd been too angry. He wasn't able to accept that what had happened was all his fault—even if Ingrid had thought so. It was downright unreasonable. After all, they'd planned the expedition together. It had been *their* project, their shared goals! Then the accident struck, and everything changed. Afterward, she hadn't even wanted to speak with him. When he was discharged from the hospital in Kathmandu on crutches, he'd tried to see her but was told he was unwanted. Ingrid was in no shape to see him, the nurse had said.

He'd been unharmed himself, apart from the ankle. Pure luck. But somehow that almost made it worse.

He had to go through a series of interrogations with the tourist police. Ingrid had spoken with them separately. Then he found out she'd left the country—gone off just like that, without answering any of his texts or calls. Left him to deal with questions from the press and partners on their own. Hung him out to dry.

He'd been furious. But over the months that passed, he'd become more intent on atonement. He understood her anger, her grief for Giovanni.

The Benedictine monk had been a part of Ingrid's climbing team before, and she was the one who'd argued for him to join them on some of their Seven Summits attempts, even though Preben had been skeptical at first. However, he had to admit that it had been easier to accept Giovanni's participation when Preben realized that the monk also had access to valuable sponsorships.

Giovanni had been a driving force behind several projects in the Himalayas that focused on sustainability and the coming generations. The climbers had seen firsthand how much was in the process of being destroyed in these important mountain regions and felt a responsibility to do something about it. They'd seen families disintegrate in the wake of the forces of nature and met many children growing up in extreme poverty.

"The children are the future," Giovanni had always said. "They're the ones who will save the world. But we can help them do so."

And this was what it was all about now, Preben thought. The project was bigger than him and Ingrid—*much* bigger. And now he could really take it on. He'd sworn to himself, many times ever since last year, that he would make up for things. Now he had the opportunity, and he wasn't going to let it slip away.

Borghild held the umbrella in her right hand and the bag with the flowers in her left as she crossed the cemetery in the pouring rain. She knew exactly who was in which grave without even having to look at the stones. So many people she knew were resting here now. She remembered her teacher, Mr. Thorkildsen, from her school days. The Moen family gravesite. She'd played with the Moen children back in the day, but now they were all gone, all five of them. Parish priest Tankred Röhmer. Good riddance! The village was better off without *him*.

But there were many there whom she missed.

She stopped at her own family gravesite and stood there for

a while before laying the wreath on the headstone, where the names shone white toward her in the pale morning light. She sat down on the small stone bench, even though it was wet, and looked at the inscriptions.

CHRISTIAN STUGU 5.11.1935–11.24.1985
ANGELINA BERG STUGU FOSS 1.25.1964–6.24.1992
MARIUS FOSS 8.25.1962–6.24.1992

She'd procured a new gravestone when Christian died, as the old one was already full of names and dates. She'd assumed that her own name would be next in line on the new stone, after Christian's: *Borghild Berg Stugu*, which had been her official name when she got married, even though she mostly used *Berg*, the family name at Glitter Peak. There had been every reason to believe that many, many years would pass before the names of future generations would be engraved there. But that hadn't been the case. Not even seven years after she became a widow, Borghild lost her daughter and son-in-law as well.

People in the village had frowned at Angelina's marriage to a "city boy" from Oslo, an economist from a wealthy, well-known family from the capital. Angelina and Marius met in business school. She moved to Bergen to study right after high school, also to a great deal of headshaking from many of the villagers. "So you have to go to school to be able to run a hotel now, is that it? That Glitter Peak girl is posh now," they scoffed. That perception was further strengthened when she came home to visit with her big-city boyfriend. But when they got married and came back to Glitter Peak for good, and it became clear that they were serious, opinions started to change. By then, Christian had already died of a sudden heart attack, and Marius was seen as the "new lord of Glitter Peak." By the time little Ingrid was born, all was forgiven—even the fact that Marius was from the capital. It also helped that he was an easygoing and practical man. He liked chatting with people in the village and eventually made many acquaintances, if not close friends. He didn't have time for too many, though, because the young family had been living there for only a few years when tragedy struck. They drove off the road on a steep curve one summer on their way home from a midsummer party. Both had been killed instantly when the car hit the stone scree below. Borghild had asked herself how this could have happened, time and time again, but had never come up with a good explanation. It was an accident, plain and simple, at least as far as the police could tell. Perhaps they were speeding or not paying attention. Marius had been driving. He didn't have any alcohol in his system. Neither did Angelina. The autopsy showed that she was pregnant. So three lives were lost, actually: a daughter, a son-in-law, and a little boy who never even saw the light of day.

It was a tragedy so immense that Borghild hadn't known whether she could cope with it. But she had to—because not everything was lost. Three-year-old Ingrid hadn't been in the car; she was sleeping in her crib in the hotel that night as her grandmother babysat. Her parents had thought about taking her to the party, but the little girl was tired, and Borghild said it was just as well for them to leave her at the hotel. Borghild loved watching her granddaughter. She'd had Ingrid in her arms as she said goodbye to Angelina and Marius on their way down to the village. Ingrid was wearing a flower crown. Her parents had been in a fantastic mood on that bright summer evening. Marius honked his horn as they drove off, and Angelina leaned out the car window and waved to them.

That was the last time Borghild saw them alive. And Ingrid lost a little brother in addition to her parents. She lost a future as part of a family.

Marius's parents had agreed that he should be buried here with his wife. The Foss family had loved Angelina—just like everyone else who met her—and Marius had felt more at home here in the mountains than he ever had in Oslo. So here they lay, forever twenty-eight and twenty-nine years old, and Borghild's heart had been so thoroughly shattered that it was only her responsibility for little Ingrid that had enabled her to get back on her feet at all.

Borghild had been in her fifties at the time. Now she was over eighty. She'd been a mother and grandmother, hotel manager and widow, everyone's friend and at the same time someone who had lost those closest to her. She'd scaled the operation up and down, hired and fired people, cleaned and tidied, laid baseboards and managed the finances, painstakingly built up a team of reliable employees, and always made things work—even if only barely at times. She'd done it. And now, little Ingrid had finally come back from the big world to take over.

"It was about time, Christian," she said to her husband as if he could hear her somewhere over in the hereafter. "I can't believe you never got to meet Ingrid. But you would be so proud of her."

Borghild stood up, leaned toward the gravestone, and adjusted the flowers a little. "Yes, Christian, here I am in the rain, thinking about death. Well, 'One day we shall die. But all the other days we shall be alive'—as that Swedish writer said. He's dead now, by the way. But he got a lot done first."

She took the empty bag the wreath had been in and strode firmly toward the parking lot with the umbrella over her head.

Ingrid stood in the doorway to the dining room, watching the lunch service. Sunny and the new kitchen assistant worked well together, replenishing food and carrying plates in and out. Sunny was good at creating an atmosphere. Now, she was smiling and chatting with the geology students, who were heading back to Oslo after lunch. Then she stopped in the middle of the room with plates in hand and posed for Pia P, who was taking pictures with her phone. *That'll look good on Instagram,* Ingrid thought.

Vegard was driving back to Oslo after lunch, but now he and Pia were chatting with Freya and John Wilkins as they enjoyed some coffee. That was a new grouping, and Ingrid hoped Freya wasn't talking Pia's ear off. *This curiosity of hers is probably some form of compassion,* Ingrid thought. She entered the dining room, but as she approached the table, she heard that it was actually Pia who was doing the talking and Freya answering.

"So your parents were Norwegian?" Pia asked.

"Yes, they were," Freya replied. "My mother died a long time ago, but you know, I actually have a picture of her here."

Freya rummaged around in her bag, pulled out a huge wallet, and handed something to Pia. "Here she is! Lottie Hansen from Norway."

"She was so pretty," Pia said. "You look just like her."

Ingrid was a little curious but didn't feel that she could enter the conversation at this point, so she said a quick hello before leaving the dining room again. It was nice that the guests had something to talk about, at least.

———

AS SHE CAME OUT INTO the foyer, she saw a small figure slipping out the front door dressed in a puffy jacket and hat.

Ingrid crossed the foyer and opened the door as the figure scurried across the parking lot.

"Hussein, where are you going?" she shouted.

No answer.

The figure continued on toward the path. Ingrid ran over to the cloakroom where they had hiking gear for guests to borrow, grabbed a windbreaker, and followed him. She looked down at her impractical sneakers for a moment but knew she didn't have time to change.

"Hussein! Hussein!" She ran over the path behind the hotel, where ice crusts crunched beneath her feet after yesterday's freezing rain. Hussein had to be nearby.

Suddenly, she saw him a bit farther up the hillside. She picked up the pace. Now she knew where he was heading. She caught up to him at Troll Rock.

"What are you doing up here?" she shouted, panting. It had been a long time since she'd done any real cardio, she could feel that now. Hussein squinted at her from the top of the rock.

"I wanted to see the view," he said. "And I'm practicing climbing mountains. They say I can't, but I can. I even have a headlamp, just in case. Look."

"Who's saying you can't climb mountains?" Ingrid asked.

"The kids at school. Mikkel and the others. Even though I'm the best climber in the whole school. They say I don't know anything about mountains because I come from a place that only has sand. But they don't know anything. We have mountains in Jordan, too! And in Syria! Higher than the ones in Norway!"

"Yes, that's true. I've actually been on a really high mountain called Mount Hermon," Ingrid said as she climbed up the rock and sat down next to Hussein. "That mountain is so beautiful that several countries are fighting about who owns it!"

"Have you been there?"

"Yes, I've been to that area several times. I used to travel a lot before, you know, and climbed mountains all over the place."

Hussein looked up at her admiringly. "You're the coolest person I know, Auntie Ingrid! Well, apart from my dad."

She didn't really feel all that cool. But she forced herself to smile. "And apart from you, Hussein. I think *you're* the coolest person *I* know."

"Next time, I'm going up to the top of Heaven's Horn."

"Heaven's Horn?"

"Yeah! That'll show them. And then I can't wait to call my dad and tell him I've been up there."

"Hussein," Ingrid said, putting a hand on his shoulder. She knew it was unlikely that Hussein would actually ever set off on his own, but she still felt a twinge of panic at the thought of the boy's tiny body on the steep and difficult snow-covered rock faces. "One day, you'll be able to climb Heaven's Horn. But it's a very difficult and dangerous route. You have to practice first. But right now, I don't think we should climb anymore. You haven't told your mom you're out here, have you?"

Hussein looked down at the ground. "No, she was busy on her computer," he said. "She didn't notice that I left."

They climbed down and Ingrid took Hussein's hand and led him back toward the hotel. The little child's hand was warm against hers, but she was freezing cold.

WHEN THEY ENTERED THE APARTMENT, Aisha was still at her computer, going through the accounts. She looked up and smiled at them before frowning in surprise at the sight of Hussein's outerwear.

"Where have you been, sweetie?" she asked. "You haven't gone out on your own, have you?"

"Hussein and I have just been out . . . cleaning up the parking lot a bit," Ingrid said.

She didn't want to give Aisha anything else to worry about, and Hussein's plans for climbing Heaven's Horn most certainly wouldn't go down well with his mother.

"How nice of you to help, Hussein!" Aisha beamed, and Ingrid immediately felt a little guilty about lying.

"Ingrid, do you have dinner plans?" Aisha asked, standing up. "If not, you're more than welcome to eat here with me and Hussein. I have a lentil stew on the stove. I thought we could eat now since I just finished up what I was doing."

"Oh, how nice!" Ingrid said. "I'd love to. Let me just go change my shoes first."

She ran up to her own apartment and replaced her thin socks and sneakers with woolen socks and warm slippers. Her feet were still numb from the walk in the cold. Aisha had finished setting the table by the time she came back down. The apartment smelled delicious—like fried onions and spices.

ONCE THEY WERE FINISHED, the two women sat chatting while Hussein took a bath on his mother's orders.

"It's so nice to have some time to talk about things besides finances and hotel management," Ingrid said as she sipped from a cup of strong Arabic coffee. "I'm so impressed with you and Hussein. You've adapted to life up here so well. But sometimes I think it must have been a pretty rough transition."

Aisha laughed. "Yes, it's pretty different from the Middle East," she said. "And *colder*!" She grew serious. "But we like it here, Ingrid. It's so peaceful. You know . . . that's not something we take for granted. We're from a place that's been torn apart, that's so unsafe. We miss Syria, but it's hard to think of it as home now. Most of my family is in Jordan, too. And we . . . no, we like it here."

Ingrid thought about what Hussein had said about climbing to the top of the mountain to impress his father in Jordan, and as if Aisha had read her mind, she suddenly said: "He misses his father terribly, you know. We hoped Mohammed would also be able to work in Norway, at least for a while, but we don't know if it will be possible."

"Your husband has a job in Jordan, doesn't he?" Ingrid asked. "I mean, he was already working there before the war broke out in Syria as well?"

"Yes, that's right. His family runs one of the big hotels in Aqaba, so we used to spend a lot of time there."

Aisha had mentioned the popular destination before. Aqaba was an old city that had been built up as a tourist destination in recent decades because it was located on Jordan's newly acquired—and extremely short—coastal strip on the Red Sea.

"It was doing really well for a while, but it hasn't been that easy lately. The pandemic is one thing, but all the unrest in the Middle East has also scared away a lot of the tourists. And now it's been so long since we've seen each other—not since Hussein and I went to Nepal, when I got that job running the catering company. We've tried talking on Skype, of course, but it almost seems to make things worse for Hussein. He's always so sad when we hang up. That's why I've said we have to stop."

"That's terrible!" Ingrid exclaimed. "I hope he can see his father again soon."

"When we left Syria, we thought our family was safe in Jordan," Aisha continued. "But there have been some problems there, too. Jordan has taken in so many refugees, they always have. Most of them are good people—decent. But some of them are no good. Some come to make trouble."

Ingrid nodded. She'd read quite a bit about Jordan's challenges, with refugees and a rising level of organized crime in the once peaceful country, but she didn't feel she really knew enough about the situation to say anything sensible.

Aisha was silent for a while, then she continued, "That's why I left. Took work elsewhere. Because of bad people. They come from Syria and other places and seek out the people who are struggling."

"They want young men to join the fighting in the neighboring countries?" Ingrid asked.

"Yes, that too. But also for . . . what's it called? The mafia. They're like a kind of mafia."

"In Jordan?"

"Yes, they spread fear and violence. In gangs." Aisha took a deep breath. "One of Mohammed's uncles in Amman came into conflict with one of these gangs. One day, they took his son, Mohammed's cousin. He was only fifteen years old. He survived, but they kidnapped and tortured him."

"What?!"

"Yes. It was supposed to be a kind of 'warning' to his father.

That's when I'd had enough," Aisha said. "I realized I couldn't stay there. I couldn't let the same thing happen to my son."

Preben Wexelsen lit the gas fireplace with the remote control, leaned back against the leather cushions with a whiskey glass in hand, and stared into the flames. Soft jazz rhythms flowed from the speakers on both sides of the couch. "An uncompromising music system for uncompromising music lovers," the advertisement had said. Strictly speaking, he wasn't exactly an "uncompromising music lover," but he did always like to have the best of the best. He knew it was snobby, but he could live with that.

Preben undid a button at the neck of his shirt. He rotated his stiff shoulders. They hurt less than they had earlier in the day. It was still pouring outside, but it was warm and cozy in here. Preben was happy. It was just as he'd always known: a shitty day can turn into a fruitful one.

The meeting with the international organization had gone according to plan. The sponsors were in place, and the foundation would be established shortly. They'd gone through everything: the finances, implementation, practical challenges. This meeting had been the first step of the plan. Now he was ready for step two, and it had to be done quickly. And it had to involve Ingrid.

She didn't want to see him; she'd made that clear several times. She hadn't responded to his messages or phone calls, and eventually, he'd given up. But he was going to do this. He owed it to Giovanni. He owed it to Ingrid and to himself.

So now, he *had* to talk to her. Face-to-face. Even if it meant he had to go all the way up in the boonies to find her in that ice castle of hers.

DECEMBER 16

The air was cold and the sky was overcast as Ingrid walked across the frozen heather, and there was a distinct smell in the cold gusts of wind. She recognized that smell: *snow*.

And sure enough, a flake landed on her cheek. Then another. This was the *good* snow, the kind that ignited a glimmer of the old anticipation from childhood: the first snowfall, snowball fights, sledding, skiing. Blue twilight hours outside, warmth and candle-light inside. Music, the smell of baking. The Christmas spirit.

What *had* happened to the Christmas spirit amid all of the hullabaloo with flooding and the Dalen gang and guests coming and going? Ingrid remembered the Christmases with Nana Borghild when she was little. Sometimes they'd been with relatives, and other times it was just the two of them, but they'd always been here at the hotel. Presents and dinner, always wearing bunads. "We're not dressing up for other people," her grandmother had said. "It's for ourselves. And for Christmas."

They'd usually go cross-country skiing together during the first hours of light on Christmas Day. Long, leisurely trips with hot chocolate, oranges, and gingerbread in their backpacks, solid speeds down the slopes. Her grandmother had always been so fit. Did Nana Borghild still ski? It occurred to Ingrid that she didn't actually know. If they could go skiing together this year, that was yet another reason to be happy about the snow—as long as there wasn't too much.

Once she'd grown up, Ingrid's Christmas plans had varied. She visited from time to time, but just as often, she was busy with some job or expedition and told her grandmother that she wouldn't be coming home this Christmas, either. She felt a pang of guilt when she thought about it now. But Nana Borghild had never complained. "Do what you have to, honey," she'd say. "And come home when you can. You're always welcome here."

The sky had brightened while Ingrid was out, but because of the thick cloud cover, the sunrise was a bit more discreet today. She'd taken a longer walk than usual, along the scree and all the way over to Djupemyr before she turned around and strolled back along the south side of Heaven's Horn. It was Monday and therefore a "weekend" for the hotel employees, in the sense that the hustle and bustle took an ever-so-slight pause. The weekend dinners and lunches were over, and several of the guests had left; now, things would be quiet until the coming weekend.

She'd gotten yet another request from one of the big hotel chains last night. The investment director wrote that they wanted to set up a meeting as soon as possible. What were they thinking, doing this right before Christmas? Were they hoping she was desperate enough to sell immediately, or what? Ingrid had succinctly replied that the director could send more information about what they wanted to discuss and then set up a meeting in the new year.

The new year . . . What would things look like then? Glitter Peak Lodge was in the midst of the most pivotal weeks now. She didn't really want to think about the possibility of selling—that would feel like too much of a defeat—but she couldn't shake off the thought, either. Everything bothering her right now—the financial worries, the flooding, the mice, the gang from the village, the electrical system—were they signs that she should give up? Even though she didn't believe in the supernatural or any of Maja's stories about ghosts and goblins, there was one ghost that came to her more and more often: the ghost of bankruptcy.

What if Ingrid was the one who had to throw in the towel after her family had run the hotel for 130 years? The thought was unbearable.

God doesn't give us any more than we can handle, a voice said inside her head. It was Brother Giovanni, who should have been in the monastery in Bolzano now, busy planning new trips. Well, he was in Bolzano now. But he wasn't following up on his environmental and social work. And he wasn't at the table with his fellow monks, enjoying a glass of the delicious wine that Muri-Gries was so famous for. No, he was underground, in the monastery cemetery.

She missed her friend so much. In many ways, they'd been quite different. Their worldviews contrasted, for one. But for a monk, Giovanni had been remarkably nonproselytizing—at least in words. Perhaps he had been more missionary in action. There were several times when they'd faced challenges in their work, and he'd spoken to her about his faith in God. He believed that

God always saw and supported them. Ingrid wasn't so sure—not then, and even less so now.

THE SNOWFLAKES WERE FALLING MORE densely as she approached the entrance to the kitchen. Aisha was back from dropping Hussein off at school and was cleaning up after breakfast with Sunny. There weren't that many guests to serve today, so Maja had a couple days off.

Ingrid sat down at the kitchen table, and Sunny placed a cup of coffee with milk in front of her.

"You're not working too much right now, are you, Sunny?" Ingrid asked. "You *are* supposed to be studying as well, after all."

"No, no," the young girl assured her. "The semester's over, and I couldn't be doing anything more educational besides working here at the hotel right now!" She took her phone out of her apron pocket. "Have you seen Pia P's story on Insta? There's going to be a *ton* of new bookings!"

Ingrid pulled out her own phone and opened Instagram. Pia had posted the picture of Sunny smiling radiantly in the dining room, and another of Pia herself with a white woolen hat over her honey-blond locks, standing in front of the hotel silhouetted against a gray-blue sky, with trees in the background covered with a light sprinkle of snow.

Nice place! If I didn't run it myself, I'd definitely want to visit, Ingrid thought happily, taking a sip of coffee. She scrolled through a few more posts about winter sales and Christmas gift tips, brushed aside the thought of getting started on gift shopping herself, and went to find her grandmother. Ingrid checked in the library, but it was empty, apart from Barry. She opened the shelf at the bottom of the bookcase, found what she was looking for, then went up to her grandmother's apartment and knocked on the door.

"Come in," she heard from inside.

Her grandmother was sitting at her desk with a notebook in front of her. She shut it as soon as Ingrid came through the door. "Good morning, dear," Borghild said, nodding at the kitchen counter. "You can make some coffee if you want some."

"No, thanks, I just came from breakfast." Ingrid sat down on the sofa. "There are some things I wanted to talk to you about. It hasn't been easy to find time lately . . ."

Her grandmother shoved the book into the desk, closed it, and locked it with the key she had on the gold chain around her neck. Then she sat down in the chair by the coffee table.

Ingrid went on, "I wanted to ask you about the newspaper headline Thor and I found. The one about the girl who disappeared."

"Oh?" Her grandmother's face showed no sign of any kind of reaction, and she didn't seem to want to say anything more, so Ingrid continued, "Can you tell me anything more about what happened?"

Borghild seemed to be wrestling with her thoughts. She took a deep breath.

"I suppose there's quite a bit to tell," she began. Her voice sounded a little different that it normally did—almost inaudible. She cleared her throat but stayed silent for a while.

Ingrid was about to ask more questions when they heard a thump against the wall.

"What was that?" Ingrid asked, quickly getting to her feet. "Is someone outside?"

Nana Borghild stood up, too, but Ingrid was the first to get to the door. She opened it and looked out into the hall. There, on her stomach, her face twisted to the side and her hands in front of her on the carpet, was a pale and limp Freya Wilkins, dressed in a headband, lavender tracksuit, and white tennis shoes.

Both Alfred and John Wilkins were quick to respond when Ingrid called. Alfred picked up the slender woman with ease and carried her into Borghild's room.

Freya made some sounds as he moved her, but she didn't seem to be conscious.

"Put her here," Nana Borghild said, pointing at her bed.

Alfred did as she said, and John Wilkins took off his wife's headband and sneakers before sitting down at the edge of the bed. He took her pulse and spoke to her calmly and gently. She was blinking her eyes open by now but still hadn't said anything.

"Could I ask you to please bring the medical bag that's in our room?" Wilkins said to Alfred. "She probably had a sudden drop in blood pressure."

He turned to Borghild and said, "We might have to adjust her blood pressure medication. It's been going up and down lately, and now she's gotten it into her head that she's going to start exercising, too." He gestured at the tracksuit.

He turned back to his wife and stroked her cheek. "How are you doing, honey? Sweetie, are you awake?"

It was the first time Ingrid had heard him speak that way. John Wilkins was always friendly and calm, both to his wife and to others, but now he looked worried. Was it normal to be in a daze for so long after fainting? Could something be seriously wrong with her?

Suddenly, Freya opened her eyes and looked around the room, but she was clearly having trouble focusing her gaze. Did she know where she was? She didn't seem to recognize any of the people sitting and standing around the bed, not even her husband. But as she turned her head toward the wall, a jolt went through her, and she struggled to get up onto her elbows. Then she lifted her head to see better.

Ingrid followed her gaze.

Strange. There was only an old painting hanging there, the one of the two bunad-clad young girls on either side of a birch tree. They had long braids—one blond and the other brown. There wasn't really anything special about the painting. The subject matter was traditional, and the craftsmanship seemed acceptable as far as Ingrid could tell. Painted by a traveling artist in 1961, wasn't that what her grandmother had said?

But Freya looked as though she'd seen a ghost. She stared at the picture and moved her lips. Suddenly she sang, hoarsely, but in perfect Norwegian, part of a traditional lullaby:

> *Sulla meg litt, du mamma mi,*
> *skal du få snor til trøya di.*

Then she fainted again.

Thor sat down at his usual table in the far corner. He was early. He looked around as his finger traced the grooves on the table. The furniture in the café area at Dalen Gas & Grill had been the same since the 1980s. Maybe even longer than that. Four tables and sixteen chairs. Each table had a simple candleholder and a basket with ketchup, mustard, salt, pepper, and french fry seasoning. Wagon wheels and old Coca-Cola advertisements hung on the walls. The owner, Olga Plassen, sat behind the counter, and as far as Thor could tell, she was *also* sitting in the same position as she had been since the 1980s, her sturdy legs planted on the floor, her arms crossed over her ample bosom, and her eyes fixed on the front door. Every time the bell rang, she rose heavily and fixed her gaze on whoever came in. If it was someone she knew, they were honored with a nod. If not, she was content with staring at them as though she could extract their order, payment, and all of their secrets through sheer hypnotic force.

Thor had gotten a nod when he arrived. After all, he had been a regular customer here since his teens. He paid for the gas he'd filled up his truck with outside and ordered two Cokes and two Dalen Grill Specials with cheese and double fries.

The bell rang again, and the Muskox Calf entered just as Geir Plassen, Olga's son, came out from the back room with two enormous plates of food. The Muskox Calf was still wearing his overalls from the workshop, and his thin hair was sticking up in all directions. He waved at Olga as he walked across the room. He sat down across from Thor and smiled when he saw the burgers that Geir silently placed on the table in front of him. Karl hadn't been difficult to convince when Thor dropped by the workshop earlier that day and offered to treat him to a meal after work. Fortunately, no one else from the Muskox clan had been around, and there was every indication that the thought of burgers had been just the thing to help Karl forget the caution he'd shown the past few times they'd met.

"You know what I like, Thor," Karl said.

"Yes, I know what you like, Karl," Thor replied. "Because I like the same thing."

Karl shook a generous helping of salt over the fries before diving into the food eagerly. Thor took a bite of the burger. He had to wait until they'd satisfied their hunger before he could try to steer the Muskox Calf toward the topics that had preoccupied Thor recently.

"How are things at the workshop these days?" he asked, dipping a fry into the ketchup. "Anything new?"

The Muskox Calf nodded enthusiastically.

"Got a Mercedes-Benz 220S from 1957 in last week!" he said. "Einar Langmoen bought it. My dad has kept the parts for one of those since we got a broken one years ago."

He continued on with a detailed description of the work that needed to be done on the vehicle, but Thor was only half-listening. Apparently, he needed to get straight to the point.

"Hey, that day you came to see me," he said. "Was there something you wanted to talk to me about?"

Karl's eyes wandered a bit before he started shifting around some burned fries with his index finger.

"No . . ." he said. "It was just that . . . nah, nothing really."

"Karl," Thor said. "You asked if I've been up at Glitter Peak a lot lately. I don't think that was for no reason."

Karl didn't answer.

Thor went on, "I've gotten the impression that a lot of strange things are happening up there these days. It almost seems like some people in the village are actually working *against* the hotel. Do you know anything about that?"

Karl just kept moving the fries around, driving them between salt and ketchup leftovers on his plate as if it were a racetrack and the fries were toy cars.

"Ingrid told us that there have been a lot of cancellations," Thor continued. "And then a bunch of kids were up there on Friday and scared the guests. And the flooding . . . but I guess that couldn't be . . ."

The words hung in the air. Thor cleared his throat and looked at his childhood friend again. "You haven't heard anyone say anything?"

Karl rubbed the back of his hand over the corners of his mouth and stared out the window. "You know," he said, finally fixing his gaze on Thor again, "Uncle Bernt told me not to say anything about it. He said there were so many people around asking all kinds of questions, it was best to keep my mouth shut. But I guess it's okay if I give you a little hint."

He picked up the ketchup bottle and turned it upside down, then laboriously drew two letters on the plate. An *X* and an *O*. Red ketchup on the scratched white stoneware. What on earth was that supposed to mean?

Thor didn't have time to ask before the bell rang again. The door opened, and Olga stood up and nodded. Thor felt disappointment spreading through his body—but also another, darker feeling. A broad-shouldered figure came stomping across the room toward their table. It was Hallgrim "Muskox" Dalen.

Hallgrim crossed the room, gave his grandson a stern look, and put a heavy hand on Thor's shoulder.

"Well, well, boys," he said. "Sitting here eating burgers and drinking Cokes and having a chat—without a care in the world. You should be getting home to your mother and father now, Karl. There's plenty of work to be done. And you, Seter." Hallgrim squeezed Thor's shoulder so hard that it ached. "Don't you have a farm to look after? Things'll go downhill fast with you piddling around. Seter Farm isn't quite debt-free yet, either, as I recall. Remember that your father borrowed money from me for the tractor when the bank wouldn't lend him any more. He wouldn't be happy to hear that you're wasting both time and money here."

Thor kicked off his shoes, hung up his work clothes in the mudroom, and locked the door behind him. He didn't normally do that, but today he did it almost automatically. On any other day, he might have paused for a moment in the hallway, looked at the photographs of the buildings and animals, and thought about the next step in the never-ending process of maintaining and renovating the farm. Today, however, he went straight into the bathroom, tore off the rest of his clothes, and stepped into the shower. As he let hot water run over his body, he wished he could let his anxiety run down the drain along with the soap and the smell of sheep.

But the meeting with Hallgrim Dalen churned round and round in his head.

The threats weren't exactly subtle. Seter Farm had been struggling for a long time, especially after the recent changes in agricultural subsidies. And Thor's father, Thorbjørn, hadn't ever been the best with money, to say the least. Now, Thorbjørn was retired, hoping his son would be able to run the farm better than he himself had. Hallgrim Dalen had come to their financial rescue several times—or was *rescue* the right word? You could just as well say that he set traps for gullible people like Thorbjørn. People often went to Hallgrim when the bank put its foot down and desperation set in. And Hallgrim could almost always help. But everything had its price. And this meeting was a reminder of what that price was. Hallgrim Dalen had the Seter family in his clutches, and he intended to leverage his position if Thor didn't mind his own business.

Thor pictured Ingrid's face—happy and proud as manager of the hotel. Excited and eager as they talked about the hotel's history. Serious as she sat hunched over the bills. All of the worries that hung over her, the uncertainty about what kind of game she and the hotel were wrapped up in. And when he had these thoughts, Thor wasn't so sure whether he could just mind his own business anymore.

He had to find out what this was all about, both for his own sake and for Ingrid's. Ingrid Berg, who'd smiled her bright smile and waved goodbye to Dalen and Glitter Peak so many years ago, but who was now back to run the hotel. He truly hoped she would succeed. And he would gladly—*very* gladly—be the one to help her make it happen.

Thor turned off the shower and grabbed the towel hanging on a hook on the wall. His shoulder still ached where the Muskox's fingers had grabbed it. He lifted a hand to the foggy mirror and drew the same two letters that the Muskox Calf had drawn in the ketchup: *XO*.

From Borghild Berg's diary:

> *I suppose I do know why Hallgrim is the way he is. It's all because of what happened with Charlie. He thinks it was my fault. But he doesn't know what really happened.*

I could have made it easier for myself by telling him the truth a long time ago. I made a promise, though, and I've kept it. Otherwise, I wouldn't have been able to live with myself. But now it's started coming to the surface again, everything that's been buried so deep for such a long time. And now she is here. I should have realized it right away. Those eyes.

The hand holding the pen trembled over the diary. Maybe Borghild *had* understood it right away—how it was all connected—on a subconscious level. But she hadn't been able to turn her gut feeling into a conscious train of thought, perhaps because she couldn't really believe it. And it had been far too long since she'd seen such eyes. Maybe it was a coincidence. Maybe she was remembering wrong.

Now Ingrid has started asking questions. She comes along with this newspaper and wants me to tell her more. And I'm going to. I was about to, or at least to start explaining, but then Freya fainted outside my door.

What was she doing there? Was she listening? Or was that also a coincidence?

What definitely wasn't a coincidence was Freya's reaction when she saw the picture on the wall—surely this must be proof that what I've been thinking is true? Or does it just show that she's overly excitable, and I'm making connections that aren't really there?

Borghild shut her diary, stood up, and found the thick cardboard folder at the back of the closet. It was closed with twine that felt stiff under her fingers. It had been many years since it had last been opened. She thought she smelled dust when she put it on the table in front of her. Dust and grief.

Darling B,

Last summer was a dream
A dream filled with heather and blue skies, warm days and
  bright nights,
laughter and breath and skin and warm hands.
I didn't know before. I didn't know that life could be like
  this.
That something could feel so good.

We'll be together forever, you said.
And we believed it at the time. That it could last forever.
It seems like such a long time ago. Everything has changed.

In reality, there was so little time left.
You know why I have to do this.
Thank you for helping me.

Your C

DECEMBER 17

"Say what you will about Napoleon, but the man sure knew how to make cake!"

The former editor of the *Dalen Daily*, Arnstein Barke, laughed heartily at his own joke. And Thor Seter was never going to eat Napoleon cake again—at least that's what he would have sworn if someone had asked him at that very moment, after he'd consumed what felt like a pound of phyllo pastry, vanilla cream with rum, and icing.

The pastry shop in Vrangsida was known throughout the valley for its enormous slices of cake, and this was where the retired newspaperman had wanted to meet. After a few introductory remarks about the weather, the shop, and the history of Napoleon cake, Thor had managed to steer the conversation over to the disappearance from 1962.

Arnstein Barke had to be about a hundred years old. He'd run the newspaper from after the war until the 1990s. Now he lived in

Vrangsida across the river from Dalen, and he'd been thrilled when Thor called a few days earlier and said he needed the editor's help.

Arnstein Barke had single-handedly maintained the *Dalen Daily* archives after the board no longer found it necessary to take care of such old matters. So when Thor had asked whether there might be some copies dating back to 1962 in Barke's collection, he'd enthusiastically confirmed that indeed there were. And in exchange for a slice of Napoleon cake and repeated promises to be extremely careful, he said Thor could borrow all the newspapers he needed.

"I remember that case well," Barke said when he'd pushed the empty plate aside and took a sip from his third cup of coffee. "Now let me tell you . . ."

It was still snowing. The mountaintops were now completely concealed behind gray clouds, the wind was howling, and the snow had been coming down more and more heavily throughout the day. It packed itself in drifts around the cars in the parking lot, and Ingrid was glad her own was safe in the garage.

She took a trip into the library, where she found John Wilkins and Pia P on the sofa by the fireplace. Dr. Wilkins had a cup of coffee in front of him, and Pia was holding a cup of something that resembled herbal tea. She was dressed in a champagne-colored pantsuit made from some kind of velvety fabric and looked shamefully good.

The doctor stood up courteously when Ingrid approached their table.

"Good afternoon, Miss Berg," he said.

"Good afternoon," Ingrid replied. "Please, sit. I didn't mean to interrupt. I just wanted to check in and see how your wife is doing."

"Thank you for asking. She's doing better now," Wilkins assured her, sitting back down. "But I've told her to stay in bed for a few days after the fainting and the . . . confusion she experienced. I'm quite concerned with getting her blood pressure properly regulated and don't want her to exert herself too much."

"You've clearly been having some pretty active days since you came to Norway," Ingrid said. "I just hope you'll let me know if there's anything the hotel can do to help."

"Thank you again," Dr. Wilkins said. "You're really already doing everything right here. We've gotten delicious food up in the room, and everyone is so thoughtful. Miss Seter has told me a lot about Norwegian Christmas traditions, and Miss Pihlstrøm here"—he pronounced the name with a thick American accent, *Peel-strohm*—"is telling me about modern Norwegian culture."

He took a sip of coffee. "I'm quite confident that Freya will be back on her feet soon. I don't know exactly what triggered the episode, but I'm sure that as long as she rests for a few days, she'll be shipshape by Christmas Day."

"I hope so," Ingrid said.

She went up to her apartment to get started on some paperwork but couldn't get Freya out of her head. Her concentration was nonexistent; she wanted to talk to Freya herself to get a sense of what was going on. What was it about the picture that had made her react this way? And why had she suddenly started singing that old Norwegian lullaby?

Ingrid paced back and forth, opened the kitchen cupboard, ate one caramel and then another. She picked up her phone, sat down, and looked at the Instagram updates from Sunny and Pia P. Lots of likes, but would they ever manifest themselves in actual profits?

Christmas Eve was only a week away! This was really the home stretch. It was lovely that snow had come before Christmas, but she hoped it wouldn't snow so much that it would cause problems for transportation.

There was a knock at the door, and she stood up to open it.

Thor Seter's cheeks were red from the cold, and his blue eyes shone eagerly as he stood in the hallway outside her apartment. His blond curls were tousled as he pulled off his hat.

"Hi!" he said. "I picked up the kiddo from school today, too. I guess it's kind of becoming a tradition."

"How nice of you!" Ingrid said.

"No, no, it was no trouble at all. And I have something I wanted to talk to you about. If I'm not interrupting?"

"Not at all," she assured him. "Come in! Do you want some coffee? I just made some."

"I never say no to coffee," Thor replied as he hung his jacket on the peg inside the door and unlaced his heavy winter boots. "Even though I've already had more than my fair share today. Of Napoleon cake, too. I had a meeting with Arnstein Barke."

"So you contacted him about the newspaper archive?" She glanced at the folder of loose clippings that was still lying on the coffee table, as disjointed as pieces of an unfinished jigsaw puzzle.

"Yeah, that's exactly what I've done," Thor said, settling down on the sofa. Now she saw he had a bag with him. Thor took out a stack of newspapers and spread them out on the table.

She put the coffee cups on the table and sat down next to him.

"You're not going to believe it," he said and patted his hand on the pile on the table. "This is pretty special, this stuff here. I thought I knew most things about this valley, but I've heard remarkably little about this particular case. Today, I've learned a whole lot more."

He carefully unfolded the first newspaper and laid it out on the coffee table.

They'd seen the masthead, Volkswagen ad, and headline before:

THE DALEN DAILY
Monday, March 5, 1962

YOUNG GIRL MISSING

The sheriff of Dalen and Innviken is searching for a young woman who went missing from her home without a trace two days ago. See page 5.

This time, they actually had a page 5 to see, and the old paper crinkled as Thor turned the pages. But the information about the case itself was limited.

"This doesn't say much more than what was on the front page," Ingrid said, a little disappointed. "A young girl is missing and there are few clues."

"Hang on!" Thor said, flipping through a couple of other papers in the pile. The front page that appeared two days later sent a chill down Ingrid's spine.

THE DALEN DAILY
Wednesday, March 7, 1962

YOUNG GIRL STILL MISSING

Family asks for help

The sheriff of Dalen and Innviken is looking for 19-year-old Charlotte Dalen of Dalen, who went missing from her home without a trace on Saturday.

She was supposed to get married in Dalen Church but never showed up for the ceremony. Her family and fiancé Jarand Smedplass (29) fear that something has happened to her.

The article continued inside the paper:

In recent days, the sheriff and volunteer crews have combed the area looking for Charlotte Dalen, who disappeared without a trace on Saturday when she didn't show up for her own wedding. She did not take any luggage with her, and as far as the family knows, has not contacted any relatives or friends in the district. A coat belonging to Miss Dalen was found near Styggfossen on Tuesday, but otherwise there has been no trace of the young woman. Rain and wind have made the search more difficult. Parish priest Tankred Röhmer says that Charlotte Dalen is a responsible young girl who has never previously gone missing or caused concern for her family.

"So her name was Charlotte Dalen? Who was she?" Ingrid asked, puzzled.

"This is where it gets really strange," Thor said. "The missing girl, Charlotte Dalen, was Hallgrim Dalen's little sister!"

"What?! But Nana Borghild never said anything about that," Ingrid said. "She only said that she knew her. She promised she'd tell me more when we were interrupted the other day."

"It's strange she didn't mention it," Thor said. "They were

around the same age, weren't they? If Charlotte was . . . what does it say here . . . nineteen years old in 1962, then she was only two or three years younger than Borghild."

"Yes. The fact that she's never mentioned it before makes it even stranger."

ARNSTEIN BARKE HAD CONFIRMED WHAT they already knew: that the young girl had never reappeared and that no body had ever been found. It was an unsolved mystery, plain and simple. The local newspaper had of course followed up with several articles in the time after the disappearance, and the case was even covered in the national media. It was rare for a young woman to disappear like that—without a trace. But no one had come forward with any information, and gradually, the attention died down.

Charlotte had seemingly vanished into thin air. Or maybe into the waterfall.

"Do you think she actually threw herself in?" Ingrid asked. "Killed herself, I mean?"

"Yes, or it could have been an accident," Thor suggested.

"But why would she have taken off her coat before she fell, in that case?" Ingrid asked. "And what was she doing up at Styggfossen to begin with, instead of showing up at church on what should have been her wedding day?"

"They don't state it outright, but this article seems to suggest that the groom-to-be was suspected of having something to do with the disappearance," Thor said, pointing at the newspaper he had in front of him.

"Yeah, what was his name again? Jarand Smedplass? I've never heard that name before," Ingrid said. "I'm pretty sure he doesn't live in the village anymore, at least."

"Maybe he moved away," Thor replied. "Or died before our time. But anyway, when would he have managed to push the girl into the waterfall? Charlotte Dalen was at home the morning of the wedding. Her brother Hallgrim confirmed that to the police, it says here."

"And this Smedplass was at the church when she was reported missing," Ingrid said. "It seems like the suicide theory makes the most sense, doesn't it?"

"Yeah, it looks that way. But you wouldn't report stuff like that in the papers back then."

"What does it take for someone to throw herself into Stygg-fossen instead of going to her own wedding?" Ingrid wondered.

"There's something missing here," Thor said. "What aren't we seeing?"

"You can say that again!" Ingrid exclaimed. "The fact that Charlotte was the sister of Muskox Dalen makes me think that this is more than just coincidence. Nana Borghild and Hallgrim don't even acknowledge each other if they see each other in the village, but they were actually friends once upon a time."

"I had no idea!" Thor said.

"Yup. Wait a second," Ingrid said. "Look!" Now it was her turn to show him something. She held out the brochure Sunny had found and Thor took it from her.

"*Learn to waltz, swing, and folk dance every afternoon in the ho-tel's dining room. Instructors: Borghild Berg and Hallgrim Dalen,*" Thor read aloud, looking taken aback. "Are you joking?"

"Nope! You can see it with your own eyes. I have no idea what could have happened there, though. But speaking of Hallgrim, these old coincidences are particularly striking because I have a feeling someone is actually working against us in the village right now. And I can't help thinking that Hallgrim Dalen has something to do with it."

"Ingrid," Thor said. He looked at her intently. Those blue eyes again . . . "I've been thinking the same thing. I talked to the Muskox Calf because I got the feeling there was something he wanted to tell me."

"Oh?"

"Yes. Hallgrim is trying to keep me out of it. You know how he is. Threatening and suggesting that bad things can happen if you dig around. But the Muskox Calf—well, I should probably call him Karl. Karl came to me with something on his mind, and after a lot of prodding, I got a hint. He drew an *X* and an *O* on his plate."

"*X* and *O*? As in XO Hotels?"

"Exactly. As in XO Hotels. Afterward, I did some googling and talked to a few people, and now I'm pretty sure I know how it all fits together. Muskox Machinery works with XO Hotels."

"Are you freaking kidding me?" Ingrid exclaimed. "That hotel chain contacts me all the time! I've even agreed to meet with them after Christmas."

Thor continued, "I'm sure that's part of the plan. Muskox Machinery has gotten lots of jobs from XO for things like excavation and development. So I'm sure the company will benefit if XO takes over here at Glitter Peak. There may be more, too. Maybe Muskox Machinery has even been promised shares or some other kind of bonus if things go the way XO wants them to."

So *that* was the missing piece falling into place.

"So Hallgrim Dalen and his clan have been trying to make things go poorly for the hotel because they'll profit if we have to sell?"

Despite what they say . . . Aslaug Slettebakken's words from the other day when she and her husband came up for dinner to "have a look around" suddenly made sense. Ingrid understood now. Hallgrim and Co. were trying to tarnish the hotel's reputation.

"So they're discouraging people from coming here?"

Thor nodded. "They want you to have as few guests as possible so your revenue base will suffer. You've mentioned sudden cancellations that seemingly come for no apparent reason? I wouldn't be surprised if they were sabotaging in other ways as well." Thor grabbed her hand, warm and eager. "But now that we know about it, we can stop them!" There was a twinkle in those light blue eyes.

Ingrid smiled. "It's good I have you as an ally!"

"Yes, I'm happy to be one," he assured her.

She let him hold her hand for a while. His hands were big and safe. She wanted to sit like that for a long time—maybe even lean against him.

But she felt a growing sense of unease as well. Her body stiffened, as if warning her that the closeness that was about to happen here was dangerous.

She couldn't remember the last time she'd had any physical contact with Thor. In elementary school, maybe? She didn't think they'd even kissed or anything like that. Their "relationship" mostly consisted of them running off and looking for animal tracks after school. When they graduated from high school and she moved away from the village, she must have given him a hug? But it felt like such a long time ago now.

Thor noticed that she was tensing up and let go of her hand.

"Sorry!" he said. "I didn't mean to . . ."

She laughed. "No, no, it's fine, I just . . ." She didn't know what to say. She tried to think of something to get the conversation going again, to pretend that nothing had happened, but then she was suddenly very aware of Thor's physical closeness. This large, adult version of his body was unfamiliar.

She sat quietly for a moment. Then she took his hand again.

Soap and wool. That's what he smelled like. Clean and warm. Something loosened in her, melted inside of her. She carefully moved closer to Thor, leaned her face against his shoulder, and breathed calmly. She felt the warmth of his body and his breath in her hair. She kept her eyes closed. Ever so slowly—so she wouldn't ruin the moment—she turned her face toward his throat. His skin was warm and a little rough. Her lips—what was she doing now?—her lips searched upward. She heard him make a sound, a kind of moan, as he turned his face to hers and their lips met.

When Ingrid and Thor came down the stairs, Ingrid felt as though everyone they passed could see that something had changed. Aisha was standing behind the reception desk, flipping through some papers. Ingrid almost blushed when Aisha looked up and met her gaze.

Thor hugged her by the door. For a long time. She freed herself as casually as she could. Thor moved his hands to her shoulders and smiled almost a bit shyly.

"I'd better get back down to the sheep. Say hi to Nana Borghild from me. Maybe she can tell you a bit more about what was in the newspapers?"

"Yeah, maybe," Ingrid said. She'd practically forgotten all about the newspapers and Charlotte Dalen's disappearance; now, all she could think about was the fact that she'd kissed Thor Seter.

"Drive carefully!" she said, walking toward the main door to check on how bad the snowstorm really was. But just as she opened the door, she jerked and took a step backward.

"Oh my God!" she exclaimed. She couldn't believe her eyes when she saw who was on the stairs.

STANDING JUST A FEW FEET away from her was a tall, handsome man with dark hair slicked back and a navy coat open over a white shirt. The tall figure and sharp profile were unmistakable, despite the dim lighting.

"Preben! What the hell are you doing here?"

"Nice to see you too, Ingrid," Preben Wexelsen replied, looking at her in that usual irritating way of his. "I came here because there's something I need to talk to you about."

"You can't just show up here like this," she protested.

"I can't?" he retorted. "This is a hotel, isn't it? I thought you'd be happy to have guests."

"Ingrid, is everything okay? Do you need help?" Thor asked. He looked worried.

Help? Was she supposed to need *help* here? What was he talking about? There wasn't anyone who could help her with this. Ingrid was freezing. She wasn't getting enough oxygen, despite the fresh air flowing through the wide-open door. She took a couple of steps to the side and supported herself on a chair. Her vision was blurring, and her hands felt numb. Then she pulled herself together and straightened up.

Preben had come into the foyer and stood there with his arms crossed.

Finally, she spoke. "Thank you, Thor. But this is something I need to deal with myself. I don't need any help. Thank you for everything you've done so far. You head on home, and we'll talk again soon."

"Are you sure?" Thor asked.

"Yeah, it's fine. I'll call you." She took Thor by the arm and practically shoved him out the door.

He looked at her in disbelief, and she felt guilty for being so brusque, but she had to deal with Preben Wexelsen on her own.

She chose to ignore Thor's questioning look as the door shut behind him. She'd have to explain this to him later—if it was possible to explain it at all. She didn't even know why Preben had shown up. The warmth she'd experienced with Thor just a few minutes ago had suddenly been replaced by cold and insecurity.

Preben was kicking the snow off his shiny, expensive, and most certainly handmade city shoes. Surely he realized that he wasn't welcome here. But that didn't matter. He wasn't going to leave voluntarily.

"I drove all the way from Oslo to talk to you," he said. "And I have no intention of leaving Glitter Peak until I do."

Ingrid looked at her watch—it was almost six. Preben wouldn't be back down in Oslo before midnight if she kicked him to the curb now. She could ask him to find some other accommodations at one of the chain hotels across the valley or closer to Lillehammer. She glanced toward the reception desk, where Aisha was watching them. Did she realize who Preben was? She'd only met him once before, in a completely different context . . .

Ingrid thought quickly. She had to find some excuse to get away so she could collect herself.

"I have something I have to take care of," she said shortly. "Aisha will find you a room, and we'll talk later."

Ingrid ignored Aisha's searching expression, turned around, and walked up the stairs, her heart hammering in her chest.

First, there was this thing with Thor, which had come as such a surprise—and now Preben had suddenly shown up. She felt his eyes on her back. She didn't turn around.

SHE WAS SITTING ON THE sofa in her apartment staring straight ahead when there was a knock at the door. She mumbled something, and Nana Borghild opened the door and came in.

"So here's where you've been hiding," she said. "I was looking for you."

"Preben is here!" Ingrid blurted out.

"What? Here?" Nana Borghild looked around as if Preben were hiding somewhere in the apartment. "No, Thor was the one who was here, sweetie."

Ingrid laughed humorlessly. "Yes, Thor *was* here! But now Preben is here, too."

Her grandmother looked at her like she didn't understand a word she was saying. "But why in heaven's name is *Preben* here?" Borghild asked.

"I don't know, Nana. He says there's something he needs to talk about. I tried to get rid of him, but he won't leave."

"And where is he now?"

"Probably in his room. I asked Aisha to find one for him."

"But then I suppose you have to talk to him?"

"Yes. Or no. I can't. I don't know. I don't have time."

"But you have time to hide in here?" Nana Borghild looked as though she immediately regretted saying that, as she changed her tone and said softly, "Ingrid, sweetie. Come to my apartment. We'll have a bite to eat, and you can deal with Preben afterward. You know you'll have to after he came all the way up here." She stroked Ingrid's cheek. "I'll help you if I can, Ingrid. I know there's a lot going on right now. But you can do it. We'll figure it out together."

THEY SAT AT THE DINING table in Borghild's apartment and had some food brought up from the kitchen. Once Ingrid started eating, she realized Maja's meatballs and cabbage stew were exactly what she needed on a day like this, and she felt her vitality coming back.

She told her grandmother about what Thor had found out.

"Hallgrim Dalen wants us to sell. He has a financial interest in a sale," she said. "Muskox Machinery is collaborating with XO Hotels."

Borghild looked at Ingrid. "The financial interest explains a lot," she said. "But there's more than that—a lot more. And there are things I need to tell you about now. Things from the past. Because no matter what happens with our finances and XO's takeover attempt, some things are going to come to light now, things that have been kept in the dark for a long time and that I haven't talked about before. Maybe I should have told you about these things already, but I've kept them to myself because I made a promise. I've also stayed silent to protect the hotel—to protect *you*, Ingrid."

Borghild took a deep breath and paused before continuing. "It's not just about the money with Hallgrim, Ingrid. The reason he's working against us, why he wants the hotel to fail. No, above all, it's because of an old grudge. Bad blood. You know that Hallgrim Dalen and I aren't on speaking terms, not anymore. But we were once. The thing is . . ." Nana Borghild cleared her throat. "The thing is, Hallgrim once hoped *he'd* be the one running Glitter Peak Lodge."

Ingrid stared at her grandmother uncomprehendingly.

"What? Hallgrim? But . . . I mean . . . our family has always owned the hotel!"

Nana Borghild gave her a meaningful look.

"Yes. Exactly. So the only way he would have been able to take over the hotel is by marrying into the family."

Ingrid was totally confused. What was her grandmother saying?

"Hallgrim Dalen wanted to . . . what? Marry . . . you?"

"Yes, is that so strange?" Her grandmother raised an eyebrow coquettishly. Her smile showed a glimpse of a much younger woman before she grew serious again. "Yes. It was before . . . before we had a falling out, and before I married Christian, obviously. Hallgrim has never forgiven me for that. He's always wanted Glitter Peak to be his."

Ingrid set her cutlery down on her plate. She thought about the dance lessons.

"Were you and Hallgrim Dalen . . . *together*? I mean . . . were you engaged to him before you were engaged to Grandpa?"

"No, we were just friends—good friends. At least the way I saw it. This thing with marriage was just something Hallgrim had come up with in his head."

"Is that why you had a falling out? Because you wanted to marry Christian—Grandpa? It's strange if Hallgrim can't forgive you after sixty years, when he himself has also gotten married and had children, grandchildren, and great-grandchildren."

"It's not just that," Nana Borghild said. "There's even more behind it. That newspaper story you asked me about the other day, the one about the disappearance? That's what it's really all about. It's about Charlotte Dalen."

Ingrid shut the door behind her. She was lost in her thoughts. She'd never known—or thought about—so much when it came to her grandmother's life. Ingrid had never known her grandfather; he'd died before she was born. She hadn't had parents who could describe him, either. Grandpa Christian had been black-and-white pictures in old photo albums and a name that was fondly mentioned in anecdotes, a part of the history of Glitter Peak Lodge, just like the furniture and the carvings and the stuffed bear.

Ingrid had never thought about it before—the reason Nana Borghild had chosen her grandfather, and that he might not have been her first love. It occurred to Ingrid that it wasn't the sort of thing you think about that much. Family and history simply were what they were, and the course of events seemed like the only option.

But now, she realized that the story *could* have played out quite differently.

And how will my *story play out from here?* she thought. She'd spent so much effort trying to push away the memories of what had happened, but now her own past had shown up at the hotel, and she couldn't put it off any longer. She had to go and listen to what Preben had to say—even though he was associated with so much pain that it felt as though her heart was stopping just at the thought of it.

She didn't want to be with him in the hotel, that's for sure. He didn't belong here.

"You'd better put your coat on," she said when she was standing outside his door. She was already dressed in a down jacket and hat. "We're going on a walk, and you can tell me what's so important."

"A walk? Now?" Preben looked taken aback, but she just waved him along and walked toward the stairs without saying another word. Preben didn't say anything else either but grabbed his coat and scarf and hurried after her.

A thought suddenly struck her. Could the fact that Preben was suddenly here have something to do with everything else that was happening? Did he perhaps have contacts in one of the hotel chains that kept asking her about a buyout? Was he going to sweet-talk or threaten her? Make her an offer she couldn't refuse?

There wasn't anyone at the reception desk, and fortunately, they didn't run into anyone in the foyer, either. Most people were probably in the dining room or the bar right now. She strode out onto the stairs and across the parking lot, and he followed. It had snowed so much that it was difficult to walk, but she didn't care. It wasn't her problem if Preben ruined his fancy city shoes. The snow made it brighter, so the terrain was easy to see. She trotted toward the familiar path she knew like the back of her hand and didn't stop before she reached Troll Rock.

Preben stopped beside her.

She turned to him and looked up—he was one of the few people she knew who was so tall she had to lift her gaze to look him in the eye—but he just stood there, staring at the landscape. She did the same. The dark heather moor, the scree, the mountains beyond, Heaven's Horn rising majestically among a few stars twinkling in the sky.

After a while, Ingrid was the one to break the silence. "I'm curious about what it is you want, Preben," she said. "After what happened, and after we haven't spoken in over a year and a half . . . you show up here, in the middle of the Christmas rush? These are the most important days of the whole year for the hotel. What could possibly be so urgent?"

She could hear her own pulse, feel it throbbing beneath her skin. The mere fact that Preben was so near had put her on full alert.

That's how close she'd once been to this man. Yes, she'd even thought she loved him. But now all she felt was anger. Anger and fear.

When he didn't answer right away, she started walking back down the path.

Preben was right behind her. She was tempted to shake him off; he'd need some time to find his way back to the hotel if she took the shortcut that wasn't so easy to see from the main path, especially now that it was so dark. She knew it wouldn't be dangerous for him. He'd survived worse conditions before—much worse.

But what was she going to gain from that? He was here now, and he wasn't going to leave her alone. Her stoic side got the upper hand once again: she had to face him. She stopped abruptly.

Preben raised both hands defensively. "I drove all the way from Oslo to see you. Can't we go back to the hotel and talk in peace and quiet? I came because there's something I *have* to discuss with you."

"But what if *I* don't want to talk to *you*?"

"Ingrid. I think you're going to want to talk about this. We probably should have talked before. I know you've been . . . angry with me after the accident."

She didn't say anything.

He continued, "You think it didn't have as big an effect on me as it did on you. But it did. My life was turned upside down too, Ingrid. We lost a friend, you pulled away from me, and everything we'd built together fell apart. We weren't just doing it for ourselves, Ingrid. We had so many plans. And that's why I'm here. Because an opportunity has come up that I wanted to talk to you about face-to-face. If we can't set things right, maybe we can . . ." He hesitated. "I've been working on figuring out how to contribute for a long time. Maybe it's an attempt to make amends for what happened. And now I think I may have found a way. I've been working with Brother Giovanni's fellow monks on setting up a relief organization in Nepal, a foundation that will continue the environmental and social work that he—well, the three of us, really—were so passionate about. And now I need your help—your involvement. Because the representatives from the organization that wants to sponsor us are in Oslo now, and they want to get moving with the planning before the new year!"

Sunny was sitting at the kitchen table when Ingrid came in. She was completely shaken up after her conversation with Preben. She had to sleep on what he'd suggested—but first, she was making the rounds to check on the staff.

Sunny was also going to bed soon. She was tired after so many long workdays, and it showed, Ingrid thought; even the normally fresh-faced Sunny was showing signs of dark circles under her eyes.

Alfred came in to grab a sandwich. Earlier today, he'd been down to the forest to take a look at the big spruce he'd chosen for this year's Christmas tree. It was going to be magnificent, he assured them.

It was late before Ingrid finally made her way back to her own apartment. Her sofa cushions were in disarray, and seeing them made her think of Thor—that she'd sat there and kissed him just a few hours ago. What in the world had gotten into her? But her body tingled when she thought of his big hands, his blue eyes . . .

And Preben. They'd agreed to talk more tomorrow. She'd decided that he had to get the chance to present the proposal properly after he'd come all the way up here to talk to her. His plans had come as a total surprise. While she had thought he'd left everything that had happened behind and was just surfing along in his successful life, in reality, he'd been working hard on setting up a foundation—a way of making amends. For a little while, she wondered whether he was there for personal reasons. To try to win her back, perhaps. She'd been relieved when it turned out that he wanted to propose a professional collaboration; but was the relief mixed with a bit of disappointment, too? Was she hoping, deep down, that he wanted to try again—if only so she would have the chance to say no?

Everything was spinning around in her head, jumbling with what Nana Borghild had told her. That Hallgrim Dalen had been disappointed not to marry Borghild and run Glitter Peak Lodge. And that for some reason, he also blamed Borghild for his sister's disappearance. Or was it the other way around? Was Borghild the one who blamed Hallgrim? There must be a misunderstanding, she thought as she was dozing off. But—a misunderstanding that had lasted for sixty years?

December 1961

Charlotte walked up the freshly shoveled walkway and looked up at the trees looming over her with their dark branches. When she knocked on the door of the vicarage, she expected the maid, Ellen, to answer, but it was Reverend Röhmer himself standing in the doorway.

"Good evening, Charlotte," he said. "Come in, come in."

She looked around. Was it just the two of them here?

"My wife has traveled to Lillehammer," he said, holding out a hand to take her coat. "She's happy to get away a little. So I gave the maid the day off. Now the two of us can have a conversation undisturbed."

She'd come to unburden herself. She'd been weighing sharing her secret back and forth. It was unheard of, this thing she was carrying around. She hadn't even known that it was possible. She'd heard of men who were like that—who loved other men. But women?

She shuddered at the thought of what people would think if they found out. She imagined the gossip in the village. <u>Sick</u>, people would say. <u>Unnatural.</u>

And yet—it felt so right. She woke up every day full of joy and anticipation. She wanted to thank God for this love. How could it possibly be sinful?

Perhaps the priest would be able to help her with the confusion. Reverend Röhmer had spoken so beautifully

about love in church last Sunday. *For love is from God,
and whoever loves has been born of God and knows God.*
She'd been moved and thought that if there was anyone
who could understand what she was struggling with,
it must be him. And he'd always been kind to her, ever
since confirmation classes.

They sat in the living room. He offered coffee and
cookies, and then a glass of sweet wine. He put the carafe
on the table. "Go on, have a bit more. Tell me what's on
your mind."

She told him, and he listened sympathetically. He sat
beside her on the sofa and poured her another glass. He
came closer, and she felt a hand on her knee. He moved
it up a bit.

What was he doing?

When she started to cry, he lifted his arm and put it
around her shoulders. "There, there. Come here, Charlotte, my dear. I think I know what it takes to help girls
like you."

DECEMBER 18

Ingrid lay in bed, cold and tired, but with a seed of anticipation somewhere deep down beneath the ice.

Vegard wasn't the only one who called her ice queen. People always had, when they talked behind her back—she knew that. No matter how much admiration she garnered as a result of her expeditions, she knew that a lot of people also thought of her as *too* disciplined, *too* controlled. "Unnatural," she'd heard someone say once.

And when it all went wrong, there'd been no shortage of schadenfreude. It was as if people had always sensed something inferior behind that perfect facade of hers.

This iciness came up again with Preben yesterday. "You seem so cold, Ingrid," he said. "Why won't you talk to me?" The injustice in his questions still stung, because *he* was the one who'd failed her, and who'd made her fail herself.

She'd needed to stay away from Preben, because he was bad for her. He made her weak. It was her infatuation with Preben that had made her lose control, grow careless. And she'd been punished so terribly for that. She'd lost everything—Preben, climbing, and the child. She'd lost a community, many friendships, and the involvement in the mountain areas she'd spent time in for so many years.

And now Preben was here and wanted to make up for it. Was that even possible?

She'd thought about his proposal all night.

Preben was sitting alone at a table by the window. He stared out over the mountains, whose silhouettes were now emerging against the brightening sky. He had a bowl of oatmeal, a cup of coffee, and a glass of orange juice on the table in front of him— what he always ate for breakfast.

After all these months, she now couldn't feel any resentment toward him, no matter how hard she tried. The conversation yesterday had calmed her a bit. That didn't mean everything was okay now; it never would be. But he'd made a proposal, and she was going to listen to what he had to say.

Preben looked up as she walked over to him. "Hi, Ingrid."

"Hi."

She hesitated. He pointed at the chair across from him with his right hand. "Have a seat. If you want."

She did as he said, concentrating on keeping her movements steady as she pulled out the chair and positioned herself across from the man who'd once been the center of her life and whom she now felt as if she barely knew. He took a sip of orange juice and dabbed at his mouth with the paper napkin before folding it and setting it down next to his plate.

Maybe he was also a bit nervous, she thought. Maybe that was why he'd just turned up here instead of calling or sending an email about what was on his mind.

"Thank you for taking the time to talk," he said.

She had to smile a bit. "You haven't exactly given me any choice. Should we sit here or go somewhere else?"

"It's nice here. Then the others will know you're safe, too. I saw the looks I got from that friend of yours yesterday. He almost seemed like he was trying to be your bodyguard."

"My friend? Thor?"

"Yeah, the blond guy on his way out as I was coming. Broad-shouldered fellow. Did you find yourself a real live farmer up here?"

"Preben. Stop right there. You can't show up here, in the middle of farm country, and start criticizing people for being farmers."

"I haven't criticized anyone, have I? I was only asking."

She thought she caught a glimpse of the old jokester in his eyes.

He went on, "But you're right. That's not why I'm here."

He brushed an imaginary crumb off the tablecloth before looking at her again. Then he leaned over and picked up a leather bag from the floor. He placed it in his lap, pulled out a plastic folder full of papers, and held it out across the table. "See what you think about this."

He handed her a sheet of paper with the heading *BOW: The Berg Orlando Wexelsen Foundation.*

INGRID AND PREBEN SAT AT the window table for a long time, even after the kitchen staff had finished cleaning up and the dining room slowly emptied following breakfast. Normally, Ingrid never would have just sat there this way while the staff worked around her. She also had a thousand things to do, but right now, she was certain that this was the most important. Even when Nana Borghild stopped by the dining room and raised an eyebrow at her and Preben, Ingrid chose to stay seated instead of finding out what her grandmother wanted. God knows the two of them had plenty to talk about—later.

She could feel her voice wasn't quite steady when she spoke. "This is all pretty overwhelming, Preben. I'm happy and surprised that you're suggesting this. And I'd like to contribute. I really would." She paused. "But—I still don't know how you and I would be able to work together. After what happened. We haven't even talked about it."

Preben looked at her again, serious now. "No, we haven't talked about it, and I think it's about time. It's been a year and a half, Ingrid. We're heading into the second Christmas since . . . since the accident. Without having exchanged a single word. You just disappeared and left me behind to pick up the pieces."

She looked at him. Was that how he remembered things? "But what was I supposed to do, Preben? I had to leave."

"You had to leave?"

"Yes! I was on the verge of a total breakdown. The avalanche, and the fact that Giovanni was dead . . ." She took a deep breath. "Everything they wrote in the papers. All the criticism. That it was our fault. I understood why they thought so, too. And all the speculation about the two of us."

Preben took a sudden and audible breath. "Ingrid. Don't you think it was hard for me, too? Giovanni was dead, the whole group had been put in danger, we had to stop our work, and then in the middle of all of this, you left the country without even saying goodbye. You didn't say anything. You didn't answer when I called or texted."

"I was furious with you," she said. "For what happened. For the danger you put us in. What bothers me most is that you can't admit you made a mistake. You were pushing so hard so we could break the record . . . even though we should have waited until conditions were safer. You should have known! The forecasts weren't good. We should have stayed at base camp."

She felt hot and could hear she was raising her voice now. "We almost died, Preben! We knew there was an avalanche risk. We shouldn't have gone out that day. And *definitely* not when we had a less experienced climber like Giovanni with us. That decision cost him his life. I couldn't forgive you. And I couldn't forgive myself for letting you cloud my judgment like that."

Preben's green eyes darkened. "I assume you recall that you're the one who wanted Giovanni to join the expedition. But yes—it was a miscalculation to leave base camp that day. It was the biggest mistake I've ever made. I'm never going to forgive myself, nor do I expect anyone else to. The work I've started now is just as much an attempt at reconciliation with you as it is to make amends in some way."

He sat quietly for a while. "That avalanche cost us a lot. And the fact that it also cost me . . . not just my relationship with you, but that you felt you had to break off contact completely, hate me . . . that's been difficult to handle. But what I'm doing now is trying to show you that I'm taking responsibility."

She hesitated. How much should she tell him? Should she also share what he still didn't know about that fatal trip? About the child she—they—lost?

She knew what Vegard had said was true: she needed to tell Preben. But not now.

She looked around the empty dining room. One day, she would tell him—but this was neither the time nor place. Still, she had to try to explain herself.

"I . . . I was devastated, Preben. After the avalanche and the injuries and the shock of losing Giovanni. After all the media coverage. I couldn't keep going. Not with the work. Not with you. I'm sorry."

She felt a salty taste in her throat and dabbed at her eyes with a napkin. She suddenly realized that this was the first time she'd ever cried in front of Preben. They'd been together for years and shared so much—enthusiasm, joy, passion. Wild ambitions. Anger. Obstinance. Willpower. Nerves on the way up a rock face and longing to get right back up there as soon as they were down. This urge that got them to plan the next adventure as soon as one was over. They'd shared all of these things. But grief—that was something they'd never shared. Until now.

"I know everything thinks I'm so cold," Ingrid said. "But I felt like *you* were the one who was cold up there, Preben. And afterward, I guess I thought you couldn't understand how I felt. And I . . . I didn't really think you cared, either. I felt like you were only calling because it would look bad not to. You stopped trying to contact me after a few weeks. I started over here after losing everything. And before I knew it, there you were on TV. On a reality show! Like nothing had happened."

"Yes, after a while, I chose to keep going with my life," Preben said. "And my climbing career. Even though you made a different choice, it was the right one for me. I know I'm privileged, Ingrid. I admit that both success and material rewards mean a lot to me. And I know it seems like I just get through most things unaffected. But I was. Affected."

He looked out of the window for a moment. "You know, Ingrid, I'm actually not completely devoid of emotions. I've missed you."

He didn't meet her gaze now. Were his eyes shining a bit?

What was she supposed to say? Had he actually missed her? She felt almost ashamed at how little she'd thought about how the accident must have affected Preben's life, too. She'd been so blinded by her own loss that she hadn't seen his.

He looked her in the eyes again. She felt something warm inside her. But no. She wasn't going back there. She straightened up and said nothing.

Preben said, "I'm happy that we're at least at the point where we can talk about it, Ingrid. I don't expect that . . . that things will go back to the way they were. Maybe it won't even be possible for us to be friends. But if we can at least stop being enemies, we'll have come a long way. Can we agree on that?"

Ingrid nodded. "Okay."

"Good!" He rubbed his hands together in a way she recognized from when he was pleased with a good business deal or reveling in a challenging wall that he would soon conquer. He looked around the now-empty dining room.

"By the way, it's quite a place you have here. Really great. It's nice to see it again. A venerable old hotel, a tradition to carry on. Props to you for taking it on, Ingrid. I know you can do this!"

You can do this. Now she felt it again. The warmth. The inspiration, but also the fear. The same feelings she'd had before setting off on a climb: ambition, anxiety, concentration, longing. The wild power of climbing in the face of the fear of falling. The almost incomprehensible and self-destructive urge to do what you're most afraid of.

"I'm actually *not* sure I can do it," she said. "It's too hard."

Now the tears were coming again. *God dammit.* But so be it.

When others looked at Ingrid, they saw someone in complete control, someone who knew what she was doing. Control was necessary to be a good climber—know the route, be willing to prepare, try again and again—but at the same time you had to live with the awareness that control was an illusion. At any moment, your foothold could slip, the gear could fail, the belay could come loose. This was the terror—and the fascination. The duality you had to live with. Only another climber could recognize and share those feelings. And not just any climber. Right now, it felt as though Preben Wexelsen was the only person in the world who could really understand her.

"Too hard?" Preben said. "To run the hotel? I don't believe that. I know you. You might think it's too hard right now. But you said the same thing when we were training in Västervik that one summer, too." Preben's voice was warm, almost laughing. "You spent days mastering only the first few feet there. At some point, it seemed completely impossible. You were so pissed! You even packed all your things and wanted to go back home, remember?"

She met his gaze but looked away quickly. "Yes, I remember. That wall was a bitch. Footholds the size of a dime. Crimps as thin as a credit card."

"But you didn't go home. You went back to the wall. Again and again."

"Failed again and again."

"But then one day you didn't fail anymore. You got to the top."

She smiled through her tears. "And it wasn't long before I wanted to get started planning the next trip."

Preben grinned. "Yup, then you were ready to go up to the crag in Flatanger where people spend years trying to send the most difficult routes!"

"So what you're trying to say is that if I manage this—I mean, if I succeed in running the hotel—I'm going to start planning on opening another one? A much bigger hotel?"

He chuckled. "No, I don't think you're going to open another hotel. At least not in Norway. That would just be doing the same thing all over again. When you've just climbed a mountain, you don't climb the same mountain again. You do something completely different. You take on the highest peak on another continent. Like us." He looked at her. "The next thing you open will probably be the BOW Foundation offices in Nepal. If you can forgive me enough to believe we can do this together, that is," he said. "You and I, in honor of Brother Giovanni."

"I want to forgive you," she said. "I'll work on it. And what about you? Can you forgive me?"

Preben looked at her for a long time. "I don't think I have much to forgive you for," he said. "I'm just happy we've come as far as we have."

"Preben Wexelsen," a voice said beside them. "It's been a while."

"Yes, it has, Mrs. Berg," Preben replied with a smile as he stood up, his charm turned up to the max. "It's so nice to finally see you again."

Nana Borghild held out her hand and formally, but politely, greeted Preben, whom she had met only once before.

"It must have been four years since you and Ingrid were here?" she said.

"Yes, that's right," Preben confirmed. "It was only a short visit then. And who would've thought it would be so long until the next time?"

Nana Borghild had managed to convince Preben to stay for lunch. *Not exactly a dream scenario*, Ingrid thought as they sat down at the table, but it went better than she'd feared. Preben was working his charm, and Nana Borghild was falling for it, too.

They'd just finished eating when Aisha came into the dining room and leaned over Ingrid's chair. "Sorry to disturb you," she said. "But I can't find Hussein. He had a half-day, so we came back an hour ago, but now I don't know where he's gotten off to."

"Oh gosh . . ." Ingrid exclaimed. "He hasn't gone out on his own again, has he?"

"Again?" Aisha asked, and Ingrid could have bitten her tongue off.

"I'll go check if his outerwear is gone," Aisha said. "Let me just run upstairs."

When she came back downstairs a few minutes later, her face was pale. "He's taken his jacket and outdoor pants and winter boots."

"We have to go look for him," Ingrid decided, standing up abruptly. "Preben, come with me."

She had a bad feeling. He hadn't gone toward Heaven's Horn,

had he? He'd been an eager climber from the very first time she saw him, and now she feared he was making good on what he'd said about summiting the mountain. "We have to check outside first."

Ingrid ran out the front door. It was snowing so hard that it was difficult to see and footprints would be wiped out quickly, but . . . there! Was it . . . ? Yes, she was pretty sure it was the imprint of a child's winter boots that she saw going down the stairs.

"He's out there," she said when she came back in to put on warm clothes. The others had gathered at the reception desk. "Nana, Aisha, search everywhere here in the hotel just in case. Preben and I will look for him outside."

"I should have given him a phone," Aisha said, her voice starting to shake.

"What about one of those smart watches?" Preben suggested. "The kind you can call him on? If . . . I mean . . . when we find him again?"

Thanks a lot for that, Ingrid thought, dragging Preben to the cloakroom and handing him a bag with ropes, harnesses, and a wool blanket. He got dressed quickly and took the necessary equipment. Crampons, cams, helmets.

"If we haven't called or aren't back in fifteen minutes, you need to call for help," she said to Nana Borghild.

They had a long way to go, and it was getting dark. Snow pelted them in the face as Ingrid and Preben struggled forward against the wind. The footprints had ended just past the parking lot, but Ingrid had the terrible feeling that she knew exactly where they needed to look. She and Preben moved in silence. She pulled her phone out of her pocket and checked it with stiff fingers. No service. Nana had probably called the rescue team by now, but deep down, Ingrid knew that help wouldn't be able to get there in time.

If Hussein was where she thought he was, it was urgent that they find him—fast. She stopped for a few seconds at Angelina Hill. Ingrid thought of all the times she'd stood here. As a child, she thought her mother and father had traveled up to heaven from here, and even as an adult, she continued drawing strength from this place. Now she was going to need all the strength she could get.

Preben stopped in the flurry behind her, came a little closer, and put a hand on her shoulder. She turned and met his gaze. She wanted to smile but couldn't manage it. She put her gloved hand over his.

It was getting harder to walk now, but they struggled on, past the frozen Styggfossen and up to the base of the steep wall on Heaven's Horn. She shielded her eyes with one hand and looked up, but there wasn't much visibility. The wind was howling around them, and snow stung her face.

"Do you really think the boy could have come up here alone in this weather and started climbing on his own?" Preben asked. "Maybe it's better if we wait here until the rescue team arrives."

She shook her head. "We have to check. If he's where I think he is, we don't have time to wait. Conditions are too bad for a helicopter to come now. But we can climb."

"Ingrid. *I'll* do it," Preben said firmly.

She squinted up into the snow, following the rock with her eyes. If Hussein was here, how could he possibly have managed to get up?

It looked as if some snow had recently collapsed nearby. There was probably a snow bridge that Hussein had crossed and then it had collapsed behind him. In that case, he had no chance of getting back without any help. She knew that she now had to do what she hadn't dared to do for such a long time—what she thought she'd never be able to do again. She had to climb.

"Thanks, Preben. You're a great climber. But right now, on this particular wall, I honestly don't think anyone can climb it better than me. I need to lead, in any case."

They walked across the snow, and she carefully felt for where to put her weight so she wouldn't fall through. When they reached the wall, she took a few tentative steps up, pushing off. One more hold. Then another. She stopped on the first small ledge, only a few feet above where Preben was standing. She felt the coil of rope she had on her back and checked her gear. There wouldn't be many opportunities to place any protection now, but she might be able to use some of the cams, and she might also need the rope to pull Hussein up if he'd fallen into a crack.

She shouted upward. "Hussein!"

No response. Preben shouted, too. His voice echoed up the rock and was louder than hers: "Hussein!"

And then . . . there! She heard a faint sound, far, far above her. A child's voice.

"Help!" it cried. "Auntie Ingrid! You have to help me!"

THE WHITE DRAGON HISSED AT HER, wanting to paralyze her. But she let it hiss. The only thing that mattered was grabbing the next hold. She couldn't think, only focus on where her fingers could find something to hold on to, where her foot could find purchase. She'd done this a thousand times, but she thought she'd never do it again. Cold. Snow. Ice. It was pure madness to climb Heaven's Horn in the middle of the winter without proper equipment. She could die. Hussein could die. But he was *definitely* going to die if she didn't try. She couldn't be responsible for yet another life being lost. She pushed away her thoughts about the snow, about the cold, about what would happen if Hussein lost his balance and fell. She just thought about the next little crack she could jam her foot into, the next hold wide enough for her to get her fingers around it.

Her body took over now. It remembered the details of the mountain.

She threw herself over the next ledge and reached the plateau with aching fingers and a racing pulse. She must have heard his voice up here . . . but there was no Hussein to be seen. Could he have gotten even farther up? No, that was impossible. She carefully made her way forward; it was hard to see where the edge was through the thick snowfall. One wrong step and she'd end up on the scree far, far below.

"Hussein!" she shouted. "Hussein, are you here?"

No answer.

"Hussein!"

Was that a voice?

Now she heard it again. The wind was doing its best to drown it out, but there it was: "*Help!*"

Was he over the edge? She crawled on her hands and knees and looked down.

And yes, there, on a ledge just below, she saw a red jacket.

"Hussein! Thank God!"

She leaned over and met his gaze. His eyes were like two tiny black dots in a face pinched with pain and cold.

"Auntie Ingrid! It hurts!"

"Give me your hand."

She grabbed his wrist with her left hand while she took out the rope with her right. She had to get it under his arms and secure him before she lifted so she didn't lose her grip and . . . She stopped the thought.

This was a crucial moment. Now she really had to focus. She didn't feel the cold anymore. She was completely focused on Hussein. She tied the rope around him and made sure she had solid footing. She tensed all her muscles.

"All right, Hussein. I have you now."

AS THE ALPINE RESCUE TEAM made their way toward Heaven's Horn from the hotel, they met a woman with climbing equipment and a man carrying a bundle in a wool blanket. The bundle turned out to be a half-frozen little boy with an injured foot and wrist. He'd fallen off a ledge but "miraculously seemed to have escaped without any major injuries," reported the online edition of the *Dalen Daily* shortly afterward.

AISHA AND NANA BORGHILD MET Ingrid and Preben in the foyer. Ingrid's hands were frozen, but otherwise she was warm, euphoric, even; she'd never experienced such a rush of adrenaline before.

Tears were streaming down Aisha's face when she saw Hussein in Preben's arms. "Thank you, Allah!" she cried. "Thank goodness, Hussein! I thought you were dead!"

Dr. Wilkins examined Hussein up in the apartment. Apart from a sprained wrist, a sprained ankle, and some mild frostbite on his face and fingers, the boy would be fine, the doctor assured them. He prescribed a hot bath, lots of hot chocolate with whipped cream, and a Skype call to Jordan.

"He told me he misses his dad so much he feels sick," Dr. Wilkins explained. "That contributed to this crazy idea of his. He thought that maybe he could make some kind of connection with him if he just went to the highest mountaintop possible. And . . . someone in his class had apparently challenged him and said he'd never make it. You should have a chat with the school and find out how he's really doing. But otherwise, I must say he has a unique talent for climbing. And he should be allowed to continue with that—though perhaps under more controlled conditions."

"I can practice with him," Ingrid said.

"Are *you* going to go climbing again?" Preben asked, grinning.

"Yes. I sure am," she replied. "The cold never bothered me anyway."

Thor was freezing. It would take a while for the heater to get the temperature in the car up to a tolerable level. He turned on the radio and drove slowly down the farm road. It was playing pan-flute versions of Christmas songs. He shuddered. Just as he was about to change the channel, the familiar notes signaling the news bulletin sounded: "Time for the five o'clock news. The government's offshore wind plans are being criticized by several parties."

Well. Offshore wind was something they didn't have here in Dalen. He switched over to Radio Rock. The afternoon feeding was over, and Thor was planning to drive down to Lillehammer for some Christmas shopping. Not that it was going to be much; probably a wool scarf and hand cream for Mom and new gloves for Dad. Not the most imaginative, but his parents didn't expect anything too inventive. He'd sent money to his sister, Grete, in Bergen so she could buy presents for her kids from Uncle Thor. It had been quite a big sum considering his financial situation, and especially considering that Grete and her husband, Magnus, earned about four times more than he did. But given how little he saw of the children, a generous Christmas present was the least he could offer.

His sister and her family sometimes came to visit during the summer, but they usually stayed at home in their big house for Christmas. They were visited by Magnus's family and always invited Thor and his parents, too, but Thor had the farm to take care of and his parents preferred to stay at home, so Thor celebrated with them. Sometimes Aunt Maja joined them as well, but she had to work this Christmas.

He turned onto the main road and noticed he was stepping on the gas a little too hard. Maybe he was trying to push away what had been spinning around his head since yesterday. Glitter Peak. He'd been up half the night, thinking about what had happened between him and Ingrid. The happiness he'd felt in her apartment. To think that he'd finally been able to get so close to her!

And then the comedown. This guy who'd elbowed his way in. He knew who he was—Preben Wexelsen. He'd seen him on TV. Arrogant. And Ingrid had practically shoved Thor out the door when Preben arrived. No. He wanted to think about something else. He thought about checking out some photography equipment, since he'd already be in town. His camera was good, but you could never have too much equipment. The lens he wanted most was far too expensive, but he liked browsing in the photo shop and was glad such specialty stores still existed. He usually chatted a bit with the older man who worked there. He'd run the place since before the store was bought by a big chain and long before the phone took over as the camera most people used. Thor felt they had something in common. They were two people who'd been left behind in a way, people who couldn't or wouldn't adapt to modern life.

Stores were open late in Lillehammer today, and the main shopping street was sure to be full of the holiday spirit. Music, Christmas lights between the buildings, the Salvation Army's Christmas tree, a stall selling wreaths and another serving mulled wine, people with ice skates in hand and children with anticipation shining in their eyes.

He remembered what that had been like—looking forward to Christmas.

Now, he couldn't really say he looked forward to it all that much. He knew exactly what it was going to be like: Christmas choirs on TV at his parents' house, ribs and sauerkraut, Dad drinking exactly one glass of aquavit too many so Mom got annoyed. The tragic little gift exchange, the predictable rounds of thank-yous. Mom's *kransekake*—well, that was actually a highlight, he had to admit that. Dad nodding off in the easy chair, Mom urging Thor to have another cup of coffee, until at some point he would say—just as he did every year—no thanks, now he had to get home and go to bed so he could get ready for the morning rounds.

He loved his parents, but this wasn't exactly how he'd envisioned things turning out. When he and Sandra got married, he'd dreamed of a future with lots of children, lively parties, people coming and going, lots of hustle and bustle on the farm. That had never happened. Now it was just quiet. He did have the sheep—but still.

IT WAS ALREADY PITCH-BLACK OUT. The days were so short now. The roads were fully drivable, but the plowing after the heavy snowfall earlier in the day had left large drifts along the road, especially at the edge of Dalen, where they were almost like walls in some places.

He'd plowed thoroughly at home and at his parents', but when he came back from the hotel yesterday, he noticed something strange: a lot of car tracks. And they weren't from any of his own cars. The whole yard was full of them. It looked as if someone had been driving around and around there. What on earth was that about?

He'd looked around when he got out of the car, wondering whether anyone was there. No cars, that was obvious, but could someone be inside the house? There were no strange footprints at the door and no sign of anything out of the ordinary when he let himself in. Still, he felt a strong sense of unease that lingered long after he'd come inside.

The first thing he'd done was to call his parents to check that everything was okay. His mother sounded surprised at the question. "Yes, of course, Thor. Why?"

"No reason," he said. "I just wanted to check in. With . . . the bad weather and all that. Anything you need over there?"

He couldn't say what he was really worried about—that is,

what Hallgrim and his family might do if Thor kept digging around in matters that were none of his business. He thought the Dalen family had been at the farm to send a message that they were watching him and to remind him who was in charge here in the village.

The thought made him uneasy. And on top of everything else, this Wexelsen fellow had shown up. Ingrid clearly hadn't been pleased to see him. Thor regretted that he'd let himself be pushed away so easily. He should have been there to keep watch over what was happening. Was Wexelsen still there? What if he threatened or bothered Ingrid in some way? Thor couldn't just let that happen.

He abruptly turned off the road and into a turnout by the old lumber yard. He'd changed his mind. Christmas shopping could wait. This was more urgent. He drove out onto the road again, this time in the opposite direction, toward Glitter Peak. It wouldn't hurt if he made the trip up there just to check. Ingrid had to know he was there for her if she needed him.

The rescue team was given coffee and cookies as consolation for having come up for no reason, and Ingrid and Preben changed into dry clothes and sat down in the library.

Preben gratefully accepted a glass of wine; he'd drive back down to Oslo tomorrow. He was sure that the representatives of the organization would understand why he had to postpone the meeting by a day.

"You were right, Preben," Ingrid said. "About me climbing again."

"You've been scared before, but you always wanted to get back up there again," Preben pointed out.

"When I had to do it to save Hussein, it was like the crisis won out over the fear. I didn't have time to stop to think or listen for avalanches. My body just propelled me up."

Preben took another sip of wine. "Well, it's been quite a day, that's for sure! Never a dull moment with you, Ingrid."

"I'm so grateful for everything you've done today, Preben," she said. "I felt like we were a team again out there."

They raised their glasses to each other in a silent toast.

Ingrid reached a hand across the table. Her fingers closed over Preben's, and she squeezed gently. He squeezed back.

OF COURSE IT WAS JUST THEN—as Preben and Ingrid sat hand in hand with the starry sky over Heaven's Horn as a backdrop—that Thor Seter entered the library.

He froze on the spot before abruptly turning on his heel and walking out of the room with quick steps. Ingrid stood up and ran after him. "Thor!" she said as she caught up to him in the foyer. She put a hand on his arm. "Thor, it's not what you . . ."

She stopped herself. Why did she have to explain herself to him? She hadn't done anything wrong, had she? But a voice inside her was shouting, *He's not going to forget this! Now you've ruined everything!*

Ruined what, though? she asked herself. *What is there to ruin?* She pulled her hand away.

Thor was facing her, but he was completely stiff. There was no laughter in those blue eyes now.

"I misunderstood," he said. His voice was hoarse. "I thought . . .

I just wanted to come up and see if everything was okay. But clearly it is. I'll just go back down. I should have realized I was only a backup."

"No!" she practically shouted. "Don't go!"

He looked at her skeptically. "Why not?"

"Because it's not what you think."

DECEMBER 19

"Safe travels, Preben," Ingrid said, putting a hand on his arm. "Let's talk soon."

"Let's do that, Ingrid!"

She waved as he drove off. He smiled and waved back.

She watched as his car drove down the freshly plowed road. Her heart felt strange. These past two days had changed so much.

She hadn't even considered the possibility that she and Preben could reconcile. The pain and fear had been too deep, the panic that took over when he came so strong. But now, just over twenty-four hours later, they were here. The surprise of Preben's proposal had begun to thaw her negative feelings, and their collaboration in rescuing Hussein from the mountain had swept away the last barriers like a sudden spring flood.

Things with Preben were different from anyone else she'd ever been with. There was an intense power in everything he did, and from the first time he set his green eyes on her like *that*, she'd known what it meant. Preben wanted her then. There was no mistaking that. And Preben usually got what he wanted. But now . . . did he still want her? And if so—what did *she* want?

At best, being with Preben was an adventure. He and Ingrid were like two force fields; they magnified each other's strong sides, and she often felt almost unbeatable with him. They'd made such an incredible team! Both their achievements and their relationship were thoroughly covered by the press. There was a kind of glow around them, and expedition participants and sponsors alike had lined up to be part of their team.

But they also had the same weaknesses; they were stubborn and willful, and neither of them was a particularly good listener—either to other people's opinions or to their own feelings. Both were practical and natural leaders. This made it difficult when they found themselves in a stressful situation and both believed they were in the right. When they argued, there were wild storms with lightning and thunder followed by long, frosty periods of cold. To be seen by Preben was to be warmed by the sun, but when he chose to ignore you, you were left in the shadows. And it was *very* cold there.

You could say they had their ups and downs—both literally and figuratively. Ha . . . she grimaced at her own pun. But how could she now be so sure it was *totally* over? If Preben wanted them to try again, would she be able to resist his power?

SHE DIDN'T HAVE THE CHANCE to call Vegard until late in the afternoon. She told him about what had happened—visits and rescues and drama on all fronts—interrupted only by her friend's outburst.

"I can't believe you climbed again! I knew it, Ingrid! I knew you could do it."

She didn't know what to say. It was as if it were only now that she realized what a big deal this was. She'd defied the white dragon. When it was really necessary, she did what had to be done.

But she didn't have much time to get lost in her own thoughts; Vegard kept talking enthusiastically.

"And it's *crazy* that Preben Wexelsen showed up at your door just like that! It's like a soap opera!" he laughed. "But what about Thor?"

"Thor?"

"Yeah, how did he react to Preben being there?"

"Hmm . . ." What was she supposed to say to that? "Well, he wasn't thrilled."

"No, I can believe that!" Vegard chuckled.

Fortunately, she'd managed to stop Thor from leaving right away yesterday. His anger had subsided a little when she told him about the drama with Hussein, but he still said he'd only come to see whether everything was okay and that he was going back down to the village. So on a personal level, things were still unresolved. What were his thoughts on the situation now? She still cringed at the thought of him coming in to find her holding Preben's hand, and now she didn't quite know how they should pick up the conversation.

She tried to chuckle, too, but the laugh seemed to get stuck in her throat.

"I leave the hotel for a few days and you manage to get yourself into a love triangle and a dramatic rescue," Vegard said. "It's nuts!"

"Love triangle? No, Preben and I ended things a long time ago. And Thor . . ."

"Yes, Thor! He's totally infatuated with you. And you like him, too. You just can't see it because you already friend-zoned him."

Well, if only you knew that I had just kissed Thor when Preben got here the other day, she thought—because she'd omitted that particular detail in her conversation with Vegard. She got the feeling that he had a hunch about it anyway.

"I'm still pretty shaky after what happened with Hussein," she said. "And relieved. And happy. And totally confused."

"Good thing the Owl and I are coming up tomorrow, then. You clearly need someone to look after you!"

Now it was Ingrid's turn to laugh. "And what are you and David going to do, then? Chaperone me? Or belay me in the mountains?"

Vegard chuckled, but then he grew serious. "Ingrid, you know I'm more than happy to help and support you however I can. You were a mess after the accident. I'm not going to let you get down like that ever again."

"I won't let myself, Vegard. I promise to tell you if I need help."

"Good!"

"When do you think you'll get here, by the way?"

"I think around seven," Vegard said. "Or, I guess it depends on when David's done at work. Maybe eight is more realistic."

She made a mental note that they wouldn't be there until nine at the earliest.

"But hey," Vegard said. "You mentioned that Thor brought over some old newspapers. Did you find anything out?"

"Yeah, it's all really strange," Ingrid said.

She gave Vegard as brief a summary as she could, both of what they'd read and what the old editor had told Thor.

"The sister of the village bigshot! Gone without a trace! It's just as I said—it should be a podcast," Vegard said. "Or a TV series. This is a real mystery!"

"Yeah, it really is," Ingrid said. "But there's more."

"Even more?" Vegard asked.

"Yeah, Thor also found out that Hallgrim Dalen has an economic interest in having the hotel do poorly. But the main point is that I'm becoming more and more certain that there's a connection between the old case and all the things that have been happening around here."

"What are you thinking of?"

"Well, first and foremost, the sudden cancellations," Ingrid explained, "which Hallgrim and the gang seem to be behind. But Nana Borghild says it's not just about the money, that there's history between her and Hallgrim that . . . okay, it's pretty complicated. It seems like he blames her for his sister's disappearance. I don't really understand how this is all connected. We'll have to talk about it more when you're here."

Vegard grunted triumphantly. "You see? True crime! Maybe the murderer from back in the day is threatening to strike again?"

"But we don't even know whether the girl was murdered," Ingrid objected.

Then she fell silent. Murder, suicide, accident, a disappearance with a completely different explanation—what did she really know about any of it? Only what was in the newspapers and what Nana Borghild had told her—and that wasn't much.

She sighed. "Right now, I don't really know what to make of anything, what with all the drama that's been going on here the past few days."

"Hope you're doing okay," Vegard said before they hung up. "See you tomorrow!"

Ingrid sat there for a while, thinking. Was she okay? She didn't know. She was exhausted, overwhelmed, happy, terrified, totally confused—and quite possibly falling in love.

Freya Wilkins was almost unrecognizable. The normally adventurous and colorful woman seemed to have faded somehow. She was reclining on the sofa in a gray sweater with a gray wool blanket draped over her legs. Her eyes were half open, and she didn't seem to even be registering the spectacular view of the mountains. Her hair was unkempt and revealed some gray roots at the base of her otherwise blond locks. A teacup with the bag still in it was on the table in front of her. The tea was so dark that it looked as though it had been steeping for hours.

"Hi, Freya, how are you feeling?" Ingrid asked. "I brought some samples from Maja's Christmas baking."

She set the tray on the coffee table, even though she got the feeling the treats wouldn't be touched. She sat down in the chair at the end of the table. Dr. Wilkins had opened the door when Ingrid knocked and was now sitting at the small desk facing the wall. He swiveled his chair around so that his back was to the desk and the many papers strewn across it. His doctor's bag was open next to the sofa.

"Thank you," Freya said, smiling weakly. She looked at Ingrid and the baked goods, but then her eyes fell again, as if the effort of uttering those two words had been too much for her. Was this really the same person who'd burst into the hotel with the energy of a tornado only a few days ago?

"Maja sends her best and says she hopes you'll be ready to join her in the kitchen again soon," Ingrid said. "There are all kinds of specialties being prepared now just before Christmas—and there's home-brewed beer that needs tasting," she said with a smile at Dr. Wilkins. "It's an important tradition!"

The invitation from Maja was a lie, of course. The chef had more than enough on her plate without Freya Wilkins getting in the way. She was at her wit's end with the American's constant fussing and "helping." But Ingrid hoped that the prospect of some traditional Norwegian activities might rekindle Freya's joie de vivre.

It didn't seem to help at all, though. Ingrid looked at the sofa again, where Freya now had her eyes fully closed. Ingrid wasn't sure whether Freya was asleep. Was she drugged or just exhausted? If so, from what?

"Freya is very tired," Dr. Wilkins said. He got up from his chair and sat down next to Ingrid. "The journey from the US, all the organizing, and the high level of activity here in Norway has probably been a bit too much for her. Not good for her blood pressure and quite exhausting, mentally as well."

He lowered his voice, almost to a whisper. "You know, she's had such high expectations for this trip. She spent months—well, years, actually—planning it. Getting help from all her contacts in Daughters of Norway, searching online day after day for tickets and local information. And she's been so excited about what we might find here in terms of her roots, maybe even some relatives. But then she found more than she expected . . ."

"More? What do you mean?"

Dr. Wilkins looked at his wife. "I'm sure she'll be able to tell us more herself when she gets her strength back."

Ingrid looked at Freya, who was still lying there with her eyes closed. "Well, I really hope she gets better soon," Ingrid said. "And I trust you'll let us know if there's anything the hotel can help with. Food or transportation or picking up medication from the pharmacy, anything you need."

John Wilkins nodded. "Thank you," he said. "You're already doing more than anyone could ask for. But I promise I'll let you know."

Just as Ingrid started getting up from her chair, Freya sat up abruptly and fixed her intense gray stare on her. Her eyes were wide open. She leaned forward and grabbed Ingrid's upper arm surprisingly firmly.

"It's that picture," Freya said. "I have to look at it again. The picture of my mother."

February 1962

Hallgrim's voice sounded like a thunderclap. "Of course you're going to marry Jarand Smedplass!" He leaned forward, shaking his finger in Charlotte's face in time with his words. "You! Will! Be! Happy! That! Someone! Even! Wants! You! At! All!"

"But Hallgrim! I can't. Even though he's your friend. He's too old for me."

"Twenty-nine isn't old."

"It's old when I'm only nineteen! And he's been married before."

"It's not Jarand's fault that his old lady took off."

"Isn't it?" Charlotte stared at her brother in disbelief.

"So it had nothing to do with the fact that he has a drinking problem and beat her?"

Hallgrim snorted. "You shouldn't listen to rumors."

"They're not rumors! I know it's true. She moved in with her sister and got a divorce."

"Nonsense. Gossip."

Charlotte started to cry. "I'm afraid of him!"

Hallgrim's face was now red with rage. "You ungrateful little . . ."

He took a step forward, and for a moment, she thought he was going to hit her. Now she was crying so hard she almost couldn't breathe. But he stopped abruptly, stepped back, and took a deep breath.

He turned away for a moment and looked back at her, his gaze piercing. "Charlotte. It has to be like this. Jarand has agreed. Who else will marry you now—what with the mess you've gotten yourself into?"

DECEMBER 20

Borghild Berg was closing the large book she had in her lap when the library door opened and Ingrid came in.

"Good morning, Ingrid!"

"Good morning, Nana!"

Ingrid looked determined as she crossed the room with long strides. She seemed a little tense, and it was no wonder, Borghild thought. She was impressed that her granddaughter was even on her feet at all after the dramatic events of the past few days. It was also the Friday before Christmas.

Ingrid sat down next to her grandmother and put a hand on her arm.

"Nana, I went to see Freya Wilkins yesterday. She's almost unrecognizable. It seems like she's in shock. She was so quiet . . . It was totally unlike her. But she said something that made me curious. She mentioned a picture of her mother. She said she had to see it again. What did she mean by that? Why does she think we have a picture of her mother here?"

Nana Borghild was silent for a while.

"I'm going to tell you about that picture," she said at last. "But there's so much to tell, and I need time to convey it properly. It's time for you to understand how everything is connected. But I think we'll have to do it later. There are so many interruptions here, and new guests will be arriving soon. I'll be able to explain it better when we're not so busy."

This statement didn't make Ingrid any less curious, but Nana Borghild was probably right. This was neither the time nor place. The guests would soon be at the door, and the mysteries of the past would have to be set aside for the time being. The future of the hotel depended on the guests who were expected soon, no matter what stories were hidden behind old paintings and no matter what nefarious plans Hallgrim Dalen and his cronies might have. Ingrid, Borghild, and the staff needed to concentrate on what they could do *now*.

For this pre-Christmas weekend, Ingrid had made arrangements with Dalen Transport for a bus from the train station for the guests who weren't driving their own cars, and one family was expected on the train arriving in Dalen at 10:04 a.m. When the minibus pulled up in front of the hotel at half past ten, the main door was open, the banister was decorated with pine branches, and the fireplace was crackling merrily in the library.

Maja had lunch preparations well underway, Alfred was ready to carry in the luggage, and Ingrid felt a sense of calmness. This was what she'd been preparing for. It was like before, when she was climbing; everything was a jumble of nerves, anxiety, fear, preparations, and noise in her head—until she was standing there at the base of the rock face she was about to climb, took the first step, and was *up on the wall*. Then her mind went quiet, and she concentrated on the holds, the way up, what she'd been practicing, what she knew she had to do.

And what she had to do now was welcome the guests and make sure they found their rooms, were fed, and felt well taken care of. She waited for them at the reception desk, inhaled the scent of the pine needles from the decorations and the gingerbread in the baskets on the tables, and put on her warmest smile. "Welcome to Glitter Peak Lodge!"

Suddenly, Nana Borghild was standing next to her.

Ingrid almost jumped; she'd been so lost in her thoughts that she hadn't even noticed her grandmother had come out.

"This isn't half bad, is it?" Borghild asked. "Being able to welcome people like this?"

Ingrid pulled her grandmother close.

"Nope, not bad at all," she said.

A couple of Japanese tourists who'd been disappointed when they found out there were not, in fact, any polar bears on mainland Norway had nevertheless gotten some consolation when they came to the library and found Barry, with whom they could take pictures. He was almost as good as a polar bear. And Ingrid told them they *might* even be lucky enough to see reindeer when they were here. Surely that must be just as exciting? "And the northern lights?" they asked. Yes, they shouldn't discount the possibility of seeing those, either. She couldn't guarantee anything, but sometimes they did sparkle beautifully over the mountains up here. She showed them an app where you could check the probability of seeing the northern lights wherever you were. The tourists were busy with that until the food was served.

They'd never had so many guests for lunch before. In addition to the new arrivals, the "veteran" guests, Pia P and Mr. and Mrs. Wilkins, were sitting at a separate table. Freya seemed to have recovered at least somewhat. Her blond locks were brushed and sprayed into place, and she was wearing a colorful knitted sweater. She was taking careful bites from a plate of mountain trout with cucumber salad.

After the regular service was over, Nana Borghild and Ingrid ate in the kitchen with Hussein and the rest of the staff. Hussein had insisted on going to school even though he was exhausted from everything he'd been through and had splints on both his wrist and ankle. After all, it was the last day of school before Christmas. He'd come home with a colorful card from his classmates—GET WELL HUSSEIN! YOU'RE AWESOME— and a bag full of Christmas decorations that he'd made himself. Ingrid promised he'd get his own small Christmas tree that he and Aisha could hang them on. She made a mental note to ask Alfred to get one tomorrow, when he'd be going out to get the big Christmas tree with the guests anyway.

The afternoon passed quickly. She glanced at the clock—it was already past four. She hadn't heard from Vegard yet. He said he was going to text when he and David left Oslo, but she knew that it would take some time. It would probably be pretty late when they finally got here, but there wasn't anything she could do about that. They'd get here when they got here. She just hoped nothing went wrong at the last minute. She *had* to have her best friend here with her this weekend.

❄

It was half past nine. The dinner service was over, and many of the guests had made their way to the bar, while the oldest and youngest had retired to their rooms. The guests had praised the food, and Sunny and the kitchen assistants had been running in and out all evening refilling plates, which were empty again before they knew it.

Maja was red in the face from exertion, but now the rush was over, and she and Ingrid were the only ones left in the kitchen. Ingrid decided to use the occasion to ask some more questions about the disappearance. There were some things she still couldn't quite wrap her head around.

The chef turned toward her and wiped her hands on her apron. "Hallgrim Dalen's sister? That was before my time."

"Can you tell me whatever you do know?" Ingrid asked. "It seems like . . . people would rather not talk about it."

What she actually meant was that her *grandmother* didn't want to talk about Charlotte Dalen.

The chef glanced at the door and moved a pot off the stove before pulling out a chair and sitting down. "It's probably something that's difficult for people to talk about," she said. "Maybe those who knew her thought it was better to forget about the whole thing. It must have been terrible for everyone when she disappeared. She was very young, after all, only a teenager."

"But have you heard anything about what might have happened? What do people in the village think?"

"No one knows anything for sure," Maja said. "But there have been a lot of rumors about the case. Some claim she ran off, that she had a boyfriend her family refused to let her be with. Others believe she was the victim of some kind of crime. But most people seem to think she killed herself—jumped into the waterfall. And that wasn't something you talked about in those days."

"But why would she do that?" Ingrid asked.

"There were rumors that she was pregnant," Maja said. "And that the man she was marrying wasn't the father."

The kitchen assistants had cleared out the dining room and gotten the rest of the night off, and Vegard and David's food was ready to be reheated whenever they arrived—since there was still no sign of them.

"I'll just head up to my room for now," Pia P said. Ingrid thought she looked a bit downcast; she'd probably also been looking forward to her friends' arrival. Maybe she'd even dressed up a bit more. Ingrid had admired Pia's white wool dress and noticed that she'd done her hair extra nicely tonight. Now, almost the whole evening had passed. Pia walked up the stairs quite heavily, holding onto the railing.

Ingrid sent Vegard a text and got a response that they were "*pretty close! I think!*"

It was half past ten before David's car pulled up outside the hotel. Ingrid had kept herself busy at the reception desk while she waited. She heard the music from the car before it was abruptly turned off, and Ingrid opened the main doors to welcome the guests. The torches were still lit along the staircase, creating a luminous path in the December darkness.

David opened the door, stepped out of the car, lifted a hand in greeting, and went to the back to open the trunk. Vegard jumped out of the passenger side and sprang up the stairs to give Ingrid a hug. He was finally back! She felt relief flood through her.

"You'll be staying in the Peer Gynt Suite!" she said as she hugged David. She handed him a key card. "Do you need any help with the bags?"

"No, thanks, it's fine," Vegard said. "We'll just go upstairs and drop off our stuff, and I'll tell Pia we're here."

Okay, so far, so good, Ingrid thought when she'd finally landed in her own bed. If this crucial weekend were a mountain trip, they'd be just starting the ascent.

DECEMBER 21

"Evening red and morning gray, a good sign for a fair day," Alfred said, taking a sip of coffee.

"Huh?" Ingrid asked as she came through the kitchen door. She was tired and had a pounding headache.

"That's what they say," the caretaker said. "A gray morning means it'll be nice later in the day. Right, Maja?"

"That's right," the chef said, glancing out the kitchen window. "It's going to be sunny later today, and it's started getting warmer. That's the *kakelinne* for you."

"The what now?" Sunny asked.

"The kakelinne," Maja replied. "When it gets warmer in December and you can get more baking done."

"As long as it doesn't get *too* warm," Sunny said as she was loading the dishwasher. "We can't have slush when we're picking up the Christmas tree with a horse and sleigh! It has to be really Insta-friendly."

"Really what?" Alfred asked.

"Nothing. Nice pictures," Sunny replied. She'd given up on involving the caretaker in conversations about the hotel's social media strategy, not to mention future-oriented topics in general. But she *did* trust him to pick out a nice Christmas tree.

"Can't do much about the warm weather," Maja said. "It comes every year during the Christmas baking."

"And it's Saint Thomas's day today," Alfred grumbled. "It'll be good to take a sip of that Christmas beer."

"As if you haven't tasted it already," Maja said with a scoff.

Alfred muttered something in response that they couldn't make out.

"Hi! You guys aren't grumpy, are you?" Hussein said. He was just coming into the kitchen. "If someone is grumpy, all they have to do is eat some gingerbread dough, and they'll feel much better."

He opened the refrigerator door with his bandaged hand and reached the other toward a bowl covered in plastic wrap.

"No, Hussein!" Maja said sternly. "You can't eat any more dough! We're baking it later today, and then you can decorate the gingerbread house with the other kids once we've put it together."

"Hussein, you know what David says?" Sunny asked when she saw that Hussein was about to protest. "'Eggs should not fight stones.' It's a saying from China, where he's from."

"Am I the egg, then?" Hussein countered.

Sunny winked at him.

Two families from Oslo arrived before lunch. Ingrid had just checked them in and given them the key cards to the family apartments when Pia, David, and Vegard came down to eat. David had been working in the library all morning, while Pia and Vegard hadn't made an appearance until now. Ingrid decided to eat with them.

Fresh trout and cucumber salad and a big glass of ice water kicked her headache to the curb, and the sun had come out, just as Alfred predicted. It shone over trees and mountain peaks in a clear blue sky. It was still a couple of degrees below freezing, even though the temperature was rising fast, so the snow was dry. That meant great sledding conditions. To add to the atmosphere, the hotel had borrowed horses and a sleigh to transport the Christmas tree so that the most adventurous guests could ride the sleigh back. Sunny and the new kitchen assistant would serve mulled wine and gingerbread along the way.

Pia, David, and Vegard were joining the expedition, along with several of the newly arrived guests. There weren't any spruce trees up here in the mountains, so they would drive down to Dalen to chop down the beautiful specimen Alfred had found in the fall, which would have the honor of being this year's Christmas tree at Glitter Peak. Tomorrow, the guests would help decorate the tree—another Insta-friendly opportunity, Sunny had noted—and it would be the centerpiece of the dining room this Christmas.

Just as the minibuses were about to leave, the front door opened, and a voice called out, "Wait for us!" Out came Freya Wilkins, clad in a wool cape, lace-up boots, and a bearskin hat, speeding across the parking lot. John Wilkins followed her, immaculately dressed in his navy blue winter coat. *Of course*, Ingrid thought. A "Daughter of Norway" couldn't possibly miss out on the felling of the Christmas tree. Perhaps the "picture of my mother" had just been a moment of confusion? Since Freya had clearly improved and now looked more like the robust creature who'd arrived at the hotel, Ingrid might be able to ask about that. But she could do so later.

Ingrid heard the sound of sleigh bells and opened the front door just as the sleigh pulled up outside the hotel, the minibus following close behind. The Christmas tree was just as beautiful as Alfred had promised. With the help of the farmer who owned the forest, he'd cut it down with great pomp and circumstance—carefully documented by Sunny—while the hotel guests were served mulled wine and gingerbread and took pictures. Now, it would be stored in the basement to acclimatize before being decorated tomorrow.

Voices and laughter could be heard inside the dining room, and Ingrid went in to see what was happening. She stood inside the door and watched Hussein, who'd managed to charm the three teens visiting from Oslo into decorating the gingerbread house with him. And it wasn't just any gingerbread house! It was more like a castle, with a tower and spire that were now being decorated with icing and M&Ms, gummy Santas and sprinkles. And what was that behind the castle—a kind of point? A spire? A mountain?

Ingrid remembered what Aisha had said about the gingerbread houses at the family's hotel in Aqaba. Perhaps Hussein had been involved in the decorating there, too? But he'd been pretty young at the time. She wasn't sure how much he actually remembered from his home country—or countries. Hussein had been born in Syria and taken to Jordan, then to Nepal, and now to Norway. Where was *home* to him, really? And how clear was the image he had of his father? Apart from Skype calls, Hussein hadn't seen his father in more than two years.

She heard footsteps behind her, and suddenly Aisha was standing next to her. Aisha watched her son, who was chatting away with the older children.

"It's nice to see him like this, Ingrid," she said. "I was so scared for him. But right now at least, he seems to be doing well."

Ingrid nodded. "He does," she said.

Hussein drizzled a thick blob of icing over the top of the gingerbread mountain. It flowed slowly down the mountainside. Then he picked up a small gingerbread man and placed it at the very top.

The sun was already setting behind the ridge when Thor Seter pulled into the parking lot outside the hotel. The sun had been shining all day, and the air had grown noticeably warmer and more humid.

Maja had insisted that her nephew join the Christmas beer tasting at the bar this afternoon and scoffed when Thor started going on about the sheep. "I think your father should be able to take care of that," she said firmly, then called her big brother to encourage him to be a farmer again for a day or two. "That Thorbjørn has gotten too used to Thor doing everything on the farm," she said to Alfred and Ingrid. "It's good for him to get out of that old armchair of his once in a while."

And Ingrid was happy that Thor came. Vegard had eagerly nudged her in the side and raised his eyebrows when he heard that Thor was going to spend the evening at the hotel and even stay the night.

"Wonderful," he said. "It's about time!"

"He's not spending the night with *me*, Vegard," Ingrid explained, rolling her eyes. "He'll have his own room."

But Vegard wasn't deterred. "We'll see about that," he said with a coy smirk and more nudging and eyebrow-raising. God, he could be so childish! But it could also be the case that . . . No, she shook off the thought.

Anyway, it was a bit awkward to greet Thor when they met in the foyer.

It's nice to see you again, she wanted to say. *Sorry about basically throwing you out the door when Preben came. And about acting so strangely. It's just been a bit much for me. I think about you all the time. I want to kiss you again.*

But instead she said, "How were the roads? Has it started getting slippery?"

"Yeah, in some places, because it's gotten so much warmer," Thor replied, setting a small backpack on the floor. "But it wasn't too much of an issue. And it'll freeze again soon. How's Hussein? And how are you?"

THE TRADITIONAL CHRISTMAS BEER TASTING was sacred at Glitter Peak. Beer glasses in various sizes had been set up at the hotel bar. When Ingrid and Thor peeked in, several of the guests were already in place, many of them red in the face from the Christmas tree event and other activities. Two new arrivals from Oslo walked in from the library, eagerly discussing cross-country skiing trails. They sat down at one of the tables by the bar.

Ingrid took Thor to a table where she thought they could sit with Nana Borghild and Maja. She'd reserved a table nearby for Vegard, David, and Pia, but it was currently empty.

"I hope Pia comes down, too, and that they don't just stay up in David and Vegard's room," she said to Thor. "Then there's not much point in treating people to a hotel stay."

Thor turned to her. "Oh, really? So people have to make themselves useful here if they want to visit?"

There was a twinkle in his blue eyes, and he couldn't quite manage to hide a smile. Ingrid smiled back. "Yes, but all *you* have to do is approve the Christmas beer and talk to your aunt a little, and your mission is accomplished."

"And with you too, I hope. Talk, I mean. Because I guess we have some stuff to talk about, don't we?"

"I do want to talk," she said. It felt as though her stomach was doing somersaults. "But not necessarily with everyone else around. Let's find some time afterward."

Or some other time entirely, she thought. Did they *have* to talk about things? Couldn't they just keep pretending nothing had happened?

THE BAR HAD STARTED TO fill up, and in came Nana Borghild with Maja. Ingrid placed the older ladies in the best seats next to the wall. She and Thor could sit on the wooden chairs on the other side of the table.

The bartender, Tom, was busy setting things up, but the evening's master of ceremonies would be the otherwise reserved Alfred. Maja was in charge of the brewing at the hotel, but Alfred was the best drinker, so they'd agreed he was the right man for the job. Tom would assist, along with Sunny, who would also simultaneously interpret into English. Six different types of beer were to be tasted before the beer could be officially "approved." Platters of cured ham, reindeer sausage, and home-baked flatbread were on the tables, as well as jugs of water and lots of small glasses.

The Wilkinses came in and found a seat farther away. Ingrid felt restless and did a round through the bar, where the kitchen assistants were now carrying in large jugs of different types of beer. She spotted Vegard and David with Pia in tow. Ingrid waved and breathed a sigh of relief. She worked her way through the increasingly crowded bar to show them where to sit.

"We've taken so many nice photos today," Pia said excitedly. Her cheeks were rosy after the Christmas tree excursion—and possibly from some expertly placed blush. "And I'm really excited about the tasting event here!"

"It'll be great," Vegard assured her. "Just wait and see. Maybe there will even be a surprise or two as well."

Oh no, no more surprises, Ingrid thought. But she didn't say it out loud.

"Let's hope you approve of the beer," she said. "Otherwise it won't really be Christmas, you know."

Pia P sat down on a chair and grinned at Ingrid. "I'm not really supposed to have beer, of course, but I had to catch this!"

"I think Alfred might just have something for you, too," Ingrid said with a smile.

As if on cue, Alfred stood up by the bar and struck a small gong. He was wearing a plaid shirt and vest, and with his gray sideburns, he looked like a combination of an elf and Neil Young. Sunny and Tom were making their way around the bar with jugs of the first type of beer. Ingrid hurried back to the table where Maja, Borghild, and Thor were chatting.

"Welcome to beer tasting at Glitter Peak Lodge!" Alfred's

booming voice resounded through the room, and the conversation died down. "Traditionally, Saint Thomas's Day was the day when all the brewing and baking had to be finished. With this beer tasting, we honor this tradition."

He raised a glass of golden brew. "We're starting with a light lager that Sunny and Tom are bringing around to you now. We've also made a nonalcoholic version, which is the one in the blue jugs. Can one person at each table be in charge of pouring? Both types of beer should be straw yellow with a thick foam. The taste should be fresh, with lots of carbonation."

Sunny translated and explained for the foreign guests, and clinking and appreciative murmurs spread through the room as the glasses were filled.

"Let's have a taste! Cheers! And now you have to help us: Do you approve of the beer? Yes or no?"

A unanimous "Yes!" echoed through the room.

The cheerful atmosphere got more and more lively as the guests tasted their way through dark lager (with a strong taste of hops), English brown ale (reminiscent of toffee), and Glitter Peak's smoked beer (with the taste and smell of German smoked malt). Ingrid held back—she was at work, after all, and mostly drank water—but took a few sips of the beer and the nonalcoholic pilsner, which was new this year. To finish, Alfred offered a classic Norwegian Christmas beer. The frothy, reddish-brown drink tasted sweet and rich and smelled of fruit and caramel. She took a proper sip of this one, and for the first time in these pre-Christmas weeks, Ingrid felt a tiny glimmer of Christmas spirit. Now *this* was how Christmas should taste!

When all the beers had been approved, Alfred started to sing:

*For Norge, Kjæmpers Fødeland vi denne Skaal vil
tømme*

At first, he was the only one singing Norway's traditional toast, while the audience scraped their chairs a little awkwardly and looked down at the lyric sheets, which they only now spotted on the tables in front of them. But then, a clear, young voice sounded through the room and joined in.

Ingrid turned and was surprised to see it was Sunny. She walked up to the bar as she sang, managing to get several members of the audience to join in as well. Some of the older Norwegians had heard the song before and knew the tune. Freya Wilkins was among them, and she looked moved as she lifted her small glass of beer and sang:

*Endnu en Skaal for Dig mit Fjeld
For Klipper, Snee og Bakker!*

When the applause had died down, Ingrid saw that Sunny had brought a guitar out from behind the bar and was now putting a strap over her shoulder. An expectant murmur spread throughout the room. Ingrid glanced over at Vegard, who smiled slyly and gave her a thumbs-up. So *this* was what he'd meant by a surprise!

Sunny looked out over the room. She seemed different from how she normally was—more grown-up, somehow. She brushed back her blond curls, cleared her throat, and strummed a few notes on the guitar. She didn't need a microphone or amplifier here; the silence was palpable, and her clear voice carried through the room as she sang the first lines of the beautiful, mournful "A

Kind of Christmas Card." She then transitioned straight into a traditional Christmas song that encouraged a sing-along for the chorus.

The applause lasted for a long time when Sunny was finished, and the pleasant atmosphere was amplified by both the singing and the drinking. Vegard grinned at Ingrid and waved at her from across the room. He looked as though he was taking credit for the success—had he become Sunny's manager now, too?

Ingrid picked up the jug of Christmas beer, refilled the glasses, and raised her own to toast Nana Borghild, then Maja, and then Thor. His blue gaze was intense, and it was hard to tear her eyes away. She felt her face getting warm. Probably red, too. *Dammit.*

Her grandmother looked at her with a small smile. What was Nana Borghild thinking?

Ingrid met Thor's gaze again. It felt so good to just be in the moment. Suddenly, finding out about all those old secrets didn't seem so daunting anymore. There were plenty of challenges, that was for sure, but such was life. Right now, it felt as though everything would be fine as long as they were here together—at least for a little while. Some tense muscles in her shoulders gently started to loosen. What an atmosphere, with so many good people. Maybe—just maybe—this would go well after all.

Some of the guests had started making their way out of the bar, and Ingrid followed Borghild and Maja to the foyer while Thor joined Vegard and the others. When she came back a few minutes later, the three men were engaged in lively conversation.

Ingrid sat down at the empty chair at the men's table. "Hi, guys. This went so well! But where did Pia get off to?"

"She went up to her room," Vegard said. "She's tired, but everything's fine."

"That's good. Do you want to keep going with the Christmas beer?"

They were more than happy to do that. Ingrid made sure they had a new jug at the table, and she herself had a glass of ice water. The atmosphere was nice and relaxed, and the conversation flowed easily.

"Thor, you have to show Ingrid the pictures," David said. He turned to Ingrid. "We've had time to talk about both sheep and photography while you were busy."

"Yes, it turns out they have that interest in common," Vegard said. "Photography, I mean. Not sheep."

Thor leaned toward his backpack on the floor and pulled out a folder. "I brought something I wanted to show you." He pushed a couple of glasses aside and placed the folder in front of her. She opened it and flipped through the pictures he'd selected.

"Wow! These are really good," she exclaimed.

And she meant it. Sheep, mountains, old buildings, cars—the motifs from the village were familiar, but Thor had a keen eye for capturing the beauty in everyday situations.

"Ingrid, you should consider offering photography courses or workshops for the guests here during the summer," David suggested.

Ingrid nodded. "Yeah, that's a good idea."

"It's a *great* idea!" Vegard emphasized.

Ingrid smiled and sank back in her chair.

It was rare to spend time with these three friends all together. She just hoped that Vegard wouldn't make any embarrassing hints about her and Thor. Or—even worse—about Preben. How things would be between them in the future was something they had to figure out on their own.

❄

"Ingrid?" Maja's hand on her shoulder pulled Ingrid out of her thoughts. She would have loved to sit here with the guys all evening, but now the chef needed to discuss something with her.

Ingrid could smell the delicious aromas even before the kitchen door was open. The staff had dinner preparations well underway. Tonight, they would be serving a big, traditional Christmas buffet: ribs with both red cabbage and sauerkraut, Christmas sausage and medisterkaker. Pinnekjøtt and mashed turnips, lutefisk with bacon, and almond potatoes. Rice pudding and red sauce. Kransekake. They were willing to do Christmas Eve a bit early so that the visitors could taste as much of the traditional food as possible. To satisfy guests who had what Maja called, with a snort, "newfangled food preferences," they also had nut roast and a number of different vegetables and salads.

Ingrid stopped Sunny on her way to the dishwasher, her hands full of plates.

"Sunny, thank you for a fantastic performance! What a nice surprise."

Sunny beamed. "Thanks!" She set down a tray of glasses and pulled her phone out of her pocket. "Look! Pia P shared this on Instagram. Have you ever seen so many likes and comments?!"

"That's amazing!" Ingrid said.

"I can't believe it, really," Sunny said. "So many people have seen me. And the hotel, too!" she added quickly. "I know it's Pia and not me they're following, but still."

"Yeah, that's how it works, you know," Ingrid said. "We have to be on the same team as the right people. And I'm happy I have you to help me with that."

When the staff gathered around the long table in the kitchen after dinner was over, the consensus was that this very important evening had surpassed all expectations.

"All of the guests seem really happy tonight, too," Nana Borghild said. "I guess the party will continue for some, but I'm going to head off to bed myself."

She smiled. "Good night, dear Ingrid," she said. "Now you should go and find your friends. Especially one of them."

Party in the suite, said the text from Vegard. *We're waiting for you!*

Okay, she *could* treat herself to a glass or two with the others. She could rest another time. Well, if the hotel went bankrupt, she could rest *all* the time. *Be right there*, she replied.

She took a quick glance at herself in the mirror, changed her shirt, put on some lip gloss, and headed for the Peer Gynt Suite. She hadn't gone far when she stopped abruptly, ran down two floors to the wine cabinet by the bar, pulled out a bottle of champagne, and took a tray with five glasses with her. She grabbed a bottle of Borghild's raspberry soda for Pia as well before continuing as steadily as she could up the stairs, stopping outside the door to the suite.

She heard music coming from inside before she knocked, and it grew louder when Vegard opened the door with a big smile. She didn't recognize the song, but then again, she wasn't particularly up-to-date when it came to the latest music.

"Hi, Ingrid!" Vegard called out, hugging her as if it hadn't been less than an hour since they'd last seen each other.

"Hi, Vegard! Why don't you help me with this tray before I drop it, you goof," she laughed, struggling to keep her balance.

"Ooh, champagne!" Vegard shouted in response.

He took the tray and placed it on the low coffee table by the sofa. Thor had stood up halfway when he spotted the potential crisis with the champagne, but then he sat back down next to David, who greeted Ingrid with a warm smile.

Pia was sitting in an armchair, dressed in another gorgeous wool dress with her long legs in a pair of high-heeled shoes. How was it possible to look so elegant when she was so pregnant? She was probably tired, too. *She's really making an effort*, Ingrid thought.

Ingrid sat down in the last available chair at the coffee table. She filled a glass with raspberry soda and handed it to Pia. Then she opened the champagne.

"Lovely!" Vegard sighed happily, grabbing the first glass as soon as Ingrid had filled it. He tilted his head back, and his glass was already empty before Ingrid had even had time to fill glasses for Thor, David, and herself. He held the glass up for a refill and called out, "Cheers to Glitter Peak!"

"Cheers!" the others echoed. Ingrid inhaled the aroma from her own glass; it was reminiscent of coffee and toast. The taste was fresh and fruity. Yes, Vegard was right—this *was* lovely. And Glitter Peak was worth toasting. Maybe she should run down and get another bottle right away.

IT WAS ALMOST ONE IN the morning when Pia got up from the chair and had to support herself on the backrest. "Whoa, I think I stood up a little too quickly," she said. "I almost blacked out."

"Be careful," Ingrid said. "We don't want any more people fainting around here. Come on, I'll take you back to your room." She put an arm around Pia, who leaned her head against her shoulder.

"I'll come with you," Thor said. "It's getting pretty late anyway."

Ingrid looked at the empty bottles and collection of glasses and snack bowls on the coffee table. "Maybe I should just clean this up first."

"Nope, you're not working right now," David protested. He was sitting on the sofa with Vegard's head resting in his lap. "We'll clean up in the morning!"

"Nighty-night!" Vegard said with a wink, waving goodbye.

"IT'S LATER THAN I THOUGHT. I really should have been in bed a long time ago," Ingrid said once Pia had been safely escorted to her room and she and Thor were walking through the corridors. "But we were having such a nice time."

"Yeah, it was really nice," Thor said. "Everyone feels extra at home here when they learn more about the inner life at the hotel. We almost laughed ourselves to death when you told us about Aunt Maja and Speedy. And the dry rot that was really Cheetos!"

Ingrid laughed. There *was* a lot to laugh about when it came to the dramatic episodes that had happened here recently and the strong personalities that surrounded them at the hotel. But she hadn't talked about *everything*.

They arrived at her apartment, and she unlocked the door and stood in the doorway for a moment.

"Good night, Ingrid," Thor said.

She summoned her courage. "You don't want to come in for a sec, do you?"

"So you're not so tired after all?"

She laughed again. "No, I'm pretty tired. Dead tired, really. But like you said, we have some things we need to talk about."

Once they were inside, she filled a couple of glasses with water and put them on the table before plopping down on the sofa. Thor sat down next to her. Now they finally had the chance to talk. But instead of saying something wise and mature, to her own surprise—and Thor's—she started crying.

Thor grabbed her hand. "Ingrid, what's the matter? Don't be upset! Did I say something? Do something?"

Thor really was so sweet, with his blue eyes and caring smile.

"No, it's nothing you've said or done," she said, sniffling. "I'm just so . . . *tired*! And confused because of this thing with you. And Preben. And there's so much going on here, and the electrical systems are bad, and Nana Borghild won't really explain what the Muskox wants, and certainly not why she has a picture of Freya Wilkins's mother on her wall."

Thor fell silent. For a long time.

"Wow," he said. "I'm a little lost. But I guess there's even more to talk about than I thought. Have some water, Ingrid."

It was such a relief to tell him everything. They kicked off their shoes and sat cross-legged on the sofa with their backs against the armrests. Thor got more water and listened.

Some things he already knew, other things were new to him. She felt her head clear the more she spoke.

"There's no way around having a proper talk with both

Borghild and Freya Wilkins," Thor said. "I can come with you if you want. Maybe we can make more sense of things if we work together?"

He moved closer to her, lifted her outstretched legs so they rested across his lap, and took her hand.

"Ingrid," he said. "I wonder . . . Okay, I'm just going to ask you straight out. Is there still something going on between you and Preben Wexelsen?"

She shook her head. "No," she replied.

"Not that it's any of my business," he said. "Or, I guess in a way it is. In any case, it's important for me to know where things stand." He blushed. "Because . . . I have feelings for you, Ingrid. I guess I really like you, plain and simple." He squeezed her hand. "I've felt this way ever since you came back to Glitter Peak. I hoped there could be something between us. And after what happened here in your apartment . . . But then I found you and Preben hand in hand in the library, and I felt so stupid. I mean, how could I have thought someone like you would like someone like me? When you could have someone like *him*."

"There's nothing between me and Preben anymore," she assured Thor.

He looked at her. "Are you sure about that?"

She paused. After what happened in the Himalayas, she'd been positive that her relationship with Preben was over forever. But now that he was back in her life, was she still as certain?

She thought about their last encounter. His suggestions about the foundation and the new collaboration. The fresh start it might mean. His intense gaze, his enthusiasm. The agreement to talk again soon.

But yes, she thought. She was, in fact, quite certain.

"It's over," she said. "Done. A relationship with a man like Preben is like binary code; the answer can only be one or zero. It's all or nothing. And now it's nothing. Zero. On the romantic front, that is. But I do think we could be friends. Collaborators. That's why he was here, actually." She quickly summarized the project Preben had proposed.

Thor was still holding her hand as he took in what she was saying. "It's good if you can work together," he said. "If you can make something meaningful out of what happened. But I have to admit, I'm happy to hear you say it's over. Because I think about you all the time, Ingrid. And especially since . . . we kissed."

"I've been thinking about you a lot, too," Ingrid said. "It was really nice. But I wasn't sure what it meant. I wondered if it was just a . . . whim. I wondered if I'd ruined our friendship. Because I guess I never really believed what Vegard said about you having a crush on me."

Thor looked horrified. "Did he say that? Is it really that obvious?"

She laughed. "Yeah, I guess so. At least, Vegard has been insisting on it for a long time. But he's always teasing me, you know."

"And what about you, did you know?"

"No, I don't think you've done much to show it," she said with a smile. "Before now, I mean. It's always been so easy to talk to you, so nice to be with you. I would have liked to spend more time with you. But I've never felt like you wanted there to be something more between us."

She thought for a moment. Then she went on, "I guess I've been pretty preoccupied with everything around here lately. I've been letting everything revolve around my own problems—work and loss and heartbreak. But I could have asked you about the same things. How *you* are really doing. Whether you find it lonely on the farm. Whether you miss having someone to share life with. But it always felt like it was too big to bring up. Too personal. It's been easier to talk about . . . practical things."

Thor squeezed her hand. Again, she thought about how big and strong his hands were.

"I want to talk to you about everything, Ingrid."

"I realize that now. But I guess Vegard was right. I haven't been seeing things clearly because I put you in the friend zone."

"The friend zone." He smiled wryly before growing serious again. "So is that what I am to you? Just a friend?"

"No, Thor." She looked him straight in the eye. "You're more than just a friend. Much more."

And then he kissed her, holding one hand against the back of her head and pressing the other against the small of her back. He was so warm, his lips were warm, his breath was warm, she didn't want him to stop. A dam burst, and she kissed him back, sliding her hands under his shirt, feeling his warm skin. She wanted him! For the first time in what seemed like an infinitely long time, she wanted a man.

"Ingrid," he murmured as she continued to kiss him, stroking her hands over his back, down to the waistband of his pants. He was glowing, she was in his glow, she was somewhere else.

THEY LAY ON THE COUCH AFTERWARD. Their clothes were strewn across the floor, and she stroked his hair absentmindedly as the aftermath of what she'd just experienced rippled through her. It had been a long time since she'd felt so good.

It took a while before she started getting cold.

"Come on," Thor said.

He lifted her up from the couch and carried her into the bedroom.

Her mind was racing, but she felt so relaxed with his arms around her. It was a feeling of finally being *home*.

Snow was falling gently outside the window. Early tomorrow morning, Thor would go back down to the village and resume his life as a sheep farmer, but tonight, he would be here. She fell asleep with his warm body close to hers, a single duvet spread over them both.

DECEMBER 22

Ingrid woke with Thor's breath against her neck. When she carefully twisted her arm to look at her watch, she saw it was only a few minutes past six. It was pitch-black outside. *Everything is at its coldest now*, she thought. *Dawn is hours away. And summer—still another six months. It won't get any darker than it is now. But it's warm here under the duvet. And inside me, it's as bright as a clear summer day.*

"MAYBE I SHOULD HAVE PRETENDED my bed was slept in?" Thor murmured into her ear as they embraced in the parking lot a few hours later.

She laughed. "I can go in and mess up the sheets a bit before the maid comes."

It had snowed quite a bit overnight, but both the parking lot and the road had been plowed. The sky was blue, and the air was crisp and clear.

"It's the winter solstice today!" she said. "We're moving toward brighter times."

"Yes . . ." Thor smiled at her. "Brighter times."

Then he opened the door to his truck and got in. He squeezed her hand before closing the door and waved as he started to drive across the parking lot. She watched the car until it disappeared over the hilltop and down the road toward Dalen.

Nana Borghild was waiting in the library when Ingrid came in. Her wise eyes sparkled.

"I'm glad you've finally opened your eyes to Thor," her grandmother said. "You know, Ingrid, our eyesight may deteriorate with age, but when it comes to people, we see all the more clearly."

A few hours later, after office hours and lunch, Nana Borghild and Ingrid stood in the dining room and admired the Christmas tree in all its splendor. Alfred had put it up early that morning as planned. Now, Sunny was standing on a stepladder, draping long ribbons of Christmas tinsel with the help of Hussein and the youngest guests.

It was the fourth Sunday of Advent. Carafes of mulled wine and platters of gingerbread were spread across the table in the halls. Calming music filled the room as one of the teenagers from Oslo played the piano; he was a tall, blond boy who was generally rather quiet, but at the keys, it was as if he were communicating through music rather than words. Maybe she should have asked him to play during the Christmas tree lighting, Ingrid thought, but she would never be able to bring herself to suggest that to Nana Borghild, who'd played the piano during the ceremony for as long as Ingrid could remember.

The sky had started to darken just after lunch. The clouds were rolling in again, and a few snowflakes fell, but the silhouette of the mountains was still clear against the gray-blue sky.

Ingrid went out into the foyer, where suitcases were piling up and guests were coming and going. The front door opened with a cold gust; it was one of the visitors from Oslo coming in wearing a ski suit.

"Amazing trails." He beamed as he passed Ingrid.

Pia, David, and Vegard came down the stairs. They were also going to catch the Christmas tree lighting before they headed back to Oslo. She saw a sly glint in Vegard's eyes when he greeted her and patted her on the shoulder, but fortunately, he said nothing about Thor while the others were there. She figured he'd ask all about what had happened in due time. They all headed into the dining room, where several guests had already arrived.

It was so nice, gathering around the Christmas tree. Ingrid remembered lighting the tree down in the village in the old days. Back then, the mayor was the one who lit the lights on the tree outside what was then the town hall, while the villagers sang Christmas carols. After the municipalities were merged, the old town hall had been converted into various offices—for a while even a pizza restaurant—and the traditions had disintegrated. It would be nice if some of them could be continued at the hotel, she thought, while some new traditions were introduced at the same time.

It was a much different crowd up here anyway. She looked around the room. Her grandmother was now at the piano. Vegard, David, and Pia P had settled down nearby. The guests from Oslo were gathered in a corner, while Aisha, Hussein, and the rest of the staff formed a group on the other side of the tree.

Freya and John Wilkins were sitting at a table by themselves. They had come to every event, Ingrid realized, but Freya wasn't as talkative as she had been for the first few days. After her illness—or whatever it was—it was as if something were subduing her; she seemed more thoughtful, somehow.

Nana Borghild gave her a nod, and Ingrid wished everyone welcome. Then her grandmother struck a chord on the piano, and they were off.

"O Christmas Tree, O Christmas tree, how lovely are your branches!" Nana Borghild's voice was high and clear, with a slight vibrato. And the guests sang along to the best of their ability— some a bit shakily—so it helped when Sunny stepped in. Those who didn't know the lyrics filmed with their phones instead. Some tried their hand at both.

At the end of the last verse, Alfred would put in the plug so the lights came on as the song faded out. Ingrid made eye contact with him as he stood by the wall socket, and he showed her he had the plug in hand. He was ready.

> *Your bright green leaves with festive cheer,*
> *Give hope and strength throughout the year.*
> *O Christmas tree, O Christmas tree,*
> *We learn from all your beauty.*

Bang! There was a crack and a sparkle as the Christmas tree gave off a single burst of light. Then everything went dark.

Ingrid felt it fade away that very second—the fragile hope she'd built up inside her over the past few days. The hope that everything would be okay after all. She'd lulled herself into warmth and optimism for a few days, but now reality had come back with a bang and a shower of sparks.

Brighter times—*yeah, right!* No, there would be no end to the darkness here any time soon, that was for sure.

She was next to Alfred in just a few quick steps.

"Are you kidding me? What the hell is going on here?" she groaned.

Alfred looked dazed, standing there with the cord in hand.

"This is so unbelievably embarrassing!" Ingrid said. "This was supposed to be a nice end to the stay for the weekend guests."

Alfred looked ashamed and mumbled something about power lines, new lights, and transformers.

"I thought you checked the voltage. Surely we must have enough power for some stupid old Christmas tree lights? Just make sure the lights come back on!" she said sharply, turning on her heel.

She saw Hussein staring at her, looking alarmed, and felt a hand on her back.

"Ingrid," Nana Borghild said. "Why are you speaking to Alfred like that? It won't help anything."

Suddenly, she felt ashamed of having been so rude to the old caretaker. What had gotten into her?

Together with Sunny and the rest of the staff, she served mulled wine and lit candles in an attempt to make the disaster seem a bit cozy, and it wasn't long before Alfred had found the main switch and the lights were back on. The lights on the Christmas tree were sparkling as well, but they gave off an unreliable glow, she thought, as if they might short-circuit again at any moment.

The guests from Oslo gathered in the hallway, thanked her for the stay, and assured her they'd had a fantastic time. She could only hope that both they and everyone else would be left with an overwhelmingly positive impression of Glitter Peak—despite the fiasco at the end.

She stood with Vegard and Nana Borghild for a while.

"Honey," Vegard said. "You just wrapped up a brilliant weekend. This was a huge success!"

"Apart from the Christmas tree lights, that is."

"Sure, apart from that. But that's just a minor detail."

"It's more than a detail," she objected.

"But there are only two days until Christmas Eve," Vegard said. "You won't be able to switch out the electrical system today, in any event."

Ingrid sank down on a chair. He was right. It didn't help to fuss about this now. She was so sick of thinking about all these practical problems, but she couldn't get them out of her head.

She closed her eyes. God, she was so tired. Everything felt so thick and muddy, and it was hard to remember what had happened over the past few days. All of these abrupt turns. How could everything change so suddenly?

The optimism that had surged through her several times over the past few days was gone, replaced by stress and worry. The wave of adrenaline after she saved Hussein had subsided. And Thor . . . It had been so wonderful, but now it seemed like an eternity since she had woken up warm and happy with him, not just earlier today.

Her lower back and abdomen ached. *Oh, right . . .* She realized there was another reason for her mood swing: she was about to get her period. And she hated it.

Every time she felt the blood coming, she was transported back to the hospital in the Himalayas, feeling the new life draining out of her. She experienced everything all over again—the horror from the avalanche, the pain afterward, the grief over everything she'd lost and over everything that would never be.

Maybe she should take some painkillers. The pain was getting worse now.

"You look pale, Ingrid," her grandmother pointed out. "Are you okay?"

"I . . . I don't know, actually," Ingrid said, surprising herself.

Her standard answer to this question tended to be "yes." Things were always okay with Ingrid Berg. There wasn't any room for anything else. You couldn't go around *feeling* things all the time. Besides, was anyone really interested in how she was actually doing? What mattered was that she was able to do what she needed to do.

But now that she was here with Vegard and her grandmother beside her, Christmas just around the corner and her head full of thoughts and concerns, it was as though the truth was revealing itself of its own accord.

"Maybe I'm not okay." She felt dizzy and warm.

"Oh, Ingrid, come with me. Let's go up to your apartment."

Nana Borghild took her by the arm and led her quickly toward the stairs. By the time they reached the apartment, Ingrid's hands were shaking so much that her grandmother had to take the key from her and unlock the door.

Ingrid sank down on the sofa, and her grandmother got her a glass of water, which she drank greedily.

"Have you eaten anything today?" Nana Borghild asked. "You weren't at breakfast . . ."

Ingrid blushed at the thought of what she and Thor had been doing while the others were eating breakfast. "No, not really . . . just some yogurt. I couldn't handle anything else, and now I'm a bit nauseous."

"What's the matter, sweetie? Nauseous? You're not . . ."

Nana Borghild stopped, clearly unable to bring herself to formulate the obvious explanation for morning nausea. Ingrid felt the dam burst. Tears started pouring down her hot cheeks.

"No, I'm not pregnant, Nana. But I have been. Before."

AND THERE, ON THE COUCH, she finally told her grandmother everything. As the tears flowed, she talked about the contraception that must have failed, about Aisha's realization the very first time they met, about the surprise pregnancy test at the clinic in Nepal. About how she'd shoved it aside while she and Preben continued planning the expedition. About the life-changing news that she *should* have shared with Preben—later, at a better time, a time that never came. She talked about the nausea, about the sudden pain that hit her in the abdomen when she was rescued from the avalanche area and regained consciousness. She talked about the confusion when she was in the hospital, the blood, the fear.

She told her grandmother that she'd never shared any of this with Preben, but that she wondered whether he might have understood it anyway. That they'd never talked about it. That she hadn't been *able* to talk about it with him.

"Oh, my dear girl!" Her grandmother wiped the tears from Ingrid's face with a tissue as if she were a child and wrapped her arms around her. "You've been going through this all alone. Oh, sweetie."

Nana Borghild hugged Ingrid tightly. Ingrid leaned in, accepting the embrace. Her grandmother was small but strong. She smelled of freshly ironed cotton and subtle perfume. Ingrid felt the strength in her grandmother's arms and allowed herself to be held tightly.

"I mean, it's normal," she sniffled into her grandmother's shoulder. "I'm not exactly the first person who's ever had a miscarriage."

"No, you're not," Nana Borghild said. "But the fact that others have also gone through it doesn't make it any less painful for *you*. And the circumstances under which it happened were unusual and dramatic. You could have lost your life in that avalanche. And you lost a friend. It was a lot to take in all at once."

They sat in silence for a while, and her grandmother stroked Ingrid's hair.

"What did you think . . . when you were pregnant?" Borghild asked tentatively. "Had you and Preben talked about the future, or what did you think it would be like?"

"I don't know . . . It all happened so suddenly, both the fact that I was pregnant and the fact that I lost the child. We never got as far as discussing it. It wasn't easy to imagine us having a normal family life, me and Preben and this child. Getting married and having normal jobs and so on. What Preben and I had together was based on climbing and expeditions and action and adventure. I don't know if it would have even been possible to combine that with having children. I might have been the one who had to leave my ambitions behind."

"Or maybe you both would have had *other* ambitions for a while," Nana Borghild said. "You know, I think you should tell Preben eventually, now that you're in contact again."

"Yes, I know I should."

"You may not be ready for it yet, but the loss you suffered is actually something he should be a part of. Maybe it will make it easier for him to understand. And that child you lost wasn't just yours, but his, too. I think it will be healing for both of you if you tell him."

"Yeah, maybe you're right. But I've had to keep it to myself to survive, to deal with everything else. I felt like I lost *everything*," Ingrid said. "And every time I get my period, I think about it. It's like it's happening all over again."

Her grandmother kept stroking Ingrid's hair and looked at her with those keen eyes of hers. "It may not be any consolation right now," Borghild said, "but the fact that you bleed every month means that things are working properly down there—that you can get pregnant again. I don't mean right now, of course," she added quickly when she realized that Ingrid was about to protest. "But later, if you want to. You still have time."

Ingrid couldn't stop crying. Now that the dam had burst, there was nothing holding back the tears and grief. She rested her face against Nana Borghild's shoulder and smelled the mild and familiar scent.

After a while, she was utterly exhausted, and her grandmother's cardigan was covered with snot and tears.

"I think you should rest, Ingrid," Nana Borghild said. "Here, drink some more water, then get in bed."

Ingrid was so warm and so tired but gathered enough strength to protest.

"Get in bed? *Now?* Not possible."

"Yes, it is. I'll say goodbye to Vegard and David from you and take over for a few hours while you sleep this off. It'll be fine. I've run a hotel before, you know."

And before Ingrid knew it, she was in bed and felt like a little girl again. She felt her grandmother's soft hand stroking her head until sleep took over.

Dalen, Spring 1962

Borghild walked calmly across the cemetery. She couldn't show what was going on inside her. Everything had to seem normal.

It was such a beautiful day. Birds were chirping and her shiny black bunad shoes crunched in the dry gravel. She made sure to walk with her back straight and her head held high. She noticed every detail—how some of the trees had started turning green, how her sølje glistened in the sunlight. Storms had been forecast for the weekend. It was only March, after all, but there was no sign of rain yet. Anyone who didn't know better would think this was the perfect day for a wedding.

They'd realized what needed to be done a few days earlier, while walking up by Styggfossen. There was still snow up there, and it was rugged and dangerous terrain, but it was where Charlotte wanted to go.

"I've started showing—look!" she cried. "I can't even button up anymore!" She tugged at the lapels of her ocher woolen coat. It was so elegant, the latest fashion; she'd been so proud of it only a few months before. But now it was tight over her stomach, and all the joy was gone.

316 · CHRISTMAS AT GLITTER PEAK LODGE

Charlotte had tears in her eyes. "I can't do it, Borghild. I can't! I'd rather jump into the waterfall than marry Jarand. And have the ceremony officiated by that . . . bastard."

Borghild put a hand on her arm. "Charlie!"

But Charlie shook her hand off. "There's no point, Borghild!"

Suddenly, she tore off her coat and threw it down the scree toward the waterfall. There was a flash when Borghild imagined Charlie herself flying toward death. Her Charlie.

"No! No! I'll help you!" Borghild cried. "I'll do anything. I love you, and I'm going to help you."

And now it was done—what she'd promised—and Borghild walked toward the church. She'd told her parents she needed a couple of hours to help Charlotte get ready and that they should go ahead to the church. They were in there now. So was Christian Stugu and the rest of their group of friends. But no one needed to save a seat for Borghild, because she was the bride's maid of honor and would be sitting at the very front.

The groom, Jarand Smedplass, was also waiting in the church, with his best man, Hallgrim Dalen, standing beside him. Borghild didn't know which one of them she despised the most. Charlie's older brother, who'd once been her close friend—and who'd even suggested that they get married—or this "groom," the brutal alcoholic black-smith who'd already beaten one wife so badly that she was forced to flee from Dalen. But apparently it was still better for Hallgrim and the family that Charlie marry Jarand than for her to be an unwed mother. Because that would be far too shameful . . .

Borghild now knew for certain that Charlie would rather die than consummate the marriage Hallgrim had pressured her into. Charlie couldn't live with being married to a violent man. And cer-

tainly not with the fact that the person who was officiating the ceremony was him—Reverend Röhmer—the bastard who'd assaulted her when she went to him for advice. The pig who'd gotten her pregnant.

How would Charlie have been able to go through with this? Hall-grim might as well have pushed her off the cliff and into Styggfossen.

Borghild slowed her pace to stall for time before she had to play her part in the last act of this grotesque charade. She knew that around the same time as she walked through the church doors, the driver, Hansdalen, would be swinging his freshly polished Mercedes in front of the Dalen family's house to pick up Charlotte and drive her the short distance to the church. But he wasn't going to find anyone there. Because Charlotte was already long gone—farther away than those waiting for her would ever know.

And Borghild would never be able to look into her beloved's eyes again.

From Borghild Berg's diary:

. . . I knew I'd never look into her eyes ever again. Until now. A few weeks ago, I saw those eyes once again. Deep granite gray, with golden flecks. It took me a while to realize what it meant, but deep down, I think I've understood it ever since I first saw Freya. She does have Charlie's eyes, after all.

DECEMBER 23

It was after noon when Ingrid opened her eyes. She'd slept soundly and dreamed of snow and blood again, but her mom and dad had been there, Angelina and Marius. She rarely dreamed about them, perhaps because she'd been so young when they died and her memories of them were hazy. In the dream, they were dressed in their wedding clothes, as in the picture of them in the photo album. Her mother had a long, burgundy dress and wavy brown hair. Her father was in a tuxedo and had a mustache and gentle eyes. The snow melted wherever they walked. Flowers floated around them, roses from the bridal bouquet and heather from the heath. Everything smelled of flowers. They'd picked her up and held her close between them. She felt the warmth of their bodies and smelled the scent of roses even after she'd woken up.

She reached for her phone on the bedside table. No texts—not even from Thor. That was strange. But she couldn't think straight. She was *starving*! Not too surprising, though; she'd slept for eighteen hours and hadn't eaten since lunch the day before. She was also hot and clammy. She needed a shower.

Again, she smelled the strong floral scent that filled the room. Wait a minute. This wasn't a dream. It wasn't roses, either. Was it . . . hyacinths? Pine needles and hyacinths.

There was a large arrangement in a glass bowl on her coffee table. Someone must have snuck in while she was asleep.

A small envelope was tucked in between the pine branches. *Dalen Flowers* was printed on it. She picked it up and pulled out the small card inside.

Thanks for a lovely evening. T.

She inhaled the scent and smiled.

AFTER A SHOWER AND A large glass of water, she felt that she was finally able to move downstairs.

"I'm so happy you're still here!" she said to Vegard as they sat in the library with coffee a few minutes later. She'd thought he and David had left the night before, but now realized they'd postponed their departure because she was unwell. They were such good friends.

"Of *course* we're here, hon!" he said, putting his hand over hers.

She felt the tears welling up again. What was going on with her?

"How are you doing, Ingrid?" he asked.

"I guess I'm okay. In a way. But . . . I'm pretty exhausted. And I can't bear the thought of Nana Borghild and me celebrating Christmas with the Wilkinses. It's not exactly what I was imagining when we decided to stay open for the holidays."

Vegard looked at her, and she knew he was about to give her a pep talk, but she lifted a hand to stop him.

"I'll let them know that we have to close for Christmas. We can blame it on the damage from the water leak or something and then find something else for them at one of the hotels in Lille-hammer. Then I'll spend Christmas thinking about the meeting I'm having with XO in a few days. We should probably tell them we're interested in discussing a sale."

Vegard looked at her intently. "I don't think you really mean that," he said. "You're just tired."

She was ready to keep arguing, but he just said: "Wait a sec," and stood up. "Let me talk to the Owl."

"About what?" she asked.

But Vegard was already out the door.

Twenty minutes later, she'd eaten half a bag of caramels she found in a cupboard. Her teeth were aching from all the sugar when Vegard came back and sat down next to her on the sofa.

"We're staying," he said.

"What?"

"We're staying here for Christmas."

She gaped at him. "What? But you and David were supposed to go to your sister's!"

"We did say we'd eat at hers tomorrow, yes, on Christmas Eve. But I called her and explained the situation. It's fine. There are so many people in the family anyway, you know. It's not like the dining room will be empty if David and I aren't there. Everyone will be happy as long as the gifts from us arrive." He smiled wryly.

"But Vegard!"

"Ingrid . . . *you* are *also* my sister." He looked at her and ran a hand through his hair. "You do have room for us, right? Just say the word if it's inconvenient. I kind of just assumed."

"Yes, oh my God, of *course* we have room! Do you really want to celebrate Christmas with us? It's almost too good to be true!" She threw herself around his neck.

Vegard smiled happily. "Of course. What are brothers for? But there's one condition."

"What?"

"That you wait until after New Year's to decide whether to sell the hotel."

"Okay."

She had her own thoughts about just that, but it was still an easy promise to make. They were almost there. Almost at the finish line. Now that Vegard was staying, she'd be able to get through Christmas—and that was what it was all about now. Getting through it. She thought about the big Christmas dinner they'd be having tomorrow. Surely there wasn't much more that could go wrong before then? The hotel was still standing, if only barely. The decision to sell would have to wait for a while. She didn't need to bring it up with Nana Borghild until after New Year's.

The smell of food had started wafting from the kitchen. Today, smoked salmon fillet with a brandy sauce and turkey breast with Maja's Waldorf salad were on the menu. Ingrid's stomach was rumbling, but dinner was still a few hours away. First, coffee and cookies would be served in the library. Nana Borghild was probably already in there.

But where were the Wilkinses? They'd left a while ago and

hadn't said anything about when they were planning on coming back. She didn't like that they were out in this weather, even though Freya kept claiming that John was an exceptionally good driver.

Ingrid walked through the foyer and opened the front door. As she looked out across the parking lot, an old white pickup came into view through the snow. It swung in front of the hotel going far too fast and parked in front of a couple other cars. Her heart skipped a beat. Had Thor come back? No. The car wasn't all that unlike the ones that Thor and half the other men in the village drove, but this one had *Muskox Machinery* written on the side.

The door on the driver's side opened, and an ox of a man climbed out. From a distance, it almost looked as if his shoulders were as broad as he was tall. He slammed the car door shut and started walking toward the hotel. Ingrid stood in the doorway and watched him approach. He walked heavily, not seeming to notice the snow whipping against his face. Now he was so close that she could see the outdoor lights reflecting off the top of his balding head. He looked at Ingrid when he reached the top of the stairs, narrowing his eyes. They were sharp beneath his heavy brow.

"Is Borghild here?" he asked without looking away. "You can tell her Hallgrim Dalen has come to visit."

At that very moment, Freya and John Wilkins's Range Rover pulled into the parking lot. The couple were quick to hop out of the car and leap up the stairs while Ingrid still stood in the doorway, staring at Hallgrim "Muskox" Dalen in amazement.

Then another car came, another pickup. And this time, it really *was* Thor Seter.

❄

"What is going on?" Ingrid asked.

She looked at the small crowd that had entered the foyer, from Hallgrim Dalen to Freya and John Wilkins, over to Thor Seter, and back to Hallgrim.

"What do you want to talk to Nana Borghild about?" she asked.

Hallgrim Dalen gestured toward Freya, John, and Thor and said, "Ask them."

Ingrid looked questioningly at Freya, who calmly met her gaze. "We had to go down and get him," she said. "But when we arrived at his house, this young man was already there."

Ingrid looked at her and Thor in disbelief. "You went down to get him? Why? And what on earth were you doing there, Thor?"

Had everyone lost their minds? No, Thor met her eyes calmly and Freya didn't seem particularly crazy, standing there in her green woolen coat while the snowflakes thawed in her hair. On the contrary, she seemed more collected than she had since her arrival.

"There are things we need to talk about," Freya said. "Together."

"Let's go up to my apartment," Ingrid said. "There are guests in the library, and if you really need to talk to Nana Borghild, wouldn't it be better to do it somewhere where the guests or staff aren't present?"

Thor seemed to be thinking the same thing. He put a hand on Hallgrim's shoulder without saying anything. But Hallgrim shook him off.

"No, we'll go in and get this over with, whatever it is. Doesn't matter where," he said, stomping toward the library.

"Do you know what's going on?" Ingrid asked Thor as they hurried after him.

"I thought that enough is enough," Thor said. "I'm tired of sneaking around and trying to pick up hints and rumors, so I went over to Hallgrim's to hear what he himself had to say about XO and the whole situation. But I'd barely gotten inside the door when these two showed up. There was a bit of shouting before Hallgrim went out to his car and the others drove after him in the Range Rover. So I followed too. And just like that, everyone was up here at Glitter Peak . . ."

He paused when Hallgrim threw open the library door with a bang. Borghild had been chatting with Vegard, David, and Pia on the sofas at the other end of the room while Sunny served them coffee. But everyone fell silent when the door slammed open.

Borghild stood up and stared at Hallgrim. Between them stood Barry in his regular place by the fireplace, like an impartial and immovable linesman. The snow was melting off Hallgrim's dark gray jacket and heavy lace-up boots and pooling around him on the parquet.

"*I* shot that beast!" Hallgrim proclaimed, pointing at the bear.

The room was completely silent.

Hallgrim went on, "He ended up here because of a bet! You won that time, Borghild! But you won't be winning again."

He took a step into the library. Ingrid and Thor stayed close to him in case something happened. (What would they do, though? Call the sheriff? What would she even say? That they'd gotten an unexpected visitor—who'd actually been brought up here by some of their guests? Hardly a reason for the sheriff to drive all the way up here. And he wouldn't get here for another half an hour anyway—maybe even forty-five minutes. By then, anything could have happened.)

Freya and John Wilkins had entered the room. They moved past Ingrid and Thor and stood with their eyes fixed on the enormous old man, who dominated the room with his presence alone. His body was so massive and his head so deep between his shoulders that it almost looked as though he had no neck at all.

Sunny was still standing by the coffee table, wide-eyed. Ingrid could hear the coffee cups clinking on the serving tray Sunny was still holding.

Ingrid could have sworn that the Muskox was actually stomping his feet now. He took another step closer to Borghild. John Wilkins followed. He was obviously thinking about intervening, but then again, he was involved in all this, too. Why on earth had he and Freya dragged Hallgrim up here? Ingrid simply couldn't understand. Dr. Wilkins generally seemed to be a sensible and level-headed man. Now, he had one hand on a backrest and was watching the situation closely, ready to make a move. Hallgrim snorted and turned toward the Wilkinses.

"Now you can explain what it is that you want," he said in surprisingly good English. "Why did you drag me up here to talk to this monster—this . . . *freak*?"

That's a strange choice of words, Ingrid thought.

"I just think the two of you have to talk," Freya said.

It was as if the room were frozen, but Nana Borghild wouldn't let herself be intimidated. She straightened up to her full height—which admittedly wasn't all that impressive—and tilted her head back so she could look the old Muskox straight in the eye.

"*Monster.* As if *you* can go around calling people that, Hallgrim,"

Borghild said. Her voice was as cold as the ice in Styggfossen. "If there's anyone who's monstrous here, it's you."

He glared at her. "These people are going around the village digging around and asking questions," he said. "And then they show up at my house and say we need to talk to you about things that concern my family. Like *you* haven't already destroyed my family!"

"I have no desire to harm your family," Borghild said. "You're capable of doing that all on your own."

He didn't answer. She held his gaze.

"You have to stop all this," she continued. "It's already gone too far."

She looked at Freya, then back at Hallgrim. "All these years, I thought the best thing was to leave the past behind. But I was sadly mistaken about that. Because the past is here among us."

Hallgrim took a step toward her, but Borghild stood her ground. "While *you*, on the other hand, Hallgrim," she said. "*You* have been trying to harm *my* family. So tell me now: Why are you conspiring against us and allying with XO Hotels? Why are you spreading rumors to get people to cancel bookings? Why have you tried to sabotage things for Ingrid and the hotel?"

"I thought you'd come to your senses," Hallgrim said. "Sell the hotel. Let *competent* people take over here."

"So that you could pocket a few extra kroner in bribes, Hallgrim? Or is there something else behind it?"

Alfred came in through the side door just then and stopped abruptly when he saw who was there. Ingrid almost thought she even saw fear flash through his eyes. The Muskox fixed his intense stare on Alfred for a moment. Then Hallgrim turned back to Borghild.

"I have helpers, you know, Borghild. People in Dalen are on my side. I don't think I need to remind you who's in charge in the village."

Borghild's laughter seemed to surprise everyone in the room. "You *were* in charge of the village," she said. "But you won't be after this."

Ingrid saw the muscles tensing in Thor's jaw; his fists were clenched so tightly that his knuckles were white. She put a hand over his to signal that he needed to stay calm. First and foremost, they just had to find out what was going on here; they would deal with the consequences afterward. She'd thought they were done with the series of strange events happening here at Glitter Peak this Christmas, but now, it seemed as if they were only getting started.

Her grandmother walked over to the large bookshelf at the back of the room. She opened one of the lower cabinets and took out a stack of papers. Then she walked toward Hallgrim so that she was standing right in front of the fireplace. Her glossy white hair had a reddish tint from the light of the fire. Her face was pale, but her hand was steady as she pointed her right index finger at the pile of papers she held in her left hand. Then she raised her hand and pointed at Freya Wilkins.

"Here, Hallgrim," she said. "And here. Here, you can see what's going to take away your power."

"What the hell are you talking about?" Hallgrim growled.

"I mean it, Hallgrim—now you have to give up half your empire. The one you snatched up when Charlotte left."

It was as if all the air went out of the man. The Muskox seemed to shrink before their eyes. He was left standing there like a shaggy, old farm bull wondering why no one was afraid of him anymore, staring at Borghild with his mouth hanging open.

For a moment, it looked as if the huge body was about to collapse, but Dr. Wilkins took a few quick steps forward and steered Hallgrim toward a seat on the sofa closest to the fireplace. He sat there for a few seconds, breathing heavily, before asking, in a voice that was noticeably less authoritative than before, "When Charlotte *left*?"

Borghild stood in the center of the room, her arms crossed. She answered loud and clear: "Yes. When Charlotte left because she couldn't live with what had happened. And because she couldn't live with the new injustice you wanted to force her into."

"But Charlotte didn't leave!" Hallgrim's face was bright red again. "Charlotte didn't leave! She died! She jumped into Styggfossen because of *you*!"

"So that's what you thought, Hallgrim. That she killed herself. Because of me." Borghild took a deep breath, now looking at Hallgrim with a completely different expression. It almost looked like compassion. "That's why you've hated me so much all these years."

"Charlotte couldn't bear the shame any longer," Hallgrim said. "And you . . ." He pointed at Borghild with a trembling finger. "*You* pitted her against marriage. The marriage that could have saved her. But no, it was better for you if she went into the waterfall."

Hallgrim looked as though he was sinking into the sofa, and Borghild sat with her back straight on one of the chairs opposite him, at the very edge of the seat. The Wilkinses had settled down at the table with Vegard, Pia, and David. Ingrid and Thor were standing behind Nana Borghild while Alfred stood next to Barry, his back to the fireplace. No one touched the coffee and cookies on the tray that Sunny had finally managed to set down. Sunny herself had retreated to a chair against the wall. She was watching the drama unfold with wide eyes.

"It's true that she couldn't stand the shame," Borghild said. Her voice was strained, but she continued. "The shame and pain that *you* helped inflict on her. You and your buddies. You wanted to marry her off to that drunkard Jarand Smedplass. So that *you* wouldn't be embarrassed by your sister having a child out of wedlock, she had to marry a man she didn't love, Hallgrim! Not only that, she had to marry a man she was terrified of—a man who was violent and dangerous."

"She messed up. Got into trouble. I was only trying to help her," Hallgrim protested.

"Messed up! Help her! Jesus Christ. Sure, she got a lot of help in this village. Did she ever tell you who got her pregnant, Hallgrim? Or maybe she didn't dare?"

"She wouldn't tell me. She was probably embarrassed for having been so stupid. But I always thought it was that traveling painter."

"Then you thought wrong." Borghild sighed heavily. "Did you really not understand, Hallgrim? Then I'll tell you now. It was someone who was also trying to 'help' her. It was Röhmer."

Hallgrim flinched. "Röhmer? The parish priest?"

"Yes!" Borghild's voice was now quivering with rage. "Yes, her own parish priest and adviser whom she went to when she was in need. And who repaid her trust by assaulting her! And he was married, too! His wife probably had no idea what he was really like. Or maybe she just looked the other way. It certainly suited Röhmer that you decided to force Charlotte into a false, unhappy marriage with Jarand Smedplass. Then he could keep up his appearance as the guardian of religion and family values, and at the same time cover up his own crime."

Borghild leaned back in her chair and crossed her legs. She was no longer as tense. On the contrary, Ingrid thought she saw a glimmer of relief in her grandmother's posture. Not all that strange considering she'd been carrying this around for sixty years.

Borghild continued, her voice softer now. "Charlotte didn't kill herself, Hallgrim. She didn't jump into the waterfall. How could you have thought that? Surely her body would have been found?"

"But . . . the coat . . ."

"Hah! The coat. She threw it days before in a fit of rage and fear. Yes, for a while, I was also afraid she might hurt herself because of the situation she'd been forced into. *But she didn't.*"

Borghild straightened up again and fixed her eyes on Hallgrim. It was so quiet in the library you could have heard a newspaper clipping fall. "No, Charlie wasn't the type to kill herself, Hallgrim. Charlie was stronger than that. She left. For America."

"What?!"

Ingrid realized only afterward that this outburst came from her own mouth. She looked at the Wilkinses, then back at Borghild. What was her grandmother saying?

"She *had* to leave because she couldn't go on living here after everything that happened. You should have understood that, Hallgrim," Borghild said. "Charlie couldn't live like that."

"She couldn't live the way *you* were living!" Hallgrim spat. "I thought that was part of why she jumped into the waterfall."

"What's that, then, Hallgrim?"

"What you and she were getting up to. Ugh! It was sick! Unnatural! You fooled everyone. I came up here and tried to curry favor with you, and you were doing *that*, with my *sister* . . ."

He looked away abruptly and lowered his head. Was he crying? Was he going to be sick?

Ingrid's mind was racing. She exchanged glances with Thor, who also looked completely stunned, but who had the presence of mind to put his arm around her and guide her to a chair. She sat there with Thor standing next to her, his hand still on her shoulder.

That? The way you were? Unnatural? Did Hallgrim mean that this Charlotte . . . had been Borghild's secret lover? Ingrid took a deep breath and felt the initial dismay melting into a trembling excitement. Now, some pieces were finally starting to fall into place . . .

Hallgrim lifted his head suddenly and looked at Borghild again, fury blazing in his eyes. "You're telling me she went to America? And that you knew about it? So you've let us go around thinking she was dead all these years?"

"I'd sworn to keep her secret, Hallgrim. She wanted it to be unresolved. She thought people had no right to know what had happened. But she said would write to you when she'd made a life for herself somewhere else. She promised me that."

"She didn't," Hallgrim said, his voice rough as sandpaper. "I never heard from her again. Did you? Is she still alive?"

Borghild turned to Freya Wilkins, and now her voice was no longer as steady. "I don't actually know. So I have to ask you, Freya: Is Charlie Dalen still alive?"

"No, she's not." Freya Wilkins's voice carried through the room, loud and clear. "My mother died many years ago."

All faces were turned toward Freya, who was now standing opposite the sofa from Hallgrim.

"Your . . . mother?" Hallgrim asked, his face pale now. "You're saying that Charlotte was your mother? That you . . . are the child who . . ."

"That's right. The child who was conceived in that unfortunate way—is me."

Ingrid could hardly believe her ears. She looked around at her friends. They were all staring at Freya now. Talk about a drama! There was *plenty* of material for the podcast Vegard wanted to make, she thought—but not much Pia and Sunny could post about on Instagram.

"My mother came to America with two empty hands and a growing belly," Freya continued. "But she created a whole new life for herself. Shortly after arriving in New York, she met a Norwegian man, a friend of her landlord in Brooklyn. That's where most of the Norwegians in New York were at the time. They got married soon after they met, on May 17, 1962. My father knew she was pregnant when they got married. That goes without saying. She was six months along, after all. He told me everything when I was an adult. He was childless, a widower, wealthy, much older than her. He thought she was the most beautiful thing he'd ever seen. When she wanted to be his wife, taking on a child that wasn't his was a price he was more than willing to pay."

"But you said her name was Lottie Hansen," Pia said. "Wasn't her name Charlotte Dalen?"

"Yes, but she married Peter Hansen, whom I came to know as my father," Freya said. "They were wonderful parents and stayed together until my mother passed in 2004."

Ingrid thought, *Charlotte Dalen became Lottie Hansen . . .*

"So Charlie . . . Lottie . . . has been dead for almost twenty years," Borghild said almost inaudibly.

"Yes, she was only sixty. Cancer. It was difficult, but I was a grown woman myself and had married John more than ten years earlier." Freya turned and looked at her husband lovingly. "Both we and my parents were living in California at the time," she said. "They moved out there when my dad retired, and my dad stayed there until he died in 2010. He was well into his eighties. But he told me he'd never loved anyone but my mother."

"But . . . did Charlie . . . Lottie . . . ever tell you about her background?" Ingrid asked. "Did you know where you came from?"

Freya turned to her. "My mother taught me a lot about Norwegian culture. She loved Norway and spoke a little about where she came from, but she was more guarded when it came to personal details. It was as if it was a door she'd closed. But on her deathbed, she said something I didn't understand at first. She spoke Norwegian, and I thought she was saying something about *climbing a glittering mountain.* I assumed it was some kind of metaphor, that maybe she meant heaven. It was only much later that I realized the connection. She wrote letters, you see. Letters to a person she just called B . . . which she obviously never sent. I didn't know about them until my father had also passed and I found them in the attic. When I read the letters, I started getting an idea of why my mother had left Norway, why she could no longer live in this place she loved so much. The letters were cryptic, almost written in code. They were in Norwegian. And they had no address. But they piqued my curiosity. The letters were the reason I got interested in genealogy and led me to getting involved in Norwegian associations. And because of the place names she kept referring to in the letters, I also realized what it was she'd *actually* said before she died. She said she always wanted to go to *Glitter Peak* again."

Ingrid looked at her grandmother. Tears were rolling down Nana Borghild's cheeks.

"So . . ." Ingrid looked between her grandmother, Hallgrim, and Freya before settling her gaze on the American. "Hallgrim's sister Charlotte, who disappeared in 1962, was your mother?"

"Yes."

"So Hallgrim is your uncle?"

Freya looked at Hallgrim, at first without saying anything. "I wasn't sure when I came here," she said hesitantly. "But now it's quite obvious."

Borghild nodded and wiped away her tears. She cleared her throat and said: "And Freya is heir to half the properties Hallgrim and Charlotte inherited from their parents. And which Hallgrim has taken ownership of since Charlotte disappeared. Freya therefore owns half of the Muskox properties."

Hallgrim looked at her in dismay. "Owns . . . ? Taken . . . ? But I thought Charlie was dead!"

Borghild's voice was authoritative once again. "Yes, but it was never declared legally, was it? Anyway, you're obligated to share. Otherwise you'll have me *and* the legal system to deal with. Because I've put in the work, Hallgrim. I've been doing some investigating and found a number of cases that show you've been making illegal and fraudulent real estate decisions for years, not to mention tricking people into debt and financial hardship."

She looked at Thor. "Your family knows all about that, don't they, Thor?"

Thor nodded silently.

Borghild went on, "You think of yourself as this tycoon, Hallgrim. Like the king of the village and protector of the family name. But you've built your estate on shady business and threats. You've taken more than what's yours. I also understand that in addition to the old grudge against me, you now have a financial interest in pushing us out of the hotel business. Because you want us to sell to your partner, XO Hotels! But that's never going to happen."

"Was that why you came down to my place the other night?" Hallgrim asked.

"I came down there to warn you and ask you to leave Glitter Peak alone," Borghild said. "Also for your own sake. But it wasn't just that . . . When Freya showed up, I knew there would be some big changes here. The snowball had started rolling. We *had* to talk. But you wouldn't listen. And my courage failed me."

"Why didn't you tell me sooner?"

"I promised Charlie I wouldn't tell you that she left. And I've kept that promise for sixty years. But now I *had* to do it. And *you* . . . you have the chance to make things right."

The snow was still falling outside the window.

The silence was palpable.

"Excuse me," Sunny said, picking up cups and saucers and loading them onto the serving tray. "I'll just go get some fresh coffee."

No one had touched the now cold cups.

Alfred stood up and tossed a couple of logs on the dwindling fire. He straightened up and looked around the room. "Hallgrim said it would be safest for our jobs if the Berg family was convinced to sell the hotel. As a part of the XO chain, we would get to keep our jobs, and it would be a better situation for everyone."

Sunny and Maja came in from the kitchen with more coffee but were struck by the silence in the room and set the tray down without a word. They stood there, staring at the caretaker along with everyone else.

A thousand thoughts were running through Ingrid's head.

"Have you been sabotaging us?" she asked. "The flooding? Did *you* clog the drain and cause tens of thousands of kroner worth of damage?"

Alfred shook his head so vigorously that his gray tufts of hair fluttered in the glow from the fireplace. He looked genuinely shaken.

"No, no! I didn't want to actually harm anything or anyone." Alfred looked at Hallgrim, who was sitting silently with a dogged look on his face. "Even though he said we had to stand together, the locals from Dalen. And that the people at Glitter Peak would ruin the hotel if they didn't sell. And . . . that he would make sure I lost my job if I didn't do as he said. He even suggested that I try to arrange for some food poisoning. But I'd never do that to Maja!"

Everyone turned and looked at the chef, whose face had turned bright red. Alfred's tone when he said her name had been so affectionate—maybe even . . . loving?

I can't believe I haven't seen it before! Ingrid thought. *He's in love with her!*

Suddenly, she saw things in a new light—all the morning hours when the aging caretaker sat with a cup of coffee in the kitchen while the chef chattered away. Alfred had applied for a job at the hotel years ago, just after Maja was widowed. He himself had never been married. Ingrid had never thought about it before, but she'd been blind—once again, love was right under her nose.

There was a kind of rumbling, and it took a while before they realized that Hallgrim was laughing. "We worked pretty hard to persuade people not to come here," he said. "We thought it would make you throw in the towel. But we haven't managed that yet."

After a few hiccups of laughter, he was guffawing so hard that he had to wipe away tears with the back of his hand. Ingrid almost had to laugh, too.

THE FRIENDSHIP THAT HAD ONCE existed between the young Borghild Berg and a young Hallgrim Dalen was hard to imagine when she looked at them now. To think that Borghild, Hallgrim, and their friends—most of whom were now deceased— were the same boys and girls who had worked and danced and spent time together here at Glitter Peak sixty years ago! They had been so young—much younger than Ingrid was now.

Dr. Wilkins hadn't said a word during the confrontation, but he now had a supportive hand on his wife's arm. Ingrid didn't know how much he had caught of the conversation, which had mostly been in Norwegian, but he seemed to understand everything that was going on.

"I knew it when I saw the painting!" Freya explained. "When I recognized my mother in the picture in Borghild's room, I understood how it was all connected. I'd started piecing things together, and I suppose I was sleeping poorly and was maybe even a little manic. John was so worried about me." She stroked her husband's hand tenderly. "We went to the National Archives and searched online, but it wasn't until we got here that I really felt I was getting close to something. I wandered around the corridors, thinking and listening and trying to find out as much as possible. I didn't even have the energy to eat. It was so overwhelming to be here, at this Glitter Peak my mother had longed for. And then I fainted and woke up to the picture of her and Borghild!"

"Your mother and Borghild?"

Ingrid stopped herself and looked toward her grandmother, who was sitting on the sofa across from them. How could Ingrid possibly be *so* slow? Of *course* they were the ones depicted in the painting that had hung there all these years—the girls in bunads. How could she not have seen it? She hadn't even recognized her grandmother; she'd just seen a couple of random models in bunads in the Norwegian countryside, young girls with long braids—one dark and one light. It was Borghild and Charlotte in the painting, her grandmother and the love of her life, Charlotte, who had been nineteen when she disappeared, whom Nana Borghild had never seen again, and whom she may have never stopped loving.

"Hidden in plain sight," Freya Wilkins said.

She took her wallet out of her purse and pulled something out. Then she stood up and walked over to Borghild, holding out an old photograph. Borghild stood up, too; she took the picture and studied it carefully before embracing Freya. They stood there for a long time with their arms around each other. Ingrid was certain they were both crying.

It ended up being a long afternoon in the library. After a while, Sunny went out for more fresh coffee and some waffles, which seemed to be just the thing to lighten the mood a bit. The conversation continued. There were still so many questions.

"What happened to the groom, then?" Thor asked.

It turned out that the jilted Jarand Smedplass had left Dalen the year after the wedding that never took place. He died sometime in the 1970s. Hallgrim heard he drank himself to death. "Things in the village weren't the same for him after he was left at the altar," Hallgrim said.

"That makes sense," Thor said, taking a waffle.

"Good riddance," Nana Borghild said sharply. "Jarand Smedplass was a bad man. Reverend Röhmer, too. He died in 1963."

Ingrid shuddered. If she'd understood things correctly, Röhmer was the priest who'd assaulted Charlie, and who was supposed to have officiated Charlie and Jarand's wedding! It was truly sick. So Freya's biological father was a rapist. What was it like for her to take this all in?

As if she'd read Ingrid's mind, Freya said: "I had a good father. Peter Hansen raised me as his own and loved me dearly, and I've never needed anyone else." She squeezed her husband's hand. "John and I were never blessed with children, but John has two grown daughters and three wonderful grandchildren. And now we've also found all of you."

Hallgrim studied Freya carefully. "I can't believe I have a niece. Wait until the boys find out—a cousin from America! You look just like her, you know. Like Charlie."

Ingrid wasn't sure that the "boys" would be all that excited about a surprise cousin with whom they had to share their inheritance. But one thing she *was* sure of was that Hallgrim Dalen now had tears in his eyes.

And he was absolutely right about the resemblance. Even with only the bunad painting and the old photograph for comparison, Ingrid could see that Freya Wilkins looked a lot like her mother. The blond hair, the soft facial features, the big gray eyes . . . What had it been like for Nana Borghild to see Freya when she came bursting through the doors a few weeks ago? Was that why Borghild had become so withdrawn and avoided the American? Had she figured out the connection right away? Had she been happy? Scared? Overwhelmed by this visit from the past?

There was going to be a lot to talk about moving forward; Ingrid and Borghild had wasted so much time keeping secrets from each other. But that was going to end now.

SUDDENLY, VEGARD STOOD UP. He leaned toward Ingrid and whispered, "Why don't you and Thor come up and join us afterward? There's something else we need to take care of here if we want the Christmas celebrations to be just right."

He winked at David and Pia and headed for the door.

Ingrid was curious. When she stood up a little while later and walked toward the foyer, Thor came with her.

"What a drama," he said quietly.

She met his gaze and whispered: "Yeah, we sure got more mystery than we were expecting!"

His blue eyes sparkled.

Thorbjørn Seter scratched his head as he put down the phone and walked over to his wife.

"This is strange, Thoril. It was someone from the hotel," he said.

"From the hotel?"

"Yes, someone named Vegard Vang. He spoke in that fancy Oslo accent, you know. 'I'm calling from Glitter Peak Lodge—on behalf of hotel manager Ingrid Berg.'"

"On behalf of Ingrid? But what did he want, then?"

"I'm getting to that. He said he knew it was short notice, but he wondered if we wanted to go up there tomorrow."

"Tomorrow? On Christmas Eve?"

"Yes, I guess they want us to celebrate Christmas with Thor and Ingrid and the guests at the hotel."

"What in the world . . . we can't do that!"

"But why not, Thoril? Really? Maja will be there and everything. I said yes."

Dinner was served later that evening. It took more than some family drama to put Maja Seter out of action. Ingrid walked Thor out to his car afterward, again. It was apparently becoming a habit. In the future, she would also make a habit of wishing him a proper welcome.

The snow had subsided a bit, and Thor was sure it was okay to drive even though the roads hadn't been plowed yet. Hallgrim Dalen had left a couple of hours ago with a new niece to tell people about and an old feud more or less put to rest.

Ingrid put her hand on Thor's arm. "So that nut Vegard has invited your parents here for Christmas Eve! You can of course say no."

Thor looked at her. "Would you rather we not come?" he asked, seeming a bit concerned.

"Yes, yes, of course you can come!" she exclaimed. "I mean, you're most welcome! I just meant that . . . you probably had your own plans already, and are used to being at home, and . . ."

He took her hand. "Never mind that, Ingrid. Never mind what we're used to! I can celebrate Christmas anywhere, as long as it's with you."

She saw a deep seriousness in his usually jovial eyes. They were standing close now, so close she could feel his warm breath on her face. With Thor, it felt okay to be so close to another person. More than okay, actually. It felt . . . right. She wanted to be close to Thor. Her body was soft and warm. It was as if a barrier had disappeared. She leaned forward and kissed him.

From Borghild Berg's diary:

I'm sitting here, looking at the painting of the two of us.

When Mother and Father were so happy with the painting of Styggfossen and Heaven's Horn, they decided to commission another painting from the painter, Antonsen. They'd originally intended for me to pose alone. Their only child, the heir to the hotel. But I didn't want that. I wanted Charlie in the painting. And so she was. I guess I was pretty stubborn and spoiled. It turned out just the way I wanted it to.

It was so exciting, being a model! But we didn't get to look while it was being painted. It was only when Mother and Father asked us to come into the living room one afternoon that we got to see what the finished painting looked like. There we were in our bunads. We could see for ourselves that we were beautiful. That everything around us was beautiful. That we belonged together. We felt so grown up then. Now I can see how young we were.

I remember grabbing her hand. "I'll love you forever," I said quietly, so that Mother and Father couldn't hear it. I was so certain. So sure that we would find a way to be together.

It was only afterward that I realized that Charlie had been more insecure than I was. That was why she went to the priest. She was so young, torn between emotions and what was expected of her. She knew that what we were doing wasn't something people would accept. She'd had a good relationship with the priest ever since her confirmation. She trusted him.

I can't believe that Hallgrim didn't know the priest was the father of the child Charlie was expecting. But she had never told him what happened. She blamed herself for trusting the priest. The man she went to so she could have someone to talk to about what was troubling her— and who assaulted her. Like the wolf he was. Like the lamb she was. He was supposed to be the shepherd.

Jarand probably didn't know who the child's father was, either. Hallgrim had only told him that Charlotte had ended up "in a delicate condition" and promised him a lucrative deal if he took on the paternity and showed up in the church. And she was good wife material, Charlie. Young and beautiful and the heir to half of the Dalen family estate. Jarand must have thought he'd hit the jackpot.

I knew I had to stop it. And I did, even though it was painful. At least I managed to prevent the one bastard who had assaulted her from officiating her marriage to the bastard who would then ruin the rest of her life.

But, and this is hard to believe, it was Röhmer who married me and Christian only a few months later. We had no other priests to choose from, and in the midst of my grief over Charlie, I did what I had to do: I came to my senses and married the kind, faithful Christian.

I'd always known I couldn't marry the person I really loved. So I might as well marry a friend. He was a good man. Our wedding was a discreet affair. Anything else would have seemed strange in light of what had just happened. We mourned Charlie, all of us, in our own ways. Röhmer didn't grow old, by the way, but that's another matter. We got better priests after him.

Hallgrim was still disappointed—no, shocked!— when I chose Christian; after all, he'd always hoped that he and I would end up together. Whether it was me or the hotel that was most appealing, I don't know. But Hallgrim Dalen wasn't used to being denied something he wanted. And it didn't help that he'd realized there was something between me and Charlie. It made his rage grow, and he thought that it—the "perversity"!—had also contributed to her taking her life. How he could think that he and I should marry is beyond me. It was as if he couldn't quite come to terms with reality. He simply couldn't understand that two women could actually love each other.

But I should have let him know that she wasn't dead.

"*I didn't hate you,*" *Hallgrim said when we sat in the library tonight.* "*I loved you.*"

"*I know,*" *I told him.* "*And I was very fond of you, too. Once.*"

"*I thought you were,*" *he said then.* "*But not in that way. Because it wasn't me you loved—it was my sister.*"

DECEMBER 24

The snow glittered in the sun. Pia P's latest Instagram post showed the Christmas tree in the dining room, silhouetted against a blue sky outside the big windows. The next photos in the series were of the snowcapped tip of Heaven's Horn, a candelabra with lit candles, and the small exhibition in the foyer with pine branches and elves. The hashtags: *#christmasjoy #christmasatglitterpeaklodge #merrychristmas*. The post had already gotten almost five thousand likes.

"I CALLED MY MOM AND DAD," Pia told Ingrid when they were having a cup of tea together after breakfast.

"Today?"

"Yeah, earlier this morning. I told them everything."

They'd spent hours in the Peer Gynt Suite last night, analyzing the drama that had unfolded in the library. Then Vegard— the little troublemaker—told them he'd invited Thor's parents to

Christmas dinner. Tonight! It was insane. But kind of nice, too. It wouldn't be surprising if all the family talk had freed something in Pia, too.

"I've been thinking about it since the last time we spoke," Pia said. "About how I should try to involve them. They're crazy, but they are my parents, after all."

"How did they react?" Ingrid asked.

"You know what? They were so happy! I could hear my mom crying on the other end when I told her she was going to be a grandmother. I thought it was despair at first and was about to hang up, but then she said she'd never been so thrilled." Pia took a deep breath. "Oh my God, I'm getting all emotional. But I can't ruin my makeup now that I'm going to take Christmas pictures and everything."

She carefully dabbed a tissue at the corner of her eye.

"That's great!" Ingrid said. "I'm so glad you got in touch."

"Yes," Pia said. "My mom wants to visit after the holidays. She started talking about a stroller and all sorts of things she was going to buy. And even though I think it'll be pretty stressful, I'm happy about it too." She took a sip of tea. "You know, at the beginning, I'd been envisioning this pregnancy completely differently. I was sure I'd be in total control and that everything would be fine. But it's been so incredibly hard. I've felt so alone. I even thought this might be the biggest mistake of my life. And I *definitely* haven't had the energy to go out and buy baby stuff." She smiled. "Instead, I've been hiding up here in the mountains. So it'll be nice to get some help when I come back down. With a stroller and all that."

"You'll probably get a sponsored stroller just by telling people about this on Instagram." Ingrid grinned. "But I get what you mean."

❄

"We talked to Dad on Skype today!" Hussein beamed as he came into the dining room, his hands full of presents to put under the tree. "He says he'll come to Norway after Christmas!"

"Yes, we hope we can make it work," Aisha said.

She turned to Ingrid and lowered her voice. "It's so uncertain, all of this. I don't dare go back there, but I don't know if we'll get permanent residence here. I don't want to tell Hussein about how unsure everything is. Right now, we're just going to enjoy the holiday season, and he can look forward to seeing his father again. Then we'll take it from there."

Ingrid took Aisha's hand and squeezed it. "That's a good place to start," she said.

Then they went into the dining room for lunch. *Risgrøt*, of course. A Christmas Eve favorite.

Maja placed large tureens on the table but insisted on serving everyone. The rice porridge was piping hot, and Maja had been stirring it for hours. She winked at Ingrid as she added a toasted almond to Hussein's bowl.

"I got some very nice news today," Vegard said once he'd tasted the porridge. "That is, I hope you'll also think it's nice. Hanna—the musician, you know—and her boyfriend, PX, want to visit the hotel on New Year's Eve. They were invited to some big events, but they need to chill after a busy season. So they want to spend a couple of days up here. Maybe they'll get a taste for more and we'll have a Hanna and the Hearts concert here in the summer!"

"*Hanna and PX?!*" Sunny shouted. "For New Year's? Here? Okay, I changed my mind. I don't want the night off anymore!"

Ingrid laughed. "You *will* take the night off!" she said. "But you're more than welcome to come here as a guest."

"That's great news, Vegard!" Pia said. "I know Hanna. She's a lot of fun. A real party girl—just like me, once upon a time."

She laughed and patted her stomach.

"Your party days aren't over yet," said Freya. "Just you wait and see." She put her hand over her husband's and smiled. Then she grew serious again.

"I have a few things I'd like to say," she said. "I found so much more than I was looking for here at Glitter Peak. It's going to take more than a Christmas visit to digest all of this—and I don't just mean the food."

She cleared her throat.

"As you know, the past few days have been quite overwhelming for me," Freya continued. "I must admit that I'm not quite sure how to react to *Uncle Hallgrim* and my new cousins. What happened to my mother is painful to think about, and she herself chose to cut off contact with her family here. But we'll have to wait and see what happens. First and foremost, I'm grateful to have found the place my mother came from and that she loved so much. And *the person* she loved." She looked at Borghild, her eyes shining. "I hope to come back here to Glitter Peak many more times. I've already thought about taking my Daughters of Norway lodge with me on a trip to Norway!"

Freya took a sip from her glass of juice. "But there's one more thing. I understand if this comes as a surprise, but I've managed to persuade this young lady"—she nodded at Sunny, who was about to pour more coffee—"to come to the US next year. I think my contacts can provide her with some good job opportunities there."

"In California?" Ingrid asked.

"Yes! A young woman with such drive and talent will do well there."

Hmm, it's a bit sudden, Ingrid thought—and she wasn't sure whether the US was exactly the place she'd recommend for someone to move to in these turbulent times. But the move also made sense. Sunny was made for the big world. She had to go out and stretch her wings.

"What an opportunity! Congratulations, Sunny. But you're not quitting right away, are you?"

"No, I'm going to finish my studies first," Sunny replied. "So I'd like to keep working here until the summer if I can. And then I'll hand in my thesis."

"The one about toolboxes?" Alfred asked.

"Yes, that's right, the one about toolboxes," Sunny said with a smile.

"I got the almond!" Hussein shouted suddenly.

"No way, really? How lucky!" Maja said, taking a bag out from under her chair. "Then you're the one who gets the prize!" She pulled a large marzipan cat wrapped in cellophane out of the bag. "Real, homemade marzipan," she proclaimed. "Inspired by Mewsephina."

"Meow," Mewsephina said from under the table.

After lunch, Ingrid found an excuse to retreat to her apartment for a while. She took out her phone and stared at it for a long time. Then she found Preben's number.

She thought about the Himalaya project, about the new foundation they were about to establish. In many ways, it would be their attempt at atonement, but it was also so much more than that. It was about shouldering the burden. The challenges of climate change, erosion, poverty, and environmental degradation were so rampant that it was easy to feel powerless, but they weren't going to give into powerlessness. She thought of Giovanni's words: *God doesn't give us more than we can handle.* She didn't know about the God part, but she would handle what she could.

Then she thought of something Nana Borghild always used to say: "Joy shared is joy doubled. Sorrow shared is sorrow halved."

"Preben Wexelsen," said the familiar voice at the other end.

"Hi, Preben." She felt her voice trembling, but she'd made up her mind. "How's it going? Yeah, great. Here, too. Almost time for Christmas celebrations. Are you busy right now? No? Are you alone? I hope you don't think it's weird that I'm calling on Christmas Eve. But there's something I have to tell you. Something you deserve to know."

The bells were ringing over Dalen. From the tower in the old brown church, the deep sound echoed over snow-covered fields and meadows, over farms and forests: *come-come, come-come, come-come!*

And people came—from the big farm up the hill, from the new housing development, and from neighboring villages. In their finest garb, driving and walking, some even on kick-sleds, all making their way between the naked birch trees lining the avenue. They went through the gate and across the churchyard, where candles flickered on the graves. People poured in through the church doors, which were wide open—because it was Christmas Eve and time to ring in the holiday spirit.

They even came from Glitter Peak. All eyes were on old Borghild Berg and her granddaughter, Ingrid, as they walked up the church aisle together with the blond American woman—the one who'd been going around the village talking to everyone she could and digging into family history and old traditions. All three were clad in bunads with tinkling sølje. They were joined by a mixed gang of hotel guests. An older gentleman—that was the American's husband. A couple of younger men in suits who looked like city folk. A beautiful woman in a white dress, high-heeled booties, and with honey-blond curls that caught the attention of the youngest girls in the church: *Isn't that . . . ? Yes, it's her! And is she . . . ? It looks like it. Yeah, definitely. Oh my god! But she hasn't shared it anywhere . . . ?*

Something else people talked about afterward was the fact that Borghild had turned on her way in and nodded to Hallgrim Dalen and the Muskox clan, who had already taken their seats in the church. As far as residents of Dalen knew, those two hadn't so much as looked each other in the eye in decades, so it made quite a sensation.

And there was the Seter family, too. Thorbjørn, Thoril, and their son Thor. They weren't often seen in church, but tonight, they sat together with the people from Glitter Peak.

In the sacristy, the new parish priest, Hanne Kristoffersen, was going through the day's sermon in her head. It was her first Christmas service in Dalen Church, and she was bound to be nervous. She and her spouse, Marie, had been living there for only a couple of months.

She could hear there were a lot of people in the church. Now the bells chimed three times. Time to go in.

❄

"And it came to pass in those days," Reverend Kristoffersen read, "that there went out a decree from Caesar Augustus, that all the world should be taxed." The congregation fell silent as the familiar words from the Christmas gospel rang out over the church. "And all went to be taxed, every one into his own city. And Joseph also went up from Galilee, out of the city of Nazareth, into Judaea, unto the city of David, which is called Bethlehem (because he was of the house and lineage of David), to be taxed with Mary his espoused wife, being great with child. And so it was, that, while they were there, the days were accomplished that she should be delivered. And she brought forth her firstborn son, and wrapped him in swaddling clothes, and laid him in a manger; because there was no room for them in the inn."

THE MERRY TONES OF "Joy to the World" faded out, and then it was officially Christmas Eve. The sky was dark when the group from Glitter Peak left the church, and they could see the stars glittering over Heaven's Horn when they got back. The light of the full moon was reflected in the snow. Lanterns cast their flickering light over the entrance of the hotel.

It was nice and warm inside. Maja had prepared mulled wine, and they each took a mug and went to the dining room as soon as they'd hung up their coats and changed their shoes.

The Christmas lights sparkled brightly on the tree behind them, and a large pile of presents lay beneath the heavy branches. Bach's *Christmas Oratorio* sounded from the small speakers on the corner tables.

Alfred, Aisha, Hussein, and Maja had set things up, and even the chef was going to take part in the Christmas meal as soon as she was finished in the kitchen. The delectable scent of pinnekjøtt wafted through the room, and the tables were set with white tablecloths, crystal, porcelain, pine branches, and red candles.

It's so beautiful, Ingrid thought. *I'm so lucky to be able to experience this with the people closest to me.* A black shadow slipped past her. Mewsephina strutted through the dining room and into the library. Ingrid had pretended not to see her over the past few days. Keeping unregulated cats at the hotel was a problem she had no intention of dealing with right now. And she had to admit—if only to herself—that it was kind of nice having a cat around here.

She looked around. It was quite a gathering: Nana Borghild, Freya and John Wilkins, Ingrid's friends, Thor's family. John Wilkins was wearing a suit and waistcoat and looked like a distinguished gentleman—which he was, Ingrid thought. Freya Wilkins looked radiant in Charlotte's bunad. It turned out that Borghild had had it hanging in the hotel ever since she and Charlotte modeled for the painting in 1961. It was supposed to be worn on Charlotte's wedding day in 1962, but that never happened.

Pia, Vegard, and David had settled down on a row of chairs by the windows. Vegard and David had helped themselves to mulled wine, but Pia had declined even the alcohol-free version. She'd ridden with Vegard and David to and from the church, having insisted on going even though they'd suggested she could stay at the hotel and rest. She'd been so happy and enthusiastic when she told them about the phone call with her parents this morning. She seemed tired now, though, and looked quite pale despite her expertly applied makeup.

Thor and his parents were in a small cluster by themselves. Thor looked terribly handsome in his dark trousers, white shirt, vest, and tie. It was strange to see him like this. She'd even caught a faint whiff of cologne when he hugged her at the church. His parents had been so nervous when they came through the hotel door, mumbling something about not wanting to intrude, but Ingrid had smiled and reminded them that they had been invited, after all. She'd said—and it really was true—that she was very happy they could come.

But it felt . . . strange as well. As if they were suddenly related somehow.

Ingrid tapped her glass to welcome everyone and call people to the table, but she got no further than a few introductory phrases when Pia abruptly stood up from her chair and leaned against the backrest, making a kind of choking noise.

The entire group's attention was focused on her.

"Excuse me for a moment," Pia said in a strange voice. She walked quickly across the floor. "I just need to go upstairs. Don't wait for me, please get started."

She waddled toward the door, leaving a wet trail on the floor behind her.

Vegard sprang up and was the first at her side. "But . . . but . . . this is the kind of thing you see in the movies! What's it called? Your water broke? Honey, you're in *labor*!"

He turned to the others: "Someone call an ambulance!"

It didn't take long before John Wilkins was beside them. "I'm a doctor," he said simply. "I can help her. First, we need to see how far along she is and how quickly things seem to be progressing. Call the hospital anyway. Ms. Berg and Mr. Vang, come with me."

Together, Ingrid and Vegard supported a confused Pia out of the dining room.

"We need a clean room with a big bathroom," Dr. Wilkins said as he took off his suit jacket and vest and handed them to his wife. He popped his silver cuff links in his pocket and folded up his shirtsleeves.

"Freya, can you get my medical bag?" he asked his wife.

"Will she need to be driven somewhere?" Thor asked.

"No, I don't think she'll make it down to the hospital," the doctor replied. "Maybe afterward, if the midwife thinks she needs to be admitted."

"The ambulance is on its way, and your mother is talking to a midwife," Ingrid said to Thor.

They agreed that Pia's room could be converted into a delivery room, and Thoril Seter offered her assistance. She was the mother of two children and therefore better qualified to help than most of the others who were present, apart from the doctor. She quickly changed from her formal dress into a pair of sweatpants and a cotton sweatshirt Ingrid brought from her own closet. The quiet older woman seemed to be in her element now that she was needed, and she was on the phone with the maternity ward at the hospital in Lillehammer.

Ingrid and Aisha ran into the laundry room to find towels and other items needed for the birth.

"Are you okay?" Aisha asked. "I mean, it's . . ."

Her eyes were filled with compassion and concern.

"Yes, I'm fine!" Ingrid replied. "There was a second there when I was bracing myself to be able to assist during the actual birth, but I'm kind of glad I don't have to."

"I understand," Aisha said. "We can make ourselves useful in other ways."

When they got up to the second floor, the screams of pain coming from Pia's room revealed that the birth was underway. It was apparently happening a lot faster than anyone could have expected. Vegard and David were pacing back and forth in the hallway like two anxious fathers, but when Dr. Wilkins opened the door to get the towels, he asked Ingrid if she "for God's sake" could take them downstairs and give them a drink instead.

"Gladly!" Ingrid said.

Now, everyone who hadn't been appointed as assistants had gathered in the library. Sitting down for dinner was unthinkable at this point, but they helped themselves to mulled wine and other drinks. Maja was naturally flustered over both someone giving birth at the hotel and the deviation from the dinner plans (*Again! After all the fuss yesterday!*) but she kept the food warm. Freya Wilkins remained surprisingly calm. She was probably used to stepping aside when her husband practiced medicine, Ingrid thought.

By the time the ambulance was pulling up outside, John Wilkins had already come down from the second floor. He'd washed up, changed into a clean white shirt, and announced that Pia had given birth to a beautiful and healthy baby girl.

Never before had there been such a Christmas celebration at Glitter Peak. The pinnekjøtt arrived on the table four hours late, and the guests took turns visiting Pia until the doctor put his foot down and said she needed rest. The midwife had confirmed that everything was fine, that there was no need for Pia to be admitted to the hospital, and that she would come back the next day.

Now, both Pia and the baby were asleep. Pia had FaceTimed her parents and showed off their new grandchild. Ingrid had helped her with the phone and let the tears flow freely as she looked at Pia with the little pink baby and heard her parents' overwhelmed outbursts in the background. They planned to get in the car the next morning and be at Glitter Peak as soon as possible.

"I can't think of a better Christmas present for Pia and the little one than having parents and grandparents in their lives," she told Vegard. "Conspiracy theories or not."

Thor's mother was back in her party outfit and had gratefully accepted a shot of aquavit after the ordeal.

"I usually don't drink much," she told the Wilkinses. "But this isn't exactly an everyday occurrence."

"You're right about that," Dr. Wilkins replied, taking a hearty sip from his own glass of aquavit. "I guess you could say this Christmas is a bit out of the ordinary."

They moved into the library after dinner.

"The way to a man's heart really is through his stomach," Alfred said, patting his stomach happily.

Kransekake and coffee were served, and Hussein—who looked like a fine little gentleman in his suit and tie—took on the job of cracking all the party poppers and reading the jokes aloud. Crowns and hats were placed on guests and staff, and Aisha got the best crown, which was pink.

Then it was time to open presents, which was another job Hussein took quite seriously. He darted back and forth between the Christmas tree and the coffee table and read aloud from the gift tags.

Nana Borghild's gift to Ingrid was a draft of the first chapter of *Sky High: The Unknown Story of Glitter Peak Lodge*, which Borghild intended to complete over the next two years with Thor's help.

"There's a gift for you from Thor," Hussein said, handing Ingrid a flat, square package. *Oh no!* She hadn't bought a gift for Thor or his parents; she hadn't had time to think about that.

When she unwrapped the gift, she was overwhelmed. It was a framed picture of her on her way up the stairs to Glitter Peak Lodge. The hotel towered against the blue sky with its spires and dragon heads, and she looked like she was a natural part of it. Thor must have taken the photo one day after she'd walked him to his car. But when had he managed to get it developed and framed? He just smiled slyly when she asked. "It's proof that you belong here," he said.

The shape of Hussein's gift from his mother was unmistakable: a new pair of cross-country skis. He beamed with joy as he tore off the paper.

"I'll be the first one out when they prep the tracks next to the hotel," he exclaimed.

"I'll go with you," Ingrid said.

Ingrid's gift to Hussein was a smartwatch with GPS. It was probably the first and only time she'd accepted a Christmas gift tip from Preben.

Then Hussein ran out and got a small package, which he held out to Ingrid while jumping up and down with excitement. *To Ingrid from Hussein.*

It was a rock. A compact, heavy gray rock. And on it was a tiny little elf figure with blond curls sticking out of its hat, with mountaineering gear on its back.

"I thought this stone could be a mountain in the fairy-tale forest," Hussein said. "So it had to have a real mountaineer, too!"

"YOU LOOK FANTASTIC IN A BUNAD," Ingrid said to Freya. "Like you were born to wear it. And I suppose you were."

Freya took her hand. "I came to Norway to find my roots," she said. "But I never thought I would find a family and a *home* like this. Because that's what I did. I've found home."

Ingrid squeezed her hand. "I'm glad you feel that way," she said. "It must have been quite overwhelming to learn about all of this."

"Yes, it has been. But the way I see it, it's first and foremost a great gift. And before I go back to California, I'm going to pay another visit to Uncle Hallgrim," Freya said.

Uncle Hallgrim! That was going to take some getting used to, Ingrid thought, picturing the grumpy, scowling old bull.

"The next time I come to Norway, we'll have dancing here! With him and Borghild as instructors," Freya vowed.

Ingrid had to laugh. "Dancing? Do you really think you can talk them into it?"

"I can talk people into quite a lot, let me tell you!" Freya assured her.

"I believe it!" Ingrid replied.

"Did you know that the dance is the reason the bear is here?" Freya asked.

"But . . . what? What do you mean by that?" Ingrid replied.

"They had a bet!" Freya said. "Hallgrim thought no one would come to their dance course. If more than ten people signed up, Borghild would get the stuffed bear he shot the previous summer. Then thirty people showed up. He drove it up here on New Year's Eve."

Ingrid laughed out loud. "I wonder what Borghild bet."

"Uncle Hallgrim wouldn't get into that," Freya said.

It almost looked as if Barry was smiling at them from his corner.

Ingrid and Thor had gone out to the stairs in front of the main entrance when fullness and fatigue started setting in. They had to go back inside soon, but it was nice to stand there for a while and enjoy the peace and quiet with his arms around her.

"I was thinking about something. Would you be up for helping Hussein a little?" Ingrid suggested. "You know what it's like to be a boy here in the village. Maybe you can talk to him and Aisha and see if there's anything we can do to make things easier for him?"

Thor nodded. "I'd love to," he said. "Because he's a good kid. But mostly because you're the one asking."

She nodded and allowed herself to take in the warmth behind his words. She rested her head on his shoulder and took a deep breath. Then she looked up and Thor bent down and kissed her gently on the mouth.

The northern lights blazed green across the sky and cast their glow over the mountain peaks.

"And Christmas magic was in the air at Glitter Peak Lodge," a small voice said behind them.

Ingrid and Thor turned around at the same time and laughed.

"Indeed," Thor said, patting the little boy on the head. "Merry Christmas, Hussein!"

The six-year-old grinned at them and pulled something brown from his pocket. "Merry Christmas! Do you like gingerbread? Speedy does. I left some for him by his hole in the kitchen. But don't tell Miss Maja!"

Acknowledgments

Many thanks to Ida Cleve and the rest of the staff at Cappelen Damm, who have always believed in Ingrid Berg, Glitter Peak Lodge, and me.

Thanks to Alf Roar Rasmussen and Anne Marte Hagen for reading and commenting on early drafts of the manuscript, and thanks to my family and friends for their patience and encouragement—and for lending me their cabins and apartments so I could get the peace and quiet I needed to write.

A big thanks to Cappelen Damm Agency and Victoria Sanders & Associates, who helped *Glitter Peak* find the right home, and to Gretchen Schmid for including me on the HarperVia list. I can barely believe how lucky I've been!

Thank you to Olivia Lasky, who has worked tirelessly and meticulously to make sure the book has found its true form in English (and who is also responsible for the English edition containing even *more* delicious recipes than the original!).

And last but not least, a heartfelt thanks to all the readers who've picked up the book. You're the ones who make it all worthwhile.

Glossary

FOOD

Bordstabel: A rectangular cookie that can be served stacked. One of the seven traditional types of Norwegian Christmas cookies.

Fattigmann: Thin, deep-fried pastries made from a dough consisting of flour, sugar, eggs, cream, and cardamom. One of the seven traditional types of Norwegian Christmas cookies.

Goro: A thin, flat cross between a cookie, cracker, and waffle baked in a special "goro iron." One of the seven traditional types of Norwegian Christmas cookies.

Hjortetakk: A traditional Norwegian donut with a sort of "deer antler" design.

Kransekake: A "tower" or "wreath" cake served on special occasions. The chewy dough has an almond base and is formed into rings that are stacked on top of one another to form a cake.

Krumkaker: A waffle or cookie that is baked in a special iron and formed into a cone. One of the seven traditional types of Norwegian Christmas cookies.

Lefse: A flatbread made with potatoes, flour, butter, and sometimes milk or cream and baked on a flat griddle.

Lussekatt: A saffron bun traditionally baked for Saint Lucia's Day.

Lutefisk: Dried codfish that has been reconstituted in lye, giving it a gelatinous texture.

Medisterkaker: A flat sausage made from pork and spices.

Mølje: The broth from cooking pinnekjøtt.

Møljebrød: Crackers served with mølje.

Pinnekjøtt: Christmas dish made from cured and dried lamb or sheep ribs that are then steamed over a rack or sticks (*pinner* in Norwegian, hence the name *pinnekjøtt*, or "stick meat") until tender.

Rakfisk: Traditional dish made from fermented fish, usually trout or char.

Risgrøt: Rice pudding served with butter, cinnamon, and sugar on top, a popular lunch meal on Christmas Eve (often with a marzipan pig as a prize for the one who finds the almond hidden in the porridge).

Sandkaker: A sugar cookie baked in fluted tins. One of the seven traditional types of Norwegian Christmas cookies.

Sirupsnipper: Diamond-shaped spiced cookies flavored with dark syrup or molasses. One of the seven traditional types of Norwegian Christmas cookies.

Skummet kulturmelk: Skimmed cultured milk or soured milk, similar to buttermilk.

HOLIDAYS

Anna pissihose: December 9, also known as Anna's Day. Beer brewing often starts on this day.

Barbromesse: December 4, also known as Saint Barbara's feast day. People used to say that the sun disappeared on this day and didn't return until Saint Lucia's Day on December 13.

Lussi langnatt: The night between December 12 and 13, known as the most dangerous night of the year. According to folklore, if Christmas preparations weren't complete by this time, the demonlike female creature Lussi and her entourage might pay you an unwanted visit.

Saint Lucia's Day: December 13, also known as the Feast of Saint Lucia or "Santa Lucia." Girls often dress as Saint Lucia (clad in white gowns with candle wreaths on their heads) and boys as "star boys" (with cone-shaped hats decorated with stars). Saffron buns are often served in connection with this holiday.

Saint Thomas's Day: December 21, also known as *tomasmesse* or *Tomas fulltønne*. Traditionally, beer brewing must be completed by this time.

OTHER

Åsgårdsreien: Also known as the "Wild Hunt" or "Odin's Hunt"— a mythical procession of restless, deceased souls who ride during the night, particularly around Christmas and on Lussi langnatt.

Bunad: Traditional Norwegian folk costume often worn for special occasions such as weddings, confirmations, Constitution Day, and other holidays. Each region has a unique style, and the bunad typically consists of a dress or suit made from wool, silk, or both and adorned with intricate embroidery, worn with decorative silver or gold jewelry (sølje).

Hulder: A mythical creature often portrayed as a beautiful, seductive woman. These creatures are believed to live in deep forests and mountainous areas and have tails that they hide from humans.

Kakelinne: A term used to describe a period of mild weather that often occurs in December, before Christmas. In earlier times, it was claimed that kakelinne was caused by all the baking; all the ovens brought about the mild weather.

Sølje: Decorative silver and gold jewelry most commonly worn with a bunad.

Recipes

FREYA WILKINS'S NORWEGIAN AMERICAN PANCAKES WITH "SKUMMEL" BUTTERMILK

3 eggs

1$\frac{1}{4}$ cups skimmed buttermilk

3 tablespoons sugar

1 teaspoon baking soda

1$\frac{1}{2}$ cups all-purpose flour

$\frac{1}{2}$ teaspoon salt

$\frac{1}{4}$ cup melted butter

3 tablespoons butter for frying

7 ounces thick bacon slices, or
   fruit and berries

Maple syrup

Melt the butter. Separate the eggs and whisk the egg yolks in a large bowl. Add skimmed buttermilk, sugar, baking soda, flour, and salt while whisking.

Whisk in the melted butter. Beat the egg whites until stiff, and fold them into the batter. Let the batter rest for 20 minutes before frying.

Fry the pancakes in a frying pan with a little butter over medium heat. Flip them after 2–3 minutes when bubbles start to form on the surface. Fry them quickly on the other side.

Place bacon in a clean frying pan and heat slowly. Once the fat starts to render from the bacon slices, increase the heat. Cook until crispy. Serve the pancakes with bacon and maple syrup.

Alternatively, you can serve the pancakes with fruit and berries instead of bacon.

THOR SETER'S PINNEKJØTT
WITH MASHED RUTABAGA

12–18 ounces pinnekjøtt per person   3 good potatoes per person

Soak the pinnekjøtt in plenty of cold water for approximately 30 hours.

Place birch sticks (or a rack) on the bottom of a large stock-pot. Pour water in the pot until it reaches just below the level of the rack or the top of the birch sticks. Place the pinnekjøtt on top and cover tightly with a lid. Bring to a boil and steam-cook the meat over high heat for 2–3 hours.

Add water to the pot as needed to prevent it from boiling dry. Never pour water directly on the meat, but along the sides of the pot. The meat is done when it easily comes off the bone.

Thoroughly wash the potatoes and boil them until tender, approximately 20–30 minutes.

$4^{1}/_{2}$ pounds rutabagas   1 teaspoon freshly ground pepper
8 cups water   6 tablespoons butter
4 teaspoons salt

Peel the rutabagas and cut into pieces. Boil in lightly salted water until the pieces are soft. Drain the water and mash the rutabagas. Season with salt, pepper, and butter to taste.

MAJA SETER'S KRUMKAKER

8 tablespoons butter

3 eggs

$^1/_2$ cup sugar

$^3/_4$ cup all-purpose flour

$^1/_2$ cup potato starch

1 heaping teaspoon vanilla sugar

$^1/_2$ cup water

Melt the butter and let it cool. Whisk the eggs and sugar together until thick and creamy. Mix in the melted butter.

Combine the flour, potato starch, and vanilla sugar, then fold into the batter along with the water. Let the batter rise for a while.

Place a tablespoon of batter into a hot krumkake iron. Press it firmly. Add more water to the batter if it becomes too thick, which will result in excessively thick cakes.

Cook the cakes until they are golden brown over low to medium heat.

Quickly shape the cakes into cones around a krumkake cone or a wooden or steel form as soon as they are removed from the iron. You can also use the bottom of cups to shape them into small bowls.

Store the krumkaker in an airtight container (or enjoy them immediately and make another batch).

HUSSEIN'S GIGANTIC GINGERBREAD HOUSE WITH MOUNTAINS

$5\frac{1}{4}$ sticks butter

3 cups sugar

$2\frac{1}{2}$ cups dark cane syrup

2 teaspoons ground cloves

4 teaspoons ground ginger

4 teaspoons freshly ground pepper

4 teaspoons ground cinnamon

4 eggs

8 teaspoons baking soda

$8\frac{1}{2}$ cups all-purpose flour

CARAMEL FOR ASSEMBLY

$4\frac{1}{2}$ cups sugar

ICING

8 room-temperature egg whites

3 tablespoons lemon juice

$8\frac{1}{2}$ cups powdered sugar

Christmas elves for decoration

In a large saucepan, combine butter, syrup, and sugar. Heat until the sugar is melted. Add cloves, ginger, pepper, and cinnamon, and stir well.

Remove the saucepan from the heat, and let the mixture cool slightly. Stir in the eggs. Add baking soda, and sift in the flour. Stir everything together until you have a smooth dough. Adjust the thickness of the dough with more flour if necessary. The dough should be fairly soft; it will become much firmer when cooled.

Cover the dough with plastic wrap and let it rest in a cool place for a few hours, preferably overnight.

Knead the dough with some flour on the table, and roll it out to approximately ⅛-inch thickness. Cut out the parts for the gingerbread house and mountains using a paper template that you have prepared in advance, and place them on a baking sheet lined with parchment paper.

Bake the house parts and the mountain in the middle of the oven at 350°F for about 10 minutes. Adjust the walls with a knife if needed as soon as you take the baking sheet out of the oven. Cool on a wire rack.

In a large, heavy-bottomed saucepan, melt sugar over medium heat until it turns a light golden-brown color. Once the caramel is ready, reduce the heat to low. Assemble the gingerbread house parts using the caramel. Be very careful not to burn yourself. If the caramel hardens faster than you can assemble the house, increase the heat slightly.

In a clean bowl, whisk the egg whites on low speed until they start to foam. Add lemon juice. Sift in powdered sugar gradually to avoid lumps. Mix everything together at low to medium speed. When the icing becomes white and thick and clings slightly to the edges, it is ready. Add more lemon juice or water if the icing is too thick.

Transfer the icing into a piping bag and pipe "roof tiles" on the house and snow on the mountain. Decorate the scene with Christmas elves, trolls, and mountain climbers according to your preference.

SUNNY'S LUSSEKATTER

6¼ cups wheat flour	Generous pinch saffron
2 heaping cups sugar	1¾ sticks butter
1 teaspoon salt	2 tablespoons raisins for
2⅛ cups whole milk	decoration
2 eggs	1 egg for egg wash
3⅓ tablespoons yeast	

In a mixing bowl, combine flour, sugar, and salt. Stir quickly to mix. You may reserve half a cup of flour to add later if the dough becomes too sticky.

Whisk together milk and eggs. Use room-temperature ingredients, or gently warm the mixture to 75–85°F. Crumble the yeast into the milk mixture and stir until completely dissolved. If dry yeast is used, it can be added to the bowl with the dry ingredients.

Add saffron to the milk mixture and stir well, until the milk has a nice yellow color. Pour the milk mixture into the bowl with the dry ingredients, and knead for 5–10 minutes on low speed until the dough comes together and releases slightly from the bowl. If the dough is very sticky, you can add the remaining flour.

Add diced room-temperature butter, and knead until the dough is smooth and has a shiny surface, about 10 minutes. Cover the mixing bowl with plastic wrap, and let the dough rise in a warm place until doubled in size, about 1–1.5 hours.

Transfer the dough to a floured surface. Roll into thin sausages, form them into lussekatter, and decorate with raisins. Use some flour on the kitchen counter to prevent sticking. Place the buns on a baking sheet lined with parchment paper. Let them rise under a cloth for 15–20 minutes. Brush with beaten egg.

Bake the lussekatter in the middle of the oven at 430°F for 8–10 minutes until they are lightly golden. Cool on a wire rack.

ALFRED HAUG'S FATTIGMANN
(POOR MAN'S COOKIES)

5 egg yolks

5 tablespoons sugar

5 tablespoons heavy cream

1-2 tablespoons cognac or
brandy

$^1/_4$ teaspoon ground cinnamon

$^1/_4$ teaspoon ground cardamom

1 egg white

$2^3/_4$ cups all-purpose flour

$2^1/_4$ cups lard for frying

Alfred's favorite Christmas cookies! Don't be fooled by the name. These are lard-fried Christmas cookies with a touch of luxury: Maja Seter uses egg yolks, heavy cream, and even a splash of brandy in the batter.

Whisk egg yolks and sugar. Whip the heavy cream, and mix it into the egg mixture. Add the brandy and spices. Beat the egg white until stiff peaks form, and gently fold it into the mixture. Stir in about $1^1/_2$ cups flour, and let the dough rest, covered and chilled, until the next day.

Use the remaining flour (as little as possible) for rolling out the dough. Roll it out very thinly and only a little at a time. Cut out diamond-shaped pieces using a pastry wheel or cookie cutter.

Make a slit in the middle of each piece and carefully thread one end through the hole, creating a bow-shaped cookie. Fry the cookies in the lard until pale yellow, then cool them on a wire rack.

Note: Be careful when frying in lard. The fat gets extremely hot, and it is easy to burn yourself! Never pour water into hot fat, and always have a lid ready that fits the pot.

INGRID BERG'S FLØTEKARAMELLER
(CREAM CARAMELS)

³/₄ cup heavy cream   ³/₄ cup sugar
³/₄ cup golden syrup   2 tablespoons butter

In a saucepan, combine the heavy cream, sugar, and golden syrup. (Lactose-free alternatives can be substituted for both the heavy cream and the butter if desired.) Bring the mixture to a boil while stirring. Let it simmer for at least 20 minutes, until the caramel mixture passes the droplet test.

Droplet test: Drop a small amount of caramel mixture into a glass of cold water. The caramel is ready if the droplet quickly hardens and can be formed into a ball.

Once the caramel mixture passes the droplet test, add the butter and mix well. Then, pour the mixture into individual molds or a small, greased baking pan. When the caramel sets, cut it into squares of the desired size.

Individually wrap the caramels in cellophane.

Tips: To add your own twist, you can incorporate chopped almonds, a few teaspoons of lime zest, or crushed peppermint candy. However, Ingrid prefers the original version!

A Note from the Translator

It's July, the temperature is well above 80 degrees in my apartment in Oslo—and I have Christmas songs on repeat.

I often find that having a soundtrack that matches the text I'm working on can help me get into the atmosphere of the book, and seasonally inappropriate as it may have been, it was exactly what I needed to work through my final edits of Kjersti Herland Johnsen's *Christmas at Glitter Peak Lodge*.

Given that you've made it to this translator's note, you've most likely already finished the book—and are hopefully filled to the brim with all the warmth, emotion, and Christmas spirit it contains. Translators often end up being the readers who get closest to the text (apart from the author, of course!), and this can often present its challenges—for example, if you're sitting with a book with a heavier theme. However, I can safely say it was nothing but a festive joy to work with Kjersti's text during the time I had.

You may have heard of the Norwegian/Danish term *hygge*; it's become something of an international phenomenon in recent years. It's one of these words that people like to claim is "untranslatable," but it means something along the lines of comfort, coziness, and general enjoyment—and Kjersti's book oozes hygge from start to finish, which was part of what made it so enjoyable to work with. The characters are warm and likable, the scenery captivating and rich, and don't even get me started on all the delicious food . . .

I also had a lot of fun with names; for example, in the original, Sunniva "Sunny" Pedersen is called Erle "Perle" Pedersen. *Perle* means "pearl" in Norwegian and rhymes with Erle—not to mention suits the girl's effervescent personality—but "Erle" doesn't quite rhyme with "Pearl" in English, so I had to find another solution. "Sunny" ended up working perfectly! Coming up with a whole slew of punny names for the various cats in the story was also a blast, and I'm lucky to have a lot of cat-loving friends I could bounce ideas off of. Perhaps there's a Mewsephina in someone's future?

Being a climber myself (although not quite as daring as Ingrid!), translating the climbing and mountaineering passages was particularly thrilling. I *may* have even allowed myself the freedom to make the English version slightly more technically accurate than the original when it comes to climbing terminology—a translator's dilemma in itself! This text in particular didn't present too many such dilemmas, but that being said, translation is never without its challenges. Norwegian is a language rich in dialects, and several of the characters in this book (for example, Maja and Alfred) "speak" in a dialect reminiscent of the Gudbrandsdal region of central Norway. Translating dialects is always a bit of a pickle, and in this case, I ultimately decided to forgo the dialects altogether so as to not incorrectly set the reader's imagination in the wrong place. I'm not sure how I'd feel about Alfred speaking with a Southern accent!

There were also several cultural references to navigate; for example, I imagine most American readers aren't familiar with the tradition of searching for an almond in your Christmas rice cream and winning a marzipan pig! For the most part, I chose to keep things as "Norwegian" as possible to preserve the true feeling of the book. This also included a lot of the food, names, and places, and hopefully it sparks your curiosity to learn a bit more about Norwegian culture.

I hope you've enjoyed reading *Christmas at Glitter Peak Lodge* and that it's gotten you into the Christmas spirit—no matter what time of year it may be!

—Olivia Lasky

Here ends Kjersti Herland Johnsen's
Christmas at Glitter Peak Lodge.

The first edition of this book was printed
and bound at Lakeside Book Company
in Harrisonburg, Virginia, in September 2024.

A NOTE ON THE TYPE

This book is set in Adobe Garamond Pro. Garamond is a group of old-style serif typefaces popular with manuscript writers everywhere; there are many variations, all named after and inspired by sixteenth-century French engraver Claude Garamond, who created punches that resembled pen-and-ink handwriting. Adobe Garamond Pro, designed by Robert Slimbach and released in 1989 as Adobe's first historical revival font, is one such variation. With its low x-height, distinctive slanted e's and a's, tall ascenders, and scooped serifs, it is a delicate, regal typeface with Old World appeal. Its letters are ornamented as elegantly as the Christmas tree at Glitter Peak Lodge.

HARPERVIA

An imprint dedicated to publishing international voices, offering readers a chance to encounter other lives and other points of view via the language of the imagination.